BLACK AUTUMN TRAVELERS

BLACK AUTUMN BOOK 2

JEFF KIRKHAM (SPECIAL FORCES, RET.) & JASON ROSS

ReadyMan
PUBLISHING

THE BLACK AUTUMN SERIES

PROLOGUE

*"History will conclude the American Empire fell
because of two poor villagers and an idiot."*

— *THE AMERICAN DARK AGES*, BY
WILLIAM BELLAHER NORTH
AMERICAN TEXTBOOKS, 2037

VILLAGE OF PARANG, SULU ARCHIPELAGO, PHILIPPINES
Seven Months Ago

BOLAT NABIYEV INSISTED on running the outboard motor
himself. Truthfully, he had never piloted a boat of any kind,
but he couldn't bring himself to trust the junior agent nor the
filthy Filipino fisherman to take control of his cargo. He had
been forced to step aside to allow the fisherman to start the

engine because it required a befuddling series of actions, including pumping a bulb, delicately rocking a choke lever back and forth, then giving the pull-starting rope a brisk snap. But, once the engine caught, the Kazakh KNB agent took control, even though he repeatedly over-corrected, steering them in a serpentine course toward the fishing dock.

The small crate sitting in the bottom of their *panga* fishing boat represented the enormous trust placed in him by the Kazakh KNB, the intelligence agency that had resumed the role of the KGB when Soviet Russian influence rolled back in Kazakhstan in the early 1990s. Only three of the deadly crates had been in possession of the KNB, now secretly under the control of Al Qaeda in Pakistan. Having learned their lesson from the assassination of Osama bin Laden, Al Qaeda now ran a quieter strategy, spreading their fundamentalist Sunni Islam by infiltrating sympathetic Muslim nations like Kazakhstan. Through their control of the KNB, Al Qaeda inherited an RDS-451 "suitcase" nuclear weapon that had disappeared from the Russian arsenal during the fall of the Soviet Union.

Uncharacteristically, Al Qaeda leadership had taken a full year to decide what to do with their nuclear weapon windfall from Kazakhstan. At the end of their decision-making, they arrived at a subtle plan—the organization's new *modus operandi*—that favored impact rather than acclaim.

For once, thought Bolat, the Arabs were rationalizing rather than romanticizing. Even so, he felt certain that little thought had been spared to protect he and his Filipino men from the radiation that undoubtedly poured off the crate in waves. He imagined he could feel his belly sickening with nausea.

But none of that mattered. Today, the crate would be loaded aboard a sailboat bound for the sparkling cities of California. Unobtrusive and plain, the little crate seemed the perfect harbinger of destruction—a small gift of honesty to be delivered to a nation of liars.

Agent Nabiyev had no idea who had come up with the idea of sending nuclear weapons across the Pacific Ocean in sailboats. The idea struck him as both brilliant and poetic. He had been assured by his superiors that small sailboats crossed the Pacific Ocean all the time, usually captained by Western adventurers sailing toward a life of leisure on the hundreds of tiny islands and atolls dotting the expanse of the Pacific. Completed in the proper season, the journey back toward America was relatively safe and not overly long, requiring just ninety days of good weather and a little luck.

In an added twist of brilliance, the sailboat was to be owned and piloted by nameless Filipino Muslims with no connection to Kazakhstan whatsoever. The sailors wouldn't even know that Al Qaeda had been involved in the scheme; even the writing on the crate was in English.

The secrecy would cost Al Qaeda. Once the crate went aboard the sailboat, they would no longer control its destiny. They would have to trust the fanatical Filipino Muslim hatred of America to ensure proper delivery of the weapon. Timing would be anyone's guess. But time was on the side of Islam. America had to win against Islam at every turn. Considering the weakness of American wealth and leisure, Islam had to win only once to destroy the lie that sin leads to riches.

Bolat motioned to the fisherman to resume control of the fishing boat. They were nearing the dock, and he had strict orders to avoid any contact with the Filipino sailors who would deliver the bomb to America. Sitting in the *panga*, this was as close as he would ever be to the nuclear weapon. In the back of his mind, he wondered if he would regret the half-hour of exposure.

As they pulled up to the dock, Bolat and his companion lowered the brims of their straw hats and stepped off onto the dock, walking away as though the *panga* had carried them as simple passengers. Once they reached the shore, the agents stopped next to a large stack of fish traps and lit Filipino cigarettes. Bolat didn't smoke, but he had learned to for moments like these when he was conducting surveillance and wanted to look inconspicuous.

The agents monitored the crate as the nuke passed onto the dock and was loaded into a large sailboat on the other side. The Filipino sailors' instructions from their tribal imam had been to set sail immediately, but the sailors dithered around on the dock for the next hour, joking with other sailors and bargaining with a fisherman on some fresh catch. The agents were forced to relocate several times on the quay to avoid drawing attention. Bolat suppressed the urge to storm down to the dock and beat the sailors for their stupidity. According to the tribal imam, the sailors had been told they carried a bomb and Bolat had been told by the imam that the men he had chosen for the mission were his most faithful followers.

If they had known the importance of the mission, wouldn't they cast off immediately? The risk of discovery alone would make most men take the task seriously. Bolat had spent the last year in the jungles, learning that Filipinos deserved their poverty-stricken lives. They had no discipline, no urgency.

The sailors eventually completed their quayside mean-derings and set sail. As Bolat watched the forty-five-foot sailboat chug out of the small harbor under engine power, he wondered if this would be the bomb to reach American soil. He had his doubts after watching the natives behave like teenage idiots on the dock.

Bolat stubbed out his cigarette on a piling and shook his head, thinking again about the Filipino villagers. They were fools. But he supposed only fools would sail across the Pacific with a nuclear bomb leaking radiation in the hold of their boat.

OUTSIDE THE BIG **Thicket Federal Nature Preserve,** Kountze, Texas

OFFICER JEREMY HELLMUND had been lying in the dirt for twenty minutes, and he was dying to scratch his nuts.

How long could a Marine sniper sit still before he had to redeploy his position and his balls? The cable TV show about Marine scout snipers made it sound like they were required to stay still for at least two hours before they could pass scout sniper school.

As a trained federal officer, Jeremy figured he could do that much. It felt like there was an ant crawling on his balls. Maybe it had crawled up his leg.

He raised the binos back up to his eyes. The black panty hose covers he had fashioned for the lenses made the image blurry. He had heard about this little hack on YouTube—panty hose eliminated glare and prevented detection.

The militia men were at it again. Training.

Jeremy was nearly certain this militia group was building up to a terrorist attack. He had been tracking their movements and infiltrating their comms network for more than a year. They frequently talked about "taking down" federal agents, and even the U.S. president, in their closed Facebook group.

When Jeremy went to his supervisor with copies of the group's terrorist chatter, it hadn't gone well. His boss, generally a pretty good guy, was obviously too lazy to pull the trigger on some real law enforcement.

"That's not your job. You're a park ranger, Jeremy." His boss had pushed back on the intel. "Just do your job, okay?"

"Park Ranger," he repeated quietly. *I'm a trained federal officer.*

As he watched the militia practice their maneuvers, he felt the reassuring weight of his handgun jammed between a buckthorn sapling and his ass. He daydreamed about what would happen the day he finally put together enough evidence to put these guys away. He pictured himself making the call. He kept a business card on the nightstand in his apartment of an FBI agent he met at a fundraiser for Red-Cockaded Woodpeckers for the Big Thicket National Preserve where he worked. Once he had something concrete, Jeremy would make the call. The FBI. The Big Time.

His ball-itch reached a crescendo and he mashed down his urge to scratch.

Just like a Marine scout sniper.

He glanced downrange to distract himself. He couldn't figure out what the militia dirtbags were doing. They looked like they were practicing maneuvers, shooting at each other, but with no *bang-bang*. When the wind changed direction, he heard an intermittent mechanical whine.

Every militia guy was equipped like a hard-core operator. Multi-cam. Plate carrier vests. Heavy stacks of .223 magazines. Bump helmets. Oakley wraparound sunglasses. Every guy carried an AR-15 assault rifle with a flashlight, laser, vertical grip, and an ACOG scope.

His curiosity got the best of him and he slowly reached forward and ever-so-gently removed one of the panty hose makeshift screens from the left objective lens. The difference was immediate. Now he could see detail. He noticed orange flash hiders on the ends of the barrels.

Oh, damn. The militia guys were running airsoft rifles with orange flash-hiders. That was it. They were training with airsoft.

Jeremy remembered back to the days before he had completed his Seasonal Law Enforcement Training Program, or SLETP, to become a federal ranger. He had definitely done his share of airsoft, even becoming something of a local legend back in Vermont.

Training with airsoft. Very clever. The perfect way to train for an attack, mused Jeremy. He slowly set the binos in the weeds and dipped into a pocket, pulling out a tiny notebook. He scribbled a couple notes.

Sept. 17th: Airsoft Combat Training
17 men, 8 vehicles

After twenty minutes of exfil, Jeremy made it back to his Subaru. He plucked at the cockleburs in his pants and gear while turning his phone on to check his messages. He grabbed a Slim Jim, which had reached a warm and oily state, from the front seat. While he unwrapped it, Jeremy popped over to Facebook, a little disappointed that he hadn't seen anything truly actionable today.

He made it a habit to check the militia's Facebook Group several times a day. Munching the Slim Jim and poking at his phone, Jeremy clicked over to the Hardin County Regulators Facebook group, or *HCR*, as they called themselves.

There was a ton of new comms traffic. Something was up. The guys were sounding off about a friend who was going before a judge Monday morning, tomorrow. He had been busted by one of Jeremy's fellow rangers. The militia suspect had drunk alcohol in an open container in a Day Use Area. The perp had been tying one on like the white trash Texan he was—pounding one big bottle of Mexican beer after another —as though the rules of the park meant nothing to him.

Jeremy's fellow ranger had challenged him, and the guy just kept drinking. The ranger called for backup and it got pretty tense, causing his fellow ranger to move up the line to the local sheriff. Charges against the drunk included resisting arrest.

The HCR boys ranted a blue streak on Facebook about how the "feds" had no right to put a man in chains on Texas soil, and how somebody, presumably the HCR, should put a stop to it.

That evening, Jeremy watched the rhetoric escalate on Facebook until one man, Morris Chittendon, the sergeant at arms of the HCR, threw down the gauntlet. As a come-one, come-all militia, the HCR found suitable assignments for everyone, even if they were too fat and too old to run seventy-five yards, as was the case with Morris Chittendon. When the injustices being done to their hard-drinking associate became too much to bear, Chittendon called for direct action.

"Enough talk," Morris messaged the group. "I'm going

down to the courthouse tomorrow morning, and *I'm going in hot.*"

Either nobody noticed or cared to comment upon the inconvenient reality that they were talking about a *county* courthouse and that their friend was being prosecuted by a *county* sheriff and a *county* judge. The feds weren't party to the prosecution. The county sheriff had taken over almost right from the start.

Later that night, back at his apartment, Jeremy again checked the HCR group on Facebook. After reading Chittendon's most recent comment, Jeremy's eyes nearly bugged out of his head. He went straight for the FBI guy's business card, sitting on his nightstand gathering dust. The glowing red numerals of his alarm clock gave him a moment's pause. It was 9:47 p.m., and terrorist plot or not, social convention required that he wait until morning before calling an FBI agent. The guy was legit FBI and there was no way Jeremy would interrupt his family time. Jeremy pictured the phone ringing while the agent was banging his wife, and he set the business card back down like it was red hot.

"Tomorrow morning," he whispered. "First thing."

As soon as Jeremy sat up in bed at 7:30 a.m. on September 18th, his first impulse was to grab the business card.

"Still too early."

Jeremy jumped out of bed and began his morning ablutions—shit, shower, shave—in that order. The courthouse opened at 9:00 a.m. and the drunk's trial would be first on the docket. If they were going to nab Chittendon before a terrorist act, they would have to execute quickly.

By 8:05 a.m., Jeremy couldn't wait any longer. He grabbed the card and tapped in the agent's number. It went straight to voicemail. After an uncomfortable pause, Jeremy decided to leave a message, explaining to the federal agent that he had a suspect who was planning on shooting up the county courthouse that very morning. Jeremy left every detail he could think of, telling about his investigative work on Facebook, the Regulator militia, the airsoft training and about Chittendon's Facebook threat. The message machine eventually cut him off, but Jeremy felt like he had supplied the salient details.

By 8:32 a.m., Jeremy still hadn't heard back from Fred at the FBI, and he was as nervous as a cat chasing a mouse in a cowboy dance hall. With visions of an imminent terrorist attack, Jeremy grabbed a fourth coffee, skipped breakfast, and raced out to his Park Service SUV.

He knew Chittendon's car from his many recon missions observing the Regulators—a bronze Ford Taurus with a Confederate bumper sticker. Jeremy would have to make the interdiction himself. He pulled out his phone and placed it on the passenger seat, praying it would ring.

Time was short, so Jeremy headed down Highway 69, looking for a good spot to cover the main approach into Hardin.

AT 9:00 A.M. SHARP, Agent Fred Castellanos awoke to his alarm clock. It was his day off, and he had planned a day of jogging, lawn mowing and knocking back brews. Since he wouldn't be driving into Beaumont for work, he felt like a million bucks, the world at his feet, with nothing to do but catch up on sleep and putter around the house.

Then he looked over at his phone and saw he had a message. *Goddammit.*

Fred snatched the phone and touched the message from an unknown number. After a long pause, someone on the other end launched into a rant about terrorists, militia, and the Hardin Courthouse. He listened to the message twice more and it still didn't make sense.

Why would anyone hit the Hardin courthouse? And, more important, why would anyone call him, part of a child pornography taskforce, about suspicious militia activity?

Fred listened to the message a third time, like a gold miner panning for nuggets.

Who the hell was this fucktard calling him on his day off?

There. There it was. Jeremy Hellmutt or Hellmud or Hellmund from the Park Service. Why in God's holy name was a park ranger calling him?

Without really thinking about it, he picked up his holster, and slid his Glock onto his belt. Hardin was just a couple towns over and he might as well head that way. He had a gnawing desire to complement his day with a sausage McGriddle, and Hardin had the only McDonalds for ten miles.

Morris Chittendon's bronze Ford Taurus blew past Jeremy Hellmund with a whoosh.

Chittendon was just five blocks from the courthouse, presumably "going in hot." Jeremy slammed his hand against the switch on the dash, firing up his law enforcement light bar. He sped out of the bar pit and gave chase behind Chittendon.

Within moments, Chittendon pulled over to the side of Highway 69, and Jeremy jumped out of his SUV, hand on his pistol. As he cleared his SUV front fender, his phone buzzed, the incoming call from FBI Agent Fred Castellanos.

But Jeremy was out of earshot and so pumped on adrenaline and caffeine that the only thing he could see was a sputtering-mad Morris Chittendon glaring back at him through his side window, literally ready to explode with pent-up patriot angst.

This Texas roadside conflict quickly ramped into a defining moment for both men—a chance to live out their most passionate warrior fantasies. One of the men was an ardent, though preposterously heavy fighter for the American way. The other man was a sincere, liberally-educated East Coast naturalist and law enforcement officer. Both men had firearms within easy reach, and the psychological power of the guns emanated from the weapons like a magic spell. Conflict was in the air.

"Mr. Chittendon, step out of the vehicle," Jeremy ordered.

The words gushing from Morris' mouth were so tightly wrapped in righteous indignation and years of forethought and intensity, that they came out close to gibberish.

"My rights as a sovereign citizen of the state of Texas, give me no leave to honor your authori-*tay* in this, the county of Hardin... Constitutional State of Texas. You have no sway here, you pig-fucking excuse of a... go back to your nature preserve, federal invader..."

What else could Jeremy do? The man wouldn't follow his order to get out of the car. Jeremy drew his gun.

The appearance of the handgun launched Morris into an even greater tempest. "Now, by force of arms, you invade... my vehicle and... my rights as a citizen of the state of Texas..."

Jeremy was flustered. He had never seen more anger in a man than Morris Chittendon. Spittle flew every which way. Chittendon's heavy hands beat furiously against the steering wheel, emphasizing his constitutional rights.

Jeremy's pistol began to shake, the ultimate divining rod of his adrenaline, righteous conviction and caffeine.

"Please step out of the vehicle," Jeremy repeated, jumping two octaves in one sentence.

Morris Chittendon held forth on his rights as a Texan, but the exact words had become meaningless. His face, apoplectic and beet-red, belied both his anger and his frustration at not being able to articulate his points in this, his defining hour.

Jeremy's indignation at not being obeyed gave way to wonder at the intensity of the heavyset man's anger. Morris looked like he might explode, like he might actually be foaming at the mouth.

Morris began to clutch at his left arm, and his rants became a raging mewl. Almost shrieking, Chittendon slumped over the center console, wheezing loudly.

Jeremy panicked. He jumped into the middle of Highway 69 and waved his arms wildly, flagging down anyone who might stop to help. He never thought to re-holster, so he was waving his handgun when the next car approached.

THE EIGHTIES-ERA CHEVY TRUCK, piloted by a nineteen-year old local pothead named Thomas Oaks, stopped abruptly in the middle of the highway far back from the gun-wielding ranger. Besides enjoying a thrice-daily sojourn with cannabis, Thomas Oaks frequently played airsoft with the younger guys from the Hardin County Regulators. The last thing he was going to do was stop and talk to a federal officer. For starters, Thomas was high as a kite.

It took young Thomas a moment to understand what he was seeing. There, in all his glory, was a park ranger, waving a gun looking like he had seen a ghost. The ranger's brown-and-tan cruiser sat behind the Ford Taurus of Morris Chittendon, blue lights flashing. From this far back, Thomas could see Big Morris flopping around in his Taurus, definitely injured and in pain. It wasn't hard to connect the dots.

Thomas stomped on the gas and roared past Ranger Jeremy while screaming out his window.

"Fuck you, pig! We're coming!"

WHILE THE DOPPLER effect of the passing truck garbled the boy's war cry, Jeremy understood enough to send a chill down his spine. His adrenaline kicked into such a high gear that he almost dropped the gun on the pavement. He could barely feel his fingers, and his face tingled like it was being pelted by high-speed snowflakes.

Jeremy whipped back to his suspect, realizing that there was probably a firearm in the Taurus. He threw open the driver side door, still training his pistol on Morris, who was now flopping like a fish out of water.

His first idea was to pull Morris out, handcuff him and place him in the back of the Park Service SUV. Jeremy grabbed a fistful of Morris' belt and pulled, instantly revealing the futility of the plan. There was no way Jeremy would be able to drag Chittendon anywhere.

Jeremy was drowning in a primal urge to get off the road

and call for backup. He forced his legs and torso under the big man's ass and shoved him up and over the console, dumping him sideways into the passenger seat.

Jeremy re-holstered his handgun and jumped in the driver's seat of the Taurus. He cranked on Morris' massive key ring, causing the starter solenoid to grind like a squealing hog. The engine had been running the whole time. Jeremy stomped on the gas and bounced up and out of the bar pit.

Why he didn't go straight to the medical clinic in Hardin or the hospital in Beaumont was known only to the Lord Almighty. Instead, in a full-blown panic, Jeremy raced to the courthouse—probably because it was the last destination on his mind while he still possessed rational thought.

———

THE LOCAL POTHEAD suffered no chemical impairment whatsoever when it came to navigating social media. Within moments of blasting around the park ranger, giving him a generous helping of the middle finger, Thomas Oaks Tweeted, Facebooked, and Snap-Chatted an urgent call to the redneck underbelly of Hardin County society. Pings, buzzes and lit-screens across the county alerted the Regulators. One of their brothers was in trouble, being oppressed by the federal government itself.

Come in hot! the chain message screamed.

———

AGENT CASTELLANOS DROVE through the small town of Hardin, eyeing his McDonalds bag. He finally succumbed to temptation and pulled out a McGriddle, starting his breakfast while he drove.

He made the turn onto Monroe Street just in time to see something that made him double-blink. A Ford Taurus plowed over the center island, bucking like an angry bull, flew across the parking lot and smashed into the curb in front of the courthouse.

"Holy Jesus," blurted the FBI agent.

He put down his sandwich and pulled in beside the Taurus. More curious than concerned, he stepped out of his car and walked around to the driver's side. The brown-shirted park ranger in the front seat sparked a connection in his mind.

Agent Castallenos rapped on the side window, and the junior ranger just about jumped out of his skin. He had been furiously dialing his cell phone, looking into his lap, and hadn't seen the FBI agent pull into the parking lot.

As he put the phone to his ear, the ranger searched madly for the window switch. By the time he found it, he was already yelling into his phone.

"Come right now. We have a Code 15 at the Hardin County Courthouse. Yes! At the courthouse. Backup required, RIGHT NOW!"

"Whoa, whoa, whoa, buddy. Take a breath." The hair on the back of Agent Castalleno's neck stood straight up. His hand drifted toward his Glock. "What the hell is going on?"

The ranger looked at him with panic-stricken eyes, and the FBI agent noticed the big man piled up in the passenger seat.

"Who is that man?" Fred asked.

A look of recognition washed over the forest ranger and he burst out, "You're the FBI guy... Call for backup."

"Take a breath, buddy." Agent Castellanos repeated. "What's going on? Is that guy okay?"

"They're co... coming... coming hot!" the ranger stammered.

Suddenly, several cars caterwauled across the median and into the courthouse parking lot—a Jeep first, followed by a late model pickup truck and a Dodge Neon.

The park ranger jumped out of the Taurus, pushing the FBI agent back, and scrambled for his handgun. The drivers of the approaching cars slammed on their brakes and doors flew open. Men with rifles leapt out, using the cars as barricades.

"What in God's name is going on?" Agent Castellanos yelled.

Nobody answered. Everyone's attention fixated on the guns. Guns in their hands. Guns pointing back. The guns charged the very air around them, like an electrical surge passing through the atmosphere, buzzing in their ears and vibrating the primordial core of their brains.

More militiamen came. Within the next sixty seconds, ten more vehicles roared up to the courthouse and piled around the militia contingent already there. The scene looked like a tornado had touched down in a used car lot, except for rifle barrels bristling from every window and every door.

The FBI agent struggled to place a call to his own office while he ducked and scrambled back toward his car, hiding behind any cover he could find.

The last of the militiamen had exited their vehicles and taken cover behind them. A tense quiet descended on the scene.

Agent Castellanos broke the silence when the office girl answered at the Beaumont FBI office. "I'm at the Hardin

County Courthouse and I need backup..." he trailed off, realizing how pointless it was to call the office, thirty-five miles away. "Send backup," he repeated hopelessly before ending the call. He scanned the parking area, counting almost two-dozen guns pointed at him and the park ranger. Out of the corner of his eye, he saw the ranger squirm into the doorway of the Taurus, trying to gain a little extra cover, his handgun trembling.

A door slammed.

A rifle boomed, shattering the charged silence.

THE PARKING LOT erupted in chaos. One of the first bullets from the Regulators passed through the rear quarter panel of the Taurus, spalling as it smashed the corner of the tire jack and cartwheeled through the backseat, through the front seat and directly into the lower brain stem of Morris Chittendon, ending his life about ten minutes before his heart attack would've killed him anyway.

Ranger Jeremy Hellmund was shot fifteen times in five seconds. He succeeded in busting a headlamp on the Jeep with three rounds before taking a round to his chest.

As Hellmund fell to the ground, another Park Ranger SUV that had been in Hardin that morning raced into the parking lot just in time to see the man in the brown uniform slump beside the Taurus. The two rangers inside jumped from their vehicle, drew their sidearms, and mistakenly shot Agent Castellanos as he crouched behind his car.

The rangers' fire drew a bullet whirlwind from the Regulators, perforating their Blazer with more than a hundred rounds, killing both men instantly.

In the moment of silence that followed after the rangers fell, the door of the courthouse burst open and two constables and a sheriff's deputy stepped out, saw the carnage, and ducked back inside to call for backup.

Half the Regulators piled back into their cars and sped away. The other half walked toward the three pock-marked cars in the parking lot, guns at the ready. They found the body of Morris Chittendon, shot in the back of the head.

Thomas Oaks was there, iPhone in hand, taking pictures of the dead militiaman and the park ranger, his handgun on the ground beside his body. Nobody rendered aid to Agent Fred Castellanos as he slowly died, slumped against the rear hubcap of his personal vehicle.

Thomas Oaks' meme went out two minutes later, and it was almost immediately picked up by conservative patriot blogs across America.

"This is what happens when you stand up to the federal government," the meme, displayed across a picture of the deceased Morris Chittendon, threatened.

"But this is what happens when a federal agent kills a Texan," the meme finished, showing a picture of the bullet-riddled body of Ranger Jeremy Hellmund.

Sometimes human history unfolds reliant on the thinnest of moments. If only Ranger Jeremey Hellmund had taken the dying militiaman to the *hospital* instead of the *courthouse*, there might still be a United States of America.

———

HIGHWAY 6 ROADBLOCK, Delta, Utah

. . .

DALE TRENTON, commander of the Delta Desert Patriots militia, contemplated the endless column of semi-trucks stretching beyond the horizon on Highway 6.

In the parlance of militia-speak, *the flag had gone up*. Within forty-eight hours, two events had shattered the self-absorption of America. In Dale's mind, the events connected through an interlocking scheme of the Deep State, the Illuminati and Neocon Zionists. He didn't have enough information to follow the bouncing ball, but it would only be a matter of time before the patriot commentators of the internet figured out the connection between the slaughter of one Texan patriot, a dirty bomb recently exploding in Saudi Arabia, and the death spiral of the stock market.

The bomb in Saudi Arabia screamed *false flag operation*. Russia, Israel, or the United States itself had orchestrated the dirty bomb that took out a pipeline junction, probably just to pin it on someone else. That's how secret societies operated. The international banking syndicate had been working overtime for years to generate a stock market failure in order to launch the New World Order, so maybe they had played a part. No doubt George Soros, may his soul rot in hell, had something to do with it all.

Dale stretched his leg and flexed his hip as he watched the semi-trucks, loaded with coal, moldering in the morning sun behind the roadblock he had erected. His one big regret, now that the shit had finally hit the proverbial fan, was that he hadn't replaced his bad hip in time. With the collapse upon America, hip replacement surgeries wouldn't be happening again for a long, long time.

Yet, Dale had prepared for this day. Given his apocalyptic religious upbringing, he had always kept food storage stashed in the crawl space of his double-wide trailer. On top of the food, he and his wife stockpiled water, gasoline, guns, ammunition, and just about everything else one might need during the collapse of society. Most important, Dale had started his own "well-regulated militia," just as the Constitution suggested. The Delta Desert Patriots numbered around 300 squared-away men and women who could be ready in ten minutes to defend their hometown.

Just the day before, Dale had called up the full militia to defend the town against an incursion of California National Guard who had come to take over the Delta coal power plant for the benefit of the state of California. Because of the massacre of militiamen in Texas, raging in hundreds of internet memes, his militia had already been placed on high alert. Within ten minutes of their arrival, Delta Desert Patriots had confronted and disarmed the California invaders. Now Dale waited on a hill overlooking his roadblock to see what else California would throw at him. With the power plant shut down—out of coal and understaffed because of the roadblock—the rich people of Southern California would be crying in their lattes, with no electricity to run their cappuccino machines.

He took no pleasure in their suffering, he told himself, but they had it coming, polluting the community of Delta, Utah with a huge coal power plant for far too many years. California had run their air conditioners and the children of Delta had breathed their coal smoke for twenty years too many. The time for patriots to stand up and say "no" had arrived.

The Second Coming of the Lord Jesus was upon them, any way you sliced it, and those whoring folks in California were going to burn sooner or later. Living without air conditioning for a few days would be the least of their worries.

THREE MILES Outside of Alameda Harbor, Alameda, California

THE HELICOPTER CIRCLED the two Muslim villagers and their sailboat again, and it became clear that they were the subject of the helicopter's interest. The gut-thumping throb of the rotor blades threw the Filipino sailors into a panic. Njay steered the boat while Miguel rushed to complete his ablutions to Allah in preparation for his death at the attack of the helicopter.

Njay shaded his eyes, searching for weapons. He knew little about military aircraft, but the helicopter was painted blue and white and had bulbous pods above the landing skids. Unless the pods were bombs, Njay could see no obvious threat.

Even louder than the howling rotors, a loudspeaker blared from the aircraft. "Sailing craft, cut your engine immediately. We detect radiation aboard your vessel. Cut your engine immediately and wait to be boarded."

Miguel paused in his ritual cleansing and shouted something to Njay that he probably couldn't hear over the roar of the helicopter. Neither man understood the words coming from the loudspeaker, but the intent was clear. They were being intercepted. They would not reach Los Angeles before the Americans destroyed them. Njay ducked low behind the steering wheel and motored directly toward Alameda Harbor, full steam.

Miguel shouted again and pointed off their bow. In the

distance, a large boat with a blue light bar raced to block their course.

Njay's bowels tightened like an angry snake. He muttered prayers to Allah as he rushed down the narrow stairs into the hold.

As the prayer reached its end, Njay opened the simple trap door and pressed the red inset button.

1

_____

"Live for liposuction, detox for your rent
Overdose for Christmas and give it up for Lent
My friends are all so cynical
Refuse to keep the faith
We all enjoy the madness
'Cause we know we're gonna fade away."

— *MILLENNIUM*, ROBBIE WILLIAMS,
I'VE BEEN EXPECTING YOU, 1998

57 FREEWAY, ANAHEIM, CALIFORNIA

CAMERON SHOULD'VE LEFT last night.

Now it might be too late, he fumed.

He groaned as he merged onto the freeway. He could think of only one reason for the 57 to be packed with cars at

11:00 a.m. on a weekday. Some tiny percentage of Los Angelenos had seen the same news and had come to the same conclusion; their world was on the ropes and, if it absorbed one more punch, the whole thing would crumple like a rotted roof on a slapdash casino.

One half of one percent of eighteen million residents of Los Angeles apparently had the same hunch as Cameron. Instead of making him feel smart, it made him feel like another dipshit crammed into the smoggy basin of tract homes and strip malls that made up southern California. The endless train of idling cars on the asphalt smoldered like a portent of doom.

He had stuck to the plan he and Tommy had laid out: drive north along the 57 Freeway until San Dimas, pass through the mountains near the Firestone Scout Camp, and drop into the northern suburbs of Los Angeles. Then run straight east, skirting the base of the San Bernardino Mountains, taking the 210 Freeway all the way to the mouth of Cajon Pass and the I-15 Interstate—hopefully pulling off an escape from the snapping jaws of Los Angeles—if this turned out to be the real deal.

A holiday, roadwork, or even a big Las Vegas weekend could turn the I-15 into a 250-mile chain of humanity, crated in their climate-controlled metal boxes, every one of them fuming with desire to get past the masses standing between them and their ambitions. This time, it felt very different. Today was just another Tuesday—except the instincts of tens of thousands of people had obviously shouted down normalcy.

Get out, their subconscious minds had screamed.

His eyes plastered open, forgetting to blink, and drying

out while he inventoried his personal failures, like gravel in his soul.

He looked into his rearview mirror at the two boys sleeping in their car seats, and his hands tightened on the steering wheel, his knuckles turning white. This time, Vegas wasn't about copious alcohol and grab-ass with his softball buddies. This time, he needed to get there to safeguard his family. His brain cooked with a feverish desire to get them clear of whatever bad thing might come next. The fact that it would be happening to everyone at the same time, if his fears turned out to be real this time, didn't factor into his equation.

"We're going to be okay," his wife said, working to draw down the anger coming off him in waves. She had a knack for sensing his worry, even though Cameron doubted she grasped its ferocity. "Let's just keep moving. The freeway will open up in a bit."

The ground shook with a deep baritone and Julie stifled a scream. "It's just an earthquake," she said. A lot of times Julie did that: blurted out what she hoped was true in an effort to fill emotional space.

But Cameron knew that earthquakes couldn't usually be felt in a moving vehicle. He had lived in California his whole life and had ample experience. This was something different.

He stared intently at the radio, his brain scrambling to place the tune, as though it might help him understand his sudden sense of dread.

"...No reason to get excited, the thief he kindly spoke. There are many here among us who feel that life is but a joke..."

Cameron pawed at the controls, punching buttons until

he managed to sever Julie's Bluetooth link with her phone and change over to regular radio.

The emergency alert tone screeched, waking the boys in the backseat.

"Why'd you do that?" Julie's protest trailed off. Cameron raced through radio stations, using the presets that he almost never used anymore, each station braying with the same emergency broadcast alert. Finally he found someone talking.

"A nuclear bomb has been detonated off the coast of Los Angeles. Please remain in your homes and stay calm. The governor will provide more details and advise citizens how to proceed. Until then, please stay calm and remain in your homes. If you are at work, please return to your homes in an orderly fashion. I repeat. A nuclear bomb has been detonated off the coast of Los Angeles..."

What had started as a precaution, leaving Los Angeles because of some incomprehensible chain of events in the world, had now side-slipped into a parallel reality. A *real* nuke had gone off, and his family had been close enough to feel the earth groan.

The other events—a dirty bomb in the Middle East, some scary news about stock prices, and some blackouts in southern California—had been enough to get Cameron and Julie moving east in their SUV, just as a precaution. Those three pieces of news together had sounded bad, so he and his family had left their home in Los Angeles the night before.

The traffic choking the 57 hit Cameron as another in a long line of personal failures; another reminder of his inability to make the right decisions for his family.

Getting busted while high on 'shrooms in his twenties.

Being rejected from police academy because of his record.

Quitting his good job at the hotel to start his own business.

Failing at the business and stiffing his father-in-law for the eight grand he invested.

He should've paid more attention to the news and bailed out of SoCal the moment the dirty bomb torched off in the Middle East. Add that one to the list.

The weather in his head reminded him of the jerky, swirling video they show of a hurricane as it spins its way toward landfall. Every waking moment of every day, Cameron had to position his ass in the clear center spot—the eye in the midst of fury. Instead, more often than he cared to admit, he subjected his family to the lashing rains instead.

Thirty-five years old and he still didn't know when to be Johnny-Be-Good and when to let the wolf off its fucking leash.

But all those bits of internal recrimination could've been written off the account against him as a husband and father if only this had been another false alarm. With a bass rumble coming from the earth's core and the high-pitched squeal coming from the radio, he knew he had screwed the pooch for real this time.

Cameron pounded on the dashboard as Julie leaned away, backing against the passenger door. A chunk of plastic from one of the air vents popped off and disappeared between the driver's seat and the center console.

The rumbling ceased. A blank silence fell over the idling cars of the 57 Freeway blockade. The quiet felt like God putting Cameron on notice.

Last chance, asshole.

RICKERSON HOME, Port Angeles, Washington

"WHAT DO YOU WANT, DAD?" Sage Ross seethed into the kitchen phone, the long spiral cord snaking from the handset back to the wall. His grandparents had retreated into the family room to give him some privacy while he spoke to his father.

The week prior, one of the cleaning ladies had found a bag of weed in the bottom of Sage's underwear drawer. His dad had sent him to stay with his grandparents in Port Angeles, Washington to give Sage "some time away from his questionable friends" in Utah.

Before sending him, Jason took away Sage's smartphone, cutting him off from the digital world. The teenager was madder than a cat in a clothes dryer.

"You and I need to talk," Jason said over the landline.

"Whatever. You're going to lecture me about college and adult life and blah, blah, blah. I already told you; I'm not going to college. Not everyone cares about money as much as you do."

After a pause, Jason continued. "I wasn't going to talk to you about college. I wanted to talk about what's going on with the stock market and with California..."

Sage interrupted, "I don't care about the stock market. I told you; I'm not about money like you are." Sage was on a roll, tapping into the kind of self-righteous passion known only to Italians, rock stars, and teenagers.

"Hold up, son. I'm not talking about money. Do you know the stock market crashed? Have you heard that a nuclear bomb went off near Los Angeles?"

There was a long pause as Sage tried to fit the new information into his diatribe.

"No. What does that even mean? Does that mean you lost all your money, because I honestly don't care."

Sage was Teenager Number Four in the Ross family, and he hated how Jason played out his phony parenting strategies rather than joining him in an honest argument. With Sage's older brother, now a United States Marine, Jason hadn't been quite so metered, and Sage got a front row seat to many hurly-burly arguments about his brother's teenage mess-ups. For Sage, talking to Jason was like talking to a professional father. It pissed him off.

"Did you hear the part about a nuclear bomb going off in Los Angeles?" Jason asked Sage. "I'm worried about you getting home."

"Then maybe you shouldn't have sent me off to butt-fucking Egypt to punish me."

"I suppose that's true," Jason agreed without addressing the disrespect. "This turned out to be a bad time to send you to Grandma and Grandpa's. We need you home as soon as possible. I'm afraid bad things are happening in the world, and I need you back in Utah."

"You don't get to control me. If things go bad, I'm staying here to help Grandma and Grandpa." Sage had Jason on the ropes, an opportunity he wasn't going to waste. Taking away Sage's phone was an attempt to control him, and sooner or later his dad would have to learn that he didn't get to control his kids. Sage had become a man, and he would be making his own decisions about what to smoke and what not to smoke, when to go and when to stay.

"Think about it, son. If things do go totally bad, Grandma and Grandpa will sacrifice their own safety and their own resources to keep you alive. I agree with you; you are an asset, but they'll put your life ahead of their own, and that could be the end of them. Come home where you can contribute like a man—protect your family here. Grandpa knows the Olympic Peninsula like the back of his hand. They'll be okay. With you there, it might compromise them."

The piss and vinegar went out of Sage. With Jason apologizing and admitting that it had been a bad idea to send him to Port Angeles, Sage could move on. Jason had admitted that Sage was a man—a man with a bona fide contribution to make to the family. That was all he really wanted to hear.

"How do I get home?"

"You need to move fast. You'll be racing the clock. I FedExed Grandpa your iPhone the same day you left. He has it now. You're going to need it to travel. Let me talk to Grandpa, okay?"

Sage called out to the living room and Grandpa Bob picked up the living room extension while Sage listened quietly to the conversation from the kitchen phone.

"Hey, Bob, how're you doing?" Jason asked his father-in-law.

"We're going to be okay. We're packing up the fifth wheel trailer and we're moving up the coast to our campground. We can take Sage with us, if that's what you want."

Grandpa Bob was in his seventies and Sage knew he had already suffered one heart attack. A former fireman, he was otherwise physically fit and a skilled outdoorsman, but the unstated truth was that Bob couldn't count on his fitness like the fireman he once was.

"I'm thinking we should get him on the road to Salt Lake City," Jason said.

"I can gear him up and send him in Glenda's Taurus in an

hour or two. The Taurus is at three-quarters of a tank and it's just been tuned up. But the engine has over a hundred fifty thousand miles on it. Do you think it's worth the risk?"

Jason went quiet for a moment. "I think the risks of sending him home are less than the risks of him staying in Washington," he said finally.

"Okay," Bob agreed. "I can see that it's a close call either way. We have a little cash we can give him for gas. Are credit cards still working?"

"I don't know," Jason answered. "You sure you don't want to come to Utah with him?"

"No," Bob said in a slow drawl, "we're best off here. This is our home and we've been preparing, little by little, for a long time. We'll be pretty safe on the Olympic Peninsula. I think we'll be all right."

Sage guessed that Bob and Glenda probably thought they would be a hindrance in Salt Lake City, and they weren't the kind of people who tolerated that. Port Angeles was Bob's hometown in the old-fashioned sense of the word. He knew the woods and the waters, and there was a fair chance they would be safe once the four million people of Seattle couldn't cross Puget Sound on a ferry. In any case, if Jason couldn't talk Bob into going to Utah, Sage probably couldn't either.

"We'll miss you. I think we're going to need men like you in the days to come. Would you get Sage set up and give me a call before he heads out?"

"Yep. Let me get to work. I'll call you soon." Bob hung up and so did Sage.

Over the next hour, Sage and his grandpa filled the Taurus with as much camping gear as they could fit into the trunk and the backseat. When everything else had been loaded, Grandpa Bob took Sage back to the bedroom and opened a gun safe inside the closet. He pulled out a perfectly maintained Winchester 30-30 with a scope and three boxes of bullets.

"This is my best rifle," Bob said. "I've killed a lot of deer and one elk with this Winchester." He handed Sage one of the boxes of bullets with his free hand and Sage put it in his back pocket.

Bob ran a finger down the barrel of the Winchester. "I planned on leaving this rifle to you when I passed."

"Why don't you keep it until then? I'll be okay without a gun. It's not like I'm going to have to shoot anything," Sage argued, not comfortable with the gift and not comfortable thinking about his Grandpa Bob passing away someday.

"I hope that's true. I hope this is all one big misunderstanding and that nobody will need guns. But sometimes we don't get what we hope." Bob looked at the rifle, sadness in his eyes and the wisdom of years pulling at the corners of his mouth. "It wouldn't be the first time a seventeen-year-old boy had to carry a gun to survive."

Sage shrugged off his Grandpa's heaviness. "That's never going to happen now, though. Right? That was back in old times. There's no way I will ever point a gun at another person."

Grandpa Bob had apparently run out of words. He looked up from the rifle into Sage's eyes and slowly handed the gleaming steel weapon from grandfather to grandson, along with the other two boxes of bullets.

"Thanks, Grandpa," Sage said reflexively, knowing it was the wrong thing to say, but nothing else came to mind. His grandpa's expression brought out that old, boyish bubbling in his chest and he turned away before Bob could see the upwelling of tears building in the corners of Sage's eyes.

When the Taurus was loaded, Bob called Jason. Sage joined the call from the kitchen extension.

"He's ready," Bob said.

"What's he carrying?" Jason asked.

Bob rattled off the list. He had raided his own camping supplies, gun safe and food pantry, no doubt cutting into Glenda's and his own survival plan: freeze-dried food, water, camping supplies, and the Winchester. Sage thought it was enough food to get him through three months, which was major overkill, considering he would likely be home in a day. He felt guilty that Bob had decimated his survival supplies.

Most important, Bob had given Sage their car.

"Are you sure you can spare the car?" Jason asked.

"We have our truck and our fifth wheel trailer. That's all we need. If things recover, you can bring the car back... So what do you think? Will things recover?"

"You probably already know what I think," Jason answered. "I'd be surprised if we ever speak again, Bob."

Sage's eyes went wide, and a bolt of fear shot up his back. No matter his teenage angst, some part of him still took anything his dad said as gospel truth.

"Yeah..." Bob reluctantly agreed.

"So let me thank you now for putting my son's life ahead of your own," Jason said. "That's way more food and supplies than he will probably need. You and Glenda are cutting it close to give him a better chance in a worse-case scenario. He'll probably be home by this time tomorrow. But you packed what I would've packed, and I know you went deep into your supplies to set Sage up."

"Of course. That's what family does," Bob answered, getting ready to hang up. "I love you, son-in-law. I'll have

Glenda call Jenna a little later. You can talk to Sage alone now. Goodbye."

Bob hung up the living room phone with a click and Sage spoke for the first time. "Grandpa's giving me way too much stuff, Dad. I should give some of it back."

"Keep it," Jason said. "Your grandma and grandpa know their own hearts."

Sage went silent for a moment, struggling to pull himself together. The old Sage cracked through the crust of pissed-off teenager.

"Okay, Dad... What's the best route for me to get home?"

Jason talked Sage through the route, outlining the most direct path from Seattle to Utah. Bob had given Sage a hard copy map of the western U.S.—a rarity in the days of GPS and cell phones.

"Make a run for eastern Washington. Anything on the coastal side of the mountain range will probably get dangerous. There'll be millions of urbanites and technology workers, all wondering where to get their next meal. Don't head south to Portland. It might implode just like Seattle. Drive straight east on the 410 to Yakima. Hopefully you can fuel up there. How much cash do you have?"

"Grandpa gave me almost eight-hundred dollars."

"Tuck half of that cash under a dish on their kitchen table before you leave," Jason told his son.

"Okay. Where do I go after Highway 410?"

"Head for Boise, then cut over to the 15 Freeway. It runs straight south to Salt Lake City."

"How long will that take?"

"If nothing goes wrong, it'll take you about twelve hours to get home. But, son, everything's going wrong... I wish I had more time to teach you things..."

"You taught me lots of things, Dad. I'm going to be fine."

There was a long pause. Then Jason said, "I love you, son."

"I love you, too, Dad. Sorry I swore at you before."

"Don't worry about it. I want you to promise me something: promise me that you will do whatever it takes to survive and to make it home. No matter what happens. Give me your word on it."

"I promise, Dad," Sage said.

"You promise what? Please say the words."

Sage straightened his back. "I promise I will do whatever I have to do to survive and make it home. It's only twelve hours away, though, right?"

"Yes, but I have a bad feeling about this. Do I have your word as a gentleman?" A bleakness rang in the question, even over the phone line, the true terror of their predicament starting to take hold.

"Yes, you have my word."

"Get going. Leave now. I love you. Goodbye."

"Goodbye, Dad."

---

12 NEW WINDSOR PIKE ST., Westminster, Maryland

MAT BEST WATCHED the naked girl snoring on his couch. The fist pump in his head never quite materialized. It had been like this for a couple of months now—all conquest and no spoils of war.

The light from the fireplace danced over her perfect breasts and her gaping mouth as she breathed loudly, adrift in post-coital slumber. He felt fairly certain she wasn't ten years younger than him. Definitely over eighteen, he assured himself.

He had been stuck in Westminster, Maryland for over a year, caretaking his grandmother's home. She passed away the year before and Mat and his brother decided to wait until the housing market improved before selling the house she left them as an inheritance. With nowhere else to be after almost a decade of service with the Army Rangers and contracting for the State Department, Mat had run aground here, in the house he had once visited every summer as a child, sleeping under the loud tick-tock of his Grandma's clock. It had been the same clock that had kept a metronome beat while he serviced his latest love conquest on his grandma's couch less than an hour before.

He wasn't going to lie. It had been a little weird.

Not ready for sleep, Mat picked up his phone and began scrolling through Facebook. He'd spent most of the day convincing this young co-ed—Caroline—that he was the kind of suave war hero who would fulfill all her Special Forces fantasies. It didn't usually take this much work for Mat, but apparently she was a southern girl who liked to play hard to get. Mat had been up for the challenge and it had blotted out his entire day, preventing him from checking his Facebook feed.

He was startled when he saw there was only one thing anyone was talking about on Facebook: a nuclear bomb had been detonated off the coast of Los Angeles. Turning immediately to his phone app, he panicked at the half dozen calls from his family in Santa Barbara, a mere two-and-a-half hours from where the bomb had killed some boaters and blew out thousands of windows. He called his brother Tye. It was three hours earlier on the west coast.

Tye answered on the first ring. "Mat, are you okay? You weren't answering your phone."

"Sorry." Mat headed into the kitchen so he wouldn't wake the girl. He was going to have to wake her soon anyway, he realized. They'd been driving in the countryside all day enjoying the fall leaves, making out and having sex in his truck. They hadn't spoken to anyone, and both of them had been too occupied to check their phones. "Is everyone okay?" he asked.

"Yeah. Mom and dad are fine and so are Alisa and Ben. The fallout's blowing out to sea, we think. Are you at Grandma's?"

"Yes, I'm in Westminster. Are you going to be able to stay there? Is it safe in Santa Barbara? What if the wind changes?"

"We don't know for sure," Tye replied. "We're north and west of the explosion and watching the winds. The fallout pattern isn't far offshore from us. But the 101 Highway is jammed with cars as far as the eye can see. There are thousands of people from L.A. pouring into town, even into our neighborhood. Dude, it's getting creepy around here. I don't think we should stay."

Worry got the better of Mat, and he forgot to keep his voice down. "Where are you thinking of going? You're taking Mom and Dad with you, right?"

"We've been talking about loading up and heading toward Uncle Tony's place in Porterville," Tye told him. We'll take everyone, but that means we have to get on the highway. Maybe we'll head back toward Ventura and then cut north from there. Nobody's driving south on the 101, so it should be doable."

"Mat... what's going on?" the naked girl interrupted, standing in the doorway of the kitchen.

"Hold on, Tye." Mat turned to her. "Babe, there's been a bomb in California and things are going crazy on the west coast. I'm talking to my brother in Santa Barbara. Let me talk to my family for a bit and I'll take you back to your dorm, or you can spend the night here, okay?" With a worried look, she headed back to the living room, probably to find her own phone.

"Sorry, Tye. When are you thinking about leaving the house?"

"Uncle Tony says we can come any time, but he doesn't have enough food for all of us for more than a couple days. Since Aunt Marilyn died, he doesn't do a lot of cooking at home. So we're trying to gather as much food as we can here before we hit the road."

Mat didn't like the sound of it, but there wasn't anything he could do from three thousand miles away.

"Will you call me when you guys leave?" Mat asked.

"Sure. Answer your phone, okay? Mom was worried about you."

"Will do. Stay safe. Give Mom and Dad my love."

Mat ended the call and walked back to the living room where the girl had put her panties on and was scrolling through her phone with mounting concern, her perfect tits looking even more perfect as she sat on the couch.

"This is really bad, Mat. I need to call my family in Louisville." She began dressing as though she needed to be clothed to speak to her parents.

"Hi, Mom. Are you okay?" she said.

Mat headed to his room, following an unconscious urge to check his gear. He pulled his duffle bag from beneath a pair of skis in his closet and threw it on the bed. Only then did he realize what he was doing: *kitting up for war.*

Somewhere in the dark, warrior corner of his mind, Mat knew they faced something more than a "west coast problem."

"Yeah, Mom," Mat heard the girl say. "I'll come home right away. I'll book a flight tonight." Mat slowed down packing his bag. Something about the conversation wormed its way into his head, casting shadows on his action plan.

"I will, Mom. Don't worry, and please don't let Dad worry. I promise I will be home tomorrow at the latest."

Mat knew it was a promise she would break. He had been in Santa Barbara, California, United States of America, when those camel-fuckers hit the twin towers in 2001. All flights had been cancelled almost immediately, protecting the airspace over the U.S. from follow-on attacks. With a true nuke strike on the continental U.S., the president would be in the air right now on Air Force One, and there wouldn't be many, if any, flights pinging around the United States to clutter up the airspace. Not for a good bit, at least.

Nine-eleven reminded him of the day he enlisted, which reminded him of Ranger School, which reminded him of the Ranger Creed.

I will shoulder more than my fair share of the task, whatever it should be...

Like a flash flood rushing into the sea, two versions of Mat collided in his head. In one version, Mat chased tail and drank way too much. In the other, he lived the highest ideals of honor and shouldered more than his fair share of any task.

Like when the World Trade Center had been hit by two

giant missiles filled with mothers and daughters, sons and fathers, Mat's world flipped. Fifteen minutes before, he had been content to get laid and get going. Now, with nuclear fallout sprinkling down from the sky in Los Angeles, the co-ed sitting on his grandmother's couch, naked from the waist up, represented an issue of honor to him.

He had spent his short adult life taking personal responsibility for the safety of Americans. But that mission had been thousands of miles away, in an alien land smelling of death and raw sewage. What did that mission have to do with right here, right now, in the heart of America?

Maybe everything.

2

"Fret for your figure and fret for your latte and
Fret for your lawsuit and fret for your hair-
    piece and
Fret for your Prozac and fret for your pilot and
Fret for your contract and fret for your car
It's a bullshit three ring circus sideshow.
Of freaks here in this fucking hole we call L.A.
The only way to fix it is to flush it all away..."

— *"ÆNEMA"*, TOOL, ÆNEMA, 1996 ZOO
ENTERTAINMENT

HIGHWAY 12, STATE OF WASHINGTON

SAGE DROVE through the night on the mountain highway
skirting Mount Rainier. The traffic inched up and over the
Cascade Mountains like a line of sparkling ants. When he
finally reached the city of Yakima, he merged onto the free-

way. He had never driven a car on a cross-country trip like this before. At fifteen miles an hour, there was nothing exciting about road tripping.

At six in the morning, he was contemplating pulling over for some sleep near the town of Wallula when his car started coughing. He checked the gas gauge and saw he had a quarter tank, but an indicator lit up on the dashboard saying, "Check Engine." He didn't know what that meant. He had never had a car do that before.

His stomach lurched as he looked in the rearview mirror. With dawn's light, he could see a plume of smoke billowing behind the Taurus, enfolding the other cars in a blue haze.

He pulled onto the shoulder and shut the car off. Half-dazed by fatigue, he forced himself to think. He grabbed his cell phone from the console and spoke into the phone.

"Call Dad."

The automated voice replied. "I'm sorry. You have no service."

Sage looked around and saw a field of trees in a neat line stretching off into the misty dawn. The slow march of traffic continued past his window. The car filled with an acrid smell.

He pushed sleep aside and forced himself to think. Something major was wrong with the car. He couldn't reach anyone by cell phone. He was somewhere in the middle of Washington.

Year before last, when he was fifteen, his dad offered to rebuild a 1967 Ford Bronco with him. They even found a Bronco, paid the owner seven thousand dollars, and drove it home. He and his dad called a Bronco restoration shop in Colorado and spent an hour on the phone with an expert detailing everything the car needed for a frame-up rebuild. His dad agreed to pay for the parts if Sage did the work.

After that, Sage did nothing. Every day, when confronted with the opportunity to work on the Bronco or lie in bed messing with social media on his phone, he had always chosen Instagram or Snapchat. He never ordered any of the parts nor did he lift a finger to start the bodywork.

When Sage turned sixteen, his dad sold the Bronco and his mom bought him a much newer Audi instead. Beyond changing the oil and the brakes, there wasn't anything an owner could do mechanically with a 2012 Audi besides change out the rims. It was a black box that only a trained technician with a special computer could access.

While Sage's Grandpa Burke had passed down knowledge about cars to his own sons, that knowledge had died with Sage and that Ford Bronco. He knew nothing about cars and it was his own fault.

Sage couldn't think of one good thing to come out of all those hours on his phone. A good-looking boy, with a topknot of brown hair, slim build and budding muscles, he had no problem getting the hottest girls in school to burn up the SnapChat lines with him all afternoon, every day of the week.

As he sat beside the road in a car that smelled like burning tires, he had no clue what was wrong or what to do. Like an ignorant child, he'd have to go find help—find someone competent enough to tell him what to do next.

Tired and angry with himself, Sage stepped out of the car and began the process of gathering his gear. He didn't want to make another mistake—leaving things in the car to be stolen. But a problem arose: there was no way to carry so much stuff. Grandpa Bob had loaded him down with enough camping supplies to fill five backpacks. The trunk and backseat of the Taurus were filled to the brim with food, water, tent, rifle, water purifier, sleeping bag, shovel, knives, cookware, Coleman stove and fuel... The list went on and on.

Sage hoped to walk until he found a farmhouse where he could call his dad on a landline. But he couldn't do that without leaving his supplies unprotected. He knew enough about road trips to know that an endless line of cars was not normal. People had to be fleeing Seattle, given the gridlock. It meant people were desperate. Even with a thousand prying eyes along the interstate, someone might still rob his car. Grandpa Bob and Grandma Glenda had sacrificed a lot to supply him. He couldn't risk losing what they had given him.

Sage slumped against the Taurus on the side opposite the interstate. He didn't want people to see how helpless he felt. Without his parents or a phone, he felt utterly lost. His eyes welled with tears, and he fought the urge to let frustration carry him away.

He sat up against the rear wheel of the Taurus for ten minutes before an ancient Chevy Suburban broke out of the line of cars and rolled up behind the Taurus. Sage looked up and rubbed his face vigorously, hoping to erase the telltale signs of his despair.

A grizzled old man in an army jacket and a long, gray beard opened the driver's door of the Suburban, hinges shrieking, and climbed down. Working out the kinks from a long drive, the old man limbered up as he trundled over to Sage. He must have noticed Sage's swollen eyes and flushed cheeks. He turned his gaze away before talking.

"You got car troubles, son?"

Sage was on guard. "Yeah, but I got it handled."

"You do, huh?" the old guy said, doubt in his voice.

"I got someone coming," Sage lied.

"Well, that's good," the old guy said, obviously not

believing him. "How'd you manage that with all the cell towers busted?"

The question stumped Sage, so he said nothing.

"Anyway," the old guy continued, "by the smell of things, I'd say you've got either a blown head gasket or you've fried a cylinder. In either case, your car's dying."

Sage gave the old man a sideways glance, unsure what to do next.

The man pulled his hand from his jacket pocket and thrust it toward Sage. "I'm Leroy Rockwood."

Sage returned the handshake. "My name's Sage."

"Well, Sage, I have a grandson about your age. I'm going to guess you're seventeen. Right?"

"Right."

"Come 'round over here." Leroy turned toward his Suburban. "I want to show you something."

Sage followed cautiously. Leroy struggled with the rear handle of the Suburban for a second, and finally the back gate flew open. Sage peered inside. The cargo space was cram-packed with survival equipment—boxes of military meals-ready-to-eat, ammunition, gas masks and big water jugs. The Suburban smelled like moldy canvas.

"As you can see," Leroy strutted, "I'm a survivalist, and proud of it, especially now with the world going straight down the shitter. I was right all along, and to hell with all those commie bastards who made fun of me. I hope they choke on their Armani leather belts when they're finally forced to eat 'em."

Sage smiled despite himself.

"Young man, you can rest assured that I'm all stocked up, and I won't be stealing from you this morning," Leroy said, intuiting Sage's distrust of strangers.

Happy to be convinced the man could be trusted, Sage off-loaded his list of troubles. "Mister Rockwood... here's the thing. My grandpa gave me this car to drive home to Utah. Now the car's having trouble. What should I do?"

"Son, you'll be answering all your own questions from here on out. I hope your daddy taught you well."

"How about I go with you and we travel together?" Sage asked, suddenly hopeful.

Leroy laughed out loud. "That wouldn't be any fun for you would it? Besides, I'm off to my bug-out location and I got OPSEC to think of."

"What's OPSEC?"

"Operational Security. You know, keeping my secrets so I don't get overrun by city folk."

"I wouldn't tell anyone about your bug-out place, Mister Rockwood."

Leroy laughed again. "Sure you wouldn't, especially if some beautiful female asked you real nice. I bet you'd keep your mouth shut tight as a tick. No, sir, I may have been born at night, but I wasn't born last night."

"Please?" Sage implored.

"Begging might have worked with your momma, but that ain't going to work with Uncle Leroy. Here's what I'll tell you, then I'll get outta your hair. Get back in that piece of shit you're driving, and get off at the next exit. Keep driving down dirt roads until the engine dies. You need to get away from the interstate. That car will probably still go a bit, and then it'll be dead forever. Alongside the freeway is not where you wanna end up. In a few days, people will tear you to pieces for the stuff you got in that trunk. Now get going. Oh, and get your ass ready for winter, son. It's coming." With that, Leroy Rockwood turned around and strode back to his Suburban.

Before climbing in, he shouted back at Sage. "Maintain OPSEC. Your daddy shoulda taught you that."

He climbed back into his Suburban and joined the slow exodus out of Washington State.

I doubt my daddy even knows what OPSEC means, Sage thought.

He considered the old guy's advice about getting off the interstate. Driving away from the interstate or preparing for the winter wouldn't put him any closer to Utah, but he was fresh out of ideas. He could wait here until another person stopped, and they might give him a ride, but odds were fair he would get robbed instead.

Sage got back into the acrid Taurus and cranked the key. The engine fired, but made a sickly rattle. Billowing smoke, he pulled back into traffic. Within half a mile, he exited onto a country road. The car kept going, skipping and coughing, but moving forward nonetheless. He passed by a farmhouse and, after a few miles, the fields along the dirt road changed to recently tilled soil. Sage drove past a small trailer park full of what looked like families of migrant workers. A mile later, the fields gave way to barren hillsides with nothing but rock and sagebrush.

The Taurus rattled and died.

Sage had exhausted everything in his list of possible actions and, with the death of the Taurus, he had reached the end of the line. He stepped out of the car and looked around. He had driven onto a road that crossed a hillside perched above a freshly-tilled field. A mile or two below, a wide and sluggish river cut the landscape in two. He had no idea what the river was called.

As the morning sun covered the dirt fields in light, Sage felt only hopelessness. He had the means to eat, the means to drink, and even the means to defend himself. Yet he lacked the one thing he hungered for most: the means to move toward home.

He hadn't a clue how far it was from this place to his home in Utah, but measured in footfalls, it felt like a million miles.

CAJON PASS, San Bernardino, California

CAMERON AWOKE to the early morning sun, feeling like someone had chucked a handful of sand in his eyes.

"Where are we?" he asked Julie, looking around, not recognizing a thing.

"We're almost into Cajon Pass."

"That's it? Motherfucker!" Cameron shouted.

"Cameron, you're waking up the boys."

"Why haven't we made more distance? You've only covered like thirty miles," Cameron said accusingly. "How long was I asleep?"

Julie defended herself. "Well, I can't very well drive over the top of other cars, can I? It's been bumper to bumper this entire time. You slept about three hours."

"Sonofabitch!" Cameron's worry kicked into overdrive. They were barely out of Los Angeles, and there was a ton of desert to cover between El Cajon and Las Vegas. If it was gridlock all the way to Vegas, the trip would take days.

Jason and Jenna Ross, his sister and brother-in-law, owned a second home in Las Vegas. Cameron, Julie and the kids could hang out there if they made it that far. But what good would that do them? Las Vegas might be as bad as Los Angeles, maybe worse.

The thought made Cameron worry about his friends and family back in L.A. Guilt rose in his throat, making that not-enough-sleep nausea in his stomach even worse. Could he have done more to help them? When he gathered his family and ran, he had left many friends and co-workers behind, maybe not taking the situation as seriously as he should've. Another boner committed in a life with more than its fair share of boners.

The day before, Cameron Stewart had been sorting and stacking torch accessories at the WeldMore Store #36 in Anaheim, California when the shit-ball first began to roll.

He enjoyed the menial tasks in the welding supply store. Though he had been promoted to store manager two years back, he needed the guys to see him as labor instead of management. There was something about admitting to being "management" that made Cameron think of all the things he thought he should've accomplished at thirty-five years old. Better to keep thinking he was preparing to launch his career than to think it had already launched and had landed him as a manager of a welding store.

He found peace in doing simple jobs that didn't require leadership. Being the nice guy exhausted him. There were days when he would much rather have punched people in the face.

His looks belied the heat he carried inside. A tall, blonde-haired, blue-eyed all-American man with an athletic build had bought Cameron easy access to minor positions of leadership. It had also bought him a smokin' hot California Girl as his wife. Looking in the mirror, Cameron didn't see himself as handsome. He saw a fraud playing up his good looks for all they were worth.

A little over a day ago he had reached down to grab another bundle of gas diffusers and something happened in the store that he hadn't seen in ages. The lights went out. It was only for ten seconds, but even that would be enough to crash the piece of shit computer in the place. It would take him an hour to reenter the inventory he had just logged.

"Son of a bitch." After ten thousand humiliating repetitions, Cameron had learned to keep his temper to himself. At work, he was the model manager, but nobody understood what that cost him in terms of self-control. He had seen an article on the internet about how parents who controlled their tempers around their kids experienced a heightened inflammatory response. Refusing to yell at your kids dumped a shit-ton of cortisol into the brain. Being a good parent, it turned out, shortened one's lifespan.

That made perfect sense to Cameron. He spent a big chunk of his life reining himself in, and nobody gave him credit for the effort. It was assumed that an adult should control himself and keep face-punching to a minimum.

With two little ones and a wife at home, plus finishing his degree at the local college, Cameron lived a life practically drowning in cortisol. For him, the mundane work of restocking the shelves felt like a mini-vacation.

The lights flickered again, then went dark.

Cameron walked to the stockroom and popped open the breaker box. All the breakers looked good, but he flipped a couple just to make sure.

He dug his cell phone out of his pocket and called the regional office. The secretary answered and told him that power was off all over the county. Cameron pocketed the phone and called his guys together.

"Take a smoke break," he told them. "Hang close, though. This should pass quickly. It's just too many people running their air conditioners at the same time." It was still summer in California—September could be one of the hottest months of the year—and power outages due to air conditioning had happened a lot back when Cameron was a kid.

Two hours later, the store was still dark and Cameron began to worry. Most men would chalk it up to a day off, but Cameron was a champion worrier. His mind wandered, and he recalled conversations with his brother Tommy.

They both loved to shoot guns. Their trips to the desert to shoot at milk jugs and pumpkins often dipped into conversations about what they would do if the world went to hell in a handbasket. There was something about the idea of society failing that worried and fascinated them.

Tommy lived in Arizona. He had started as an Anaheim street punk, just like Cameron, hanging around the small-time street gangs that sprouted up in metropolitan Orange County as it began its slide into urban squalor. But, like many street-smart guys, Tommy had eventually grown up and worked the lessons of street life into a career in business. After fifteen years and a passel of promotions, Tommy lived in Phoenix and was knocking back six figures in senior management.

Cameron preferred to stay close to their Anaheim home, where he felt more comfortable. He lived in the same house where his parents raised two brothers and a sister.

His sister, Jenna, left Anaheim at her first opportunity. She attended the Mormon university in Utah and eventually married a guy they knew growing up.

Jason Ross, her husband, was an Anaheim kid, too. He had done the dot-com business thing, made a pile of money, and now did whatever he wanted. He and Jenna visited Disneyland a couple times a year with their seven kids, catching up with Cameron and his wife Julie whenever they came into town to see Mickey Mouse.

Last Christmas, Jason and Jenna had sent them the weirdest Christmas present ever: six buckets of freeze-dried food. It was enough food storage for Cameron's family to eat for a month. The odds of the bucketed food turning into slightly edible cardboard in the next thirty years were almost one hundred percent. But, with the power still off that morning in Orange County, Cameron couldn't help thinking about those buckets.

Just then, the lights popped back on and the computer began to whir through its long restart sequence. Cameron breathed a sigh of relief.

Two hours later, the lights in the store had gone out again and Cameron's worry returned with a vengeance. He did what he always did when he felt things slipping; he called his brother Tommy.

"Hey, Tee, how's it hanging?" Based on the background noise, Tommy was driving.

"Hey, big brother! What's up? How you doing?"

Cameron did a quick calculation, converting Phoenix time to Anaheim time. Tommy should be heading to lunch. Hopefully he could talk.

"I'm good, bro. Just here at the store, living like the other half. How's the promotion treating you?" Cameron really wanted to talk about the power outage, but it wasn't in his character to put his own needs first. He felt more comfortable letting Tommy talk for a bit about his kick-ass corporate life.

"It's all good, bro. Just like on the streets but wearing a tie, you know?"

Their family culture emphasized several cardinal rules. On the top ten: *listen to the other person first.* So the call played out like a wrestling match of consideration. Cameron felt bad for interrupting Tommy's day, so he let Tommy talk. Tommy, on the other hand, knew that Cameron wouldn't have called him for nothing.

"What's up, brother? You okay?" Tommy pushed.

"Yeah, I'm good. It's just that the power is off. Actually, it's been off for most the morning."

"No kidding?" Tommy sounded sincerely concerned.

Cameron continued. "The news said it was just a glitch with the power company computers but, along with the problems in the stock market... I'm a little rattled."

"Have you talked to Jason or Jenna about it?"

"No, I didn't want to bother them."

Tommy went quiet for a second. "I think you should call Jason. He likes to hear about stuff like this. He's one of those Doomsday Preppers, right?"

"You're probably right," Cameron replied. "I'll call him when we're done talking. I got nothing else to do. I can't sell welding supplies with the computers down."

"All right, brother. Will you call me later and let me know what happens with the power?"

"No problem. I'll talk to you tonight." Cameron hung up.

Cameron's brother-in-law, Jason Ross, hadn't heard anything about problems with the electrical grid. Even so, they both knew something big was happening in the stock market because of the dirty bomb that had gone off in the Middle East. Someone, maybe the Iranians, had detonated a dirty nuke over a big Saudi oil processing terminal. The power going out in California might have nothing to do with the bomb, but Jason told Cameron to get ready in case he had to bail out of SoCal in a hurry.

Jason and Jenna were prepped for social unrest. They had a killer spread in the mountains outside of Salt Lake City, and they had set the place up for their family and a couple hundred of their closest friends. They even had a bunch of Special Forces guys in charge of security.

Jason gave Cameron a list of things to do. "Buy water bottles. Fill the cars and every available gas can with fuel. Get as much cash out of the bank as possible. Buy all the ammo you can find. Make sure your wife and kids were ready for a road trip in less than an hour's notice. Maybe go shopping and fill the pantry and buy canned food, not frozen."

Some of that might be hard to do without power in Orange County, Cameron thought, but he typed the list into his phone just the same.

On his lunch break, Cameron ran over to the gun store on Beach Boulevard. The place was a madhouse. The display cabinets were empty except for a few expensive target handguns.

He managed to pick up some ammo for his Beretta 92 handgun—some sort of expanding ammunition. It ran thirty bucks a box, cash only, but it was all the store had.

At 5:30 p.m., the lights were still out at the welding supply store. Cameron sent the guys home and decided to hang out so he could turn customers away, but no one came by.

His local gas station was running on generator power, so Cameron filled up his Toyota 4Runner after sitting in line for almost an hour. Everyone was saying the same thing: "Just a power outage. They'll have it handled in a few hours."

Over the years, Cameron, Tommy, and Jason had talked a

lot about the dangers of living in southern California. They all agreed that SoCal would be a death trap if things turned bad. The quickest way out of town was Interstate 15. It started in Long Beach, California as the 91 Freeway and passed through Riverside and San Bernardino Counties, heading straight north into the heart of Nevada, Utah, and Idaho. All the areas bordering the I-15 in southern California had become densely populated, and making headway on the freeway was tough enough even during regular times. If the shit hit the fan, the boys figured the I-15 would become a two-hundred-mile-long parking lot.

Cameron and Tommy had pored over maps, trying to figure a better way out. Even though southern California looked like a spider web of freeways, everything heading east passed through one choke point in the San Bernardino Mountains before opening onto the high desert. Caltrans had tried to correct the problem by creating an alternate route for trucks, but the choke point still existed. There was virtually no easy way around Cajon Pass if you were trying to get out of Orange County.

Cameron, Tommy, and Jason agreed that the survival of Cameron's family might depend on escaping before the other eighteen million people panicked. If even one percent of the population of the greater Los Angeles area got the urge to leave, the roads would be totally impassable, maybe forever.

Cameron decided right then, leaving the gas station, that this would be a great time for an impromptu vacation. He might lose his job over the decision, but that would be a problem for another day. He called his wife. She argued a bit, but Cameron was steadfast.

"We leave as soon as we pack."

Despite the early hour, Cameron checked his cell and

found it was miraculously still working. He placed a call to his closest friend, Beto.

"Hey, Beto, how's it going down there?" Beto lived in Buena Park, just a few miles from Cameron and Julie's house in Anaheim.

"Yo, *hermano*. It's pretty bad. The lights are still out and we're hearing gun shots every few minutes out toward Stanton. It smells like some shit is burning. We haven't had any rain, but the mist this morning smelled funky. Maybe it's from the ocean. Maybe it's radioactive, *'mano*."

"Oh, shit. Do you have your Kimber? You have rounds for it?" Cameron asked, not knowing what else to say.

"You bet your ass. Anyone comes down our street trying some shit, I'm going to pop a cap in their ass. I'll be honest, *'mano*, I'm pretty freaked right now. I'm glad you got Julie and the kids out when you did."

"We're not out yet," Cameron said, worry coming through. "We're stuck at the mouth of El Cajon and traffic is totally screwed. Have you taped around your windows?"

"I ran out of duct tape, but I got most of 'em. I gotta go. You take care, brother. Be strong," Beto ended the call, sounding eager to get off the phone and back to scanning the street for danger.

"*Vaya con Dios*." Cameron spoke to a dead phone, unable to hold back a lonely tear of frustration.

Overhearing the call and frantic with worry for her family in L.A., Julie pleaded for more information. "What's going on?"

"It sounds bad. Really bad."

Julie began to cry, probably imagining her mom and dad in Downey, on the edge of the scary part of Los Angeles. Her parents were in their sixties, and they had been in the same house during the L.A. riots. They often talked about how terrifying the riots had been.

"Why, Cameron? Why is this happening?" Julie cried.

"I have no idea, baby. Sometimes bad things happen to good people."

MOUNT SAINT MARY'S UNIVERSITY, Emmitsburg, Maryland

FOR SOME REASON that hovered just out of reach in his mind, Mat Best didn't drive home after he dropped the girl off at her dorm. He sat outside the residence hall, his Ford Raptor idling, the radio crackling with the scariest news he'd heard this side of Iraq.

The banks had taken a "bank holiday" and the stock markets had closed in the middle of the week for no good reason. Not only had rioting enveloped several of the large cities in California, but rolling blackouts had begun to hit the eastern seaboard as well. To Mat, this didn't sound like a disaster. It sounded like an attack.

He grabbed his phone out of the cup holder and stared at it, trying to make a decision. On his home screen, he had uploaded a picture of a recent tattoo on his back—one of the fancied-up Army Ranger logos with crossed M4 rifles and a skull with wings. He felt a bit self-conscious, uploading a picture of his own tattoo as his home screen. It probably couldn't be seen as anything but self-absorbed. Mat smiled, wrestling with the twin desires that had plagued him as he transitioned from being a punk Army Ranger to someone maybe with something to offer the world beyond killing bad guys.

The tattoos covering his arms and torso had a purpose. While they told the story of his military career, they also covered the scars he had inherited from a poorly treated skin affliction he picked up overseas. Any way you cut it, Mat admitted to himself, the tats were a vanity. Not only was Mat movie-star good looking, but he had never slowed down at the gym. If a woman couldn't be pulled into bed by Mat's perfect brown hair, dazzling smile, and rock-hard physique, she probably was a lesbian. He had even managed to pull a couple of those into the sack.

Again, Mat smiled at his blatant narcissism, still looking at his home screen. He had earned the narcissism honestly and he could still laugh at himself. But the words on the tattoo, *Rangers Lead The Way*, put a finer point on his self-examination. Mat knew good looks and charm would run dry in the end. He suspected life had more on deck for him than idling his jets at his grandmother's home, banging female conquests, sometimes several in a day.

The Ranger Creed, campy though it may be, haunted him. Words like *honor*, *gallantry* and *moral rectitude* had left their mark on his soul and no amount of whiskey and women would erase those values, dug in deep like the ticks that had burrowed into his crotch and armpits during Ranger School.

He swiped up on his phone and clicked over to "Recent Calls." He didn't even have the girl's name in his contact list. He clicked on the 502 area code call from yesterday, assuming it was a Louisville, Kentucky number, and would be hers. He punched *Call Back*, committing himself.

"Hey, Caroline. Mat here." A shock of fear inched up his spine as he worried he might have gotten her name wrong.

No part of him wanted to be that guy—the clichéd poon-hound who forgot girls' names.

"Hey, Mat. What's up?" she asked, a little confusion in her voice. He had just left her at her dorm fifteen minutes ago.

"I'm listening to the news here in my truck, and I'm worried about you. I hope that doesn't sound like a stalker. We just met and I'm already talking like a protective big brother. I guess I don't blame you if that makes me sound like a creeper..." Mat realized he was rambling.

"No. No, Mat, that doesn't sound creepy. What's up?"

"This thing in California has turned ugly. The banks are closed and we're having power outages along the eastern seaboard. I was about to get on the freeway," Mat fudged the truth, "and I pulled over because I don't want to just dump you so far away from your family. Is that crazy of me? Kind of creeper-guy, right?"

"Really? You turned around because you're worried about me? I'll be honest; I thought we were just going to screw and move on. I mean, that's the deal, right?"

Mat laughed, but the words stung. "Yeah. Maybe that was the deal... But here I am outside your dorm. Knight in rusty armor, I guess. Why don't you grab some clothes and hang out for a day or two at my place? Maybe we should play it safe and chill until we see what happens?"

"Hmm," Caroline seemed to be thinking through the implications. "They cancelled class. I'll grab some clothes and stuff. Hanging out sounds like fun. I'll be down in ten minutes. Maybe fifteen. Can you wait that long?"

"Sure. No problem. I'll be the stalker in the big, black truck."

They both chuckled and Mat ended the call.

3

"And it's time we saw a miracle
Come on, it's time for something biblical"

— APOCALYPSE PLEASE, MUSE,
ABSOLUTION, 2004

INTERSTATE 15, HESPERIA, CALIFORNIA

IT HAD TAKEN the entire day to inch up the I-15 to the top of
Cajon Pass.

Logically, Cameron knew they should keep going,
crawling along the I-15 all night. But he and Julie had
exhausted their ability to keep it together. Stress and fear
gnawed through any mental reserves they once had. Between
that and sleep deprivation, he knew driving through the
night would be a bad idea.

He pulled off the interstate and turned onto a series of
dirt roads running into the featureless California high desert.

With nothing but rolling washes, mesquite bushes, and the occasional yucca plant, Cameron was betting they would be left alone to get some sleep.

During the day, he had dug out his handgun and wedged it between his seat and the center console. He vaguely recalled it being illegal in California to carry a loaded firearm in the car, but he loaded the Beretta anyway, running the slide and racking a bullet into the chamber.

As soon as they shut the car off in the pitch-black heart of the desert, Cameron and Julie fell asleep.

CAMERON AWOKE to a blinding light and a brutal headache. At first he couldn't figure out where he was.

As his sleep-addled mind assembled the nightmare—the nuclear strike on L.A. and their endless drive through the California desert—he lunged for his gun and twisted around in his seat. The light drilled him from his driver's side mirror, coming from a vehicle behind the 4Runner.

His first thought was that cops were shining their spotlight into his back window. He shoved the loaded gun under his thigh, hiding it.

As minutes ticked by without an officer knocking on his window, Cameron began to doubt the spotlight came from the police. For one thing, the light was wrong. As he shielded his eyes, he could see a massive bank of lights on top of a truck about sixty feet back. Then it dawned on him; he was looking at an off-road pickup truck with a light bar.

A chill went down Cameron's spine. Someone in an off-road vehicle was sitting behind them, planning who knew what. He cranked his keys and stomped on the gas, making his 4Runner roar to life, but going nowhere. In his panic, he hadn't taken it out of "park." He threw the SUV into gear. Julie and the kids jolted awake. Gravel and dust blasted out the back as he tore off down the dirt road, escaping the off-road truck.

The truck followed, keeping its distance.

"What's happening? Who's behind us?" Julie trilled, keying off Cameron's intensity.

"I don't know. It's someone in a truck," shouted as he raced deeper into the desert with no idea where they were headed.

After twenty minutes of high-speed chase, the futility of running slowly dawned on him. The truck wasn't backing off, nor was it closing the distance. Worse yet, he had no idea where they were or how to find a way out of the desert. He couldn't see city lights anywhere.

"What're we going to do?" Julie sobbed. Cameron ignored her.

"What the hell are they doing?" he raged. He went down the list of possibilities as he plunged farther into the desert. It could be gangsters looking to rob them, though that seemed unlikely out here in Hicksville. It could be local kids dicking around. It could be some outlandish threat from a world where people detonated nuclear bombs over Los Angeles. He had no idea.

The unknowable motives of his pursuers teased at his self-control, picking at the fine threads of reason, leaving them frayed. An impulse grew to slam on his brakes, jump out of the car, and empty his gun into the truck.

If he stopped to shoot, lots could go wrong. He could kill some high school kid for doing nothing more than following him on a dirt road. What were the odds he would go to jail for shooting at some local yokel teenager? *Probably pretty good*, Cameron thought, even if he only put a couple of bullets in the fender.

Or, he could get shot by his pursuers. If he were killed, what would happen to his family? He shuddered to imagine the many paths things could take out here in the desert, his family defenseless.

A war waged inside him. Was it time to think or time to rage? Therein lay the rub. The gun, still tucked under his thigh, called to him, begging to be fired, aching to propel the anger from Cameron into whomever threatened his family.

But, if the civilized world persisted, maddeningly relentless in punishing Cameron's past lawlessness, he would pay a dear price. Could he release the hounds snarling in his head and not suffer at the hands of plodding members of polite society?

When he was younger, he had dabbled in the underworld, roaming the streets of Orange County, partying hard, brawling in bars, and smoking more than his fair share of weed. But he had never crossed that line, that line where a man became *a bad man*.

Many of his friends had crossed that line and Cameron knew, at this moment, thousands of bad men were cutting loose and burning it all down. One little snag in the safety net surrounding the weak and neighborly was all it would take for predators to enter among them, shooting first and laughing later. Cameron understood what drove them.

With his cell phone dead, he worried that the greatest risk to his family might be running out of gas in the endless desert. Every mile they ran from their pursuers, they pressed farther from the interstate and deeper into the unknown.

"Fuck it." Cameron stood on the brakes, launching Julie

and the kids into their seat belts. A Tupperware tub of Cheerios from the back seat flew onto the dashboard, impacted, and blew cereal across the dash.

Cameron unbuckled, grabbing the door handle in one hand and his Beretta in the other. The vehicle shuddered to a stop and he jumped out of his seat, bringing the gun up, turning and opening fire on the pickup truck.

BLAM, BLAM, BLAM, BLAM...

The pursuing truck slammed on its brakes, swerving from side to side. It lurched to a stop still eighty feet from Cameron. With a tell-tale grind of the transmission and a whining reverse, it fled backward a hundred yards and bounced into a ditch beside the road. The driver slammed the truck into drive, lurched out of the ditch, and skittered away from the gunfire, heading back the way he had come.

Cameron shot the handgun dry into the fleeing truck while Julie and the kids screamed in terror. Standing in the middle of the desert night, empty gun hanging from his hand, Cameron felt a wave of release. Something as old as mankind had broken free.

He could breathe. The tension melted away and calm settled over him.

He wasn't *a bad man*. But he wasn't a *good man*, either. Standing on that dark road in the desert, he was something else.

———

IT TOOK three hours for Cameron to find his way back to the interstate. The coming dawn eventually revealed the highway. When they reached pavement, he looked down at the gas gauge for the hundredth time. It was at a quarter of a tank.

The fool's errand into the desert might well have cost them the ability to reach Las Vegas.

Before returning to the barely-moving exodus along I-15, Cameron stopped the SUV and popped the rear hatch. He had grabbed everything his brother-in-law suggested back in Orange County. The 4Runner was packed to the gills with dried food, canned food, milk jugs with water, gas cans, and camping gear.

Cameron thought about it for a minute and decided to reorganize.

"What're you doing?" Julie asked. Cameron hadn't said much since the shooting. She shifted anxiously in her seat, apparently freaked out by the night before. "Should we call the cops?"

Truth was, Cameron felt totally on top of things. "No cops," he answered, busy with his thoughts. "We're fine."

"How're we fine?" Julie almost shrieked. "You just shot at people!"

"Sweetheart, please be still. We're fine. I need to think for a minute. I'm sorry. I just need to think."

Julie broke into tears, and the boys started crying. Cameron tuned them out. He considered the supplies and the 4Runner. He looked around. Like most of Hesperia, trash spread alongside the road, resembling a flotilla of garbage on an endless sea of sand. He spotted some old telephone books next to an abandoned trailer several hundred paces away.

"Julie, I'll be right back." He broke into a run.

"Wait!" she shouted.

"Just hang tight," he yelled. "You'll be fine."

Cameron ran over to the trailer and stacked up the old, weathered telephone books, as many as he could carry. He struggled back to the SUV and then made another trip, bringing more phone books.

"What're you doing?" Julie asked.

"I'm putting together some protection. The 4Runner won't stop a bullet and I'm afraid we'll have more shooting before we make it to Utah."

"More shooting?" she said, fear rising in her voice.

"We'll be okay. Give me ten minutes. Get the boys ready to travel. Take a walk and stretch your legs. Thanks, babe." Truth was, he hadn't felt this clear in a long time. Back in the real world, anger clouded everything, circling his thoughts like a vulture ready to pounce. This morning, he could think straight.

He pulled everything from the backseat and the rear cargo area and stacked his supplies into neat piles. He finished with five rough stacks: the telephone books, the canned food, the water, the gas, and everything else.

Cameron never missed the *MythBusters* television show. Those dudes had shot a gun at everything imaginable on that show, making it a poor man's encyclopedia of ballistics. He knew books served as excellent bullet-stopper. He also knew from *MythBusters* that water made bullets do crazy things— causing them to twist, bleeding off energy like an Olympic runner in molasses. What he saw on the ground, in five piles, was plenty of both: water and books.

He pictured the slow-motion videos he had seen of bullets going through books and bullets going through water. If a bullet hit a book first, it would slow it down a lot, but it would still be going straight, pointy end first. Cameron didn't know much about physics, but he was pretty sure that a bullet, with all its force concentrated in a pointy tip, was pretty powerful. But, going through water, a bullet turned sideways, even if it was a big rifle bullet.

What would a bullet do if it hit water first and went crossways or sideways into a book?

Horse sense told him that a thick book would stop a sideways bullet.

Cameron began stacking "miscellaneous" gear in the center of the cargo area: the freeze-dried food Jason had given them for Christmas, the camping gear and their luggage.

He unbuckled the boys' car seats.

"What're you doing now?" Julie was perplexed.

"I'm going to wedge both the car seats into the center of the backseat."

Julie was beginning to calm down. "Won't that be unsafe? They won't be belted."

"Yeah, but we're only going five miles an hour and, honestly, I'm more worried about gunfire than a car accident."

"Really? Why?" Julie clearly hated the thought they would face gunfire again.

"Because shit got real, babe. We're going to be okay, though. I just need a few minutes. Put the boys back in their car seats."

Cameron grabbed some luggage and pushed two suitcases up against the kids, one on each side of the mashed-together car seats.

He stacked the phone books outside of the luggage, standing them on end. He still had a bunch more phone books, so he stacked those in the cargo area, facing the back of the car. He dumped the last six phone books on the driver's seat.

Last, Cameron stacked the canned food, two cans deep,

up against the phone books, the last layer of gear on the outside by the car doors.

When he jammed the passenger doors closed, the cans slouched against the door and window, barely fitting. The water jugs and gas cans were the last things left, and he stacked them around the outside of the rear cargo area, the first line of defense.

When Cameron was done, he could see that it was far from perfect armor. But, with any luck, a bullet would hit the canned food, gas or water first, yaw like he had seen on *Myth-Busters*, then slam sideways into the phone books. If a bullet fragment made it through the books, it might hit the clothes or the camping gear. From the right angle, he figured the junk he had stacked up might stop a rifle round.

Cameron leaned in, grabbed the telephone books on his seat and put them on the floor beneath the kids' legs.

"If we get into anything scary, I want you to grab these books and put them between you and the door," Cameron instructed Julie.

Julie made a worried face. "What about you?"

"I'll be driving like a bat out of hell, so I probably won't have free hands. Besides, this is all just a precaution."

Five hours later, they had progressed almost fifteen miles. The gas gauge bobbed near empty. Up ahead, a gas station appeared in the distance with a giant, hand-made sign painted on a four-by-eight sheet of plywood. "Cash Only," it said. "$10 a gallon."

"Sons of bitches," Cameron swore, but he was happy he had grabbed all the cash from their bank in Anaheim three days back. He'd cleaned out their checking account, even taking their rent money. He had almost four grand.

An hour later, he made it to the front of the line and refueled. His mistake turning onto the desert road and burning up half their gas hadn't cost them their lives after all.

WALLULA, Washington

SAGE ROSS ABANDONED the plan to try for Utah.

With his current resources, it seemed impossible; he would have to walk all the way from Washington to Utah. After consulting his map, he realized that meant traversing a fortress of pines eighty miles wide and six thousand feet high, plus another five hundred miles of flatland.

Some people might survive the winter trapped in alpine mountains, but Sage's thin Boy Scout training didn't even come close. According to the map, he would cross either the Nez Perce or the Umatilla Mountains and, no matter how many times he repacked his backpack, he couldn't find a way to carry more than five or six days' worth of dried food.

He supposed a superior mountain man might be able to forage enough food in the winter pines, but Sage wracked his brain, remembering the limited time he had spent in alpine forests. He couldn't remember seeing much in the way of edible plants or edible animals. At least here, among the fields, he knew where to find water. He might even be able to scavenge crops.

Raised in the period of western child psychology that demanded parents protect their children from every form of failure, Sage used to view life as his oyster, and he was the beautiful little pearl cradled inside. Everything had pretty much always gone his way.

With his car dead and his phone not working, a new realization descended upon him: stuff in this world might actually be out to kill him. For the first time, some long-dormant part of his psyche that worried and fretted about the future began to wake up and stretch its arms.

For years, Sage helped his dad work their hobby farm. He complained the entire time, but he had begrudgingly learned a few things about the production of food. He and his dad had spent time in the forests of Utah and Wyoming, backpacking, fly fishing, and tinkering with wilderness survival. In that time, Sage gained a passing familiarity with the edible plants of the West and could probably identify a quarter of the edible mushrooms, roots, and berries common to the Rockies.

With even that tidbit of knowledge, he admitted how difficult it would be to cover even the most stripped-down caloric requirements while living off the land. In round numbers, he ate between twenty-five hundred and thirty-five hundred calories a day. It would be painful, but he could trim that down to two thousand calories a day if he was careful about how much energy he expended.

He guessed that gathering food consumed huge amounts of energy. The easiest calories he and his dad found in the wilderness had been roots. But a lot of the best roots, like sego lily and dandelion, were a bitch to get out of the ground. With each root delivering around five or ten calories, and the process of digging them up costing nearly that much energy, it penciled out to a losing proposition. He might fill his belly, but he would never gain net energy.

Roots growing in wet, loose soil, like cattails, were somewhat easier. Sage had seen some cattails down by the canal that ran along the fields. He could harvest the cattails for carbohydrates, but he knew he would burn through the local supply within a matter of days, and pulling cattails from wetlands was cold and dirty work.

One of his most despised farm jobs back home had been butchering rabbits. His dad built a rabbit-breeding system, and Sage became the designated rabbit slaughterer. When his dad forced him to do it, he could kill, skin, and clean one rabbit every ten minutes.

Sage recalled his dad droning on about survival butchery while he taught Sage how to slaughter rabbits. The truth about all animals, except for carefully fattened cows and pigs, was that they were naturally lean, with very little fat and scant calories. Wild animals, and even cage-raised rabbits, rarely grew much fat. Their bodies didn't contain as many calories as one would think. Without simple sugars like roots, berries and bread, Sage would slowly starve to death, even if he stuffed his face full of deer and rabbit. The calories in wild animals weren't sufficient to sustain human life for long. At least that's what his dad had said.

While Sage might succeed in identifying some wilderness plants, and maybe catch fish, rabbits and kill the occasional deer, he knew the process of surviving in the mountains would be a slide into nutritional suicide. Once winter closed in, hypothermia and illness would also raise their ugly heads.

Sage decided to stay put until the press of humanity slackened. He might be making the biggest mistake of his life, but there was nobody else to consult. He would have to trust what little knowledge and instinct he had learned.

He spent almost two days moving his gear from the Taurus to a hide-out. Taking the old man's advice about OPSEC, Sage found a shallow cave that was a quarter of a mile from the dead carcass of his car. The distance forced him to make a lot of trips back and forth, but that was better than staying too near the Taurus. The car would be a dead giveaway that Sage was close. He even used a different route each time he carried a load so he wouldn't cut an obvious trail for anyone tracking him.

As the sun set, Sage plopped down on a rock above his hide, totally exhausted. He took inventory of the situation. He had chosen to make his home in the nook of a rocky outcropping on a little ridge—a volcanic protuberance overlooking a pond a quarter-mile below. The pond filled from a pipe poking out of the hillside. It would provide water close to his hide-out, but not too close. Any source of water would draw people. The rocks made it possible to stay off the ridge, where his silhouette would stand out, but still maintain a view for miles around. Luckily, Grandpa Bob had given him a camouflage tarp, and Sage used it to conceal his stack of gear.

OPSEC, Sage reminded himself. Operational Security. In other words, *stay hidden.*

The nook didn't provide much overhead cover from weather, but it would be a good backstop for a fire. Once while backpacking, he and his dad were stranded in a rainstorm. After the storm passed, they were wet and cold, so they built a fire against a big boulder. The reflected heat dried them out and Sage hoped for the same here.

Using his buckets of food as support columns, Sage suspended another big tarp overhead, making a small room extending out from the shallow cave. He used up almost all the paracord Grandpa Bob had given him in the process. The big tarp was brown and didn't match the color of the lava rock, so Sage did his best to face the camo tarp toward the road and the brown tarp away from the road.

He walked downhill to check it out. From the pond below,

he scanned for his hideout. For a moment, he couldn't even find it. Then he picked out one of the straight lines made by the tautly-stretched tarp. He'd have to work on his camouflage job. Somebody could still find him if they knew where to look.

On his way back to the hide, he gathered as much dead sagebrush as he could carry. Firewood would be a problem here. The barren hillside was dotted with dead sage and bitterbrush, and it would burn fast. After a short while, he would denude the entire area. He would have to stretch the Coleman propane as long as possible.

When he returned to his hide, Sage strategically placed the dead sagebrush to improve his camo. He stepped back and realized it would take him twenty armloads of sagebrush to do a half-decent job.

With his energy running out and the sun dipping behind the flat plain to the west, he couldn't make himself work anymore. He had already worked harder than any day before in his life. He sat down on a rock and stared out at the bleak landscape—miles and miles of tilled ground, sagebrush, and dirt roads. The magnitude of his isolation dawned on him. He would not be going home for many months. He would have to live here alone. He would have to scratch his survival, somehow, from this raw ground. He couldn't see how that would even be possible.

Would this be his life now working his ass off from dawn to dusk just to survive? This wasn't supposed to happen. He was just a kid. He should have been hanging out with high school friends or paddling around in his mom's swimming pool. Why had his dad sent him to fucking Washington? All he had done was smoke a little weed. Who hadn't? He wasn't a bad kid.

His anger pushed tears and he sobbed loudly, sitting alone in his desolate hiding place. The injustice of his predicament and exhaustion overwhelmed him. He focused all his indignation on the easiest target: his father.

Why did his dad have to be such a dick? Why did he make him work all the time on the farm and follow his stupid rules? Did he really think his kids needed to be rich pricks like him? What a douchebag, to think that his kids would even want his life—working all the time just to keep a big house, nice cars, and to make people like him. Couldn't he see? His kids just wanted to enjoy their lives. They didn't even want all that money.

What did his dad hope to accomplish by sending him away? He might even die out here, all because his dad was a fucking control freak. Why did his dad have to treat him like a bad kid and fucking maroon him in the middle of nowhere, probably to die of starvation at seventeen years old. He wasn't supposed to have to fight for his survival. He was supposed to be enjoying proms and basketball and summer flings.

Sage's rage boiled over and he started kicking his stacks of supplies. The more he kicked, the more his anger accelerated. With surprising speed, he flew into a tantrum, knocking down the tarps and booting his supplies across the ground, sending them rolling down the hillside.

When he finally ran out of energy, Sage slumped down on the ground. His rolled-up sleeping bag was nearby. He grabbed it and jammed it under his head. Right there, he fell asleep, angry and crying.

Several hours later, he awoke, freezing cold with his mouth parched from thirst. The stars blazed overhead and he could feel his body heat pouring off him in waves, disappearing into the cold Milky Way Galaxy shimmering overhead. He had no idea where his flashlight had gone during his tantrum. He groped around in the dark until he found a bottle of water and he downed the whole thing.

With his thirst handled, he returned to his sleeping bag, yanked it from its sack and lay down in the dirt without a tarp or sleeping pad. He could taste the dust as he breathed, but he returned to sleep anyway.

Several times that night, his thirst woke him, but he ignored it. After many hours, he finally awoke to the light of morning. As consciousness dawned, he heard people talking and laughing. Wakefulness came hard and he realized he was in danger.

He had no idea how visible or vulnerable he was to the intruders.

HIGHWAY 97, Westminster, Maryland

MAT AND CAROLINE decided to leave Maryland the next afternoon. It had probably been the first time he watched broadcast TV since he'd been at his grandmother's house. With televised news of looting in New York City and Baltimore, on top of the chaos his brother described in California, Mat was motivated to get the hell out of Dodge. He didn't know where to go, but heading closer to his family felt like the right thing to do.

They were barely outside of town, driving west on Highway 97, when Mat's phone chimed. He looked down at a text from a strange phone number in the 801 area code:

*"I left a bunch of gear you're going to want in storage unit A5 at the
Hampden EZ Storage. Bring a pair of bolt cutters. Thank you for
taking care of Emily. Merry Christmas. Enjoy the NVGs."*

"What's that?" Caroline asked, edgy.

"I'm not sure. I think it's a text from a rich guy I know in
Utah. I used to train his daughter."

"You used to *train* his daughter. Is that what you call it?"
She smirked.

"No, seriously. He paid me to train her in shooting and
riding motorcycles. She's a medical student at Johns Hopkins
in Baltimore."

"Well, that's weird. Is she still there? Do we have to go get
her?"

"I don't know," Mat answered, thinking it through. "Her
dad isn't asking me to check on her, so I guess she's okay. The
text says I can have his daughter's stuff in her storage unit in
Baltimore."

"We're not going to Baltimore, though, right?"

"We should consider it. We have a long drive and things
are getting more fucked up by the minute. I saw the stuff he
put in that storage unit and we might be better off taking a
small detour to get it."

"But they're looting in Baltimore, aren't they?" Her eyes
went wide. "Will we be safe?"

Mat patted his AR-15 rifle, nestled between his seat and
the center console. "This baby might be as illegal as fuck in
Maryland, but I'm glad I have it. We should be all right." He
had also stashed a Glock in the door, along with three extra
mags.

Mat had all the weapons he needed, but the last line of
the text convinced him that it would be worth the detour to

hit the rich guy's storage unit. Many times in the sand box, his night vision goggles, or NVGs, had transformed him into a superman of combat death, scything through enemy combatants like the God of the Old Testament. Even without all the other cool swag in that storage unit, Mat would have made the trip just for the NVGs.

When they hit Highway 70, Mat turned east instead of west, barreling toward Baltimore.

HAMPDEN EZ STORAGE, Baltimore, Maryland

TWENTY FEET inside the Hampden EZ Storage gates, Mat drew down on three men. His girl lay curled up in the passenger footwell, hiding behind the engine block.

"GET THE FUCK BACK OR I WILL KILL YOU!" Mat screamed.

The men stood, frozen, in front of Mat's truck grill, their arms loaded with stuff they had apparently stolen from a storage locker. One by one they dropped their booty and ran back the way they had come, toward the back of the storage complex. Mat heard the chain-link fence rattle as one, two, then three men scampered over, somehow pushing through the barbed wire on top.

Getting into Baltimore had been easy, since the gridlock was traveling only one way—*out* of Baltimore. Getting out of the city would be much more difficult than getting in. They would have to take side roads, and that meant more risk of confrontation. This latest altercation inside the storage center had been the third stare-down Mat and Caroline had made with local punks since getting off the interstate. They boiled it down to a system: Mat would jump out and point his Glock at the punks, Caroline would curl up in the footwell, and he would scream his intent to shoot them. So far, nobody had called his bluff, which was good, because he hadn't been bluffing at all.

Mat devolved into the well-worn tempo of combat. Most people thought of Army Rangers as something less than Navy SEALS, Delta Force and Marine Raiders—kind of a minor league version of American Special Forces operators. While there was some truth to the fact that the higher tiers of Special Forces often pulled from the ranks of Rangers, public perception ignored the reality that Rangers got more work than almost anyone. In terms of SOF combat, "more work" penciled out to highly desirable opportunities to trade hot rocks with the enemy.

The officers at the Head Shed didn't need as much intel to send in Army Rangers as they might need for the SEALs or Delta guys, presumably because those Tier One guys shit gold bricks or something. The Head Shed could send the Rangers any old time they felt like an enemy compound needed a look-see, and they would be more inclined to let the Rangers conduct "recon by fire," hitting likely targets just to see what was what. The result: Army Rangers got a lot of work, and long-timers like Mat Best had fought countless direct action missions.

After serving as an Army Ranger for five deployments, Mat cut over to the CIA, where the action ran hot and the money came in heavy. As an expendable pipe hitter for the State Department, he had seen plenty.

So, when it came time to stare down bad guys at the barrel of a gun, it didn't strike him as any more traumatic than getting in a tussle at a bar. After hundreds of repetitions, the endorphins of threatening and killing enemy combatants lost that old gut wrench. It wasn't that Mat thought lightly of taking a life—quite the contrary. But his mind was largely anesthetized to the adrenaline hit of lethal combat. He could take incoming fire and laugh about it two minutes later.

Once the hoodlums had run out of the EZ Storage, no doubt leaving chunks of their asses on the razor fence, Mat pulled around to Unit A5 and was pleased to see the lock unbroken, the door closed.

"You're good. You can sit up," he reassured the girl. "We're clear."

"How can you do that and just move on like it's nothing?" she asked as she sat back in the seat, scanning for the looters who had disappeared while she was hiding. "How can you point a gun at people and then mosey down the road?"

Mat recalled how civilians felt about conflict. "I've had a lot of those moments. I hope you don't think I'm some kind of sociopath."

"No," she answered, but the tone in her voice said maybe.

"I'm a decent guy," he reassured her as he dug around in the backseat for his bolt cutters. "I promise. I really am. I'm just... good at this stuff." Mat stepped down from his truck, Glock in one hand, bolt cutters in the other, and checked his 360-degree perimeter for threats.

He didn't know how to explain his life to her, or to anyone else for that matter.

He holstered his gun and popped the lock with the cutters. He rolled up the door and, as his eyes adjusted to the shadows, he could see that all the Ross girl's stuff was there, neatly stacked on wire shelves and loaded onto a motorcycle trailer. Right off he could see twin motorbikes, six cans of gas, ammo canisters, two AK-47s, backpacks, cases of freeze-dried food, and a Pelican case that he hoped held a pair of NVGs. Mat pulled the Pelican case down, set it on the fender of the trailer, and popped it open with the hiss of equalizing air pressure. Inside he found a pair of white phosphor NVGs.

Mat whistled. He'd expected the normal Gen 3 NVGs. The white phosphors must have set that rich dude back at least ten grand a pop. He had never been issued white phosphor. The Army had been too cheap to give Rangers top-of-the-line swag like this. He looked forward to driving his truck blacked out while sporting these babies. He had heard these NODs were the shiz-nizzle.

He backed his Raptor up to the trailer and, luckily, had the right ball hitch for the trailer's receiver. He didn't want to linger in the storage center any longer than he had to—worried the looters would come back with friends and maybe take potshots at him through the perimeter fence. He hurried to get all the goods thrown in the back of his truck, including the fifty gallons of water stored in water cubes. When he came to the pair of REI backpacks, Mat tossed them into the backseat of the cab, curious about what they held inside. The Ross dude had been right about the storage shed—it was like the best Christmas ever for an Army Ranger.

When the storage unit had been pillaged down to the last piece of gear, Mat hopped into the cab and drove away, leaving the rolling door open.

ON THE CORNER of Pennsylvania and Fulton, Mat saw his first American murder.

Neither he nor the girl knew enough about Baltimore to

avoid the "bad areas" as they wove their way out of town, roughly paralleling the gridlocked I-70 freeway. As fate would have it, they had driven Mat's Ford Raptor, loaded with vital supplies and pulling a trailer carrying two motorcycles, right into the heart of the worst looting and rioting he had ever seen.

The corner shop where the murder happened ironically advertised itself as the "Friendly Fried Lake Trout, Chicken and Subs." As Mat nudged through the intersection in bumper-to-bumper traffic, two men ran out of the shop, both armed with revolvers. An aging black man, his hair graying around the edges, burst through the door behind them and leveled a shotgun in their direction. The blast of the shotgun dropped one of the young men, no older than twenty, on the sidewalk, not fifty yards from Mat's truck. The other kid ran away, something cradled in his arms.

The middle-aged man, hopping in agitation, bounced up to the dead kid, viciously kicked him until he flipped face-up, and dug a wad of cash out of the young man's front pocket. He kicked the kid again for good measure, causing him to flop back face-down, his legs akimbo.

The man argued out loud with himself, justifying the killing of the kid to anyone who might be listening and, without knowing what else to do, headed back into his shop.

Mat's first impulse was to stop his truck and render aid, but he thought better of it, especially in this neighborhood. He had seen enough dead men to know one when he saw one. The close-range buckshot had ripped off the top half of the kid's shirt, chewing into his chest cavity and lower face, revealing bits of the vital organs once protected by the ribcage.

"Keep driving, keep driving, keep driving," Caroline begged in a whimper, hunched down in her seat, terrified.

Mat inched along in his truck, passing through the intersection as he cradled the Glock in his lap. The neighborhood people kept moving, too, looking down at the boy but not gathering around the scene of the body to help or call the cops. They must have instinctively understood the new level of danger, and they kept walking down the street, speeding up their pace if anything.

As Mat's truck crawled past the "Friendly" store, a heavyset African-American woman ran past them, wailing, her hands flailing the air. She turned the corner where the young man had been killed and disappeared from view.

Probably the mother, Mat thought to himself. He scanned his threat angles, checking the mirrors every ten seconds.

———

THREE HOURS LATER, Mat cleared the city proper and edged out into the suburbs, the road choked with traffic bailing out of Baltimore. The suburban residents loaded their cars in their driveways, meandering about, restless to take some action to protect themselves and their families, but with no idea what to do or where to go. The impression Mat got was of hundreds of thousands of people in utter confusion.

In that sense, this was a more savage environment than Iraq. At least in Iraq, people knew what to expect from civil disorder, looting and chaos. In an American suburb, civil disorder hadn't occurred in twenty generations—from Western European pre-industrialization to American colonization. The primitive instinct to head for cover had been winnowed down to zero after fifty generations of society and safety.

At least the African-Americans in Baltimore knew better than to wander around clutching their cappuccino makers. Maybe it was DNA with fewer generations separating them from tribal Africa. Maybe it was the environment of urban crime and police "brutality." Either way, generational immigrants to America knew what was up. Long-time residents knew jack shit.

For the twentieth time since they left the EZ Storage, Mat heard gunfire. Caroline moaned, curling into a ball on the seat.

"Look at me, honey." Mat left the Glock in his lap and reached out to touch her. She jumped a little at his touch. "We're going to be okay. I have this under control. We're going to be all right."

She looked at him, her eyes darting. With his continued touch, her eyes rounded and her breathing slowed. "But what about my family in Louisville?" she worried. "Are they going to be okay?"

4

"Crying parents tell their children
If you survive, don't do as we did
A son exclaims there'll be nothing to do to
Her daughter says she'll be dead with you."

— *STAND OR FALL*, THE FIXX, THE
SHUTTERED ROOM, 1982

WALLULA, WASHINGTON

SAGE SAT up in his sleeping bag, still lying in the dirt where
he had slept the night. He heard voices echoing from the
pond below his rocky outcrop.

The sleep sand had clotted copiously in the corners of his
eyes like an accusation. It had been idiotic to flop down on
the ground, falling asleep after a tantrum. If he was going to
survive, he would have to do something about controlling his
emotions.

The voices from the pond were a mixed group of males and females, and they sounded strangely normal, like a bunch of everyday campers. An SUV had backed up to the edge of the pond, and they had set up lawn chairs around a would-be fire circle. The group probably moved in below him sometime in the night, while he slept off his indignation.

Sage decided to watch for a while before he made himself known. Maybe he could tell if they were a threat just by listening. It seemed unlikely they were dangerous, based on the carefree way they chatted. The group was young, maybe in their twenties. For some reason, their age made Sage feel better. They belonged to his tribe.

Still cautious, he looked about slowly, hoping to locate his backpack. That was where he had stashed his grandpa's binoculars. He vaguely remembered kicking the backpack down the hill. He could see it against a bush, too far to reach without getting up.

He listened instead. If he laid stock-still, he could pick out words, even from a quarter mile away.

"...where'd you put the stove? I need my morning cup..."

"Who drank my Mountain Dew? Come on, guys..."

"Justin, did you remember to bring a shade fly?"

After half an hour of listening, Sage had a sense of the group: a bunch of young adults, probably from Seattle. He decided to approach and make friends, but he would hold off telling them about his hideout and his cache of supplies.

There wasn't much he could do to conceal his camp since he had kicked his stuff around the hillside the night before. If he stood to straighten the mess, they would see him for sure. Instead, he scooted around on his butt, using the sagebrush for cover, and hid as much of his gear as he could. He scooped up the backpack and crawled into the shoulder straps. Sage made his way carefully through a gap in the rocks, putting the outcropping between himself and the new people. By their conversation, he felt pretty sure they hadn't seen him.

He walked around the back side of the rocky knoll, made a wide loop down to the dirt road, and approached them from the direction of the interstate.

"Good morning," Sage hollered.

"Hey, what's up?" one of the girls hailed back without concern.

"My car died." Sage pointed back toward the interstate.

"Oh, yeah?" One of the men stepped toward Sage. "What can we do for you?"

"I'm looking for a place to camp until cell phones start working again."

"Yeah? What do you have for supplies?" The guy nodded toward Sage's backpack.

"Just some camping gear..."

"You got any food?"

Sage made a non-committal gesture. "I have some freeze-dried. My name's Sage."

The guy visibly relaxed and shook Sage's hand. "If you're willing to share, you can camp here. My name's Justin. That's Penny. There's Tyson, Nora and Condie."

"Hey, guys." Sage waved. "I'm definitely cool sharing." He stepped into their camp and lowered his backpack to the ground, still too unsure to sit in one of their lawn chairs. "Where are you all from?"

The first guy, Justin, continued to speak for the group. Two of the girls drifted toward the conversation with the newcomer, and the other girl and guy went about their camp business. "We're from Seattle. We work at the Starbucks over on Fisher Street. When the lights went out, we grabbed some stuff from the store and headed camping. Figured we'd hang out for a couple days until things blew over."

"How was Seattle when you left?"

One of the girls, Penny, answered, "Things were a little crazy. People were rioting downtown and in a few of the low-income districts. We figured it was time to bail for a bit. The police were out of control. You know, bashing heads like always."

Sage dug into his backpack and pulled out a Mountain House meal—egg-and-red pepper. "Are you guys making breakfast?"

"We're trying to get some coffee going. We have plenty of coffee." Penny smiled and shrugged, as though being Starbucks employees guaranteed that they would never run short of coffee. Sage accepted her offer, and Penny dug around in the back of the SUV and pulled out a backpacker's stove. She set it up on the tailgate while they talked.

The three girls and two guys were in their early twenties, except for the one named Nora. She looked like she might be closer to thirty.

"So what's your story?" Penny asked Sage, making conversation.

"I was staying with my grandparents in Port Angeles and took off toward my home in Salt Lake City when the bomb went off in California. I ran out of gas back on the interstate."

Sage told his first big lie. He wanted to trust these people, but he felt reluctant to commit. He sensed that they were probably underestimating the severity of "things going on in Seattle" and that they were living in a bit of a fantasy world. He wasn't in a hurry to correct their mistake. It gave him a small advantage.

With some difficulty, Penny got the backpacker's stove working and poured water into the little pot that came with the stove. At that rate, it would take several pots to make coffee for everyone.

"How're you set for supplies?" With five people and only one SUV, Sage didn't see how they could have much, especially if they had used up so much room by packing lawn chairs.

Justin had gone off to set up their tent. Penny answered, "We borrowed lots of food from the store, and then we went by Justin's house for camping supplies. He's our outdoors guy."

Sage had spent his life around "outdoors guys," and he hadn't seen anything that would make him think Justin knew what he was doing. The gear they had looked like "tailgater" camping gear. But, at seventeen years old, Sage was by far the youngest person in camp. Even though he probably knew more than anyone about camping, the social situation suggested he behave like a guest. Plus, the guys were around twenty-five. They had to know a thing or two he didn't.

"How about you?" Penny asked Sage. "Are you into camping?"

"A bit," he demurred, "I was a Boy Scout, and my dad tried to get me to go camping with him a lot."

"Cool." Penny turned back to her boiling water and dug around for the packets of instant coffee. "You want a cup?"

Sage loved coffee, but he didn't know if he would like the instant kind the girl was making. His dad was a coffee snob and had typically been Sage's coffee supplier. Other than McDonalds and Starbucks, his dad's coffee was all he had ever tasted.

"Okay. What kind of coffee is that?"

"It's our Starbucks instant. Try it." Penny handed him a paper Starbucks cup, half-filled with dark, instant coffee. "There's some cream and sugar in there." She pointed to a box on the ground.

Sage dug around, found powdered cream and sugar, and mixed them with his coffee. He took a sip. "Wow, that's really good. I can't believe that's instant coffee."

"Yeah," Penny smiled, "it's not fresh brew, but it's good all the same." Sage liked her smile. Too bad she was so much older than him. The other girl, Condie, was a bit awkward-looking, with stringy blonde hair and a long face. Nora, the older one, was straight-up chubby.

"You got coffee?" Justin came back around, having made progress with the tent. Both guys in the group were rail thin and both had voluminous hipster beards. Justin's mustache curled up at the tips, like a fancy lumberjack going out on the town. Both wore plaid shirts with pearlescent cowboy snaps. Tyson had a brown beanie pulled down over his ears. He hadn't said a word or even gotten up from his lawn chair since Sage arrived. He would have pegged Justin and Tyson as a gay couple, except there was something possessive about the way Justin regarded Penny, like a dog that never takes his eyes off the sandwich sitting on the counter.

After boiling water three times over the stove, everyone had coffee. Sage noticed that Penny filled the pot from single-serving water bottles. He didn't see any other water around camp.

"What's the water plan?" Sage aimed the question at the group. Justin jumped on the answer.

"We're gonna fill water bottles with the spigot at the farm-house we passed a ways back. We decided not to buy more flats of water bottles, since they add plastic to the landfills."

Sage nodded, but wondered how wise it had been to count on the permission of the farmer. He might not like that they were camped on his land.

"We're running low," Penny said. "We should head up this morning and introduce ourselves."

Sage didn't want the farmer to know he was camped on his land but, if these guys were going to meet the locals, he thought he ought to tag along. "I'll go with you and help," he said.

Later, after a breakfast that included Sage's Mountain House eggs and a few cold Starbucks sandwiches, the whole group jammed into the SUV and headed to the farmhouse two miles back toward the interstate.

The farm consisted of several outbuildings with tractors, wood piles, farm animals, and barns. There was a chicken coop, and a pig sty with six or seven pigs. One dairy cow stood in a small enclosure, tied to the railing. As they pulled up, a big man in tan Carhart coveralls strolled onto the porch. Sage saw him set a shotgun within easy reach inside the screen door.

"Hello," Justin called as he approached the porch.

"Hello to you," replied the farmer. "Is there something I can help you with?"

"We're camped just down the road and were wondering if we could use your spigot to fill our water bottles."

The farmer squinted. "All the land around here for a few miles belongs to us. There ain't any campgrounds, except all the way back at the Gap near Wallula."

"We're just staying near the pond down the road. We won't be any bother."

The farmer appeared unconvinced. "Help yourself to water today, but we'd rather not have squatters on our land.

You should head back toward town or move on to Walla Walla. There are campgrounds up that way."

"We'll look into it," Justin said noncommittally. "Is this the spigot we can use?" He pointed to a pipe sticking out of the ground with a big red handle and a hose bib.

"Yeah," the farmer said. "For today."

Justin motioned for Sage and the girls to come fill up twenty small bottles. They carried them in a grocery sack. While the farmer watched from the porch, Sage and the girls filled the bottles and shuttled them back to the car.

"Thank you." Justin waved his goodbye. The farmer held his hand up, but didn't actually wave.

On the drive back, Justin weighed in on the farmer. "Who does that guy think he is? It's like he thinks he owns Mother Earth. Just because he cultivates the surface of the land, does that make him the lord of the manor?"

Sage didn't follow. "But he owns the place, right? He bought it at some point."

"Just because a rich guy plunks down money does not give him ownership over the land. The ground belongs to us all. We're all guests of Mother Earth." The girls nodded. "That guy may have a title to the land, but a piece of paper doesn't give him the right to treat it like personal property."

"I doubt the police would agree with you on that one." Sage let his contrarian nature get the best of him. He probably should have kept his mouth shut, he thought, as soon as the words left his mouth.

"Who cares what the racist police think? They're part of the problem," Justin sneered.

Nora changed the subject. "When are we returning to Seattle? I didn't make arrangements for anyone to feed my cats."

Justin grabbed his cell phone from the center console and stared at it. "I'm still not getting cell service. Maybe we can head down the highway to the gas station by Wallula. We need to fuel up anyway. I can ask there and find out if things have calmed down in Seattle. Let's drop off the water bottles in camp and I'll make a trip for gas and supplies."

Back at the campsite, they pooled some cash for fuel and food. Everyone chipped in twenty dollars, including Sage.

"Any special requests?" Justin asked, heading toward the SUV.

"Yeah," Tyson spoke up for the first time. "Can you pick up some weed?"

Justin laughed. "The county sheriff will throw you in jail forever for buying marijuana in this part of the state, Tyson."

Condie spoke up. "I brought a big Ziploc of grass and a bong. We should be set for a few days."

The group said their goodbyes and Justin drove down the road, the car shooting a feather of dust into the sky. Sage worried that the farmer would see the car and it would aggravate his sense of trespass. With Justin gone, Sage peppered Penny with questions about their camping plan.

"Why didn't you guys bring jugs of water? Like big jugs?"

"We're just camping. It's not like it's the end of the world," Penny answered.

"How much fuel for the stove did Justin bring?"

"Just whatever's screwed onto the stove. That should be enough, right?"

Sage grunted. "Where's the rain fly for the tent?"

"What's a rain fly?" Penny asked.

"It's the thing that keeps rain from getting into the tent. I'm just saying; you guys might be in trouble if you don't get back to Seattle soon."

"What do you mean *us guys*," Penny fired back. "I thought you were with us."

"Sure," Sage agreed, "while you're in camp."

An hour later, Sage saw another plume of dust rising from the road heading their way. Justin's SUV appeared in the distance.

As soon as Justin got out of the car, it was obvious he bore bad news.

"The gas station's closed. Same with the little store in town. Their power's out and they won't take credit cards. I couldn't go any farther looking for supplies because I was afraid I wouldn't make it back on the gas we have left."

"Oh, no," Nora said. "Did you find out how Seattle's doing?"

"According to the old guy I talked to, Seattle's gotten even worse than before. He said a lot of the city's burning and the military has gone in."

Condie covered her mouth, her eyes wide. Nora began to cry.

"What're we going to do?" Penny asked. "How long can we stay here? Where are we going to go?" Everyone but Sage turned to Justin for answers.

INTERSTATE 15, Las Vegas, Nevada

CAMERON AND JULIE passed thousands of cars on the shoulder of the I-15, mostly abandoned. Since the high desert, they hadn't seen a single open gas station. The blackouts apparently had made their way as far east as Hesperia. The stop they'd made for gas outside Hesperia saved them. They would have run out around Barstow otherwise.

In maybe two dozen road trips to party with his buddies in Vegas, Cameron had never once noticed how this endless stretch of desert epitomized despair. For as far as the eye could see, oatmeal gravel stretched off into the horizon, broken only by distant, drab mountains. It was as though an entire planet of discarded, ground-up granite had been dumped between San Bernardino and Las Vegas. The thin switches of mesquite struggled out of the soil over decades, lucky for a sprinkle of water a few times a year. Where man had passed, by the highways and roads, trash endured forever, without rain or anyone to remove it. The only thing this piece of desolation had going for it was the incessant compulsion of Californians to gamble. Otherwise, it might as well have been Mars. Except on Mars, the baking sun wasn't slaughtering people one drop of sweat at a time.

The thought of his family walking down the interstate, sunburned and dragging luggage, like they had seen hundreds of times that morning, sent chills up Cameron's spine. The desert would take peoples' lives in the next few days, and it was by a slim margin that Cameron's family would escape that fate, at least for now.

For Cameron and Julie, the thousands of dead cars meant traffic had thinned, even though the exodus out of California had probably multiplied a hundred times since the nuke. Cameron figured that fleeing Californians were reaching a simple, physical limit: they were running out of gas, blocking the road westward from Cajon Pass back to Los Angeles. Even using the southbound lanes, dirt margins and side roads, an all-out migration from Los Angeles had undoubtedly choked every inch of blacktop.

Leaving southern California had probably become impossible.

Before the nukes, very few people could have accurately guessed the range of the gas tanks in their cars. In the desert exodus out of California, that minor statistic—an asterisk in the vehicle's owner's manual—had meant life or death. People who had recently filled their tanks, or who had braved the massive lines at gas stations, had achieved a greater distance from the violent caldron of southern California. But no vehicle had enough capacity in one tank to clear the chaos bubbling out of the Los Angeles basin.

In perfect road conditions, with a full tank of gas, light sedans with top-of-the-line fuel economy could reach six hundred miles. Stop-and-go traffic traded fuel for forward progress, burning at least a quarter gallon per hour. The simple physics of internal combustion would leave hundreds of thousands stranded.

With cars dropping like flies and northbound cars overtaking the southbound lanes, the stop-and-go rhythm increased, and the 4Runner started making fifty feet at a time. Cameron and Julie had logged more miles that day than the previous three days combined.

Survival of the fullest tank, Cameron thought to himself.

At last they neared the final stretch of highway into Las Vegas. Dead cars littered the roadside like a desiccated army, riven with people stumbling slowly northward.

As they crested the final rise, Cameron's heart sank. Vegas looked like a dying fire pit, with hundreds of buildings smoldering across the valley, sending up tendrils of smoke, all conjoining to form a disc of muddy gray haze over the desert metropolis.

"Oh, my God," Julie whispered.

Cars poured out of Vegas in every direction except back toward southern California. The southbound lanes were filled with the California exodus. Even as Vegas died, people knew better than to head toward L.A.

"Are we going straight to Jason and Jenna's place?" Julie asked. They both understood she meant Jason and Jenna's second home in Henderson, a few miles south of the Las Vegas strip. The golf resort home had acquired mythical dimensions in Cameron's mind, a respite in this struggle to survive. Knowing Jason's penchant for "prepping," the Henderson home would offer them resupply—food, water, and gasoline, assuming nobody had looted it out. Once again, Cameron bet his family's life on the whim of fate.

—*Spin the wheel and, praise the Lord, Jenna's house still has gas. Spin it again, and, ah shucks, your family dies from thirst in a burned-out version of Sin City.*—

Cameron felt compelled to run directly to Jenna's vacation house to see if they lived or died; he wanted to see if the gas had been discovered by looters or not.

This Cameron, the one who had emptied his Beretta into those assholes in the desert—weighed his options. Strangely, the killer in him could stop and think, less afraid and more cagey.

"We need to make a decision about which road to take tomorrow to reach Utah. Assuming we find gas tonight, tomorrow we can either go the normal way up I-15 through Saint George, or we can go around the Grand Canyon. With this traffic, it might be quicker to go east around the Grand Canyon and cross into Utah on back roads. Let's drive through Vegas a little and see how bad traffic gets on the other side of the Strip. We can always double back."

Julie's face slid into a frown, eager to escape the highway

nightmare they had endured for three days. "Cam, the boys need to get out of the car."

Cameron knew that wasn't her real concern. She wanted to get under cover, exhausted from the constant stress of driving through *The Death Valley Death March*. He didn't blame her for being tapped out, but he also knew that they would have to answer the question about the I-15 sooner or later.

An hour later, they inched into the Las Vegas Strip, shadowed in the deep channel cut by Interstate 15 between high rises and luxury hotels. As soon as the Aria Hotel loomed over the freeway, it became clear he had made a terrible mistake.

Hotels burned unchecked, whole floors gushing soot like black demon tongues licking the sky. As the family drove by the Bellagio Hotel, Cameron saw something fall from a burning floor, ominously sculling in mid-air, almost certainly a human form.

—Spin the wheel of fate and, whoops. You win a visit to Purgatory—

Even amidst the destruction, people flooded the streets and rooftops—partying, looting, rioting. They saw a couple having flagrant sex on a freeway overpass, flaunting their naked pubis precariously over the edge of the guard rail, oblivious to the hundreds of cars passing below.

As they passed by the towering glass City Center Hotel, locked into slow-moving traffic, someone opened fire with a rifle from one of the top floors. There was nothing Cameron could do to escape the gunfire. They were completely blocked in on all sides by plodding vehicles. A person's head exploded in the car next to them, splattering the passenger side window with blood and brain matter. A half-second later, a bullet thunked into the 4Runner, somewhere near the rear quarter panel.

"Check the kids!" Cameron screamed at Julie, afraid to let go of the steering wheel, as though clutching it could somehow protect them. Julie ripped both crying children from their car seats and shielded them with her body while searching them for blood. Unhurt, the kids shrieked, echoing the feral terror of their parents. Another bullet slammed into the front half of the 4Runner, and Cameron prayed it hadn't hit the engine. Stalling right then, under rifle fire, could prove fatal.

—Spin the wheel once more and you get an all-expense paid trip to Sniper Alley. Remember, medical attention will cost you extra—

The traffic gave a little and Cameron inched under an overpass, shielded from the sniper by asphalt and concrete. "Shit, hell," he yelled into his vinyl-wrapped steering wheel, projecting his rage onto the embossed Toyota symbol. Never before had he felt so much like a rag doll caught in a hurricane. He hungered to stop the car right here, climb every step in the City Center Hotel, find that gunman and wrench his neck until he could feel nothing but vertebrae.

Other than abandoning their car and their supplies, Cameron could think of no alternative but to drive straight ahead. A three-foot concrete barrier separated the north and southbound lanes, and there was nowhere else for him to go. They were caught in a concrete slalom. They drove on, everyone panting from the come-down of absolute terror. The car beside them nudged past with its slain passenger smeared across the window, howls of grief and terror resonating like a pack of dogs, wild and unchecked.

As they nudged out the far side of the overpass, they saw

a body hanging from a lamp post on the Flamingo Road Bridge, a smudged sign around her neck branding her *Bitch* for some inconceivable offense.

Thankfully, the shooting seemed to focus on the side of the overpass they had already cleared. The spinning gameshow of death had moved on to other lucky contestants.

Music pulsed from atop one of the hotels. Cameron couldn't tell which, but the falling bodies seemed most frequent from the top of Trump Tower as a contingent of Vegas visitors partied their way into the Apocalypse.

Fatigued through and through by horror, Cameron's mind drifted back to the Prince song.

"The sky was all purple, there were people runnin' everywhere. Tryin' to run from the destruction, you know I didn't even care."

Cameron felt the tidal shift of emotion pulling him toward nihilism and apathy. Then he looked in the rearview mirror, caught sight of Benny and Barkley's terrified children's eyes, and snapped back to reality.

Gotta hang on, Cameron reminded himself. *First guy to lose his shit loses his family. Last guy to lose his shit, maybe his people make it.*

Thinking about this like a Discovery Channel show helped calm him, tricking his mind into a peace that it had no business finding.

Cameron wondered what had pushed the Strip into debauchery and murder in a mere matter of days. The criminal underbelly of Vegas had likely descended on the Strip—preying upon unprotected visitors. Overwhelmed and opting to protect their own families, Vegas police must have abandoned the stranded visitors to their terrible fate.

Before the first commercial on the Discovery Show about the cataclysmic destruction of Vegas, they would showcase the gap left by civilization retreating. As they rolled wordlessly forward through the chaos, Cameron heard the Discovery Channel voiceover in his head.

—*Some sleeping evil awakened, sweeping before it the drunk, drugged and vicious. Human predators mingled with the thousands of vacationers, and the weak and elderly hid themselves like doomed rabbits in their hotel room warrens. The Hell of Dante had come to America.—*

That would be the last line of voiceover before they transitioned to the commercial break.

Cameron and Julie's eyes glazed. The couple grew silent, except for the occasional sob from Julie, shell-shocked after witnessing five miles of human destruction and evil.

A few miles later, the towering hotels gave way and the freeway merged onto the 515-belt route, climbing out of Purgatory, and ramping toward a subtler hell. The 515 looped east of the Strip, back toward Jenna's golf resort home. While the horror lessened considerably, hundreds of businesses and homes still burned, drifting waves of smoke across the freeway.

His mind addled and adrenaline subsiding, leaving numbness and confusion, Cameron flipped to the television documentary he had been playing in his head.

Commercial ends, fade from black.

—*Most visitors to Las Vegas failed to realize the racial tension and poverty just a couple miles from the decadence of the Strip. Glamor turned gristmill, the outlying areas had likewise devoured themselves like a snake eating itself tail-first. Even on the freeway, burning cars evidenced the roving attacks reaching out from low-income neighborhoods.—*

On every street, from their raised vantage on the belt route causeway, Cameron and Julie could see barely moving cars and walkers from Las Vegas, stumbling eastward. Where were they going?

It dawned on Cameron: the people walked toward water. That would definitely make it onto the documentary. He tapped some long-forgotten show he had seen about Hoover Dam and the Las Vegas Valley:

—In Vegas, millions of desert animals came from the surrounding desert every summer to indulge in the water provided by the humans of the city. Lawns, lakes, golf course ponds, even zero-scaped yuccas and creosote brush along the sculpted parkways in the wealthy areas—all drew a share of the water flowing into Las Vegas by the grace of county engineers.

Now, with the grid broken, the flow of water and creatures reversed. People poured into the desert, seeking the one thing they couldn't live without for more than a couple of days: water.

Without power to pump, Vegas withered in the desert basin, except for those people ending lives neck deep in the alcohol stored on the Strip.

For sixty years, Vegas had flourished at the sole mercy of Lake Mead, piled behind Hoover Dam, back-filling dozens of miles of what had once been the Colorado River. But Lake Mead couldn't be counted upon to give up its water with ease. The River Mountains stood between the lake and Las Vegas. Pulling the water up and over the mountains required massive piping, pumps and electrical power—power that had died on the pyre of the stock market.

To get water, the sun-dappled, silicone-breasted people of Las Vegas would literally be forced to walk twenty miles to put their hands in the water of Lake Mead. When the taps guttered to a stop, the blackjack dealers, car salesmen, telemarketers and transmission repairmen of Sin City turned desperately toward the only place they knew held water: the lake.—

Tens of thousands of human souls moved sullenly down both sides of Warm Springs Road toward Lake Mead, dying of thirst. Watching the mass exodus from a freeway overpass, every east-bound street filled with humanity, Cameron's mind stutter-stepped.

Cameron couldn't afford to care. It was as though he had awakened to find a world where mothers ate their young and God gutted puppies alive. Stuck in bumper-to-bumper traffic, heading toward his sister's vacation home, a sign hung over his limbic brain reading: *Out to Lunch.*

For a moment, Cameron forgot how to drive. He looked over at Julie and could see the same schism in her slack jaw and glossed-over eyes, as though all the muscles in her face had suddenly ceased to function. Time stopped and his ears rang.

After several miles, the auto pilot in Cameron's brain must have failed because he slammed slowly into the back of a Nissan Altima in front of him. Neither Cameron nor the Altima bothered to pull over to the shoulder—settling instead on giving the middle finger out the window.

Cameron's rage at the gesture pulled him back from his stupor.

"Mother FUCKER!"

"What's wrong, Cameron?" Julie asked reflexively, a profoundly stupid question given that *everything* was wrong.

"We need to get out of here." Cameron slammed back into reality. "We need to get the fuck out of here pronto. This place is dying and pulling everyone with it."

Julie looked at her hands. "How could this happen? Why didn't the government fix this?"

"Babe, you're talking about the same people who work the counter at the DMV. You expect them to give a shit—to stay up nights staring at the ceiling, imagining all the ways the world could come undone? Hell, the authorities do their jobs, then go home and watch a shit-load of TV just like the rest of us."

"They were supposed to keep us safe. That was their job," Julie argued, still staring at the floorboards.

Cameron's stutter from childhood returned briefly. "I g-g-guess they never imagined it would come to this."

Finally, the 515 belt route banked to the west and the traffic disappeared, apparently not foolish enough to re-enter the hell of the Las Vegas Strip. From there, Cameron and Julie would have an open shot at reaching Jenna's house, assuming they could survive the surface streets.

Assuming Cameron's mind didn't slip sideways off the ledge.

WALLULA, WASHINGTON, "STARBUCKS CAMP"

THAT NIGHT SAGE slipped out of the camp by the pond and made his way quietly back to his hide on the rocky ridge. He had opted to sleep outside under the starlight instead of packing into the six-man tent with the Starbucks people. He wouldn't mind being packed in there with the girls, but not with the hipster guys. He knew from personal experience that a six-man tent was really a six-midget tent. For six people to fit, they would be belly to butt.

Under the moonlight and without a flashlight, he carefully cleaned up the supplies he had tossed around in his tantrum the night before and tucked them against the rocky nook. He pulled a trash bag from his backpack and wrapped his rifle and ammunition, protecting them from moisture. With his gear stacked tightly, Sage re-secured the camouflage tarp so that everything was hidden from view, piling up dried sagebrush to improve concealment.

Once he was done caching his supplies, he sat down to think. On the one hand, the Starbucks Clan, as he had begun to think of them, had little to offer him. They were going to run out of food soon and their camping equipment was a joke. At this point, there was no way he was going to tell them about his own food cache and his gun. They were too near a cliff of desperation, and they didn't even know it.

On the other hand, he liked the idea of being around the girls, especially Penny. She was probably too old for him, but he had a rising sense that, in a failing world, age wouldn't be the deciding factor. Justin certainly wasn't going to save them from starvation.

Sage worried they were headed for a confrontation with the farmer. He had already asked them to leave. The Starbucks Clan would increase the chances of Sage being kicked off the land, too. But there was nothing he could do to get rid of the Starbucks Clan, so he might as well hang out and see what happened next. He could always sneak back to his hidden camp at night, even if the farmer ran them off.

For now, Sage decided upon a mission. He would show the Starbucks Clan how to live in the wilds. If nothing else, being around young people helped blunt the edge of his dread of being alone. Living by himself was a rising factor, he had been forced to admit.

A thought dawned on him, and he went back to his stack

of supplies and dug around. His grandpa had added a seventies-era Boy Scout Handbook to his backpack. Sage leafed through it and noticed that the old BSA book, with a picture of a gleaming Boy Scout hiker on the cover, kicked butt on his own modern Boy Scout Handbook.

Back in the sixties, the Boy Scouts of America were more concerned with becoming competent in the wilderness than becoming politically correct citizens of the eco-obsessed world of the 2000s. The old book had no-nonsense instruction on how to live in the woods. Of course, the old handbook allowed for cutting down saplings and maybe even killing animals in the process of survival. The modern BSA lawyers would have a stroke if they thought a Boy Scout might kill a plant to survive.

Right beside the vintage Boy Scout Handbook in his pack, Sage found an old wilderness survival book called *Outdoor Survival Skills*. It looked promising. He dug out a tiny LED flashlight and did some light reading before sneaking back to the Starbucks Camp for the night.

Probably for the first time ever in the history of a survival skills book, that knowledge might just get a guy laid.

INTERSTATE 70, Near Warfordsburg, Maryland/Pennsylvania Border

AT THIS RATE, it would take Mat and the girl at least six days to reach Louisville. They were averaging little more than five miles per hour in the stop-and-go exodus from the big cities of the east. Forests, rivers and parks kept forcing Mat back onto the interstate. For the last dozen miles, he had been rolling alongside a big river that he guessed was the Potomac. A West Coast boy would think the Potomac River flowed through the nation's capital, not deep inland. It made Mat feel like he was making no progress, that they were still trapped in the human web of Baltimore, D.C. and the over-populated eastern seaboard. Being close to the nation's capital made his skin crawl.

The sun set slowly in the west, making it hard to concentrate on the maddening process of rolling forward ten feet, waiting two minutes, then rolling forward another ten feet. The glaring sun added a jagged edge of headache to Mat's slow-motion torture. With the constant stress of the traffic and civil disorder, Caroline drew visibly inward, like a flower drying out.

"How're you doing? Are you hanging in there?"

"Yeah. I'm fine," she said, pushing back her long dark hair. Even in horrible traffic, Mat couldn't help but notice she had incredible tits.

"Don't shut me out. We're in this together."

"Are we? Why didn't you just leave me in my dorm? You didn't have to take me to Louisville. I'm sure it's making you drive out of your way, and you don't owe me anything. I was just a one-night stand."

A rush of guilt hit Mat. "Don't say that. Helping you get to your parents is literally the best thing I could be doing right now."

"Bullshit. I know what I am. I'm a great piece of ass. I have nothing to add to our survival. I'm like a mouth with no hands."

"I'm not going to lie and say that you're not hot. I'm not

going to say that I'm not attracted to you. Of course I'm attracted to you. But I think you're selling yourself short."

"Don't let it bother you." She waved him off. "Everyone makes me feel like a sex object."

Mat went silent. Things had gotten more real than he was prepared to address. Right now, with people being murdered in the street and cities rioting, a hot girl feeling bad because people saw her as a hot girl sounded like a first-world problem. It bothered him anyway. Mat retreated to his old standby —humor. "Actually, I need your *hands* for something right now. Something very useful. Especially useful for a man *with needs*." Mat leered.

The girl made the universal expression for "what the fuck?"—throwing her hands up and scrunching her brows.

"No... young lady. Check your dirty mind." Mat continued, "I need you to go through the backpacks I threw in the back seat. I'm curious what the rich guy packed for the Apocalypse. What did you think I meant?"

Her face relaxed, a smile returning. "I thought you were going to ask me to make you a sandwich," she joked, uncurling her legs and reaching back to grab one of the backpacks.

Fantastic ass, too, Mat noticed as she reached across the console.

"When you're done with the backpacks, I could actually use a sandwich," Mat said.

"That's how you see women, huh? Good for hand jobs and kitchen work," she sighed dramatically. "What's a modern feminist to do?"

"I'm your knight in shining armor, carrying you back to your father's castle on my trusty steed." Mat patted the steering wheel. "Feminism might have to take a breather."

"Pretty much true, I suppose," she said as she figured out the combination of buckles and drawstrings at the top of the backpack. "Let's see what a crazy prepper person thinks will save him from the end of the world."

"Right now, those 'crazy preppers' are thinking they're the smartest people on the damned planet. Kind of hard to argue the point, considering..." Mat waved his hand at the traffic.

"First up: we have extra clips for the big guns," the girl held up a heavy chunk of stamped metal, filled with 7.62 bullets.

Mat faked a lisp and whipped his hand around like an interior decorator. "Young lady, that would be a *magazine*, not a *clip*. And the 'big guns' are AK-47 rifles. Let's get our terminology straight, okay, if we're going to be traveling the end of the world together. That'd be just fabulous, sweetheart."

She laughed as she fished out the next item, a blue stuffed sack. She pulled the drawstring open and peered inside. "A bunch of laminated maps," she reported. One by one she opened the maps, puzzling out their purpose. For the next few minutes, Mat drove silently while Caroline went back and forth between half-a-dozen maps.

"The rich guy drew a black line on the maps going from Baltimore all the way to Salt Lake City, Utah." She showed Mat a line across one of the maps, probably drawn with a Sharpie. "That must be home for the med student."

"I think that's what they told me; that they live some-where in Utah," Mat recalled.

"Why are there two backpacks and two motorcycles if only one daughter was at school?" she wondered aloud.

"Her dad must've thought it'd be too dangerous for her to travel alone. He must've planned for her to find a traveling companion. Maybe that was going to be me. She never mentioned it, though."

"Probably because it would've made her sound like a loony," Caroline chuckled. "If she already had a car, why did she have motorcycles, too?"

"Traffic and gas, Miss Hot Tits. Traffic and gas. More than a dozen motorcycles have passed us in the last couple hours like we're standing still. If we ditched the truck and got on the motorcycles, we'd be making a lot better time. Also, you saw the lines at the gas stations we drove by? Soon, gasoline will be scarce. Those two bikes are light—almost mopeds. I'll bet they get over a hundred miles per gallon."

"So why not leave the truck and head out on the motorcycles?" she suggested.

"Hush. You'll make Vanessa sad," Mat soothed the dashboard. "We won't abandon you, Vanessa. Don't listen to Miss Hot Tits. I wouldn't give you up if my life depended on it. There are a lot of advantages to having wheels and those motorcycles barely qualify as wheels. For one thing, we can't hop into the cab and get out of the weather on motorcycles."

"I'm not Miss Hot Tits. I told you, I don't like how that sounds."

"Sorry. I'm joking. I'm trying to lighten up this whole end of the world scenario. Did you ever see Land of the Lost?"

"Nope."

"You're too young. I'm too young, too, but I'm into vintage television. *Land of the Lost* was a seventies TV show where a family falls through a portal and into a parallel dimension of dinosaurs and *Sleestak* lizard, zombie-monsters. Maybe that's us. We're like the Marshall family. We need to be thinking about all the people in these cars turning into Sleestaks. I've seen it happen, honey pie."

"You've seen people turn into Sleestaks?"

"Yep. One day, the Iraqis were living their lives, waiting for the next Ironman movie to come out in Baghdad, and the next they were trying to blow up every American they could find. I'm not sure how it happens, but people can turn into Sleestaks."

"You're scaring me, Mat. I don't see how that could happen in America."

"I don't mean to scare you. I just don't want us to get caught behind the times. If that happens—if people start going zombie, like we saw in Baltimore—I don't want us to miss the turn signal."

She looked down, studying the floor mat. "I don't think I can make it in a world like that."

Mat thought about it for a second. He had seen the first signs of grit in this girl. He wasn't so sure she wouldn't make it in a world like Iraq. Maybe with a little experience and some training, she might be okay.

"I'm not sure you're giving yourself a fair shake," Mat argued. "Anyway, that's why you have me."

Too late, he realized that he had just committed himself.

5

_____

"Soon to fill our lungs, the hot winds of death
The gods are laughing, so take your last breath
Fight fire with fire, the ending is near
Fight fire with fire, bursting with fear."

— _FIGHT FIRE WITH FIRE_,
METALLICA, RIDE THE LIGHTNING,
1984

HIGHWAY 68, NEAR ICES FERRY, WEST VIRGINIA

"COULD you show me how to use this?" Caroline asked, holding the AK-47 assault rifle like a dead rat by the tail. They had pulled off the highway onto a dirt access road to get a little sleep and now, with morning dawning, they were ready to get rolling again.

"We'll be back on the road soon, so I doubt the police

could get here before we head out. Yeah. I suppose we can shoot here."

They had passed homes half-a-mile back in the night and then parked the truck in a gravel quarry. Mat figured they could shoot safely into one of the embankments without any risk of sending lead caroming into a house. Someone might still call the cops but, given the chaos pouring into the hill country like a rising tidal wave, Mat wasn't too worried about police intervention. The AKs might be illegal in West Virginia—but on second thought, who knew? Maybe a redneck state like West Virginia tilted more red than blue. In any case, Mat smelled lawlessness in the air and it wasn't a smell he entirely disliked.

"Rock and roll, Sister Christian." Mat looked around and stretched his back. Driving all day and then sleeping sitting up in the driver's seat wasn't as easy as it had been when he was a younger man. He was creeping up on thirty years old— something he would prefer to forget.

"I'm Catholic, just so you know," she said, smiling.

"Yeah. I've noticed you're quite a saint," Mat made eyes at her, obviously referring to the backseat gymnastics they had shared before going to sleep the night before. "Sister Christian's an eighties song, in case you were wondering. You're at least eighteen, right?" Mat shot her an expression of mock concern.

Caroline gave him the bird, simultaneously sweeping the rifle playfully in his direction.

"Whoa, whoa." Mat grabbed the muzzle and pushed it downrange. "Rule Number Two of Firearm Safety: don't point the gun at anything you don't intend to destroy."

"It wasn't loaded," she argued.

"Rule Number One: treat every gun as though it's loaded. You with me?"

"Yep. What's Rule Number Three?"

Mat reached in and gently removed her finger from the trigger. "Keep your finger off the trigger until you're ready to fire. Rule Four: know your target, what's behind it and what might step in front of it. This berm right here," Mat motioned to the cut-back wall of the gravel pit, "is a safe backstop. Let's pop a mag in and go Ted Nugent."

"What's a Ted Nugent?"

Mat sighed, confronted by their age gap for the fourth time in ten minutes. "Ted Nugent is a *who*. He's a seventies rock star. You know, spokesman for the NRA? Reality show host? *Cat Scratch Fever?*"

"How old are you?" She laughed, this time minding the muzzle of the AK.

"I'm old enough to know good music from bad, young Padawan learner. Now, rock the mag into the mag well like this, run the bolt like this and defeat the safety like this. Got it?" Mat popped the mag out, ejected the round and returned the gun to safe. "You do it."

Caroline executed the sequence perfectly, even clicking down the stiff clacker bar safety with the long side of her thumb like Mat had done. Mat reached around and reset the safety.

"Color me impressed, young lady. Not only are you beautiful, but you follow instructions like a natural. Let's shoot. When you're ready, you're going to defeat the safety again, line up the sights on that white, bowling ball-sized rock and squeeze the trigger."

"How do the sights work?" she asked.

"Great question. I'll show you." Mat dove into teaching

her the basics of sight picture—the art of focusing on what matters when sighting a firearm. Then he had her dry-fire the AK until her trigger press was smooth as butter.

Within fifteen minutes, she had chewed the white rock into half a dozen chunks, blasting through an entire magazine of 7.62 bullets.

Mat took the rifle and launched into his best southern accent. "Why, Miss Caroline, I do declare, you are a fine natural shooter. I do say, I may have misjudged your aptitude for the charms of combat."

"Why, Mister Rhett Butler, you've gone and made me blush," Caroline replied, quick as a whip, in a perfect southern belle accent.

Mat dropped the accent. "I thought you were from Kentucky."

"I say, a well-bred gentleman like yourself should know when he's courting a southern lady. I was born and raised in Charleston, South Carolina. My parents and my brother only recently relocated to Kentucky." She nailed it, proving without a doubt that southern English was her maiden tongue.

"Goddamn. You are beautiful on many levels. Miss Caroline, I would love nothing more than to take another run under your petticoats, but I'm afraid we've overstayed our welcome by burning through that magazine. Let's saddle up and get moving down the road."

As Mat walked to the driver side, he puzzled over the feeling in the pit of his stomach, a sensation like he had just emerged the winner from a gunfight. He knew what it meant to find a girl attractive, but this had bumped to another level.

What's wrong with me? he wondered as he stepped up into

the cab, marveling at the girl sitting across from him. He felt his capacity for rational thought get a little fuzzy.

WALLULA, WASHINGTON, "STARBUCKS CAMP"

"WE'RE OUT OF WATER AGAIN," Penny informed the Starbucks Clan. By the time they were done with breakfast coffee, one little pot at a time, it was almost time for lunch. "And we're running out of food."

Justin groaned. "I can go check the store again today. Maybe they're getting back to normal."

Sage doubted it. He had carefully shepherded his cell phone battery, and twice a day he checked for a signal. He checked half an hour ago. Nothing.

"Maybe we can start foraging for food," Sage floated the idea.

"Hah!" Tyson jeered, "like you're going to find anything edible out here in Sticksville. Good luck with that."

Sage ignored the insult. "If the farmer comes around, he's going to freak out. This camp's starting to look like a bunch of homeless people live here." Clothes were strewn about and some kind of animal had busted into their trash bag overnight, chewing a hole in the side and dragging garbage around the camp.

"That farmer can suck a bag of dicks," Justin answered. He glared at Sage, daring him to make another comment.

Sage shut up and went back to whittling sticks.

"Whatcha making?" Penny asked. Sage had been whittling where she would be most likely to notice him. Penny had warmed to him this morning. He took it as a good sign.

"I'm making figure-four deadfalls," he said, fishing for a follow-on question.

"What's that?"

Sage smiled. "They're small animal traps. Let me show you." He put one of the delicate traps together and pressed down on the top of the figure-four shape made by the sticks. His downward pressure simulated the weight of a rock.

"I put a piece of bait on this pointy stick here, then set a big, flat rock here and, when the animal touches the bait..." Sage tapped the "baited" stick and the whole figure-four shape collapsed. "Wham! The rock falls."

He had been working on figure-four deadfalls since the crack of dawn. Truth was, he had never made one before, and it had taken him several tries before he got it to work.

Penny looked impressed. "Wow! What kind of animal will you kill with that?"

"Maybe a squirrel or a mouse. Maybe the raccoon that got into our trash."

Penny screwed up her nose. "We can eat those? Do they taste okay?"

Sage figured any animal he would kill with the dead fall trap would taste like shit on a shingle, especially compared to the Mountain House freeze-dried hidden in his cache. He had radically exaggerated the size of the animal he might kill, too. It would take a two-hundred-pound rock to kill a raccoon, not that anyone in camp could call him on his bullshit. "Anything tastes good when you're hungry enough," Sage claimed, not at all sure that was true.

Penny looked dubious, but Sage had already accomplished his mission, to look like a badass in front of the girl.

By the time Justin got back from town, Sage had returned from a several-mile walkabout around the camp. Justin slammed the car door, obviously pissed. "Not only is the store closed, but the redneck gun fanatics around here are psychos. One guy in town almost shot me. When I drove by the farmer's house, men with guns were standing in his front yard."

"So what about Seattle?" Condie, the girl with the horse face whined at Justin.

"How the hell should I know about Seattle? The locals have gone *Red Dawn*. I was lucky they didn't blow me away. As though there's not enough bad news, the car started sputtering the last quarter mile. I think it's out of gas."

The news alarmed Sage, but it wasn't unexpected. He had grown up listening to his dad, grandpas, and their friends talk about the fall of civilization or "When the Shit Hits the Fan" or "SHTF," as they called it. To Sage, this series of events was like a scary bedtime story turned real life. He knew each chapter, and he suspected things were going to go from *bad* to *inconceivably bad*. Once things went pear-shaped with modern society, getting back to "normal" might take years, or even decades. Or so he had been told around his father's campfire.

"There is one piece of good news," Sage chimed in. Justin turned on him with a sneer. He was probably sick of Sage contradicting him. "I found onions."

"What do you mean, you found onions?" Justin asked.

"In the dirt field over there." Sage pointed to the field on the other side of the road with the stick he had been whittling. "There are a few onions still in the ground. The harvester machine must've let them pass. We can sift through the soil and pick out the ones they missed."

"I hate onions," Tyson remarked from his lawn chair.

Justin marched over to Sage's pack. "You can eat reject onions if you want, but you better not be holding out on us with your food in that backpack. What do you have in there?"

All eyes turned to Sage's backpack leaning against a rock.

"I have a couple more Mountain Houses, but that's about it."

Justin started pulling stuff out and tossing it on the ground.

"Hey, bro, that's my stuff. Take it easy." Sage stood.

"We agreed when you came in here—you're sharing everything, remember? We've shared our stuff with you; now you're going to share back." Justin continued tearing the pack apart.

"I *have* been sharing," Sage argued.

"Yeah? Then what's this?" Justin pulled out a Mountain House berry cobbler. "You didn't tell us you had this."

"Nobody asked," Sage answered.

"Right. You sound like a selfish capitalist asshole. When we invited you into this camp, everything you owned became ours. Why would you keep this for yourself?" Justin held up the cobbler like an indictment.

"Whatever, bro. When I joined you, this was just a camping trip. Take whatever you want. It's not going to matter. We need a long-term plan for food and water or we're screwed."

"Don't you worry, little man, I have a plan." Justin took the berry cobbler and left the mess on the ground. Sage got up and repacked his gear.

"You don't have to be mean, Justin," chubby Nora defended Sage. "At least he's looking for options." Her defense made Sage squirm. Maybe he hadn't been fair with her, writing her off as someone too old to relate.

When Sage had his backpack together, he turned to Penny. "I'm going to dig up some onions. I want to see what we can do with them. I'll figure out the best way to do it and come get you guys, if you want." He marched out of camp, churning through options in his mind. He wasn't going to let Justin treat him like that. Not for long, anyway.

It took Sage an hour to collect more onions than he could carry in his shirt. When he came back, things had settled down.

"Sorry I got so intense with you," Justin apologized. "I'm just worried. Maybe we should try some of those onions." He pointed at Sage's shirt and smiled.

"Yeah, I was thinking we might try cooking them over the coals," Sage said, accepting the apology.

"Sounds good. I'll help you collect firewood." Sage and Justin did a quick circuit of the surrounding area and brought back a bunch of dry sagebrush. Everyone was hungry since they had skipped lunch, so the group gathered around as Sage and Justin stacked the sagebrush into their makeshift fire pit.

"What are you doing?" Sage looked up from the fire to see Penny pouring water from one bottle to another bottle, passing the water through her shirt.

"I'm screening the pond water. We can't get water from the farmer because we're out of gas, so we're filtering this."

"Did anyone drink that?" Sage asked, concern in his voice.

"Yeah. We made a bottle earlier for coffee when we ran out of bottled water."

"Who drank it?" Sage stopped working on the fire and focused on Penny.

"Just me. I drank the last pot." Penny shrugged. "Did I do something wrong?"

"Maybe. How hot did you get the coffee?"

"Not quite boiling. We ran out of gas. Why?" She looked puzzled.

Sage shook his head and exhaled loudly. "I don't know for sure, but that water is likely to have bacteria and stuff. You can't drink it unless it's thoroughly filtered, then boiled."

"I feel fine," Penny said. "It looks good. It comes out of that pipe. Justin said it was a spring."

"It might be a spring, all right, but that doesn't mean it's pure. Let us know if you start feeling sick. Nobody else drink that water unless it's brought to a full boil for several minutes. Okay?" Sage looked around and everyone seemed to be listening except Tyson. He was hitting the bong.

Justin squinted at Sage, his hands on his hips. "I said it was a spring. I didn't say it was okay to drink from it." The man covered his possible error.

"Also, where's everyone pooping?" Sage asked.

Nobody 'fessed up. "Listen, we can't relieve ourselves anywhere near the pond or we'll get sick, no matter how carefully we boil the water. We need to set a specific crapping area." Sage sensed his detente with Justin slipping.

"Justin, where do you want us to take our dumps?" Sage turned to him, acting as though he was their leader.

"Let's crap over behind that big bush on the other side of the dirt road. Okay, guys?" Everyone nodded. "We'll dig a pit there after we eat."

Sage turned back to the fire pit and got the sagebrush burning. After half an hour, they had burned the sagebrush down to coals. Sage put the onions directly on the hot coals.

"Isn't that going to burn them?" Condie asked.

"I don't think so," Sage said. "It should burn the outer layers and cook the inside. It's almost like steaming them in their husks. Do we have any salt?" Nobody seemed to know, which meant they didn't.

They ate all the onions. With the smoky flavor, salt would have been nice. Everyone but Tyson thanked Sage. Tyson insisted he hated onions and refused to try any.

After lunch, Nora suggested they bathe. "Would it hurt if we bathed in the pond, Sage? We're starting to smell bad. The tent at night... it's gross."

Sage had no idea if bathing in the pond would be a health risk, but he was suddenly seized by the prospect of seeing the girls naked, so he put on his most expert-sounding voice. "I think we should be okay. Just nobody crap or pee in there."

"Great," Nora said. "Then I'm taking a bath. Who's with me?"

Sage looked sideways at Penny. "Yeah," Penny said, "I'm in."

As the group queued up to go into the pond, the moment of truth came. Nobody wanted to seem prudish, so everyone slowly undressed until it came down to underwear. An unspoken hesitation passed through the group as they stood on the rocky edge of the pond in their underwear, their feet uncomfortable on the stones. Finally, Justin pulled off his underwear, his penis dangling, and jumped into the water. Everyone followed suit, with Sage running last in line as he furtively checked out naked Penny.

She was just full-figured enough to look exotic—not the picture-perfect nudes he was used to seeing on internet porn. Her unshaved bush, and the fact that it had been a while since he had seen a naked girl, turned him on in a mad rush. He had to jump into the pond to hide his erection.

Penny swam up to Sage as they played and splashed. "So, Mountain Man, what're we going to do next?"

Sage felt the warmth of her approval amplified by her nakedness. The question seemed incredibly intimate to him. Somewhere in the back of his head, he suspected the implied intimacy was intentional on her part, but he went with it, more or less helpless.

He thought for a few seconds, then began. "We need to improve our shelter situation. That tent's not going to cut it. One big rain will soak all the sleeping bags, and then we'll have a hypothermia problem. So that's a top priority. As far as food, we can live off onions for a while. There are tons of them in that field, plus there are other fields. Water's going to be an issue. We need to come up with a better filtration system, and then we have to boil everything. I'll start work on that tomorrow."

As she looked at him expectantly, he got the impression she wasn't really listening. She just wanted to know someone was handling her survival. Apparently he had risen to the position of "Mountain Man" in her mind, just as he had hoped. With this latest development, things felt strangely okay.

The group tired of swimming and climbed out of the pond, picking their way across the rocks and back to their clothes. Sage was the last out, getting a solid eyeful of the naked women. He needed a minute before he could climb out after them.

An hour later, an onslaught of diarrhea hit Penny. The slurry of biota in her morning coffee triggered an all-out counter-offensive by her intestinal tract, and she blew liquid out the top and bottom ends of her system. Every ten minutes, she ran back to the crapper bush to expel another jet of liquefied coffee and onions. They could hear the pop and rush of her bowel explosions all the way from camp.

ROSS HOME, Henderson, Nevada

WHEN CAMERON and Julie pulled into the country club in Henderson, Nevada, the gate hung open, smashed and buckled. Papers billowed out of the gatehouse and spread across the once-impeccable entryway; hundreds of little slips of paper, like waterlogged lily pads, speckled the pond.

Until the world went to hell, this home owners' association prowled the grounds like a golf-tanned grandma gestapo, catching any infraction of the rules within hours, if not minutes. Cameron celebrated each piece of garbage alongside the otherwise pristine streets of the golfer's paradise. The rich pricks were running scared, just like everyone else, and it gave his soul small respite. As fate would have it, all men were equal before Master Mayhem.

The spinning wheel of fate chattered to a stop on "Winner," and Cameron found everything he needed and more at the resort home his sister would never see again. The house hadn't been touched. Several boxes of freeze-dried sat on the garage shelves. Alongside the food, he found chlorine-preserved water in big, square jugs. While everything in the fridge and freezer was warm and fetid, the cupboard gave up a bounty of canned food; weird stuff, like canned olives and refried beans, but it would be a welcome complement to the freeze-dried food they had been eating. Best of all, they found a dozen bottles of good wine. They wouldn't be drinking much alcohol, but the wine might come in handy for trade.

Out back, Cameron saw the first sign of theft. A hose snaked up and over the wall and into Jenna's pool—some desperate neighbor siphoning their pool water away to stave off the inevitable refugee journey to Lake Mead. Cameron didn't plan on staying long enough to use the pool water, so he let it be.

The home owners' association would have given spontaneous birth to kittens if they had discovered the gasoline his brother-in-law had secretly stored alongside his garage —a huge no-no in the Cult of Safety that had saturated America since around the year 2000. A fifty-five-gallon drum of unleaded had been concealed inside a pool toy locker, complete with a hand pump. Cameron assumed the gas had been preserved with STA-BIL. It wasn't like his brother-in-law to leave something like gasoline storage to chance.

Best of all, the gun safe was untouched, and Cameron knew the code. Inside, he found an AR-15 assault rifle, six mags and an entire case of .223 ammunition. Up top, his brother-in-law had stashed a handgun—a Kimber 1911 .45ACP, with five mags and four boxes of shells. Cameron would keep his Beretta, but the AR-15 made him feel a lot better about things in general. He bundled up the guns and loaded them in the 4Runner. He stuffed the AR-15 alongside the driver's seat.

"How long are we staying?" Julie came up beside him while he was loading the guns and ammo.

"We should get out of here as soon as I fuel up. Every minute, things get dicier on the road."

"Are we going to head through Vegas again?" she asked,

an edge of panic in her voice. There was probably nothing Julie wouldn't do to avoid going through the Strip again.

"No, we're heading toward Hoover Dam," Cameron told her. "If that doesn't work, we'll cut back and try to cross the Colorado River at Laughlin."

Julie seemed okay with any plan that headed away from the living hell on I-15.

Cameron rolled the big gas barrel out to the driveway, noticing that it was only partially full. That suited him fine. His SUV only took about twenty-five gallons anyway. He would refill his gas cans if there was any left. Next time he went to buy an SUV, if there ever *was* a next time, he would pay more attention to the range of the fuel tank. The maximum range on the 4Runner was a joke.

Thirty minutes later, the car was packed, the gas cans full and the additional food added to their cache. Cameron rolled the tank back around to the side yard, and out of respect for his brother-in-law and sister, locked up the house.

The traffic heading out Highway 93 was bumper to bumper, but it moved along better than the I-15, ten miles per hour instead of two. In a couple of hours, they arrived at the Hoover Dam crossing. Cameron already knew it was open or the highway wouldn't have been moving at all.

Someone, presumably the government, had tried to block off the suspension bridge with concrete barricades. Why they would do that, Cameron had no idea. With so many people fleeing Vegas, it had only been a matter of time before someone came by with something big enough to shove the barricades out of the way. By then, nobody was still on duty. Cameron could see cars crossing the dam itself, like back in the eighties, unconcerned with terrorist bomb threats.

Making the most of their good fortune, he pushed hard,

driving late into the night. The traffic lightened, and he reached Kaibab National Park before he became too exhausted to drive.

They pulled off where their road map showed a campground at Cataract Lake. Cameron thanked his dad over and over in his mind for badgering him about keeping maps in his car. It was one of the more useful "Dad-isms" as it turned out, since his Apple maps had stopped working somewhere in the California desert.

Cataract Lake Campground overflowed with refugees from Vegas. Beneath the Ponderosa pines, cars parked willy-nilly, ignoring designated camp sites and parking spaces. Cameron pulled in beside a Ford F-250 truck with a California Angels bumper sticker. Even though the guy had Vegas plates, Cameron figured he would do okay next to another Angels' fan. The guy was still awake by the fire, rolling a joint. It felt like providence.

They pulled in and the guy looked up, bothered by the intrusion. Cameron tucked his Beretta into his waistband around back and jumped out of the 4Runner with a winning smile. "Angels' fan, huh?" he commented.

"Yeah, sure am, dyed in the wool." The guy licked the paper and finished off his joint.

"I was born and raised in Anaheim."

"You got here from Anaheim? You musta seen some horrible shit."

"Yeah, more than I care to say. My name's Cameron, by the way."

"I'm Sal. From Los Angeles, too, but right now from Vegas." The men shook hands without Sal getting up.

"No family?" Cameron looked around and didn't see any tents or camping equipment near Sal's truck.

"Nope. My kid lives in Vacaville with her mom. I'm on my own." Sal lit the joint and hit it.

"It's gotta be better in Vacaville than here," Cameron mused.

"Couldn't be worse. You want a toke?" Sal reached out to Cameron with the joint.

Cameron didn't hesitate. "I sure do. I'm wound up tighter than a monkey's nuts." He took a hit and passed it back. "Where you headed?"

"I'm going to Burley, Idaho. I got cousins who own a farm up there. I figure I can work for them until things get back to normal. I don't think things will get cleaned up in Vegas for a while. I'm done there, anyway. You traveling with kids?" One of Cameron's little ones had woken up and was squawking. Julie struggled to get them back to sleep in the cramped SUV, since Cameron didn't feel like digging out the tent. They would be leaving as early in the morning as possible.

Cameron and Sal chatted while they worked down the joint. On impulse, Cameron asked Sal to hold on a second. He dug around in the car and pulled out his brother-in-law's Kimber, stored in its plastic case.

"You have a gun?" Cameron asked, carrying the plastic case over to the campfire.

"Nope. Never got around to buying one."

By the look of things, Cameron guessed his new friend was probably a felon from way back and couldn't get a gun even if he did "get around to it."

"How about I loan you this one? It's my brother-in-law's gun, and I have my own Beretta. I don't think he'd mind if you took care of her for a couple days. Maybe she'll take care of you."

"Seriously?" Sal gawked at the gun case.

"Yeah. Here you go." Cameron handed him the case and a box of shells. "That's a .45, so hang on tight when you shoot."

"How do I get this back to you?" Sal popped open the case and stared at the gun, reluctant to touch it.

"We're heading in the same direction, so you can give it back in Salt Lake City. If we get separated... here, I'll write my brother-in-law's address on this box." Cameron grabbed a pen from the 4Runner and wrote Jason and Jenna's address on the carton of .45 ammunition.

"Dude, thank you. I don't know how I can repay you," Sal said. "Tell you what, take anything you want out of the back of my truck. *Anything you want.*"

Cameron cast a glance at Sal's truck but reconsidered. "Naw, I'm good. I couldn't fit any more in my rig than I got already. What time you planning on leaving in the morning?"

"First light."

"Sounds good. I'll catch you then." Cameron slapped both knees and walked around to the driver's side of the SUV for a few hours of uncomfortable shut-eye.

6

"There was thunder, there was lightning
Then the stars went out and the moon fell
   from the sky
It rained mackerel, it rained trout
And the great day of wrath has come
And here's mud in your big red eye
The poker's in the fire and the locusts take
   the sky"

— *EARTH DIED SCREAMING*, TOM
WAITS, BONE MACHINE, 1992

WALLULA, WASHINGTON, "STARBUCKS CAMP"

PENNY STRUGGLED all night and all the next day with
uncontrollable diarrhea. Sage began to worry that it might be

life-threatening. By mid-afternoon, she seemed to be running to the crapper less often.

Thanks to the survival manual his grandpa had given him, Sage took the morning to build a better water filter for the camp. After wandering about the fields, he found a couple of metal drums—about fifteen gallons each. He took one of the drums and hammered the bottom with a rock, making a funnel-shaped depression. At the lowest point, he punched a small hole with his Leatherman multi-tool, ruining the edge on the leather punch in the process. He scooped the cold coals out of their fire pit and filled a third of the drum, tamping them down. He found fine sand and filled the drum the rest of the way to the top. He tested the filter with pond water and the water dribbled out of the funnel clear.

"The water still needs to be boiled, okay?" Sage held up the water bottle, stating the obvious and relishing the success of his filter. The ladies looked duly impressed.

"Yeah, we get it. Filter the water, then boil the hell out of it. None of us wants the Hershey Squirts like Penny." Justin took the water bottle from Sage and held it up to the sky. "Looks pretty good, little man."

Sage had heard his dad call an open campfire the "white man's cooking fire." By that, he supposed his dad meant that an open campfire was big and wasteful, not that a campfire could carry racist implications.

There had to be a more efficient way to boil water than over an open campfire. The water they boiled that morning for coffee required a huge pile of sagebrush to achieve a full boil. At that rate, they would spend most their day gathering firewood.

The same afternoon, a group of new people wandered

into camp—thirty-five people of all ages and genders. Most of them had no food and were well on their way to starvation. Their arrival set alarm bells ringing in Sage's head.

"The farmer is definitely going to come and kick us out if we let these people stay," Sage reminded everyone.

"We can't send them away. They're people," Nora argued. "We're all children of Gaia. We have no right to run them off as though we own this place."

"I have no idea what Gaia thinks," Sage replied. "I don't even know who Gaia is."

"Gaia is the spiritual talisman of Mother Earth," Nora explained patiently. "She was the Greek goddess of the Earth. Saying we're all children of Gaia is another way of saying that we all belong at the pond, or anywhere on the planet."

"I think I understand," Sage continued. "But, if we think the farmer's going to go along with us starting a refugee camp inside his farm... I'm just saying; it's going to end badly."

Justin made the decision for the group. "We'll let some of them stay, the ones like us. Then we'll send the rest away. Agreed?" Nobody wanted to take responsibility for the decision, whether they agreed or not. Sending people away felt too much like sending them to die. Everyone either nodded or said nothing.

"Then it's settled."

Justin went around to the people he liked, mostly young women, and invited them to stay. Then he shouted to the milling crowd, "The farmer gave permission for just a few of us to camp here," he said, "so only the folks I talked to can stay. The rest of you need to find another place away from the farm. I'm sorry, but only a few of us can camp here. It's out of my control."

"Who the hell are you to decide who stays and who

goes?" one guy yelled. He hadn't been picked by Justin, probably because Justin hadn't chosen anyone physically larger than himself.

"It's not my decision." Justin held his hands out in feigned helplessness. "The farmer made it clear that only a few could stay here. Plus, we're out of food."

The crowd grumbled but began to shuffle out of camp. A stroke of perverse genius, lying about the food had worked. It reminded Sage of when he certified as a Rescue SCUBA diver. He was taught that if someone panicked and grabbed him in the water, he should take a breath, deflate his buoyancy device and sink underwater. No drowning person would hold onto someone as they sank. By lying about the food, Justin gave the crowd no reason to stay.

The crowd slowly massed and headed to the road, trundling off into the hills. Six of them stayed—the ones Justin had deemed "like us." Five of the six were young women, and one of them was another slim hipster man named Felix.

Sage left the group to their socializing, the Starbucks Camp going in an even more dangerous direction. They were truthfully running out of food. Regardless of Justin's bullshit, the farmer had specifically asked them to leave. Inviting more people into camp increased the odds of expulsion.

Sage gathered his figure-four traps and the rusty snare wire he had found. The old survival book showed how to set rabbit snares and Sage wanted to give it a try.

A deadfall dropped a rock on an animal, smashing it. The design presumed a lot of things. Was the rock big enough to kill the animal? Would it fall fast enough to keep the animal from running out from underneath it? Would an edible creature even go for the bait in the first place?

In any case, Sage was learning that he would have to experiment for a while before figuring out the rhythms of any given ecosphere. The more stuff he tried, the smarter he would become. It was an advantage of staying put; he could learn the natural patterns of the area. Even a valley or two over, the patterns would probably change. Moving around meant having to relearn at each place.

Snares worked by entangling, then strangling an animal. While baited deadfalls wouldn't normally work against plant eaters, like rabbits, snares could catch herbivores.

Sage went with simple trail snares, where he would position a wire noose in the middle of a rabbit trail, then anchor it to a bush. Looking carefully, he could locate the rabbit thoroughfares, but finding good choke points with brushy walls required some work. Given the chance, a rabbit would simply hop around a snare unless Sage set it somewhere that forced it to squeeze through a gap in thick brush. He feared this would take many days of trial and error to master. The rabbits were clearly present, given the heavily-used trails. But tricking them into giving up their lives would be another matter altogether.

Sage's dad was an avid hunter. Because hunting competed for his attention with girlfriends and video games, Sage had only joined him once or twice.

"An animal is a thousand times more adept in the wild than you are," his dad preached. "For you to take an animal's life on its home turf, the animal has to make a huge mistake. In a sense, the animal has to decide to allow you to kill it."

At the time, it had sounded like Native American folklore but, as Sage looked for places to set rabbit snares in the waning fall in eastern Washington, he sensed the truth of what his dad had said. Success would require a huge stroke of luck—the rabbits would need to cooperate. Sage said a silent prayer, begging the rabbits for their consent.

He spent four hours setting deadfalls and snares. Some of the frozen Starbucks sandwiches had gone bad in the cooler, and Sage used the sausage and eggs for bait.

He placed the snares along rabbit trails going in and out of fields of alfalfa. When he finished, he didn't go back to the Starbucks Camp. Instead, he headed up to his secret stash and grabbed a Mountain House freeze-dried lasagna and his Coleman stove. He slid around to the back of the rock wall and boiled water from one of his clean water bottles to reconstitute the freeze-dried meal. He had plenty of stashed water, and there was no way he would drink the pond water, no matter how filtered and boiled it might be. Whenever he visited his cache, Sage refilled the same, blue Nalgene bottle with clean water so the others wouldn't notice he had been drinking something different than they had.

Grandpa Bob had given Sage a pump-action water puri-fier. It would purify the pond water in a single step. Problem was, Sage couldn't produce a water purifier from thin air without causing suspicion. The water purifier hadn't been in the backpack when he originally walked into camp. He should have kept it in his backpack from day one. Since he didn't know how quickly the purifier might clog up from pumping pond water, part of him was glad he held it in reserve. Perhaps it was better to keep the purifier hidden with the rest of his gear, at least for the time being.

As he enjoyed his meal, a wave of guilt washed over him. Was he cheating his friends? Sage provided way more than his fair share of food at the Starbucks Camp; he had been the one to discover the onions in the fields, after all. The thought of Penny eating only blackened onions made the lasagna stick in his throat. What kind of man had he become?

The fact remained: he couldn't trust the group not to take his food and kick him out. As much as he liked the idea of sharing, earlier that day the group had pushed a bunch of people off into uncertain wild lands with lies and deceit. Wilderness socialism wasn't the utopian dream he had hoped, and someone was always going to get the shaft. Sage had promised his father it wouldn't be him.

In any case, the supplies weren't really his to give. His grandfather and grandmother had sacrificed big for him to have so much food. Maybe it was a hollow justification, but Sage felt wrong about handing over his grandparents' supplies to the group. His grandma and grandpa wouldn't approve.

For the first time in his life, Sage weighed the value of his word. He had promised his father that he would do everything in his power to survive. Maybe he just wanted to believe that keeping food to himself penciled out as something other than selfishness. Maybe so, but he *had* promised his father, and the promise crept up on him like a chill in the night. Somehow, it mattered.

Like the rabbits that might find their way into his snares and the snow that might fall any night, giving and keeping his word tied him to the earth. Perhaps a man who kept his word might also be the kind of man who honored the rhythms of nature, a man who deserved to live in this new, harsh world.

Honesty pervaded everything outside the Starbucks Camp. Inside the camp, life depended on lies and deceit, maneuvering for sex and dominance. Outside the camp, in the rolling hills and alfalfa patchwork, honesty ruled. Nature, in a fit of virtue, had begun eroding the false human world, pounding like relentless waves against the fabrications of mankind, threatening to wash them away into something primeval and true.

It might make him less of a gentleman to allow Penny to suffer, but Sage would not tell the Starbucks people about his supplies. Above all, Sage would keep his word to his father, no matter the cost.

———

HIGHWAY 89, Outside Fredonia, Arizona

CAMERON AND SAL leaned over the warm hood of Sal's truck, studying Cameron's road map.

"Decision time, Sal," Cameron announced. "Are we going down the freeway or taking the back roads?"

"I've never been this way. I have no idea what these back roads look like. Have you been up Highway 89?"

"Once," Cameron remembered. "My brother and I rode motorcycles up there with my Pops. We went to visit my sister in Salt Lake. The road's good, but what worries me are the little towns. See? Every few miles there's one town after another all the way up 89. I'll bet most of them have set up roadblocks by now, trying to keep the city slickers from Vegas and Phoenix out of their yards. You drive through enough towns like that and you're going to hit one that won't let you through. Or maybe they'll steal your supplies and leave you in the cold."

Sal thought about it for a minute. "Can't we just drive around the roadblocks? Take side streets?"

Cameron ran his finger along the highway on the map as

he spoke. "That's the thing, hermano. Most of the towns tuck into these mountains like lint in a butt crack. There's just one way in and one way out of each town. It's not possible to drive around roadblocks on side streets. I'm guessing the townsfolk are good people, but who knows? One rotten sheriff like in *Rambo First Blood* and we're screwed." Cameron laughed and shrugged.

"What other way is there?" Sal stared at the map. "I've only ever gone straight up the interstate."

"Yeah, that might not be a bad way to go. Check it out." Cameron rotated the map to get a better look. "I'm guessing the city of Saint George blocked off the Virgin River Pass, here." Cameron pointed to a spot in the road where it passed through a tight gorge. "My brother and I assumed they'd do that when we planned how we might get to Salt Lake if the world took a shit. The traffic jam I saw in Vegas probably confirms that roadblock's up. It's probably a sixty-mile traffic jam that butts right up against a roadblock near the state line. That's bad news for folks coming out of Vegas, but it could be good news for us."

"How so?"

"Since there's no traffic making it past the Utah state line here in the Virgin River Gorge, then the towns after Saint George, north to Salt Lake, might not have road-blocks. If I remember correctly, most of the towns on the I-15 are set back a long way from the freeway. They won't barricade the interstate, especially since Saint George already shut off the flow of refugees. I-15 runs through a series of wide valleys almost all the way to Salt Lake City. And there are tons of dirt roads to get around those roadblocks."

Sal looked at the map, not really understanding it like

Cameron did. "Okay, sounds like you've thought this through. Let's do it. How do we get back to the interstate?"

"We need to cut west, going through these two small towns and then through Hurricane. We'll completely bypass the Virgin River Gorge."

"Why's that town sound familiar?" Sal pointed at the town of Colorado City on the map.

Cameron guffawed. "That's the polygamist town on the reality TV show. Remember: Warren Jeffs, hair bumps, long dresses, multiple wives?"

"Oh, yeah," Sal agreed. "Think they'd want me? I'll convert. I can handle a bunch of wives."

"I think they might want you if you were a fifteen-year-old girl. I hate to break it to you, but you're a forty-something, tatted-up, weather-beaten old man. Nobody's going to want to add you to their fundamentalist community, bro. You're *all hat, no cattle.*"

"You got a point there, Anaheim," Sal conceded. "What if they just want your wife, and leave us both out in the cold?"

"Naw. These are inbreds," Cameron laughed. "You gotta watch more TV, Sal. They're too busy building altars and trying to get with their cousins. We'll be fine. It's better than taking our chances with the towns on the 89."

An hour later, they drove through the town of Fredonia and turned left on Highway AZ 389. Cameron led out in the 4Runner and Sal followed behind in his truck. Passing through Fredonia, they didn't see a living soul. It should've given Cameron pause, but the freedom of the road prevailed and he slipped into a breezy nonchalance.

The heat of the Arizona highway cooked through the floorboards of the 4Runner. The shiny strip of jet-black asphalt gleamed in the sun, contrasting with the umber sand

and bright pops of green hackberry and juniper sprouting up in the bar pit.

Cameron marveled at how liberating it felt to finally drive sixty-five again. He cruised over the crest of a hill, descending into another long depression in the road.

As Cameron mounted the next rise, he saw three cars jumbled at the bottom, two hundred yards away, one leaking steam from under its hood. Cameron stood on the brakes, sending the 4Runner into a tire-smoking fishtail. Behind him, Sal did the same.

"What is it?" Julie had been dozing and she sprang awake.

"Not good! Not good!" Cameron shouted as he tried to jam the SUV into reverse before it had even come to a full stop. The moment after he got the transmission to cooperate, glass and plastic exploded into the passenger compartment, the windshield, hood and dash blasting inward with the angry buzz of incoming rifle rounds. Cameron flailed, trying to jam his mental transmission into reverse as well.

—*The wheel of fate spins again. Tits up, hombre. You lose.*—

Cameron stomped on the gas and the car lurched backward, clawing at the road to escape the fusillade. Before the 4Runner could retreat ten yards, a bullet found its mark, zipping through Cameron's throat and just to the left of one of the boys in the back seat. Another round punched into his chest, passing between two ribs and slamming into the plastic of the car seat behind him. Cameron's foot came off the pedal as he gasped.

A grown man working at a welding store. His two boys. His wife. His brother. His sister.

His life. Was that all it would ever be?

His body relaxed. Finally, he rested. His spine curved sideways, his always-tense body listed to port.

The 4Runner slowed, rolling in a gentle arc off the road and into the sandy shoulder with a dull thunk.

The shooting abated. Julie and the children howled, but their cries melted into background noise as Cameron's senses, one by one, abandoned him. The last thing he saw, like some kind of lurid hallucination, was a man crucified high on a telephone pole, a hundred yards up the road.

INTERSTATE 64, Outside Lexington, Kentucky

MAT SAW it as a good news/bad news scenario. The good news was that traffic had thinned. The bad news was that it meant he was going a direction nobody else wanted to go—west toward Lexington, Kentucky. The eastbound lanes of Interstate 64 stood virtually gridlocked, packed with stalled cars, their occupants camping beside the road. The campfires caused eerie, white flashes in his NVGs as Mat drove slowly through the night.

He had poured the last of the gasoline into the truck fifty miles back, the gas cans from the EZ Storage extending his truck's range well beyond that of most refugees heading out of Baltimore and D.C.. Mat hadn't seen an open gas station in two days.

"What's that glow on the horizon?" Caroline asked.

Mat stopped the truck and pulled off the NVGs. He had been running dark, his headlights off. The white phosphor NVGs had truly been *all that and the kitchen sink*, worth every penny of Mac Daddy Ross' money. He didn't have to manually focus to see his truck gauges and he wasn't getting the headache he usually got from driving under night vision. Running dark meant pissed-off campers alongside the road wouldn't get much of a chance to shoot at them if they felt so inclined. By the time anyone knew of their approach, they were already heading away, making a shot less and less likely and offering a black hole as a target. Driving blacked out was the only way to fly in the Apocalypse.

Mat's eyes adjusted to the night without his NVGs and he could see the orange glow to the west.

"Ah, fuck. That's Lexington. It looks like it's on fire."

"What about Louisville?" Caroline worried, fear creeping into her voice.

"Nah. Louisville is still eighty miles past Lexington. We're not close enough to see it." Mat didn't want to state the obvious. If Lexington was on fire, Louisville probably was, too. People fleeing from St. Louis, Cincinnati, Columbus, and even Indianapolis would escape toward Louisville and Lexington. Like a chicken coop with a fox inside, people were running everywhere without any idea where to find safety. So far, Mat wasn't sure there was such a thing as safety anymore. Lots of motion; nowhere to go. All that frustration was building, undoubtedly, into an unstoppable, continental panic.

"I'm really worried about my parents and my brother in Louisville."

"You have a brother?"

"Yeah. I told you. My parents had an 'oops' baby in their forties. He's eleven. We didn't have room in Charleston for a nursery, so my parents put the crib in my room. I got to wake up with him in the night and cuddle him back to sleep when he had nightmares. For almost a year he called me 'Mom.'" She looked wistfully out the dark windshield. "Not seeing him every day has been the hardest part about being at school."

Mat looked at Caroline, seeing her as a possible mother for the first time. The look on her face as she thought of her baby brother erased all doubt.

He deflected. "I hear you. I miss my brothers, too. They never cuddled me to sleep, but they did beat the shit out of me a few times a week. Made me the man I am today," Mat puffed up. "Hard as steel."

He scanned the near landscape without NVGs, picking out the yellow-orange glow of dozens of campfires. To the southwest, he noticed a particularly bright spot about half a click out. He wasn't aware of any city in that direction.

Mat had no desire to drive his Raptor, trailer and girl-friend—whatever she was to him—into a burning city in the middle of the night. He needed to gather more intel and figure their way around Lexington to avoid running afoul of some unforeseen peril. All the highways circled Lexington proper, and he couldn't backtrack around Lexington without a major detour and expenditure of fuel. He hadn't spoken to anyone but Caroline since leaving Baltimore. Maybe it was time to gather some human intel.

Mat turned off the Interstate and made his way carefully along an outback road, approaching the bright spot on the horizon with caution. He set his NVGs on the center console and turned his headlights on in time to see cars lined up on both sides of the road, with people walking along the shoulder in groups of fives, tens, and twenties. Everyone walked in the same direction—toward the light.

Mat drove slowly, passing a sign that read "Sycamore Creek Farms," with a long driveway packed with pedestrians, many of whom carried rifles and shotguns. Mat could see a gigantic bonfire at the head of the drive, apparently the source of the light.

"I'd like to go collect some intel at that shindig," Mat explained while pulling into a parking slot on someone's lawn a few hundred yards from the driveway.

"I hope you plan on taking me with you," she said.

Mat shook his head. "I'd love to take you, but I'm afraid that, if we leave the truck, it'll be picked clean by the time we get back. One of us needs to stay. Frankly, I think it's safer in the truck. This meeting gives me the creeps. It looks like a KKK rally."

"Come back quickly." She pulled the AK-47 from beside her seat and checked the chamber and double-checked the safety, laying it across her lap.

"Good girl," Mat praised her for her gun safety. "I'll be back in a jiffy. I don't suggest you get out of the cab for any reason. This is Indian country and I have no idea what's brewing."

Caroline nodded and Mat climbed down, checking the chamber of his Glock and slipping it into the low-viz holster under his belt. A group passed by and Mat folded into the back of the group, trying to make himself inconspicuous.

On the walk down the drive, Mat overheard enough to surmise that these folks were strangers, too, having driven in from Columbus, fleeing violence there. Somebody had come by their camp earlier looking for volunteers for a "roadside community group" and pointing everyone toward Sycamore Creek Farms.

Passing the big farmhouse, Mat noted a number of armed men standing on the porch, scowling at passersby and warning anyone from coming too close to the house. By the looks of things, this "roadside community group" had overrun the farm, probably because it was the closest place with standing water. If Mat had to guess, the farm had allowed a couple of travelers to take drinking water from the huge pond and it had become an avalanche of people, too many to evict. Mob democracy at its finest.

No good deed goes unpunished.

Mat heard shouting and ripples of anger coming from the crowd around the bonfire. He approached and the hairs stood up on the back of his neck. In the flickering firelight, he caught the glint of hundreds of gun barrels and reflected firelight in the eyes of scores of desperate people.

"If they won't share, we need to give them a REASON to share!" the man at the head of the mob exclaimed. A rousing chorus of agreement rose from the crowd. "In these times, we don't have the luxury of being selfish. Those cattle are the only food for miles, and unless we're willing to let our kids starve, we need to buy those cows whether the Stinson family wants to sell them or not!"

Mat didn't like where this meeting was going—socialism by bonfire and gun barrel: his least favorite sport. Guys like Mat, men who produced results, were *never* the beneficiaries of this kind of socialism. This group could be counted upon to take more than they gave.

He remembered an Iraqi compound they had taken down on his second deployment as a Ranger. They'd cordoned off a building intel said was a waypoint for foreign terrorists coming into Iraq.

When the interpreter yelled that the "soldiers would kill everyone in the house," at least fifteen Al Qaeda soldiers marched out of the 1,200 square-foot, concrete-and-mud building. Eventually the Rangers had been forced to go in and clear the building because the target they were looking for had dug in. The rooms were tightly packed with cabinets and bunk beds, every two paces another horror show of hiding places and bad feng shui. They lost two of their best Rangers clearing that building. Still, Mat probably felt safer there, in that shitty Iraqi hovel, than he did here among fellow Americans around this bonfire. At least in Iraq, he had a team. Here, he stood alone among pissed-off, entitled fools. When did America become the enemy, Mat wondered.

Gently, he backed his way out of the crowd. The man up front was still screaming, rousing the others to meet back at the same spot at seven in the morning to make their "final offer" to the cattle family. Mat broke free and moseyed quickly down the driveway, watching carefully to see if anyone followed. Before he made the corner back onto the street, the rattle of AK-47 fire shattered the night. Some of the people in the crowd rumbled and a couple screamed. Mat took off at a sprint toward his truck.

When he got there, he skidded to a halt. A man lay on the ground next to the bed. A rifle barrel poked out of the window of the backseat of the cab. He heard Caroline sobbing inside.

Mat pulled his Glock and his tac flashlight on the run back, and he made a wide circle around the truck, checking for additional threats. When he reached the man on the ground, Mat flicked his tac light for a moment and immediately noticed four big holes, shining red, on the man's chest.

"Caroline. Can you hear me. This is Mat. I'm coming in. Don't shoot me."

"I wo... wo...won't," she stammered.

Mat set his hand on the front sight, avoiding the hot barrel of the AK and controlling the direction of the muzzle. "Are you hurt?"

"No... I'm fine. Is he dead?" she cried.

"It's going to be fine. You did well. But we need to get out of here right now. Hop up front and let's get rolling, babe." She began talking as soon as Mat opened the driver's side door.

"He... he... he was trying to take the stuff out of the truck. I warned him and warned him but he just kept reaching inside the truck bed. I shot the ground. I promise, I shot the ground first, but he pulled a gun out of his pocket and then... I shot him. Oh, my God, Mat. I shot him. Did he die? Mat! Did he die?"

Mat fired up the Raptor and roared away from the scene just as a crowd began to form. He wasn't a hundred percent sure, but he felt a bump when he pulled away from the parking slot, probably running a wheel of the trailer over the dead man, not that it was going to bother him any.

"Caroline. Listen to me. I've been in more situations like this than I can count and I promise you—are you listening to me? You did the right thing. You handled yourself well and nobody can fault you. That dude fucked up and got shot in the process. A guy pulls a gun on you and it's either you or him. I'm very glad that it was him who took the hit. Do you understand?"

"Yes, but did he die?"

"Babe, I don't know," Mat lied. "Honestly, I don't care. He pulled a gun on my girl and, if you hadn't shot him, I would've. That's how things are supposed to go down. You comported yourself perfectly and it doesn't matter if he's dead or injured. He got what he had coming."

"Oh, God. Forgive me," she prayed as her sobs began to subside. "I never wanted to hurt anyone."

"Good people never want to hurt anyone. But good

people sometimes have to. Hey, what do you say we call it a night? Let's get far away from here and get some sleep. Things will feel better in the morning."

"I hope so, Mat," she said through sobs and hiccups.

"You're strong. You will get through this. This is something I know a lot about. You will get through this." Mat turned back onto the interstate, finally deciding it would be better to spend the fuel to backtrack, putting as much distance between them and Lexington as he could.

7

―――――――

"Mega cities still blaze in the night
Burnin' the ashes they choke
From the earth the magma will rise
Enveloped in the poisonous smoke
So the meanin' of life ends in prophecy
Premonitions of tragedy
Still no hope for humanity."

— *3 DAYS IN DARKNESS*, TESTAMENT,
THE GATHERING, 1999

MARBLE CREEK BAPTIST CHURCH, EAST OF NICOLASVILLE, Kentucky

MAT AND CAROLINE woke up in the parking lot of the Marble Creek Baptist Church. Mat quietly dropped the tailgate and started a fresh pot of coffee on his JetBoil, eager to do anything he could to comfort Caroline.

She staggered out of the truck fifteen minutes later.

"You put on your makeup, so you must be feeling a little better," Mat observed out loud.

Caroline wandered toward Mat, put her arms around him, and laid her face into his neck. "Good morning," she muttered over his shoulder, presumably to spare him her morning breath.

Mat shut up and let the moment linger, following her lead. Relief flooded him. She was recovering from the shooting. Thank God. The light of morning embraced the world, doing its healing work.

When she loosened her hold, Mat took it as permission to offer her coffee. "I've got a cup of French press," Mat presented the JetBoil on his tailgate with a flourish.

"French press... You *are* the man of my dreams," she quipped.

Mat's mental gears came to a full stop. He suddenly needed to know if she was joking or not. Then he wondered if he was being a fool, if he was being played. In this world gone mad, a guy like Mat wasn't just a pretty face. He was a ticket to survival. If she meant "man of my dreams," maybe she had only meant it as a joke. Or maybe the stress was talking. Maybe he just represented safety.

But wasn't that always part of the deal between men and women? Had mankind emerged very far from the cave, when you got right down to it?

"Don't get a boy's hopes up," he joked. "It's just a pot of coffee."

"It's much more than a pot of coffee, Mat Best, army commando," she answered as she dug her bathroom kit out of her suitcase in the back of the truck. "It's a pot of French press. A man who takes time with his coffee is a man who takes time with his woman." She presented him with a wan smile, and Mat reminded himself that she had killed a man the night before. He needed to tread lightly, to put his need for self-assurance aside for a few days at least.

"I'm your humble servant, Miss Caroline." He carefully poured the coffee into two vacuum mugs he always kept in his go-bag. Why had he packed two mugs in his go-bag months ago, he wondered? He admitted, there was rarely a time he hadn't factored in a lady companion in any given moment of any rotation home. He had spent very few days of leave alone.

"Good morning." A mid-thirties African-American male stepped cautiously out of the woods beside the parking lot. Mat's hand flew to his Glock, but he paused before drawing it.

"Good morning, friend," Mat said. "Can I please see your right hand?"

"I can't show you my right hand because it's holding my gun," the stranger replied.

Mat relaxed a bit. Any man who will tell you about his gun and who just stepped out of the woods would have killed you already if he meant to. "Thanks for letting me know. I've got a hand cannon, too, so I guess that makes us even. What can I do for you?"

"I was coming to find out what we can do for *you*. You're having breakfast at our church."

"I hope that's okay," Mat said. "We pulled into the parking lot in the middle of the night."

"I know. We've been keeping an eye on you. I'm assistant pastor Ben Fields and my family's back there in the woods a bit, waiting to make sure we're all copacetic. We eat breakfast here—the whole neighborhood—every morning. Today's my turn to set up and get started. You're invited to join us."

Mat offered the assistant pastor his own cup of joe. "Would you like some coffee?"

"I sure would," the pastor waved for his family to come out of the trees as he walked over to take the proffered cup.

A few minutes later, Mat, Caroline and the Fields family stood around the tailgate chatting while Mat made another pot of JetBoil.

When the introductions and niceties were through, Caroline asked, "Have you heard anything about Louisville?"

"Oh, sweetheart," Mrs. Fields said, "do you have people in Louisville?"

"My mom, dad, and brother."

"I pray they're okay. A big part of Louisville has been taken over by gangs and there's nobody to stop them. The police vanished from there two days ago. We know because a steady stream of refugees comes through here every day, even with us so far out in the countryside. We'll pray for your mamma and papa right now."

Mrs. Fields held hands with her daughter and husband and launched into prayer, asking God for protection over Caroline's family. Midway through the prayer, Mat and Caroline awkwardly took the nearest hand, caught up in a ritual neither had ever experienced.

"Lord, wrap your arms around these good people. Lord, take their family into your embrace and protect them from evil, Lord." The family whispered "amen" after each "Lord."

"Lord, use this horrible time—your great and terrible Armageddon—to bring us, your children, Lord, to kneel beside you. Enter our hearts, Lord. Enter our hearts and fill us up with your hope and your peace, Lord. Lift away our selfishness—the selfishness that brought us unto destruction, Lord... and accept it on this altar of pestilence, and replace it with your tender mercy. Amen."

The group mumbled their "amens" and let go of one another's hands.

"Thank you, Mrs. Fields. I'm so worried. Can we go right now, Mat?"

"Go to Louisville?" Mat stalled for time. The last thing in the world he wanted to do was head into a strange city controlled by criminal gangs without a plan how to get back out. One of the main things they pounded into an operator was "never go into a place without at least two rock-solid plans how to get the fuck out."

"Yes. I'm worried to death about my family. Can we go?"

"Okay, let's do it," Mat said. He would have a fifty-mile drive to figure out infil and exfil, if that was even possible, given he knew nothing about Louisville.

Mat and Caroline quickly said their goodbyes, packed up their stove and, less than five minutes later, they pulled out of the parking lot of the Baptist church.

FUNDAMENTALIST LATTER-DAY SAINT, Hospital Compound, Colorado City, Arizona

CAMERON STEWART AWOKE with a girl who looked like Laura Ingalls hovering over him. His dad had forced the family to watch reruns of *Little House on the Prairie* every Tuesday night until Cameron turned fourteen. He thereafter refused.

Cameron's dad couldn't get enough of the cowboy west, and those simpler, more moral times.

The girl hovering over him smiled cheerfully, her freckled face glowing. She wore a white, floor-length prairie dress with a huge, laced collar, buttoned up to the neck.

Well, Dad would love it here, Cameron thought as Laura Ingalls adjusted the pic line running into his arm. Except Cameron wasn't lying on his back in the Old West. Plastic tubing and IV bags hadn't been invented until the 1960s.

Little by little, Cameron pieced together where he was— in some kind of hospital after his car had exploded in a hail of bullets on a highway in northern Arizona.

Pain bore into him from his jaw down to his abdomen.

"Stay still, Mr. Stewart," Laura Ingalls instructed in a sweet voice. "You shouldn't move about. You need to heal."

"How do you know my name?" Cameron croaked, his throat dry as sand.

"Sister Stewart told us, of course." Laura laughed and turned to another patient in a bed next to Cameron's.

"Wait. Miss, is my family okay? Are the boys okay?"

Laura turned back to Cameron. She looked to be thirteen or fourteen years old. "Everybody's fine. They're out enjoying the sunshine at the Prophet's picnic. Hurry up and heal and you can enjoy some sunshine, too." She smiled and turned back to her other patient.

Cameron lurched forward to call the girl back for more questions, but she had already moved on.

He found himself in a medical bay with ten or fifteen other patients, a scene more akin to World War One than modern America. His head swam with the effort of lifting it and he dropped back to the pillow and faded back into unconsciousness.

WALLULA, WASHINGTON, "STARBUCKS CAMP"

THE STARBUCKS CLAN SKIPPED BREAKFAST. Penny still felt sick and now Tyson, Condie, and three of the new girls were sick as well. As best as anyone could tell, none of the others had drunk water that hadn't been filtered and boiled. Sage scratched his head; could boiled water still be infectious? He couldn't imagine how.

Considering how filthy they had let the camp become, anything was possible. Sage thought of a list of ways people might have gotten sick. They could have eaten something bad. They could have gotten a flu from the new people. They could have come in contact with rodents and vermin. Everyone was hungry, and hunger lowered immunity, his dad had told him. The camp was so dirty and out of control that he would have been surprised if people *didn't* get sick.

One time, Sage met a homeless guy who had been camping outside for six straight years: winter, spring, summer, and fall. The guy clearly demonstrated what his dad had called "obsessive compulsive behavior." The homeless guy cleaned his campsite over and over again, enforced double and triple checks on his water, and managed his human waste like a city sanitation engineer. Sage figured the guy was nuts. In retrospect, maybe that was exactly what it took to keep from getting sick in the wilderness: obsessive compulsive behavior.

Truth was, he didn't know. Sage's experience of backpacking and camping hadn't extended past a few days at a time. Camping for more than a week raised hard questions.

Would people get sick from wearing the same clothes every day? Would people get sick from not cleaning their dishes with hot, soapy water? Could people get sick from eating too many onions?

He had the finest private school education Salt Lake City could offer, but there were so many unanswered questions out here in the dirt. How much did he really know about camping or sanitation? Looking back, camping had been an amusement, done under artificial circumstances for short periods of time. *Living outdoors* turned out to be a lot different than *camping*.

Sage checked his traps and snares as soon as sunlight hit the ground. He had set up four deadfalls and six snares. It took him an hour to check them, and he had walked three miles.

Nothing.

It wasn't as though animals had defeated his snares, it was just... *nothing*. The snares and deadfalls looked just the way he had left them the evening before. On the end of the figure-four traps, the bait remained untouched.

He had burned about two hundred calories checking the trapline, and he had nothing to show for it. Even if he had killed a mouse or squirrel, how many calories would that have delivered? A hundred at most? A rabbit would be almost worth it, maybe delivering as much as a thousand calories.

Sage sat down and thought it through. He had seen signs of animals. He knew rabbits were hitting the alfalfa field because the low trails in the grass were almost certainly created by rabbits. But the field itself was acres, and rabbits could enter the field at any point. Why should they choose his particular trail?

Why would the animals he was trying to bait with deadfalls show up to take his bait? They probably spent the night scouring broad swathes of land, and they wouldn't necessarily come past his little traps. The scent of the bait would reach out maybe ten feet or so, but apparently it would take more stink to draw predators. He had never trapped game before. It was a lot harder than the movies made it look. But that was no excuse for quitting. If he kept at it, he would eventually learn how the animals behaved.

He decided to leave the traps and snares where they were. Tomorrow he would move some of the rabbit snares to other trails. The bait would continue to rot and maybe attract animals from farther away.

Wrapped in his thoughts, he made his way back toward camp. He crossed a field of stubbly grass and movement caught his eye. Something primordial in his brain knew instantly what he was seeing: a rattlesnake.

His first reaction was to back away. His second reaction won: *easy food.*

Rattlesnakes seemed terrifying because a single bite can lead to crippling sickness and even death. Land animals usually gave rattlesnakes a wide berth. As Sage watched the snake coil up, it dawned on him that the snake's defensive strategy didn't work particularly well against people.

Keeping one eye on the location of the big rattler, Sage hunted around and found a few hand-sized rocks. He hurled the first rock at the snake and missed entirely. The second rock hit the snake mid-body and did nothing but piss it off. The snake uncoiled and began to make its escape. Sage stepped closer and threw the last rock, walloping the snake on the head.

The snake writhed about, making no further progress. Sage busted off a bitterbrush stick and broke off the branches, except for a fork on the end. He moved up to the snake, wary that it could still bite even with its head smashed. He pinned the head beneath the "Y" in the stick and reached down with his Leatherman tool, carefully sawing off the head. Still the rattlesnake twisted, flicking his rattle from side to side, but the fight was over. Sage guessed he was looking at seven hundred calories. It wasn't a lot, but it would be a welcome addition to onions.

"Just goes to show you, Mister Rattler," Sage spoke to the severed snake head. "You gotta keep evolving. Once someone comes on the scene who can throw a rock, you best reconsider previous strategies. Making yourself into a bullseye and then rattling... not the best plan."

This was the first rattlesnake he had seen in Washington, but it seemed like there might be more in the chaparral. Sage took note of the time and the position of the sun. He had seen a lot of grasshoppers bouncing out from underneath his feet as he walked back from the field, especially as the morning warmed. Maybe the rattlesnakes came out as soon as they warmed up enough to catch grasshoppers. Maybe in that brief window, when the rattlers were slightly warmer than the grasshoppers, they could chow down and take the rest of the day off in the shade.

"Ain't nature just the cleverest little bitch?" Sage mused out loud, talking to himself again.

He decided to test his theory by opening the rattler's belly when he got back to camp. In any case, this was good information about the fauna of the region. Rattlesnakes were present, at least for the season, and they came out to hunt at the first rays of sun.

Happy with the new information, and feeling like he was making progress, Sage tromped into camp.

Everyone freaked out.

It took Sage a moment to realize that they were screaming and jumping to their feet because he had a big snake dangling at his side.

"What the fuck!" Justin jumped back from his chair as the women shrieked.

Sage didn't know what to say. "Check it out. I brought lunch."

"The hell you did." Justin put the chair between himself and Sage. "Nobody's going to eat that."

"Everyone knows it tastes like chicken," Sage tried.

"I'm definitely not eating *that*, Mountain Man," Penny said, still sick and wrapped in a blanket on one of the lawn chairs. Sage noticed a cloud passing over Justin's face when Penny called him "Mountain Man."

"I'll cook it up, and you guys can try it. We're going to have to get used to eating things that aren't normal," Sage said.

"Whatever, little dude," Justin replied.

Since they didn't have a frying pan, Sage cooked the snake directly on the coals in its skin. He had to admit, the meat was bland and had an "off" odor about it. But calories were calories. Ironically, Sage had thousands of calories stashed up in the rocks, yet he was the only one eating rattlesnake meat. Even though he wasn't particularly enjoying the flavor, he choked down the entire thing.

Nora approached him as he knelt by the fire forcing himself to eat. "I'm sorry we didn't eat your snake with you. It's cool that you knew how to hunt like that. I appreciate what you're doing. Maybe let me try a tiny piece?" Sage knew she didn't really want to eat it, but he pulled off a flake of the bland, alien meat anyway.

Nora slowly raised the meat to her mouth and winced as

she set it on her tongue. "Tastes like chicken," she said before chewing.

"Liar," Sage said, smiling. They both chuckled as she managed to chew twice and swallow.

"That tasted awful. Not the way I imagined breaking off being a vegetarian." Nora grinned. "Snake meat."

"You're a vegetarian?"

"Until today. Well, thank you for sharing your snake. I know Justin can be a douche, but I don't want you to think we don't see what you're doing for us."

"We?" Sage asked.

"Well, I don't want you to think that *I* don't see what you're doing for us." Nora put a hand on Sage's shoulder, then drifted back toward her lawn chair.

As he chewed his way to the last quarter of the snake tail, Condie pointed to the road and spoke. "Check out those guys."

A crowd of dozens of people shuffled up the road, kicking up dust. They moved like zombies—probably refugees from the highway. The group came into camp and barely reacted to the Starbucks Clan, moving without a word of explanation or consideration. The new people began pawing through their gear.

Sage dropped the snake and made a run for his backpack. He ripped it out of an old guy's hands, zipped up the pocket and slung on his back.

"Do you have food in there?" the old guy begged with a glazed look.

"It's not yours," Sage shouted.

All over camp, desperate people picked through boxes and bags. One of them pushed into the tent, tossing the sleeping bags, looking for food. Justin, Tyson, and the girls screamed and pushed, but it was like pushing water. The mob kept coming, picking through everything, searching listlessly for anything to eat. The Starbucks Clan was stronger and healthier than the intruders, but they were hopelessly outnumbered, maybe twenty to one.

Sage watched as one bedraggled woman snatched the remainder of the rattlesnake off the ground and set to work feverishly on the last shreds of the meat. She even tried to eat the charred skin.

"Sorry, man. Sorry, man," a guy in his mid-thirties kept saying. He wore jeans and a filthy gray teeshirt with the words *Don't worry, Be happy* below a Rastafarian happy face with dreadlocks, smoking a joint. "We're so hungry. Sorry, man."

After half an hour or so, the mob slowly moved off down the road. The camp was destroyed. Every last piece of food was gone, including their trash. The starving people had even eaten the skins of yesterday's onions. Others of the mob drank water straight out of the pond. The dawning reality was that they had just witnessed the walking dead.

"Who the hell were those guys?" Tyson asked.

"They're from the highway," Justin guessed. "Damned idiots."

Sage wondered how the Starbucks Clan saw *themselves* since, from Sage's point of view, they weren't any more prepared or capable than the people from the walking dead.

The lack of calories was starting to show in the Starbucks Clan, as well. It took them two hours to put the camp back together.

"We should go collect some onions," Justin said. "I'm slowing down."

The very idea of onions made Sage sick. He could barely

eat one without gagging, but onions were calories. As best as he could tell, there were maybe two thousand calories in ten pounds of onions. That meant they would each have to eat ten pounds of the cursed things to cover the caloric requirement for a single day. The thought made Sage want to vomit.

His irritation about eating onions blossomed into an admission that he was burning time and calories trying to help these doomed people. He had begun to see the Starbucks Clan mostly as incompetents—by choice, not by necessity. It was hard to ignore the fact that they were dying right before his eyes, but they still weren't willing to eat strange things or listen to cold, hard reason.

Didn't this all come down to the same argument he had been having with his dad for years? If his dad were here, he would point out that Sage had little to gain and a lot to lose by staying with the Starbucks Clan. He would argue that there was no profit in the relationship for Sage.

Sage would argue back that he didn't care about profit. That he thought everyone could win. That he was holding out for something better than a world where some were winners and some were losers. He could help them to survive, even without giving them his grandparents' food. He could help them to see truth and to make better decisions so that everyone would make it.

In the wake of the zombie mob, Sage couldn't deny the thinness of his argument. Considering the beating their equipment had just sustained and their complete lack of food, the Starbucks Clan had maybe forty-eight hours before they were rendered to the walking dead themselves. There was very little Sage could do to stop it, especially since the group still resisted his input on the matter of survival.

But one factor overwhelmed all reason, rising up in Sage's mind at every turn of argument: Penny.

Her smile. Her hips. Her breasts. She had been kind to him. She had *relied* on him.

Even though she had been crapping her guts out for two days, Sage still wanted her, and he felt an obligation to her. There was something about rescuing Penny—and getting in her pants—that overrode all argument. And Nora had been kind to him. They could be saved.

Sage knew he was being foolish and it might get him killed. There was nothing about hanging around the Starbucks Clan that amounted to a survival advantage. But he couldn't see a way to get Penny and Nora away from them. If he asked them to leave, the three would have to go to his hidey-hole to collect his gear and then the jig would be up. They would be seen making their getaway, and Sage would have to face the group, admitting that he had lied to them about sharing his supplies. If he even just told Penny about his stuff, she might force him to tell the others. He simply could not see how to get away from this sinking ship with Penny and Nora without tremendous risk of losing his stockpile.

But what good was survival if he was alone?

Sage shook his head, deciding to stay for now. Without him, the Starbucks Clan was doomed, and Sage couldn't live with himself if Penny or Nora ended up dead because he had been too selfish to share, at the very least, what he was quickly learning about survival. Heck, they would have been dead already if Sage hadn't found the onions or devised the water filter.

Now that they had been decimated by the wandering mob, they would listen to reason. They would accept Sage as their leader—the only choice in order to survive. Even Justin couldn't fail to see that now.

HIGHWAY 150, Outside of Mount Washington, Kentucky

MAT STARED into a skyline twined with a thousand tendrils of smoke. He stood atop a mountain and he should have been able to see the downtown high rises of Louisville. All he could see were smoky cords and a sickly haze with a few tall buildings poking through the soup. To him, it looked like Mosul, Iraq.

"Can we please go get them, Mat?" Caroline begged. "I have a really bad feeling about this."

"Babe, if we go rushing into that mess, we will lose everything and maybe get ourselves killed. Without my Raptor, we're just another pair of helpless refugees."

"I don't care about our gear. I care about my parents and my brother." Caroline didn't seem to understand Mat's training or his reluctance.

"Where do they live? In what part of the city?" Mat pulled out the Kentucky map.

"They live in Beechwood Village. I think it's right about here." Caroline pointed to the east side of the metropolis on the map.

Mat tried to picture the big city and how danger would develop after a collapse of civil order. Gangs would probably hit their own areas first, but then fan out into surrounding suburbs to scavenge, eventually ranging far into the country-side. He had seen it happen before. Gangs eventually figured out that the countryside was rich in resources and isolated in terms of defense. Ultimately the gangs would see that the countryside gave them the easiest pickings. But they would first hit the areas they knew best.

"Where's the 'wrong side of the tracks' in Louisville? Where's most the crime?"

"I didn't live there more than a year before going off to school. I grew up in Charleston." Caroline thought about it for a moment. "I'm pretty sure most of the crime comes from the west side of the 65 Freeway. Right here." She traced a line through the map of the city.

"And your parents live here?" Mat pointed to the area, maybe twenty miles to the east of the 65 Freeway.

"Yes. It's a really nice neighborhood. A long way from the bad spots," she said, obviously doing her best to convince Mat that a rescue could be accomplished.

"It's been over a week since the collapse of the stock market. Anything could be going on in that suburb." Mat sighed, exasperated with how little he knew about the tactical situation. "We'd be going in totally blind. We can't afford to lose this truck. If we do, we die. I'm sure your parents would want you to live. Let's just consider that for a moment."

Based on the look on her face and the way her hands kept wringing, Mat didn't think she heard a word he said.

She countered. "I trust you. Let's give it a try. We can always turn around and head back out if things look too dangerous."

"Actually, no. We probably won't be able to turn around and head back out if things go south. When you stumble into an ambush, it's usually already too late for anything but the crying. Trust me, this is a game I know."

Caroline stood in front of him, pleading with her big green eyes, her dark hair framing her perfect face.

"Dammit," he swore. "Let's at least *try* to get an exfil plan together before we wade into that shit sandwich." He gestured at the burning city. "We can hide the motorcycles and ditch the trailer. At least then we can run out of a death trap without making a twelve-point turn. We need to find a deep thicket, lay the bikes down and cover them with branches."

"How long is that going to take?" Caroline fretted. "I'm telling you: I feel like we need to help them *right now*, or it'll be too late."

"It's dark in an hour. We CANNOT go into Louisville at night, Caroline. That's certain death. Let's hide the bikes, get a little sleep, and head in a few hours before dawn. We'll run blacked out in the truck and hope that all the bad guys are asleep. There are more holes in that plan than a dude with five noses and ten butt holes, but that's all I got."

The next hour, Mat searched for the darkest, thickest bramble he could find. He spotted a thick patch in the middle of a twenty-acre copse of trees less than a quarter mile off the main highway. They rolled the bikes off the trailer, pushed them into the thicket in a "J" path, obscuring the line of their trail. He laid the motorcycles down, covering them with branches he hacked off the surrounding trees with a small ax from his go-bag. Mat checked the Rotopax plastic gas cans bolted to the saddlebag brackets, making sure they weren't leaking gas when laid over on their sides.

He went through the saddlebags, checking the kit the Ross girl had chosen for the bikes. He found extra mags for the AKs, two-way radios, freeze dried food, a water purifier and a couple quarts of water. He even discovered an extra

JetBoil and two spare canisters. Satisfied with the emergency cache, Mat carefully unbent the bent branches from the bramble, further hiding their trail. With any luck, no refugee would think to scavenge in the middle of a thicket.

The work done, Mat looked at the darkening sky. A bolt of fear shot through him.

What if she was right? What if they should've gone straight into Louisville?

His only job in this new world had become her safety and getting her back to her parents. If they found her parents and brother, that job would grow serious hair. He might even lose her to her family. He couldn't guess at what her dad might want to do. Mat didn't know the man.

In just a few days, Caroline turning her back on Mat mattered. He would do just about anything to get ahead of that possibility. Right now, with the night sky coating itself with weak, smoke-shaded stars, the fear tingling in his back told him he might have made a mistake. Maybe the situation had gotten ahead of him instead.

What were the odds that going into Louisville this afternoon instead of in the wee hours of morning would matter? A hundred to one? Either they were dead or they were alive. A few hours wouldn't matter.

Still, Mat weighed his stake in the big game, a bet riding on a life-or-death gamble. Before, he had just been playing along—being the Big Hero. Now he played for keeps. He hadn't even known that he cared about the jackpot before, but now he couldn't deny it. He was in, all or nothing, for Caroline.

Fuck me. How did I get in so deep?

8

"The hairs on your arm will stand up
At the terror in each sip and in each sup
Will you partake of that last offered cup?
Or disappear into the potter's ground?
When the man comes around...
Till armageddon no shalam, no shalom."

— *WHEN THE MAN COMES AROUND*,
JOHNNY CASH, AMERICAN IV: THE
MAN COMES AROUND, 2002

BRIGHTON DRIVE, LOUISVILLE, KENTUCKY

RED BRICK. White doors, white windows, and eaves. Perfect lawns and perfect trees. Even through his night vision goggles, Mat could tell that these homes were Tudor style and the neighborhood was early twenty-first century American well-to-do. Except for the trashcans overflowing the perfect country curb, and the garbage strewn about the lawns, Mat wouldn't have thought "Armageddon."

Then he came upon the first burned-out homes. Scorched brick walls, some of them collapsed, and the occasional isolated chimney. They punctuated the otherwise intact neighborhoods.

Mat tried to imagine how or why these homes had burned. Maybe the families had attempted cooking with fire indoors. Maybe criminals had hit the homes and burned them out. Maybe vandals had lit them on fire just for fun. One thing was certain: no firemen had come to stop the blaze. They had burned unchecked until the fire ran out of fuel.

As soon as he could, Mat abandoned the main roads of Louisville in favor of the dense grid of residential streets crisscrossing the manicured neighborhoods. It was four o'clock in the morning and they hadn't encountered any danger—just a city that looked as though every soul had vanished into thin air. Maybe it was like the old fire-and-brimstone preacher had warned. Maybe all the people except Mat and Caroline, unrepentant fornicators, had been taken up into the sky to greet the Coming of the Lord.

As so often occurred in the run-up to battle, Mat saw nothing specific to worry him. Still, his Spidey senses did backflips, his hand antsy on the AR-15 in his lap, a round in the chamber.

"You're going to need to head northwest pretty soon." Caroline navigated with her cell phone. For whatever reason, Google Maps began working the moment they passed the city boundaries. It was a good thing, because the big laminated map wasn't detailed enough to get them to her parents' house. "We're looking for Brindle Road, but we still need to work our way a mile north."

All the lights in the truck, including the dome light, had been turned off. The only light in the cab was Caroline's cell phone. Mat moved along at fifteen miles an hour, his Raptor nearly silent in the dewy, late September morning.

"Roll down your window, please," Mat asked.

"It's cold outside and I feel safer with it up."

"You're not safer with it up and, if I have to shoot, the back blast will cook your eardrums with the windows rolled up."

Caroline rolled all the windows down and bundled up in her wind breaker. The smell of death wafted into the cab.

"Also, I know it's a pain in the ass, but please put your backpack on." Mat reached around and handed Caroline one of the packs.

"You're worried. I can tell. What're you worried about?" she asked.

"I'm terrified, Hot Stuff. We're deep in the shit now. I can feel it. If we have to abandon the Raptor and all our supplies, we'll need these packs to survive. I made sure they had a critical load-out before we went to bed last night. If we fall into the meat grinder, we won't have time to grab packs. Run your seat all the way back and it'll be more comfortable. Will you pass me my pack, too?"

Caroline handed Mat his pack and he slipped it on while he drove, rolling his seat all the way back.

Mat made a right turn onto an inconspicuous residential street and his NVGs flared white, adjusting to a new light source. Twin fires burned in the middle of the street half a block up, and cars jammed the street in a crude barricade. Dark human forms flitted back and forth between the cars, like demons worshipping the firelight. He had driven into the voodoo night before in Iraq and knew the hideous things men were capable of doing when darkness fell. The flickering firelight and hunched shapes of men bent on mayhem lit a primordial part of his brain, drawing visions of torture, evisceration, and endless pain. Mat stomped on the brake.

He checked his flanks and suddenly recognized ominous shapes hovering over the lawn exactly beside his truck. Mat's blood ran cold.

Skewered human heads lulled on poles of some sort— probably shovel handles. The residents had lined them up along a once-manicured lawn. The closest heads were only a few feet away from the Raptor and Mat could tell they were the heads of young African-American males, at least a dozen.

"What is that?" Caroline pointed to the bonfires and roadblock, luckily keeping her attention from the severed heads.

"Get down." Mat threw the Raptor in reverse and roared backward, pulling out of the trap that would've undoubtedly killed them both—a trap likely erected by insurance salesmen, Mary Kaye representatives and social media marketing consultants trying to carve their neighborhood out of the citywide chaos. The bedroom communities of Louisville had gone feral.

"What happened?" Caroline asked, whipping her head around to understand the threat Mat had seen.

"That was a wrong turn, babe. I'm pretty sure we just saw a neighborhood that's been attacked by looters one time too many. I don't think that was a block party with weenies and marshmallows; maybe a block party where they kill anyone who they don't know from the P.T.A."

Mat shivered involuntarily, considering the ambush they had just avoided. He didn't mention the part about the severed heads to Caroline. He presumed they had been set as a warning: *Fuck with this neighborhood at your peril.*

What kind of a suburbanite, just nine days after the crash of the stock market, would chop off heads and stick them on shovel handles? Mat guessed it might be the kind of suburbanite who had already lost loved ones to criminals.

"There!" Caroline pointed to a street sign that read, "Brindle Road." Mat made a left, and rolled through the stop sign. A moment later, Caroline pointed again, "That house with the big walnut tree in front."

Mat pulled onto the lawn beneath the tree and winced as his brakes squeaked. Any noise right now dragged his nerves through hell. He felt a creeping dread, like a man who shows up to a friend's wedding in his best suit, only to find it had been the week before.

"Let me clear the house before you come in," Mat insisted. "Trust me on this. Stay in the car until I come back for you." Caroline nodded and checked the chamber of her AK. Mat stepped out, still wearing his NVGs. It made sense for him to go in first, but part of him just wanted more time— more time while she still might care for him.

Mat used the big walnut tree trunk for cover, then slipped around the tree and made his way to the side of the house past a one-car garage. The backyard held no surprises, a lawn surrounded with flower beds. Mat tried the back door and found it locked. He knocked quietly and waited. Nobody answered. He knocked again. Still no answer.

Trying to be as quiet as possible, Mat threw his weight against the door. The added weight of the backpack hit the door harder than he had anticipated and it burst inward with a loud crash. Afraid he might get shot by Caroline's parents, Mat called out in a loud whisper.

"Mr. and Mrs...." Mat suddenly realized he didn't know Caroline's last name. "...I'm a friend of Caroline. I'm Caroline's friend. Don't shoot." Mat stopped and listened. Deep inside the house, he heard a creak and his blood ran cold. Mat slung his AR-15 around outside his backpack and out of the way. Simultaneously, he cleared his Glock from the holster.

"Don't shoot. I'm a friend of Caroline's," Mat loud-whispered again. He entered a kitchen with a sink full of unwashed dishes. The kitchen smelled like rotting meat, which probably came from the refrigerator. The creak sounded again, and Mat placed it upstairs, above him in the small loft bedroom he had noticed when they pulled up. He stopped and listened again. Nothing.

"Don't shoot. I'm with Caroline." Mat side-stepped the corner of what must have been a living room, noticing a stairwell and a closed door across the room, most likely leading to the main floor bedroom. Stepping into the living room, Mat's boot punched into something that could only be human flesh. More concerned with the threats that might come bounding out of the bedroom or down the stairs, Mat cleared the living room and slowly crabbed around the one-hundred-and-eighty-degree corner at the bottom of the stairwell. Then he returned to the body.

With a quick flick from his tactical flashlight, an image burned into Mat's retinas, and it was the last thing he wanted to see: a middle-aged man on the floor. From the image still fried into his night vision, Mat couldn't deny the balding head and the pool of shiny liquid beneath the human form. Mat thought that the man—undoubtedly Caroline's father— was wearing a track suit. It might have been the closest thing to tactical wear the old man had owned, probably the best thing in his closet during a night when bad men might come into his home.

Well, the track suit hadn't saved his life,. And, if her dad had a gun, whoever killed him had probably taken it. Mat hadn't seen it on the floor.

Keeping his eyes pointed toward the threat angles, Mat levered the toe of his boot into the pool of blood. The rippling sound of medium-fresh blood broke the silence in the room as he lifted the boot.

Mat exhaled loudly. The man had probably died recently.

Pushing his regret and shame to the back of his mind, he returned to work. Somebody very definitely still breathed life in this house, and fifty-fifty that person would kill Mat, given the chance.

Mat loud-whispered up the stairs. "I'm with Caroline. Don't shoot."

Mat couldn't go up the stairs without clearing the bedroom first, unwilling to leave uncleared space behind him. He Indian-walked up to the door and, with practiced speed, opened it, flicked his tac light, and stepped into the position of dominance, sweeping the room from the deepest corner of greatest danger to the closest corner of the room. The center of the bedroom was filled with a queen-sized bed with a single human body lying half in and half out. At a glance in the dark, Mat surmised it would be Caroline's mother.

Mat couldn't dwell on the implications of her dead parents until the house was completely clear, and his mind flipped back to the creaking in the upstairs room. He hoped he would hear footfalls on the staircase if someone came down to hit him at his six. In any case, he wasn't planning on spending more than seven seconds in the bedroom and he swept the backside of the bed, noting that the dead body was a middle-aged woman. Her long, blonde hair and trim figure made sense, given how beautiful her daughter was.

Mat cleared the closet and left the room, quietly closing the bedroom door behind him.

Again, he turned to the staircase. Taking a quick peek, Mat saw nothing at the top of the stairs. There was literally no proper way to handle a staircase without tremendous risk. If someone was waiting at the top of those stairs, ready to blast him, Mat would get blasted. The longer he waited, the more likely it would be that Caroline would grow impatient and come looking for him. That would add a free radical to the situation. Mat needed to clear the top floor quickly, risky or not.

Once more he loud-whispered up the stairs. "I'm Mat. I'm Caroline's friend. Don't shoot." Mat figured the odds of Caroline's brother shooting him, if that was who was hiding upstairs, was more than there being a gangbanger lying in wait.

Drawing a breath, Mat stormed up the stairs, immediately sweeping the small anteroom to his left, then leveling his gun on a little, smiling terrier, wagging his tail on the floor.

"Jesus, buddy. I almost ventilated you."

Mat considered the door behind the dog. The door to his right was open and it revealed a small, empty bathroom that smelled like the toilet bowl was probably full of turds. He would need to clear the upstairs bedroom just like he had cleared the bedroom below. Slowly, Mat slid the dog across the hardwood floor with his boot, out from in front of the bedroom door. The terrier kept smiling and wagging, as though nothing was amiss.

With a burst, Mat opened the door and stepped into the

position of dominance, inside the room and a couple feet along the wall, sweeping from the deepest corner back toward the window on the far wall. Nothing moved. Mat took another breath.

He stepped across the room and cleared the backside of the bed, moving to the closed door of a closet. He threw open the door and cleared from side to side, seeing nothing but hanging clothes.

On instinct, Mat spoke. "Hey, buddy. Come on out of there. I'm not going to hurt you. I'm Caroline's friend."

A whimper came from the back of the closet and, slowly, the clothes parted. A boy stepped out, his eyes ghoulishly white through the NVGs.

"Are my mom and dad dead?" the boy asked, likely already knowing the answer.

MAT PULLED the truck off the street and into the driveway, backing in for immediate egress. Caroline had gone inside and Mat busied himself with prepping the truck for departure, giving her a few moments alone with her parents.

Eventually he would have to go inside and get her. They needed to hurry the fuck out of Louisville, ASAP. Dawn was breaking.

The boy had told Mat that gangbangers had gone door to door the night before, jacking homes. His mom and dad had been in bed when the gangbangers burst in the front door. His dad had struggled with someone in the living room. Shots had been fired. The men rummaged through the kitchen and checked the house over, took their mom's jewelry and some canned food in the kitchen, and left without finding the boy in the closet.

The story gave Mat a rock-hard knot in his throat, the implications undeniable. If he had gone straight to Caroline's parents' house the night before, like she had asked, her folks would still be alive.

Mat's anger with himself shunted into a short fantasy of what he would've done to those droopy-assed gang-bangers if he had been at 17 Brindle Road last night to welcome them.

He didn't know for sure if he had made a tactical mistake by not coming earlier. Whatever the case, the results were in, and he would get to live with the consequences.

As he leaned against the big walnut tree, scanning Brindle Road for threats, he couldn't see a future for himself in this shitty world without Caroline. He assumed he would figure it out, but he couldn't see it at that moment, with Caroline beside the remains of her parents inside the dark house.

Pretty much every woman he had ever known would place the blame for their deaths squarely on Mat. Something in the female psyche, in Mat's experience, defaulted to placing the blame on their primary male figure, pretty much every time. For better or worse, he had signed up for that privilege the moment he called Caroline from outside her dorm. There was a ninety-nine percent certainty that Mat would be the new bad guy in her drama.

He delayed facing Caroline and her wrath, hanging out by the walnut tree longer than he should have.

With the sky turning shades of hazel, Mat exhaled loudly and marched into the house, resigned to facing the music. As expected, Caroline and her brother sat on the side of their parents' bed weeping. Mat had dragged the bodies there earlier, and the brother and sister had covered their parents with a comforter.

"Should we bury them?" Caroline asked as Mat stepped to the foot of the bed.

Mat had already considered it. "We can put them in the truck and bury them later or we can leave them here in bed. Either way, we need to leave right now. It's getting light outside." Mat didn't want to put the bodies in the back of his truck. He knew dead bodies and he knew they would leak nasty stuff all over the truck and the gear, which could become a serious issue for them later. Even though they were loved ones, their bodies weren't going to behave any differently than Iraqis.

"I can't leave them here." Caroline began wrapping them in their bed sheets.

Mat helped, taking charge of the shroud around Caroline's father. Deep in unknown emotional territory, he said nothing.

Once they had cleared some space and laid the bodies in the back of the truck, Mat introduced himself to Caroline's brother.

"I'm Mat. I'm very sorry about your mom and dad."

The young man shook Mat's hand. "I'm William."

"William, would you like to come with us?" Mat assumed there was no other choice, but asked the young man anyway to offer him respect.

"Yes, please," the boy replied as he climbed into the backseat of Mat's truck and called the little terrier up into the footwell. Caroline ghosted around to the passenger side door and climbed into the cab.

"Good," Mat said to himself as he closed William's door, "let's get the fuck out of this deathtrap."

ASSUMING that looting would concentrate first on stores and businesses, Mat did his best to thread the gap between West Buechel and Jeffersontown, avoiding clusters of commercial buildings. He hoped to go out the same way they had come in, since at least he had a small amount of intel about that travel corridor. But Caroline had been in no condition to navigate, and Mat quickly lost his way.

As soon as he saw the red sign in the growing dawn, he recognized his mistake. Not all commercial buildings were created equal in the Apocalypse.

Freddie's Spirit Shop and Smoker's Outlet appeared out of nowhere, located in an unlikely residential crossroads. A dozen cars were in the parking lot in complete disregard for the painted lines. Flung open to the world, the glass doors of the shop were a sure sign of looting.

As Mat eased past the scene of civil disorder, he saw a "military age male" or MAM in Ranger parlance, sit up in the front seat of a lowered Honda Accord, whipping his head around to glare at Mat's truck. Reflexively, Mat tapped the gas pedal, causing the big V6 of his Ford Raptor to growl, making even more heads pop up and take notice. As he increased speed, Mat could see in his rearview mirror that gangbangers who had been sleeping off a party at the *Spirit Shop and Smoker's Outlet* scrambled to give chase. Mat had no choice but to run, balls out.

"Wake up, guys," Mat warned his passengers. "We got trouble. Caroline, you might need that AK. I blew it back there and we've got company." Caroline and William both looked up, craning and blinking, struggling to get up to speed with the latest horror.

"What's going on?" Caroline asked.

"I woke some bad guys and I think they're going to try and catch us. Both of you buckle your belts. It's going to get crazy."

"What are we going to do?" she asked again.

Mat ran through his training, but none of the options in the "vehicular response to ambush" worked in Louisville, Kentucky in the middle of a social collapse. Mat had no "hard point" where he could run for support. There would be no air support. No Quick Reaction Force awaited his mayday call. He had no team to back him up.

That wasn't exactly true. Caroline had already proven capable of killing an armed man in self-defense. They might not be a "team" for long, but they would be fighting this battle together, at least.

He assumed the gangbangers would want his Ford Raptor most of all. Using their cell phones to coordinate, they would eventually chase him down. He could already see the first Honda Accord leaving the parking lot, thundering its illegal exhaust, accelerating in his direction. With cell coverage still working in Louisville, the 'bangers could call in more guys and maybe even corral him into an ambush. Racing up and down strange streets wasn't going to work for long. The glass and thin sheet metal of a vehicle did almost nothing to stop bullets. Still, Mat would do almost anything to keep from abandoning his truck. Escaping on foot, or even on motorcycles, opened new versions of hell that he didn't want to think about. He would hold onto his wheels if possible.

The Ford Raptor roared on the straightaways, dropping the rice-rocket gang cars in a satisfying cloud of steam pouring out of the huge exhaust pipes of the truck.

His Raptor could outrun a Honda Accord in a straight

race, but every turn forced Mat to brake to keep from flipping the top-heavy truck. And every turn allowed the Honda and the 'banger cars with it to catch up. If Mat couldn't find a straight shot into the countryside, they would eventually end up within shooting range.

As Mat worked through the tactical situation, he came up with an idea.

"Caroline, put a couple of mags in your pocket." Mat shoveled a magazine for his AR-15 into his front pocket while he drove, swerving as he nudged the steering wheel at high speed.

"What are we going to do?" Caroline pleaded, her words fringed with panic.

"We'll be fine. I have an idea. You both need to bail out on the passenger side when I come to stop. Get behind the engine block on the opposite side of the car. Caroline, when you get into position, fire an entire magazine from your AK into the gangbangers chasing us. Do you copy?"

"Yes." She repeated his instructions. "Jump out and get behind the engine block. Then shoot a magazine at the gang guys."

"Roger that. You'll do fine. William, stay with your sister behind the truck. Got it?"

They nodded just as Mat snapped his head around, straining intently at a big grove of trees that appeared on the right.

"Hang on!"

Mat stomped on the brakes, the big knobby tires howling in protest as he took a right turn into a residential area at sixty miles an hour. The Raptor leaned heavily and tilted on two wheels, nearly flipping. As Mat carefully corrected, the truck slammed down, back on all fours and straightening out.

Mat could see white smoke rising as the gangbanger cars slammed on their brakes, following Mat into the ninety-degree turn.

The Raptor roared down the residential street, passing small middle-class homes that had probably been built more than a hundred years before. Mat suddenly got his wish as a ten-acre parcel of freshly tilled farm ground opened on his right. It was the "open danger area" he had been looking for. Mat stomped on the brakes, causing the tires to chirp and growl again, throwing up another white cloud of smoking rubber. Mat heaved on the steering wheel and took off across the dirt furrows, bounding through the choppy field at top speed.

"Let's see you follow me here, cock bags!" Mat yelled into the cold morning air. Despite the death and sadness of the morning, the adrenaline of combat hit him like a big hypo needle full of crank.

Mat shouted, "Keep hands and feet inside the ride at all times. *Quedanse sentados, por favor.* Get ready to bail out, kids!"

At the last second, Mat saw a small break near the tree line and he angled the Raptor toward it, slamming on the brakes. He glanced back and saw men piling out of cars back on the pavement, now running on foot across the field toward them. He heard the passenger doors fly open just as Mat dove out of the truck on the driver's side, his AR-15 roaring to life and delivering a hail of 5.56 into the approaching men. Some 'bangers dove to the ground seeking cover. Others fell to the ground limp. Mat hit at least five men in as many seconds, and his mag went dry.

Mat charged around to the back of the truck, dropping his empty mag and ramming another one home just as he rounded the tailgate. He spun at the rear tire and leaned over the sidewall of the truck bed. With a steady rest, Mat worked through the next magazine carefully, shooting men with deliberate malice, mostly in the head. Two hundred yards across an open field was an "easy day" for Mat and the AR-15. As he got about halfway through the mag, Caroline opened up with her AK-47, giving Mat his window to boogey. He ran around and hopped back in the cab of the truck, throwing it in gear.

"Get in!" he yelled.

Sister and brother piled into the cab as much-reduced gunfire popped in their direction.

Another bunch of gangbanger vehicles screeched to a stop at the road and more men appeared. Making Louisville safe for democracy wasn't Mat's mission. Keeping Caroline and William safe was, but some part of him hungered to take on the whole damned gangster army. Given that he had killed or wounded most of them, his confidence flew sky-high.

Or maybe that was just the adrenaline.

He stomped on the gas and made for a gap in the trees, an overgrown OHV road that led through the woods into another field.

The gangbangers had bitten off more than they could chew. Mat felt certain they had never received an ass whooping like this, and they would be looking for revenge. Without a doubt, Mat had killed and maimed a bunch of guys.

"Can you guide me back to the motorcycles?" Mat yelled over the noise of the bucking Raptor as it roared across another tilled field.

"On Google Maps?" Caroline asked, already digging for her phone, occasionally smacking into the headliner.

"Yeah. I'm going to put a few miles between us and those

assholes. Did you pin the location of the motorcycles on your phone?" Mat had pinned the bikes on his own phone, but he was in no position to dig it out of his pocket.

"I didn't pin it, but I think I know where they are. Google Maps might not be working this far out from the city."

Mat avoided paved roads, only crossing a few at right angles as he made his loop and resumed south. He stopped the truck to listen occasionally, and once he heard the loud bleating of a pimped-out muffler, probably searching for his Raptor.

He made his way south, weaving between clumps of trees and open fields.

"Stop!" Caroline shouted. Mat slammed on the brakes. "I think you've got yourself trapped in the bend of a river. Google Maps can't chart a path through dirt fields, so you've been off the path for a while. You're heading straight toward the motorcycles, but you're not going to be able to cross the river that's between us and them."

She handed Mat her phone and he studied the digital map. While he shrunk and expanded it, he heard a car buzz by on the street he had crossed a quarter of a mile back. For a quick flash, he saw the car appear between the trees. Hopefully, they hadn't seen the Raptor. Mat handed the phone back to Caroline and rolled the Raptor behind a small barn. The buzz of the car returned, probably after doing a U-turn. Then everything went silent.

"Fuck," Mat swore. "We've been made." He rolled the truck out from behind the barn in low gear, idling quietly in hopes that the car wouldn't see him if he used the barn as a visual screen. He crept the Raptor south, knowing that he was heading deeper into the bend of the river. After rolling for a couple of hundred yards, Mat began to see signs of wetlands. Without roads, and without bridges on the map, the Raptor had reached the end of the line.

"I don't want to leave the truck. We can't lose it. It's our lifeboat." Mat argued with no one.

"Can you beat them in a shooting fight?" Caroline asked.

"They have all day to call in buddies and pick us off. Our best bet would be to drive through them at full speed." Mat pictured running through thirty armed gangbangers in the Raptor, bullets pinging around inside the cab like angry wasps.

As horrible as that scenario seemed, losing the Raptor at the end of the world was almost as bad. But driving through a shooting gallery penciled out to a near one hundred percent chance of Caroline or her brother dying. He could not concede to that possibility.

Even so, he had a sinking feeling that people under his protection would die either way.

FUNDAMENTALIST LATTER-DAY SAINT, **Hospital Compound,** Colorado City, Arizona

CAMERON AWOKE, still in the World War One hospital, this time with his wife sitting beside him reading silently.

"Are you okay? Are the kids okay?" he jerked awake, starved for information.

"Yes. Yes. We're all fine. Lie back down. You've been shot."

Cameron remembered the car exploding, glass flying in his face. "Who shot me?"

"The Brethren. Cam, it's best not to talk about it right

now." Julie looked down at her lap then around the hospital ward, her eyes darting. "The important thing is for you to heal." She patted him on the shoulder, causing a lightning bolt of pain firing up into his jaw.

Her eyes flew open, noticing his wince. "I'm sorry. I'm sorry. Just rest. Lay back."

"What are you reading?" Cameron asked, finding it extremely strange that she would be back to reading just a few days after their car had been destroyed in a hail of bullets.

Julie perked up at the question. "Did you know these people foretold the calamity happening right now? It wasn't a chance event, the nuclear bomb and the financial collapse. These people have been preparing for it to happen and they even knew that it'd happen this year."

"Julie, what're you talking about? What people have been preparing for a calamity? Who do you mean?"

Her eyes still darting, Julie continued. "The *People of the Work*. These people. They knew the world would end. They had everything ready. The Prophet Rulon foretold that it'd be this year." She looked at Cameron, wide-eyed with expectancy.

"Listen to me very carefully, Julie," Cameron said, speaking through the dull throb in his chest. "Be careful. They shot our family. They aren't right. There's something very fucked up going on here."

"Cameron, your language." Again, she looked around, her glance settling on a fourteen-year-old girl in a prairie dress, brown hair pinned up in a towering bump. "Don't use foul language and don't criticize. I know they shot our car. But we're okay and you're going to heal. Maybe it was a blessing after all. These people aren't suffering like everyone else.

They're safe. They were ready. I'm telling you, they knew this was coming somehow."

Julie lifted her book, and he read the title, *Words of the Prophets*. "This book was written years ago and their prophets and apostles prophesied this calamity would befall the United States. Listen: 'The wicked on this land are about to be destroyed. This is the land where the new city, the city of Zion, will be built. This land must be swept clean first. After the Great Destruction, everybody's going to be wiped off, except for the priesthood people under Prophet Rulon, who have been kept sweet.' You see, Cameron? This was written years ago. How could they have known?"

Cameron gathered himself. He was in no physical state to debate anyone, though he felt surprisingly well for a man who had been shot. He must have been very lucky with the size of the bullets used and where they had hit him.

"Julie, people have been saying the world is going to end for a long time. Lots of people said the same thing. This prophet person just got lucky."

Julie folded her hands over the book. "Maybe you're right. But you told me that bad things sometimes happen to good people. What we saw in Vegas... to me that looked like *bad things* happening to *bad people*. And here we are with the *People of the Work*. We're safe. Our children are playing at the park. You're being cared for. To me, this looks like good things happening to good people and bad things happening to bad people. Can you see what I mean?"

Cameron didn't have the energy to argue. Admittedly, he didn't have a very good counter-argument anyway.

"Julie. They're polygamists. The men take more than one wife. They make girls marry old men. They're not good people."

Julie sighed and looked up toward the ceiling. "I hear what you're saying. I watched the TV show, too. But maybe the TV show got it wrong. You have to admit; there's a chance that these people were right all along. I mean, there's a chance. Just think about the world right now. This might be the only town for thousands of miles where our kids can play in a park."

Cameron sighed. "Please promise me that you'll be careful. This town is dangerous. Don't forget they shot at us. They were crucifying people along the highway. These people are nuts," he hissed the last word, trying to shock her out of her illusions.

"The people hanging on crosses were dead already from car crashes. They only put them on the crosses to scare away people from Vegas. They didn't crucify them," Julie argued. "I asked about that. Uncle Winston explained it to me. They have to defend this town from outsiders or it'll turn into the same horrible thing as Las Vegas."

"Uncle Winston?" Cameron's worry clicked up a notch. "Julie, you can't believe what they tell you. They're a cult." A wave of pain hit him and his mind swam, unable to connect his thoughts for a moment. Wracked with concern about his wife and boys, he still couldn't think clearly enough to work through it. He wanted to sit up and shake some sense into Julie, but he could barely catch his breath.

Julie appeared to notice his pain and she carefully touched his shoulder. "Honey, we're okay. Don't worry. Just focus on healing. We can figure things out later."

The wave of pain washed Cameron's mind out to sea and he gasped. Julie jumped up to get the young lady, probably for more pain medication. As far as he could tell, Cameron didn't feel like he had been given any.

Julie came back with the girl and the two spoke quietly at Cameron's bedside, but he didn't catch the words. The pain abated, leaving him again on the shores of sanity. He tried to regather his thoughts and marshal his arguments. But now the prairie girl was there and he couldn't say what he was thinking.

"I'm going to go now and let you get some rest," Julie said, hovering over his bed.

"Keep the boys close," was all Cameron could think to say.

9

"Johnny struck through the Shaolin slum
Prum-prum-prum on my Shaolin drum
Niggas don't dare to step in the square
Kids ain't playing over here, playa
Only one way, and that's my way
Grim Reaper calling, Judgment Day."

— *JUDGEMENT DAY*, METHOD MAN,
TICAL 2000: JUDGEMENT DAY, 1998

WALLULA, WASHINGTON, "STARBUCKS CAMP"

IN THE NIGHT, the cold came like a destroying angel. It started with a benign sprinkle of rain, but it was cold rain. The Starbucks Clan huddled around the dead campfire, trying to conserve energy and to draw out every minute before retreating into the tent.

There were now ten of them sleeping in a six-man tent. Sage had yet to sleep there, preferring his sleeping bag under the stars. But that night it not only rained; it snowed. Sage had no choice but to climb into the tent or disappear from camp, something he was still reluctant to do.

The group relegated Sage to the bottom of the tent where their feet bumped and prodded him all night. Once again, they treated him like a child. He did most of the work, brought in most of the food, and they still stuck him at the bottom of the tent. He should have been a full member of the group, not the guy people used to warm their feet.

The problem was Justin. He wouldn't give Sage his due as the guy keeping them alive. Justin held a jealous grip on leadership and contributed nothing. The unspoken but obvious truth: if Justin didn't keep Sage down, he might lose breeding rights to the females. As far as Sage could tell, Justin had been banging all the girls, probably even gut-sick Penny.

Why the women let Justin have sex with them, Sage would never understand. Maybe they thought Justin would keep them alive. Maybe something ancient and primitive in their minds drove them toward the Alpha Male. It made no sense. Sage kept them alive, not Justin. He only pranced and preened. Why couldn't they see that?

As he lay sleepless at the bottom of the tent with one of the men's calloused feet jammed into his lower back, Sage admitted he was playing the fool. As the morning light began to take the tent from black to gray, he decided to do something. With snow on the ground, things would go from bad to deadly bad.

As dawn came, the sun peaking weakly over the horizon, beads of water condensed inside the tent and an intermittent drizzle speckled their faces. The breath of ten sleeping people hit the icy tent walls and formed into droplets. The shells of their sleeping bags were getting soaked by the light rain. Within a night or two, they would start feeling the damp inside their bags. Without an inevitable change in weather, Sage knew from experience in Boy Scouts, hypothermia would become an issue.

As light rose, their discomfort mounted and people began to stir. The new guy, Felix, unzipped the tent fly and stepped out. He had slept in his clothes. After him, the girls started waking and picking their way outside. They hustled to their duffle bags and suitcases to find warmer things to wear.

Nobody had slept much. When Sage stepped from the tent, there were five people standing around the fire pit fumbling with kindling and matches. He left them to their catechism of endless lighter-striking and went over to his backpack to get a sweater and his Arc'teryx wind shell.

He came back to the fire and stood with the crowd, his hands stuffed into his pants pockets. Felix banged away on the lighter, hopelessly putting flame to wet wood. Sage could see that Felix's kindling was way too big and way too wet. Sage knew starting a fire in these conditions would require half an hour of shaving wood curls and carefully standing up a pile of tiny twigs and dry paper. Instead of helping, he left Felix to struggle.

"Don't just stand there like a retard. Help me get this started," Felix said, glaring at Sage.

"Fuck you, Felix." The words came out of Sage's mouth before he could stop them. He knew he was in a black mood because of his terrible night's sleep, and he knew his emotions were raw. His logical mind told him they were sinking, and helping Felix, even with this fire, was a net loss of energy. Sage would be fine without the fire, tucked in his Gore-Tex shell, conserving calories.

Justin wandered over to the wet fire pit. The snow had slowed down, leaving just an inch of white on the ground, scraped away where the group had walked. A skiff of frozen mist hung over the depression where they camped, and drifted down in fat, lazy pom-poms of snow.

"Sage, help him start the fire," Justin ordered. "Felix, don't use the word 'retard.' It's an ignorant word."

Sage didn't move, ignoring him. "I'm going to check the traps," he said as he walked away.

There it was, Sage thought as he headed toward the alfalfa field. *The first schism.*

He would never go back to being their beast of burden. He and Justin were at an impasse, and Sage wasn't going to save their asses anymore.

And this is how emotions get people killed.

Sage noticed that his internal voice was starting to sound a little like his dad.

We're making cascades of deadly mistakes because Justin insists on being in charge. His ego is going to get everyone killed. I'm reacting to his ego instead of figuring out our survival. I'd be doing us all a favor if I shot him.

As he crunched through the snow, Sage tried to distance himself from the drama. He knew Mother Nature would keep throwing punches morning, noon, and night. But she wasn't the real killer. With technology stripped back, human ego would kill millions.

Mother Nature came at a man straight on, knocking him

to the ropes by sheer force. Human ego, on the other hand, crawled out from under the canvas, slid up a man's leg and laid maggots in his brain. When it all fell apart and people died, it wasn't because of snow, water, drought, or heat. It was emotion. Mother Nature only finished the job human ego started.

He hoped Justin could see reason.

Sage smiled, hearing one of his Grandpa's overused sayings in his head: "Put hope in one hand and shit in the other. See which one gets filled first."

His smile faded. Without hope, he might have to fight Justin.

Something about that idea rang false. They no longer lived in a world where fighting someone meant pushing them around, posturing and calling names. The stakes ran too high in this world and few could afford posturing.

Unless he planned on breaking his word to his father— that he would do whatever it took to survive—Sage would have to keep bowing down or kill Justin. One or the other. Trying to find the in-between would be an invitation for Mother Nature to make the decision for him, and Sage had little doubt which she would choose.

Men with hardness lived. Men with weakness died.

Sage shivered, even beneath his top-brand outdoor clothing. He pictured, for a moment, Justin dead at his hands, a gaping hole in his chest. Sage knew what kind of wound a 30-30 Winchester caused. The rifle would easily put down a wild hog, and few rifles could claim the same. His 30-30 would tear Justin apart. The others would see his destroyed body, blood gushing into the snow. They would see Sage holding the gun.

He pushed the thought away with prejudice.

Not today. Today he would find animals to eat and buy them more time to work this out.

With the scrim of white on the ground, he had a hard time locating his snare lines. After a maddening thirty minutes, he finally spotted one loop, frosted in snow.

He already knew it would be a bust. If the rabbits had been out last night in the snow, he should have seen paw prints. It seemed unlikely that animals would be running around in the snowfall. They would probably stay in their dens until it stopped snowing and then venture out.

It was the same deal with the dead falls. All his figure-four traps were exactly as he had left them, except for one that must have fallen in the wind. He reset the trap and headed back to camp.

Sage considered alternatives.

He could leave the Starbucks Clan. He had his hiding place up on the hillside. Without Sage, the Clan would search the surrounding area, looking for food. They would eventually find Sage's stash and devour everything within a few days. He couldn't carry his supplies far enough and carefully enough to prevent the hipsters from stumbling upon them.

His nuclear option was the rifle. He had the 30-30 lever-action stashed on the rock ridge. He could always drive the Clan away by threatening them. Could he point a gun at Penny and the other girls and make them walk away to their deaths? Would they even choose to go with him if he split the group? After that, would Justin always be a threat, apt to slit his throat in the middle of the night to regain the women?

Sage still wanted to get with Penny. Maybe if he saved her life and took her away, they could be together. She wasn't doing well, waking up in the night at least a half-dozen times to go to the bathroom. She needed real food and clean water. Sage could supply both, but he would have to trust her with his secret stash. He would have to take responsibility for her, which would be a huge violation of his agreement with his father and his grandparents.

Rather than heading back to the camp empty-handed, Sage made a detour to the onion field. The plowed dirt had turned to mud. Sifting for undersized onions was now an order of magnitude more difficult because the sticky mud weighed three times as much as it had. It glommed onto everything—his hands, his boots, his pant legs.

Sage pawed through the muck, ignoring the sludge, and found eight small onions. Like so many things now, if he wasn't willing to get muddy, he wasn't worthy of survival. He stuffed the onions into the big pockets of his shell, getting the pockets filthy in the process. Then he plodded back to camp.

The group had given up on the fire and stood around in the sullen throes of hunger. As Sage arrived, some of the girls' eyes followed his movement with interest. He went to work, wordlessly, building a fire. He shaved long, paper-thin strips off the sticks Felix had abandoned. When he had a large pile of shavings, he pulled some paper out of his bag—the instructions to his water filter. Nobody noticed that he had burned water filter instructions for the last two fires, which was a good thing, since nobody knew he had a water filter.

Once he had amassed a small pile of shavings, Sage set to work with the tiniest twigs, arranging a six-inch teepee around the fine fuel. He patiently added more twigs, leaving a small opening for his lighter. He laid on slightly larger twigs, building the teepee up to ten inches tall. Sage gathered a pile of larger and larger sticks and set them within easy reach. He knew from experience: *don't start a wet fire without everything in perfect order.*

The paper instructions burned slowly at first since they weren't true paper but some kind of industrial plastic-fabric-paper. He laid his head near the muddy ground and blew gently into the pile of cinder-fringed paper. With breath so slight he could barely tell he was exhaling, he saw the pile begin to smoke. Then, with a last careful exhale, the tiny teepee crackled and flamed.

Sage looked around to see who had witnessed his small miracle of practice and patience. A few of the girls stared at him blankly. The others had lost interest. Sage shook his head and continued to add to the fire. Soon he had a small bonfire going. He wanted it to burn hot and fast, leaving a pile of coals to roast his onions. Within fifteen minutes, the sagebrush had burned down and he had his coals. He fished the onions out of his pocket and the girls slid to the edges of their lawn chairs.

"Ooh, can I have some of those?" one of the new girls pleaded. The others chimed in with their own entreaties.

"You guys know where the onion field is. You're going to have to get your own onions. These are for Penny and me, since she's too sick to get her own." Penny heard her name and perked up.

"I'm sick, too," one of the new girls whined. Sage hadn't bothered to learn her name.

"Nora and Condie can show you where to dig for onions. I suggest you get moving. You're feeling slow and lazy because you're beginning to starve. If you don't get moving now, you'll die right here in camp."

"Nobody is going to die," Justin announced. "And we don't

need your onions." He turned to Sage. "Today, we are going to the farmer's house to get our share."

"We have a share at the farmer's house?" Condie asked.

"The farmer has plenty," Justin explained. "There's no reason for us to starve when he's fat and happy just two miles down the road. Those farm animals belong to the earth and the earth belongs to all of us. Just because he enslaved animals does not make him the Lord of the Manor. It's time we make him do the right thing."

"Make him?" Sage wondered aloud.

"He needs to give us food, whether he likes it or not. The time of the ruling elite is over."

Sage scoffed "He's going to blow your ass away if you go in there thinking you can force him." The further Justin slid into malnutrition and the longer Sage stayed strong, the less he felt the need to edit his emotions with Justin.

"We'll see. Maybe we'll visit at night." Justin smiled. "You know, I've been noticing that coat of yours. Looks expensive. Are you a ruling class capitalist, too, little man?"

It suddenly struck Sage that he had no idea what a desperate, hungry person like Justin was capable of doing.

Suddenly, Sage didn't feel certain of his own safety. When faced with losing his status as leader, Justin might be capable of anything. Sage's sense of the Starbucks Clan flip-flopped. In his mind, they went from being a benign bunch of fools to a malignant pack of wounded animals.

When he was young, his older brother stole a muskrat trap out of his dad's workshop. One of the neighbors' cats often wandered into their backyard in their old home in the city. In the middle of the night, the tomcat would make a horrible ruckus for some reason Sage never understood. Now he knew that the cat had been out pursuing females to breed, yowling and mewing his sexual angst.

Sage's brother cocked the muskrat trap one night, staked its chain into the lawn, and set a chunk of hotdog on the pressure plate. The next morning, the muskrat trap had disappeared.

Sage got his brother and they went looking for the trap. They found the cat behind a coiled garden hose, leg broken and twisted in the jaws of the trap. The tomcat had yanked out the stake and backed into the first corner he could find.

The cat's eyes burned with desperation and fury. Sage had never seen a living creature so incensed. His big brother ran off and came back with an aluminum baseball bat. Sage watched, to a chorus of hollow twangs, as his brother beat the wounded animal to death. Before it died, the tomcat fought back with a devil-possessed fury Sage would never forget. Sobered by the horrible scene, but fearing the trouble they would be in if their father found out, the boys quietly buried the cat in the rose planter and headed off, late for school.

Looking at Justin, Sage remembered that tomcat.

"I'm not going into anyone's home in the middle of the night," Nora stood up, marshaling her strength. "What you're proposing isn't right, Justin. You may have the right idea about the Earth, but threatening other people to make them comply is wrong. I will not be party to violence. I'd rather die." She sat back down a little too hard and the lawn chair groaned.

Sage waited to see what would happen next. Nobody followed Nora's lead, whether for weakness of body or weakness of mind, Sage didn't know.

"I'm going to collect some more onions. I'll be back in a bit." Sage turned and walked away without waiting for a response. The scene had unnerved him and he wanted nothing more than to put some distance between himself and Justin.

"Hey, little man, stop." Justin trotted up to him with something obviously concealed in his hands. Sage came to full alert, his senses amped. Justin stepped toward him with a strange expression.

Is this it? Sage wondered.

His shoulders hunched defensively and he freed his hands from his coat pockets, suddenly very aware that he had no weapon.

Justin shoved a crushed plastic sack toward Sage. "Here's a grocery sack. Bring enough for everyone or don't come back." He slapped Sage on the back with a malicious grin.

Justin returned to the girls standing around the smoldering coals and set to work stoking up Sage's fire.

Sage barely suppressed the urge to run.

* * *

ONCE HE HAD MADE some distance from the Starbucks Clan, Sage cut a wide loop, keeping out of sight but heading back toward the pond and the ridge. He longed to get his hands on his rifle, but what good would that do him? He wasn't going to shoot Justin just because the man *might* be dangerous.

Then it clicked in his mind—an absolute line that he could not cross, under any circumstances or for any reason. No matter how this played out, Sage would not allow Justin to hurt the farmer or his family. At the end of the day, Sage was more tribe to the farmer than to the Starbucks Clan. Regardless of his hard-on for Penny, regardless of Nora's nobility and regardless of his rebellious rumblings against his own father, he wasn't going to permit Justin to ambush the farmhouse.

No matter what else happened, Sage now knew his bottom line.

He thought about his own family: his dad, his mom, his grandmas and grandpas, and his aunts and uncles. He knew his family, *his true clan,* would always side with the farmer—with people of the land over people of the city. That distinction didn't resonate precisely, but without knowing the farmer at all, he knew that the farmer would be more like his own family. More like *him.* With so much change around him, Sage's family rose as his guiding light, an immutable truth about who he was at his core.

The city people had interesting ideas, and their lifestyles seemed smart and sexy. Nora's philosophies and Justin's politics rang seductive and maybe even true to some degree. At the end of the day, though, the Ross soul that lived in Sage would not be seduced. His family, despite their failings, would always gravitate toward accountability and plainspeaking. And, regardless of women and philosophy, Sage would always be a Ross.

That was his rock bottom.

He had logged plenty of time in the world of manipulation and laziness. He admitted to himself that he had come close to taking the easy way, the city way, many times. Hungry, scared, and trotting a path toward his supplies, thoughts of his family loomed large.

One day he would face his father, his uncles, and his grandfathers, and he would account for his journey and the things he had done to stay alive and to get ahead. He had promised his dad that he would do everything necessary to survive. Yet he would account for this decision—to warn the farmer or succumb to his own lust and weakness. That fore-knowledge made the decision for him.

He would warn the farmer.

Sage kept his present course, circumnavigating the camp and the pond. Soon he reached the rock ridge and ducked behind it, heading directly for his rifle. He carefully lifted the rock away and dusted off the garbage bag, making sure no sand dropped into the mouth of the bag. He removed the rifle and pocketed the box of 30-30 shells.

Sage peeked over the rocks and looked down on the Starbucks Camp, hoping he could sneak over the ledge and grab a few more things. People still mulled about the campfire, a sickly, smoke haze wallowed in camp, the fire apparently starved out through inattention.

It was a no go. In mid-afternoon, in full light, he might be seen by the group and then he would be forced to either explain or shoot. His throat was parched and he hadn't been able to resupply his water since the day before yesterday. He would simply have to endure.

At a slow jog, Sage loped back toward the road, keeping well away from the Starbucks Camp. With the sun at his back, he eventually approached the farmhouse. Sage slid behind a run-down shed and leaned a sun-bleached pallet over the top of his backpack and his gun. The snow had completely melted away, leaving only a few wet spots in the shade. He looked around and marked the location of his gun in case he was forced to make a quick getaway.

As he walked across the front yard, two armed men stepped off the porch and moved behind two huge cotton-woods shading the house.

"Let's see your hands," one of the men shouted as he leaned around the tree with a hunting rifle. The other guy had an odd-looking rifle that Sage concluded was a pellet gun. No matter, the hunting rifle was scary enough. Sage raised his hands.

"I'm a friend," was all Sage could think to say.

"Keep your hands where I can see them and stop." The man turned to the guy with the pellet gun. "*Vete a trier mi papa*," he said in Spanish.

Pellet-gun guy trotted into the house with a slam of the screen door. A few moments later, a tall man in a Levi's jacket emerged from the farmhouse, still chewing his dinner. Sage recognized the farmer from their trip to fill up at his spigot.

"I'm Sage Ross."

"Well, hello, Sage Ross. What do you want?" the man drawled.

"I've been camped with the people at the pond up the road, but I'm not really with them."

"Okay..." The man waited on the stoop, picking at a tooth.

"They're planning on coming here tonight to do something to your family. At the very least, they're planning on stealing your food, and maybe taking your livestock."

"That so?" The farmer thought about it for a second. "So what do you want?"

"I wanted to warn you. They're getting desperate."

"How about you?" the farmer asked. "You getting desperate? Desperate enough to blow the whistle on your friends?"

Sage hesitated. He couldn't answer the question honestly without revealing his stash, which he wasn't going to do. "I've been digging through your field and eating the onions the harvester left behind. I killed and ate a rattler yesterday."

"You can put your hands down, young man." The farmer walked toward Sage. "So how many of these friends do you expect will come and bushwhack us in the night?"

"There are three men and eight women, but a couple of them are pretty sick."

"What's ailing them?" the farmer asked.

"They drank the pond water."

The farmer relaxed a little. "Ah, yeah, you shouldn't drink the pond water. It'll go through you like shit through a goose."

"I'm worried one of the girls might die." Sage didn't know why he had said that.

"Lots of people are dying, son. But you're looking pretty healthy."

"My dad taught me a couple things about camping. I was a Boy Scout for a while."

The farmer softened. "Well, Boy Scout, how about you come inside for a bite of dinner? Why don't you sponge off some of that mud on your coat over in the mud room? Antonio will show you where."

Sage took a chance. "Sir, I have a rifle stashed behind that busted-up shed. I'd like to bring the gun and my backpack inside, just in case."

The farmer stiffened again. "Do the trespassers down by the pond have guns?"

"No, sir, just me."

"Okay, then. Show Antonio where your stuff is and he will hold onto your gun."

"Okay, Mr...."

"I'm Rowland Holland." He held out his hand. Sage shook it firm like his dad had taught him.

The farmer smiled. "Get your gun, clean up and come in for dinner. We're working on the main course right now, so hustle. You might like it better than rattlesnake." The farmer turned and ambled back to his supper.

At the dinner table, Sage met the family and two of their laborer staff.

"This is my wife Thelma, my daughter Angelina and you already met my son out on the front lawn. That's Terrence. Then you got Antonio and Fernando. They're our farm supervisors."

Sage shook hands all around. The daughter looked like she was about eighteen, with long, red hair and a big port wine mark on her face. The son, Terrence, appeared a couple of years older than his sister.

Dinner consisted of country fare—fried chicken in a stick-to-your-ribs batter, mashed potatoes, bottled green beans and apple pie. Everyone but Sage had already finished the main course, but there was enough food left to make him a plate.

"How're you guys eating so well?" Sage asked in wonder.

"This is a farm, young man," the lady of the house answered. "We've always raised our own food. There's not much we need from the grocer."

"How about power?" he asked between bites.

"We miss having electricity, that's for sure," she answered. "But the well's pumped by the windmill, and we don't need to refrigerate much. We're running on candles and kerosene."

"But that's a conversation for another day," Rowland interrupted, probably uneasy sharing so much information with a stranger. "We got some work to do before the sun goes down. If you've had enough to eat, how about you come with us? We're going to invite your friends to leave."

"Now?"

The farmer scratched his head. "It wouldn't be too smart to wait until after they were sneaking up on us in the dark of night, would it?"

Sage hadn't considered confronting his friends. He imagined they would come in the night and the family would repulse the raid. Thinking about it, the farmer's plan made a lot more sense.

"Their car's out of gas. If you could spare a half a gallon of fuel, they could gather up their gear and drive out of here."

"Good idea." The farmer turned to the supervisor. "Antonio, could you please get the small gas can?"

The farmer walked around a corner and came back with Sage's 30-30. He racked the handle and breech-checked the gun, making sure there wasn't a bullet in the chamber or any in the tubular magazine.

"I'm going to hang onto your bang stick until we know each other better, okay? Doesn't sound like we'll be shooting anyone, but speak softly and carry a big stick. It was President Roosevelt that said that—the real Roosevelt, not the sissy one." Rowland looked Sage in the eyes.

"Let's go." Rowland turned and walked out the front door with Sage, his son and the two supervisors in tow. Terrence carried his hunting rifle from earlier, and Antonio had his pellet gun. Sage noticed that Rowland had strapped a six-shooter in a leather holster onto his belt.

When they pulled up to the Starbucks Camp in the farmer's pickup truck, the hipsters looked like deer caught in the headlights. Nobody made any quick moves, probably because they were so sick and hungry. Sage noticed a handful of onions burbling on the coals.

"Listen up," Rowland shouted. A couple of the girls jumped at his deep baritone. "I'm telling you to clear off my land right now. Please grab your stuff, pile it in your vehicle, and git."

Justin stepped forward. "Hey, mister, you don't own the land. It belongs to everyone."

"Is that right? Where'd you learn that? Smart-ass school? How about this, Professor Smart Ass? How about you and my boy punch it out for a camping permit here on my land?"

Justin visibly shrank.

"I didn't think so," Rowland said. "So I brought you a gallon of gas, unless you think I don't own that, either. I'm going to have Antonio here put it in your Japanese vehicle and then you're going to drive back the way you came. I'd appreciate it if you'd take the next ten minutes and clean up your God-awful mess. Sound fair enough?"

The Starbucks Clan mulled around, stunned.

"I'll take that as a yes. Now, get it up!" the farmer bellowed, and the starving baristas jumped to action, stuffing gear into the back of the SUV.

After fifteen minutes, the campsite still looked like a dump, but the sun was setting.

"That's good enough. Now get in your car and drive back that way." Rowland pointed toward the highway with Sage's rifle. The trespassers loaded into their car until it became obvious that it was physically impossible to fit eleven people into an SUV designed for five.

"A couple of you can get in the back of my truck," Holland said.

The remainder climbed into the pickup truck, including Penny. Sage helped her climb up.

"How're you doing?" Sage asked.

Penny looked at him with glazed eyes. "I'm sick."

"Yeah, I know you are. Maybe you can get medical help at the highway."

"I'm sick," she repeated. "I'm hungry."

Sage fell silent. He felt like an asshole. He had turned on Penny and the group and now he had a full belly for his treachery.

"Mr. Holland, can you wait a second?" Sage asked through the driver's side window. The farmer nodded and Sage trotted back to the campsite. He grabbed three onions from the coals, now cooling, and ran back to the truck.

He slapped the side of the truck bed twice after he jumped into the bed next to Penny. The farmer rolled slowly down the road. The SUV followed. Sage handed the onions to Penny and she unwrapped the black outer layer and nibbled on the sweet core. She should have been wolfing it down; she'd had little or nothing to eat in three days. Sage watched her closely as they bounced down the road.

When they reached the highway, Sage wasn't prepared for what he saw. Cars were bumper to bumper from one horizon to the other, like an endless dead centipede, the body beginning to decompose. Most cars were in a state of being dismantled for parts—hoods made into rain shelters, wiper/washer tanks repurposed to collect water, and upholstery ripped out for bedding. People camped right where their cars had died, doors open, hoods up, trunks flipped upright, belongings strewn across the lane of blacktop, stretching back to Seattle.

Hundreds, maybe thousands of people shuffled about, so much like zombies that Sage did a double-take. This was no dystopian television show. These were real people and they were dying. The farmer didn't linger; dropping off his load of trespassers, he doubled back on the road to come window to window, face to face, with Justin, who was driving the SUV.

"Don't come back. We won't be so helpful next time." The

farmer rolled up his window and drove on, with Justin glaring at Sage in the truck bed as they pulled away.

Sage thought of the vicious, maimed cat. He remembered the look in that tomcat's eyes, an eight-pound animal that would've given anything to launch itself at Sage and claw its way into his guts.

NEAR THIXTON LANE, South of Louisville, Kentucky

LORD KNEW, Mat had done plenty of overland infil in his day, and he knew it could be a long, arduous process. But nothing had prepared him for moving overland on foot with civilians in the middle of *Americanistan*.

The suburbs around Louisville contained thousands of patches of woods, along with a mind-bending number of mud water creeks, each forest and each creek requiring a broad detour. It had already cost them the Raptor. They had been forced to leave it in the crook of the river on the wrong side of escape from the gangbangers. They were doing everything possible to avoid homes and streets, sticking to the helter-skelter pockets of woods.

Mat regretted losing his truck almost as much as he regretted delaying going after Caroline's parents sooner. He gave up the truck in a split-second decision to balance sacrificing their mobility against risking it all in a battle against a hardened crew of criminals.

Ultimately, he had found the deepest, darkest road he could find, drove the Raptor as far into the woods as he could and covered it with a camo net from the Baltimore EZ Storage. Mat promised himself he would come back for his Raptor once this area quieted down, maybe in a couple weeks.

As they closed in on the motorcycles, Mat halted the party in a heavily wooded area and insisted they hole up for the rest of the day, catching up on the sleep they forfeited the night before. They would be better off moving at night anyway, when Mat's NVGs would give them an advantage and reduce the risk of being detected from one of the homes. They had been moving through peoples' yards, so to speak, and every step brought risk they would be shot by some dude's hunting rifle.

They searched fruitlessly the entire next night for their buried motorcycles. Mat had been wholly unable to connect the landmarks he had memorized in the daytime with the landmarks he could see through his NVGs at night. Finally reaching Thixton Lane, he had called it a night, surrendering to the fact that he would have to approach the bikes in the daytime if he was ever going to find them. The group made a hasty camp in the middle of the forest.

For almost the entire day before, they had moved in silence, the distance between Mat and Caroline seeming to grow with every passing hour. With death breathing down the back of their necks, there had been no time to discuss the disastrous repercussions of Mat's mistake. His mind worked overtime interpreting every glance. Not once had she touched him since leaving her parents' home and mostly she looked away when he turned toward her. It probably hadn't helped matters that her mother and father had been abandoned with the truck after their bodies had been tossed around while fleeing the gangbangers. They had barely taken time to straighten them out, lying side by side, before disappearing into the Kentucky woods. Odds were good that wild animals would get to them before Mat could return for the truck.

Helpless against their silence, Mat distracted himself with the business of escaping.

The dog, some kind of terrier, he supposed, had turned out to be the perfect patrol animal. Caroline's parents had either cut his vocal cords or trained him not to bark because the only sound Mat heard him make was a silky growl that couldn't be heard by anyone but the person standing next to him. The dog never once wandered more than ten yards away, and he could be relied upon to alert them if discovered.

While he set up their expedient camp, Mat struggled a little to figure out sleeping arrangements. They only had two sleeping bags, with three travelers plus the dog. The rich Ross girl from Baltimore had packed ridiculously light sleeping bags, which were also miraculously warm. In a fit of curiosity, Mat dug out his red-filtered flashlight to check the tag on the bag.

Every American operator was also a gear whore, and Mat Best was no exception. Even with modern industry in the shitter, probably for the next two decades, Mat still needed to know who had made that amazing sleeping bag. *Western Mountaineering* was a brand of gear Mat hadn't heard of, but he guessed the sleeping bags had set old man Ross back at least four hundred bucks apiece.

"Hats off to you, Mister Ross," Mat muttered to himself. Obsessing about the inevitable dew that would fall on their down bags, Mat went to work with an ultra-light canopy material he had found at the bottom of his backpack. *Kifaru* was a brand Mat recognized—makers of special operations shelters and bags. Mat loved the Kifaru *Woobie*, a waterproof and tough blanket, standard kit for an operator. Within a few minutes, Mat had the Paratarp up and camouflaged, keeping the dew and uninvited eyes off their hide. He needn't have worried about the sleeping arrangements, as Caroline and William slept together under her sleeping bag, spread open on her own tarp.

Now, with afternoon shadows lengthening, Mat packed up the tarps, hoping to find the motorbikes before the last of the autumn afternoon drained away over the horizon. He knew they were close. There could only be one "Thixton Lane." Somewhere to the south, he had hidden the bikes in the bend of small creek, the thicket made dense by the nearness of water.

After circling two homesteads, Mat stepped right into the thicket, realizing he had been within six hundred yards of the bikes the entire day.

As quietly as he could, Mat pushed the bikes out of the mass of brambles and stood them up one at a time, scanning the forest for prying eyes. The bikes had been selected for this exact mission and, as much as Mat struggled with losing his Raptor, he had to admit that Ross had assembled the perfect "Mad Max" motorcycles. The bikes were light. A woman could probably stand them up if they fell over—which wasn't true of most motorcycles. The light weight probably gave them a hundred miles to the gallon or more. Ross had mounted a tough-looking saddlebag system with Rotopax gas cans bolted onto the racking with a clever cam system. Mat inspected the mounts and concluded they had been built especially for touring. The saddlebags and gas cans put the weight over the back tire, exactly where he would want to carry extra weight on a motorbike.

"Can you teach me to ride?" They were the first words Caroline had said to Mat since they left the bodies of her parents in the back of the Raptor. With the bikes now found and the gangbangers far behind, Mat figured he might as well get it out in the open.

"I'm sorry I didn't go to your parents when you said to go back in Lexington. I feel like shit. I should've listened to you." Nobody would ever know how dangerous it might have been to infil Louisville during the afternoon, but Mat figured his only play was a full *mea culpa*. Given the death of her parents, she would probably never forgive him anyway.

"Mat..." she began, glancing at William, probably preferring privacy for the conversation. "You did what you thought was right. I would love to blame somebody for my mom and dad. Maybe if I could blame someone it'd hurt a little less. But you didn't have to come at all, and your training saved our lives... Mom and Dad are gone and I hope you'll understand if it takes me some time to grieve. Right now, it's time to think about William. I'll understand if you don't want the additional responsibility, especially given how fucked up the world is. Whatever you decide to do, please understand that I don't blame you for my parents' death. They were killed by a gang."

It took Mat a moment to grasp what he was hearing. "You don't blame me for not getting to your parents earlier?"

"You were doing your best to keep us alive. On some level, I knew my mom and dad were in danger. I can't explain it, but I knew it and I failed to make that clear to you. We will both have to live with our mistakes. I'm sure that won't be the last of them."

A crushing vice around Mat's chest backed off by degrees. "Next time you tell me you have a strong feeling about something, we go."

"I have no idea what's going on in this world, Mat. One way or another, you're the leader here."

"Even so, we make decisions together from here on out, even if all we have are gut feelings to pull from."

Maybe Mat spoke from pent-up relief. Maybe he spoke from the adrenaline come-down of two days of combat and exfil. Maybe this whole cluster-fuck world had jacked with his head. Either way, his next words sealed their fate together.

"Babe, as far as I'm concerned, William, you and me are family now. We live or we die together."

10

"There's a storm heading our way
All that's been will be gone
All your cities will sink into the ocean
You run away like cattle
But you cannot flee the battle
Wipe your ass, it's time to put on your war paint."

— *HAIL THE APOCALYPSE*, AVATAR,
HAIL THE APOCALYPSE, 2014

PRESTON HIGHWAY, OUTSIDE LEBANON JUNCTION, KENTUCKY

IT WAS high time Mat figured out where they were going. Every mile of road was like a roll of the dice, and he constantly balanced risk factors: that they would get ambushed, that they would run out of gas, that Caroline would crash her bike.

So far, he had kept her bike in second gear, afraid that shifting gears would task load her too much and she would wobble into a tree. He didn't know how far they'd come since breaking camp, but he knew two things for sure:

1. They were going really slow, and
2. They weren't going to be able to travel at night.

Girl of his dreams or not, she couldn't ride a motorcycle worth a good goddam. It was a miracle she hadn't laid the bike down already.

Outside of Lebanon Junction, Mat stopped to check in with his team. William rode on the back of Mat's bike, holding Mat around the waist and keeping the little dog wedged between them. In another miracle of canine cooperation, the terrier hadn't tried to squirm free. With his nose and elephantine ears flapping in the wind, the dog seemed perfectly content to play the bologna to Mat and William's sandwich.

Mat had given William the helmet, opting to wear his bump helmet with the NVGs removed and safely tucked in his backpack.

He shook his head as Caroline rolled to a stop and forgot to push in the clutch, stalling her bike.

She'll get better, Mat promised himself. *Everyone gets better with practice.*

Beside just taking a break, a couple of things led Mat to stop. For one thing, he felt like they made their escape from Louisville proper, and he didn't want to get too far from the Raptor. He fully intended on returning to it in a couple weeks. For another thing, dark clouds massed to the west and he worried they were headed into a storm.

Caroline popped the visor on her helmet, smiling. "I think I'm getting the hang of this."

Mat wasn't so sure. "Good work, babe. Remember to push in the clutch when you come to a stop or shift gears."

"How do I shift gears?" she asked.

Mat grimaced. "Maybe I'll show you later. Hey, we should start looking for a place to stop for the day. I'm worried about those clouds." Mat pointed to the dark half of the sky. He hadn't spent much time in the Midwest and didn't know how hard or fast rain came in this part of the country.

"I'm good," Caroline assured him. "I'm having fun. Let's keep going." She smiled through the helmet visor, her cheeks pressed up in a chipmunk grin.

"Onward, then." Mat flipped down his visor and pumped the gearshift to confirm he was in first gear. The group pulled onto the road, with Caroline managing a half-decent clutch release, especially given she was in second gear. Bikes this light had no problem with a rolling start in second, which was good, considering that they could motor along up to twenty miles an hour in second gear. Mat figured he would find a place to pull over if it started to rain.

Even a town the size of the tiny Lebanon Junction felt too risky to Mat, so he kept to side roads, weaving through farmlands, driving by lone farmhouses. He mostly ignored the maps and navigated by dead reckoning, pointing them roughly south and west, hoping to avoid any urban overflow from Nashville.

The maps provided by the Ross family had been interesting—a window into the mind of a scared prepper. Old Daddy Ross had drawn three-hundred-mile circles around each metropolitan area from Baltimore to Salt Lake City, finding the least amount of overlap and then striking a route between the circles. Mat figured the three-hundred-mile circles had something to do with the distance an average car could travel on a tank of gas. If the cars carried gas cans, or if they filled up on the road, it would screw the range estimates. But it felt like a good guess—that a very small percentage of urban refugees could make it farther than three hundred miles. The spaces between the circles would be the closest thing to safety he would find this side of the Mississippi.

The west side of the Mississippi felt like reaching the Land of Oz—a mythical dividing line between chaos and less chaos. On this side of the big river, it was like running from the Wicked Witch of the West. Mat decided he would spend more time studying the maps when they stopped for the night, solidifying their travel plan to get beyond the Mississippi.

As they puttered along backcountry Kentucky, the rain began to fall. At first, it tinkled lightly against Mat's visor. He immediately searched for a place to hole up for the night. A solid wall of pines hemmed in the road, interspersed with an occasional doublewide trailer. While Mat searched for a two-track trailing into the pines, the rain cranked up to a full downpour with only a few seconds warning.

It hadn't rained in a week, and Mat suddenly worried the new rain might float the road oil and create slicker-than-usual conditions. He searched for a place to stop and hide, wary of every farmhouse and doublewide, since they were unlikely to welcome strangers with anything other than the barrel of a gun.

At the last second, through a curtain of water on his visor, Mat spied a lonesome dirt road heading into the forest. He hit his brakes and felt the give between his tires and the road. As he feathered his brakes and down-shifted to first, Mat heard a sickening screech as metal met asphalt behind him. He finessed his bike to a stop and cranked around in his seat only to find the sight he dreaded most: Caroline and her bike splayed out on the road, horizontal and wrecked. She picked her head off the ground and struggled to get out from underneath the bike.

Mat helped William and the dog off the back, set his kickstand, and ran over to Caroline.

"Are you hurt?" he shouted over the pounding rain.

"I think I'm okay. Just a little scratched up." She hobbled back toward the bike, reaching down to pick it up.

"Let me get it." Mat lifted the bike with a grunt and rolled it over to his own bike. "Let me see your leg," he asked, noticing her pronounced limp.

"I'm fine. Just some road rash," she smiled with bravado, wrenching her helmet off. Mat inspected the wound, a solid fifteen inches of ground-up skin where the bike had pinned her calf against the road and scraped away denim and flesh.

"That needs treatment. We need to get you cleaned up. Let's get out of the rain."

Luckily for them, the road into the woods kept going, not ending at another doublewide trailer. After Mat and William walked the bikes about four hundred yards, they cut toward a small clearing in the pines.

"Let's set the poncho and get out of the rain. I want to clean you up."

Mat and William went to work setting up the Paratarp while Caroline worked on cleaning her leg. The boys battled the rain as they dug items out of their bags, trying to keep everything as dry as possible. They suspended the Paratarp taut across two trees and stashed their bags where the rain would hit from the sides and not dead-on. Somewhere during the rush to get under cover, Caroline gave up trying to roll up her jeans and took them off. She hobbled around the camp in a jacket and panties.

In the maddening complexity of working in the rain, it had taken them almost forty-five minutes to move the bikes to a campsite and set up their shelter. Mat hadn't considered the effect it would have on her wound.

Mat steered Caroline under the tarp and inspected the wound carefully with the help of his headlamp. He sighed heavily as he got a good look. Rocks, pine needles, and dirt had found their way into the road rash and it had set up in a grey, watery scab.

Mat pinched her cheek. "I think you're going to live, sweet cheeks. Let me get the first aid kit." Mat popped out of the tarp and ran through the rain over to his pack.

He had checked "first aid kit" off his list when he pre-staged the backpacks two nights back before going into Louisville. He knew exactly where to find it in the outer compartment of his pack—where it would be easy to grab in an emergency.

Mat opened the basic backpacking first aid kit to find the regular items: gauze, wet wipes, band aids, ibuprofen, an ACE bandage, and moleskin. He found himself wishing he had looked through the kit before setting out for Louisville. It was a first aid kit in name only—worthy of a weekend back-packing trip and not much more. He hadn't intended on losing the Raptor, staging the packs more as an insurance policy than a concrete plan. Now he was stuck with this underwhelming medical resource.

Somewhere in his career in the Army, he had been trained in trauma first aid by an Eighteen Delta medical sergeant. The old timer had drilled into their heads the fundamentals of a first aid kit: antiseptics, antidiarrheals, anti-inflammatories, and antibiotics.

The backpacker's kit had a few ibuprofens and four alcohol wipes. Given the size of her wound, he could go through twenty alcohol wipes in just the first cleaning. They had no antidiarrheals nor any antibiotics.

If he had thought it through properly when he set up the packs, he would have raided his big first aid kit in the Raptor and doubled down on antiseptic. He knew he didn't have antibiotics, since they were hard to come by without a prescription, but he thought he had a bottle of alcohol in the truck, and that would've been a godsend for cleaning her wound.

Mat dug out his half-full bottled water, worried that he might have just one chance to clean her wound properly. From here on out, they would be filtering water from the murky streams of southern Kentucky. Mat didn't know enough about water filters to be sure he could pull medical quality water from dirty, rain-swollen streams. Needing their tarps for shelter, he would have a very hard time collecting any substantial amount of water from the rain.

Just cleansing the wound in the pouring rain, underneath the Paratarp, became a game of Twister. He wanted to rinse the wound with water to remove most of the big chunks. Then he would do the best wipe-down possible with two of the alcohol towelettes, saving two for another wipe-down tomorrow.

What Mat really needed was a fresh toothbrush to scrub away the shit that had impacted into the wound, now trapped in the huge scab like chocolate chips. He couldn't use their toothbrushes because they had been in their mouths. Somehow, he needed to get the junk out of her wound or it would infect for sure.

"Babe, you're not going to like this, but that scab has to come off. I can't get the wound clean like this."

"It's just a road rash. It'll be fine," she smiled, looking down at the mess she had made of her leg, proud of herself for not making a big deal out of it.

"I'm not so sure... infections killed a lot of people before antibiotics came along and, if we don't take care of it, it's going to get infected."

"Do your worst, Lieutenant Best," she quipped.

"I work for a living. You can call me Sergeant Best." Mat grabbed the clean shirt he had set aside and poured bottled water into it. "Hold this on the wound. When it's good and soft, we're taking that scab off."

She grimaced. "I guess we should've cleaned it right away."

"Yep." Mat raised his eyebrows and pressed the shirt over the wound, saturating the scab with water. Even the clean shirt, Mat thought, probably carried its own host of bacteria just from being in his pack. He set up the JetBoil under the fly of the Paratarp and got it burning blue, running the back of his knife through the flame.

"You planning on doing surgery with that?" She stared at the heavy, fixed-blade knife with worry.

"I'm disinfecting the spine and I'll use it to scrape off the scab." He lifted the wet shirt and pulled her leg out into the rain, where the water, blood, and scab wouldn't get on their sleeping bags.

"Ready?" he asked. When she nodded, he went to work, scraping the back of the knife across the scab until all that remained was a bleeding pool of skin and gore. Caroline had latched onto the sleeping bag with a death grip and sweat had popped out on her forehead but, other than labored breathing, she hadn't made a sound.

"Let it bleed a little," Mat suggested. He allowed the fresh blood to run for a moment in the rain, then poured the remainder of the bottled water over the wound, hopefully clearing any last foreign matter. With a dry corner of the shirt, he dried the wound and went to work with his alcohol towelettes, wringing every bit of alcohol he could out of the swabs. Then he laid several three-inch squares of gauze over the wound and wrapped it with the ACE bandage.

"That's the best I can do given the conditions." Mat sat back.

"It's fine," she said. "Just another bike crash. I had a zillion like it when I was a girl."

Mat didn't think it was the same thing at all.

HOLLAND FARMHOUSE, Wallula, Washington

THE HOLLAND FAMILY invited Sage to stay for the winter. He would work for his food, but the farmer began to trust him and he looked forward to having an extra gun.

Either the food on the farm was incredibly delicious, or Sage was tasting his own gratitude. Either way, he ate well, with little concern for scarcity. The farm had run as a self-sufficient enterprise for several generations, and not much had changed with the collapse of modern civilization. Losing electricity was an inconvenience rather than a game-changer.

The farmer's wife, Thelma, argued for taking food out to

the highway. Her husband vetoed the idea with conviction. "If we start feeding some, the rest will lose their minds. We're already too close to that damned highway. Giving them food will draw them to our farm, and that'll be the end of us."

Sage spent most days working with the farm animals. Antonio taught him how to milk the cows, the job nobody else wanted because it necessitated waking up at the crack of dawn.

After chasing off the Starbucks Clan, Farmer Holland set up a watch schedule in case they came back. Since Sage was already waking up at dawn for milking, he drew the shift that Antonio called *la madrugada:* 4:00 a.m. until dawn. Luckily, the 30-30 had a scope that collected a little starlight. In ideal conditions, his Grandpa Bob's Bushnell scope could see well in the dark.

After milking, Sage went back to sleep for a few hours. When he awoke, Thelma presented him with a heaping plate of held-over breakfast. He had never eaten biscuits and gravy, and the sheer decadence of the dish made his eyes roll.

After a late breakfast, Sage gravitated toward Angelina, who was tending to the horses in the barn. He stepped inside the door, waiting for his eyes to adjust to the dim light. Angelina combed the coat of a horse, her back turned toward Sage.

"What kind of horse is that?" Sage asked.

"It's my mare, Patsy," Angelina answered without turning around.

"What kind of horse is your mare?" Sage clarified.

"I'm guessing you don't know the first thing about horses, so why are you asking?"

"I'm just making polite conversation."

"Well, if you're going to make conversation, you should work while you do it."

"What am I supposed to work on?" Sage looked around the barn, but nothing jumped out at him.

"I shouldn't have to tell you."

"Imagine that you did have to tell me. What would you tell me to work on?"

"You can shovel the dung out of the milking stall. Are you saying you didn't notice the cow crap when you milked this morning?"

"Yeah," Sage answered, feeling like an idiot. "I noticed."

"You didn't imagine that we leave it there, right?"

Sage hated this conversation. "Where's the shovel?"

"God put your eyes forward-facing. Lucky you." Angeline turned back to her work.

Sage looked around carefully and noticed two shovels hanging by the milking stand. He picked one off the wall, entered the milking stall and shoveled up a big dollop of ripe cow dung.

"What am I supposed to do with it now? Throw it out the door?"

Angelina guffawed, not looking up from her horse.

Sage glanced around and discovered a big wheelbarrow full of dung.

"The wheelbarrow's full. Where should I dump it?"

She exhaled loudly. "There's a large bin made of pallets over by the garden. That's the compost pile. Dump the wheelbarrow on the pile."

Sage set the shovel down, still full of cow crap. He grabbed the wheelbarrow and rolled it out of the barn. When he got back, she was still combing the horse. He lingered in the doorway.

"You liking the view?" she asked, still not turning around.

Sage startled, then continued toward the shovel. "The view of what?" Somehow, she knew her butt had caught his eye.

"You know what." Angelina hung her comb on a hook, opened the horse stall, executed a pirouette and danced out of the barn doing a ballet skip and a leap. "Enjoy shoveling the stalls." She disappeared into the sun.

Sage was left in an awkward position. Should he shovel the milking stall, even though she had walked away? Should he shovel all the stalls?

He went ahead and shoveled them all.

Later that morning, Sage took a break on the porch, sipping a glass of iced tea Thelma had given him. Angelina danced in the front yard to music only she could hear. Sage didn't think he had ever seen such an ethereal creature. There were hot girls and then there was this... person. He didn't know what had jacked up her face—he assumed it was a birth defect—but she had personality and then some. Her nice rear end couldn't compete with the sparks coming off her in showers. All the boring-ass Shakespeare they had made him read in private school suddenly made sense. His teenage worldview wobbled a little on its axis.

Farmer Holland came around the corner and climbed the stairs, apparently coming in from farm duty. His hands were covered in grease and he carried the six-shooter on his hip.

"Where'd you get that iced tea? Thelma, your man's thirsty," he yelled. Thelma came out with a glass. She slapped the big farmer on the butt as she turned back into the house.

Sage and the farmer gazed over the lawn and the cotton-woods, taking in Angelina.

"So let me give you a word of advice regarding my daughter..."

Sage had stumbled into an awkward social situation. This wasn't a conversation he wanted to have with a father, especially not after only two days at the farm.

"I like you. Any boy who'll eat a rattlesnake is probably okay as a son-in-law."

Sage said nothing. He liked admiring the girl but he wasn't thinking marriage. Maybe that's how they did things in farm country. You look. You buy.

The farmer meandered in a new direction with his thoughts. "You ever seen a lynx?"

Sage shook his head.

"We get them around here. You mostly see them in the winter. Their coats go almost completely white. They hunt rabbits. You've never seen anything as athletic as a lynx chasing a rabbit. They got these ears that point straight up with long feathery tufts. They're just gorgeous. I've never even thought to shoot one for its fur. They're such beautiful animals."

Sage didn't know what to do, so he kept staring out at the lawn and Angelina, sipping his tea.

"I caught one in a cage once as a boy and I took it up to my bedroom. Right up those stairs." The farmer nodded his head back toward the house.

"When I got tired of watching the lynx, I reached into the cage to pet it. I got a passel of stitches and a couple of good scars out of the deal. My dad had to come in and shoot that lynx just to get it out of my bedroom. The bullet's still in the floor."

The farmer stopped for a long drink of tea.

"Yeah. A lynx is a beautiful thing," he continued, his eyes

coming back to his daughter. "But, if you're going to take one into your bedroom, be ready. It's a goddamned lynx, after all."

The farmer patted Sage on the shoulder, set his glass on the railing, and walked across the yard.

Sage finished his tea, wondering what had just happened.

FUNDAMENTALIST LATTER-DAY SAINT Area of Control, Colorado City/Hildale, Arizona/Utah Border

WOUNDED OR NOT, Cameron was being put to work. Over the last two days in the hospital, he had pieced together why the polygamists had shot him and then saved his life.

The potato harvest.

Most of the beds in the hospital were filled with men and women who had been ambushed along Highway 389. As soon as a man could walk, he was hauled out of the hospital ward to what the polygamist candy stripers called "*repentance*." This time of year, apparently, *repentance* meant harvesting potatoes. The only potato harvesting machine in town had busted and the community needed slaves to work the fields.

Cameron could barely breathe without wincing, so he had no idea how he was going to do manual labor. Just the truck ride to the giant circular fields west of town felt like a three-round fight against a dude with an ice pick.

When the truck arrived at the field, another crew of "the penitent" were being herded off for lunch. Cameron's crew of a dozen men climbed down off the pickup trucks, and a man dressed like an Amish guy gave them instructions on how to pull potatoes from the tilled soil. Behind the crew of slaves stood three men with rifles. All of them appeared to be in their mid-twenties.

Once the instruction was finished—mostly teaching the workers how to handle potatoes—Cameron and two old men were separated from the group and assigned to "secondary picking." A young polygamist in a cowboy hat led the three men off to a far corner of the field where a small tractor awaited.

The more Cameron moved about, the better he felt. Something about getting up and mobile caused the pain to recede to a dull roar rather than crippling pangs.

"Secondary picking" meant picking through the already-harvested rows. The attachment behind the tractor ran powered fingers through the soil, jiggling the dirt and sifting up spuds that would float to the top. The rows had already been picked over once, so Cameron and the old men walked behind the potato digger and grabbed the occasional straggler. Two men watched for potatoes while the third man carried a crate. The polygamist kid in the cowboy hat drove the tractor, and carried an old scoped rifle at his side.

The two old men on his crew didn't know much more than Cameron about the polygamist community. The three men shouted back and forth over the chugging of the ancient tractor and the rattling of the potato harvester. They had been ambushed alongside the highway just like Cameron, though neither had been shot.

Cameron gathered that all men from the FLDS community were called "priesthood men" and the slaves were called "gentiles." The women were called "sisters," whether fundamentalist Mormon or not. The last bit set off a wave of disquiet in Cameron. The system had a distinct air of women being handled like cattle and, at this moment, his wife and boys were being held in the figurative corral. Julie's strange willingness to believe the dogma wasn't making him feel any better about things. Until he could gather more information, he would have to bide his time, play the good worker, and maybe make his way into the community system.

Much later in the afternoon, with the shadow of the Utah Mountains nibbling away at the sun-baked earth, the team stopped for water while the young man watched over them with his gun.

"When do I get to see my wife and kids?" Cameron asked his new boss.

"Oh, I wouldn't worry about that. You have plenty to worry about right here." He pointed at the dirt.

"I mean, if I do a good job here, can I work my way up into being part of this place—part of the town? This is 'repentance,' correct? Eventually, we will be able to get good with the Lord, and all that, right?"

The young man guffawed.

"When do I get to see my wife and boys?" Cameron persisted.

"Drink your water and get back to work. You need to forget about your former wife."

"Wait. What did you say?" Cameron took a step forward, dumping his cup of water onto the clotted soil. The young man ran the bolt of his rifle and pointed it at the ground in front of Cameron.

"Back off, gentile. It's not my fault you're of a wicked generation and not blessed with celestial marriage."

"You're going to have to sh... sh... shoot me, motherfucker, or explain what you just said," Cameron stammered, the blood rushing to his face. "How is she my *former* wife?"

"How dare you profane a priesthood man!" The young man leveled the rifle at Cameron's chest. "I'm not afraid of you... Fine. I'll tell you. Your wife and children were placed yesterday with the prophet Rulon's son Isaiah. She has been married into the holy bonds of celestial marriage—real marriage—and you won't ever see her again. So get back to work."

The two men stood staring at each other, the young man pointing his rifle at Cameron, his finger on the trigger. After a long, tense moment, Cameron tossed his empty water cup into the potato crate. The young polygamist slowly backed away and climbed onto the tractor.

Big mistake, Cameron thought to himself, the hot blood pounding in his ears.

The tractor fired up and the potato digger began its herky-jerky dance, fingering the dirt, drowning out the tension that had gone through the group of men like crackling electricity.

Only Cameron hadn't cooled down at all. Somewhere between discovering that his wife had been given to another man and the scorching pain in his chest, Cameron forgot about his plan to insinuate himself into the community.

A few moments later, when he picked up a potato to find it was actually a stone, the die was cast.

Cameron had played little league baseball, then high school baseball, then city league softball up until the day before the collapse. He ran center field and could throw a softball a hundred feet like a rope, burning throws from center field all the way to home plate with deadly accuracy. The rock he picked up was slightly smaller than a baseball and its weight and size felt like a nod from Satan himself.

Violence had always been part of league softball—the

draw, the juice, the unspoken *raison d'etre,* as his fancy sister might describe it. The penalties for fighting—or "emptying the dugout" in a melee—sounded stern in the rulebooks, but those punishments were barely worth consideration: forfeitures of game and suspensions of play. Somewhere in the hallowed halls of city league, there persisted a knowledge that not half the league would play if not for the promise of an occasional fistfight.

When an offense occurred on the softball field, be it a runner unnecessarily smashing into the first baseman, crossing the line with trash talk, or ripping the pitcher with one too many line drives, the dramatic tension would ramp up, harbinger of the coming conflagration.

With some final insult, gloves would be flung to the ground. Hats would be torn from heads. Sunglasses would be hurled. And violence would erupt like an orgasm long-awaited.

Yet the violence had a pageant's air to it, as though everyone had colluded to incite the conflict, but within an agreement that men should be hurt rather than wounded. It was a game, after all, and games are to be played only as a *precursor* to war. They aren't the act of war itself. Bloody, even broken noses, mangled hands, blackened eyes, and cauliflower ears were all *de rigueur*—well within the bounds of gentlemanly battle.

If a softball player ripped off an ear, bit off a finger, or stove in the knee of an opponent, that would be beyond the pale: a violation of decorum. Such a violator would be looked upon as a despicable sort of savage, and even his own softball team would gladly see him hauled off to jail.

Physically, it might be easier on the fists to punch a man in the throat and possibly collapse his esophagus, but no man would dare do it. Even with a dozen baseball bats at arm's reach, few men ever left the fight for the hospital. The level of injury adjusted itself, mostly, within reasonable limits.

Afterward, the warring teams would sometimes share a beer at the nearest watering hole, celebrating their injuries and basking in the post-coital glee of having once again survived mock combat.

Cameron had been the veteran of over a dozen such softball battles; he knew the limits and had learned the means of causing pain without injury, wounding without maiming. He had reveled many times in violence without consequence.

Standing in the red dirt rows of a northern Arizona field, the violence pounding in his head ratcheted beyond pageantry. Murder took hold. The look in Cameron's eyes would be instantly recognized by any man and would have alarmed the young slave driver, except that he had turned his back.

The old man standing beside Cameron sucked air through his teeth as Cameron wound up and rocketed the stone at over seventy miles per hour directly into the dimple where the back of the young man's skull met his spine. The young polygamist crumpled over his steering wheel like a marionette whose strings had been cut. Cameron rushed forward and jumped into the cab, triggering a massive stab of pain in his chest. He hunted for the ignition to shut the tractor off but reconsidered and left it chugging. He draped the limp man's arm over the steering wheel, stabilizing the plodding trajectory and buying himself a minute or two before the tractor pitched off the row into the scrub beyond.

Cameron grabbed the rifle and scanned the potato field, grateful no one had noticed except his fellow slaves. He searched the man's pockets, finding a box of bullets and a set of truck keys. He tossed the keys to one of the old men. Without saying a word, Cameron climbed down from the tractor and lurched away, wounded and crooked, loping to the edge of the field where a dry creek bed ran away from the potato field into the red hills above the town.

11

"Dying world of radiation, victims of mad frustration
Burning globe of oxy'n fire, like electric funeral pyre."

> *— ELECTRIC FUNERAL*, BLACK SABBATH, PARANOID, 1970

THE HOLLAND FARMHOUSE, WALLULA, WASHINGTON

IT WAS *LA MADRUGADA*—THE middle of the night. Technically, early morning. Sage's guard duty.

Guard duty meant sitting on a chair in Terrence's room, looking out the highest window in the house toward the backyard while the farmer's oldest son snored beside him in bed. The farmer's wife, Thelma, left coffee warming in the kitchen for Sage, and he had scrounged an insulated coffee mug, the kind of mug with a cup for a lid and a big "Thermos" printed on the front. It probably held six cups of coffee; apparently a farmer's dose.

Nothing in this world felt cozier to Sage than a mug in his hands. Sage would have rather been asleep but, if he couldn't be asleep, coffee with cream was an outstanding consolation prize.

If there was a paradise amid the collapse, it would be right here, living with the Hollands. Sage couldn't think of a time when he had met better people.

Even with their high-minded ideas about social equality, the Starbucks Clan hadn't necessarily been *good* people. Maybe Nora was good people and maybe Penny, but Sage understood now in a way he hadn't before. He remembered the trappings of society once important to him: skinny jeans, the hip-hop music scene, and luxury travel. He had spent time in Manhattan with his parents, and the allure of running with the elite lit him up back then.

In a rare indulgence while on that trip, his dad took him to Saks Fifth Avenue in Manhattan. Caught up in the glitz of New York, the two Ross boys splurged on matching pairs of fashionista high-top sneakers. His dad handed over his credit card and paid almost $300 a pair for the shoes. Back at school in Utah, Sage wore them like the cock of the walk, slipping the story of the high tops into any conversation he could. It was his sophomore year and, eight months later, they no longer fit his feet.

The Hollands hadn't probably ever paid more than a hundred bucks for a pair of Carhartt work boots, and that had likely been for Christmas. The way they lived and loved struck Sage as human bedrock. With darkness submerging the heartland, the Hollands—and a few hundred thousand like them—might be the final islands of American society.

His thoughts about the city and the farm felt a bit overly dramatized, and Sage knew he tended to grow sappy when he was tired. He filed the musings away to be considered again in the light of day. The last thing he wanted was to fall asleep on guard duty, so he pulled himself upright and took another sip of coffee.

The sunrise drifted begrudgingly over the farm. Sage noticed the packed firmament of stars dimming, then silently vanishing, one by one, the color of the sky going from black to dishwater gray. He had seen nothing all night, and his guard shift would be over soon.

A hundred yards out, a fence separated the backyard from an endless hayfield. The Hollands raised paddocks of hay and alfalfa to tide their animals through the winter.

At the fence line, Sage noticed something move. He focused hard on the spot, but the movement vanished. Then he heard a human voice, barely audible on the wind. At once, scores of shadows pushed through the barbed wire fence, silently trampling trails in the alfalfa. Sage didn't need to look through his scope to confirm what he saw.

"Wake up! Wake up!" Sage screamed with a trill of panic. "People are coming. Wake up!" The house stirred as feet hit the floor, family members startled from sleep. Terrence grunted and came full awake, reaching for his rifle.

"What do I do?" Sage implored.

"What's going on?" Terrence moved to the window and took in the mob of people moving across the field through the dark. Some moved furtively, but most didn't appear to have the energy; a hundred or more plodded toward the farmhouse.

"What should I do?" Sage begged.

"Shoot them," Terrence yelled. He lifted the partially raised but stubborn window with a loud creak and propped his hunting rifle against the window frame, ran the bolt, steadied, then fired.

The massive boom inside the room dizzied Sage, but he collected himself and braced his .30-30 against the other side of the window frame. The mob had already cleared most of the back field, the front wave lumbering toward them, just twenty yards from the back door.

Terrence fired again and Sage joined him.

Like a video game, Sage picked a target, squeezed the trigger, ran the lever, and picked another target. He had no idea if he was hitting anyone, but the number of sprawling bodies in the backyard grew steadily.

Just a video game, Sage repeated to himself. *Modern Combat. Medal of Honor. Just a video game.*

He ran the Winchester like a stick-shift car, more machine than weapon.

Press the clutch, shift gears, pop the clutch.

The Winchester kept doing its mechanical job, locked in its mechanical rhythm.

Finger straight, run the lever, pick the target, press the trigger.

The process repeated itself until the rifle ran dry. When that happened, it took Sage several seconds to remember what to do next.

Reload.

Sage dug in his pocket for more shiny, brass cartridges and pressed them into the little port on the side of the rifle, his hands quaking like the last leaves of fall.

The mob kept coming, unfazed by the shooting and death in their ranks. They reached the farmhouse and broke like a wave, some pouring into the house and others flowing around the building and heading toward the animal pens.

Sage heard the big farmer pounding down the steps, letting loose with his six-gun, running it dry. A long scream rang out, then another. Cacophony filled the farmhouse. Sage abandoned his shooting position and turned to help the farmer.

As Sage ran downstairs, he dared not shoot. The first floor was full of shadowy people, cloaked in darkness. He couldn't tell the difference between family and intruder. People yelled, screamed, and wailed. When Sage hit the floor, he almost fell; the wood was slick with fluids. As soon as he recovered, an onslaught of bodies jostled him. They shoved past him in the dark, hungrily climbing the stairs.

Panic gripped him, and Sage made an about-face and scrambled back up the steps, catapulting through the mob. He burst into Terrence's bedroom and scooped up his backpack, stabbing his arms through the loops and pulling it tight against his back.

"They're coming up the stairs," Sage shouted to Terrence, who was still firing out the window. Terrence turned to shoot at the door.

"Don't bother. There are more than a hundred. Get your mom out of here." So long as Terrence kept shooting, Sage felt like a coward. Better to run. Better to carry loved ones to safety than to kill.

Terrence snapped out of his bloodlust and headed toward his parents' bedroom. Muted light filtered through the window shades, a harbinger of daylight.

Sage stopped to think. The farm had been overrun. He had maybe ten bullets left. He topped off the tubular magazine of the 30-30 with two more rounds. It was probably too late to hide any of the animals or the family's food storage. He could hear a mass of people in the kitchen below, laying waste to the pantry.

The bedroom door burst open. Sage reflexively aimed the .30-30 at the tangle of bodies shoving through the doorway. The first couple of intruders noticed the gun and fell to the floor, covering their faces. The people behind pushed past, their eyes scanning for anything to eat or steal. Sage stood his ground but couldn't bring himself to shoot. The wild-eyed invaders surged into the room and went to work, tearing through the closet and nightstand, occasionally glaring up at Sage as if to say: you can shoot us, but hunger will kill us anyway.

Sage wondered at their feral recklessness. They burrowed into Terrence's drawers and closet, finding nothing edible or even useful, but they dug through clothes, magazines, and shoes anyway. With the rifle waving impotently at the pack of human animals, Sage side-stepped the savages and fled.

The hall was empty. In every room, he could hear creatures tearing at the belongings of the Holland family. Sage peeked into the master bedroom. Thelma was gone, replaced with hunched foragers digging through her nightstand and armoire. The guns had fallen silent, and the mob had more to fear from one another than they did the Hollands. Any food discovered was instantly devoured or carried off at a run to keep another person from stealing it.

With his backpack on his back and his rifle in hand, Sage felt strangely neutral, like an observer to incomprehensible chaos. More than anything, he wanted to check on the family. But, with darkness still holding sway on the ground floor of the farmhouse, and with a hundred bodies crammed and thrashing within the home, Sage couldn't tell friend from foe.

He shoved his way to the front door and looked back. He could see Farmer Holland fighting a man for a big jar of bottled peaches. Sage considered helping but, no matter who won, a bottle of peaches would be a symbolic victory at best. Sage abandoned the claustrophobic house and fled into the front yard. Terrence and Thelma stood, helpless and frustrated, near one of the huge cottonwoods.

The only member of the family Sage hadn't seen was Angelina. He assumed the laborers were with their families at the laborers' village a quarter of a mile up the dirt road. Sage looked around in the growing light. The mob grappled with animals—trying to capture and subdue cows, chickens, and geese. The goat already lay dead, people setting to it with knives in a grotesque parody of Julius Caesar.

In the distance, Sage recognized Justin. He was directing people and shouting orders, though the mob seemed largely loosed from any control. Once again, Sage considered shooting Justin and demurred. Instinct told him it would be a just and due price for the devastation of the farmhouse, yet he couldn't raise his rifle. He argued with the reality before him—Justin had made good on his threat of destruction, but Sage could not face the responsibility to kill a man, a man he knew, a man who deserved to die.

Instead, he strode across the yard toward his enemy, holding the Winchester out in front of him like a rattlesnake stuffed in a sock.

Justin noticed him coming in the dawn light. "Is that our little man? With an assault rifle, even?"

"You destroyed a good family by coming here. I hope you realize that." Sage yelped.

Justin held out his hands. "I told you. The days of the elite are over. This man is going to have to share his food.

Hundreds are starving down at the road. Who is he to keep all this for himself?"

"Those people will starve anyway," Sage answered, searching for the perfect retort but coming up short.

"Oh, so now you're God? You're going to let those people starve so this family can have plenty?"

Sage ignored the question. "Where's Penny?"

"Penny?" Justin laughed and pointed his finger at Sage. "Oh, yeah, you were hoping to bang her, weren't you? You might just have a chance now, big shot traitor with a gun. She's dead... And that's on you. You led the farmer to our camp, and now Penny is dead in a ditch next to the interstate and you killed her."

Sage struggled to take this information in as the world shifted under his feet. He barely knew Penny, but she hadn't deserved to die. His eyes filled with tears he didn't want Justin to see, so he whipped around and went back to his search for Angelina.

"See you later, turd," Justin called out behind him.

Sage trotted past the animal pens, now overrun by the mob. He ran into the barn and darkness engulfed him again. As with everywhere else, the barn was filled with the grunts of human scavengers. The sheep were all dead, and Sage assumed the horses were dead, too, because they had ceased to whinny. He looked into the stall of the mare and, as expected, she was dead, a long, ragged gash across her throat. As Sage took in the scene, he realized that a person lay pinned under her.

Fearing the worst, Sage dropped to the ground and set his shoulder to the dead horse, jamming his legs between the carcass and the wall of the barn, then pushing with all his strength. The body of the horse rolled and came away from the inert form of Angelina. Sage pulled the girl clear, and the horse rolled back to its former repose.

Angelina had bled profusely from her left ear and the front of her face, on top of her port wine scar. One of the stall shovels lay on the concrete floor, slick with her blood. As he hunted for a pulse on her neck, Sage pieced together the scene. Angelina had placed herself between the mob and the mare, and someone had slammed her aside with the shovel.

He found no pulse. Angelina was lost, having given her life to defend a doomed animal. The feral mob hadn't eaten the horse while it lay on top of the dead girl. Killing her had probably been enough to cause them to move on, at least for the present.

All the bright promise that had once drummed in her veins had poured out into the straw on the bottom of the horse stall, all in exchange for a wasted horse, a horse the mob had declined to eat anyway. Maybe if they had ever seen her dance on the lawn, they would have let her live. All they would have had to do was pass by this one stall. They could have even killed the other horses, and she probably wouldn't have stopped them. This horse had meant enough for her to give her life.

If they had seen her dance, maybe they would have thought twice about smashing in the side of her head with a dung-encrusted shovel. Or maybe they had lost the ability to know dance, to acknowledge beauty. Maybe they were no more human than vultures at this point.

He couldn't leave her in the barn with the wandering packs of human animals, so he scooped her up with a grunt, grabbing his rifle in his free hand. He simply wasn't strong enough to hold her in his arms, so he hitched up his strength and pitched her over his shoulder. He staggered into the dawn light, carrying her away from the abattoir the barn had become.

He stumbled as far from the farmhouse as he could, eventually laying Angelina's body on a stack of pallets by the woodshed. He looked up to see several laborers running toward him, led by Antonio. Most were armed with rifles, though a couple had baseball bats. Antonio carried his pellet gun.

"What happened?" Antonio asked, looking down at Angelina with horror.

"The farmhouse was overrun. She's dead."

"And Mr. Rolland? Mrs. Thelma?"

"I think they're okay. Stay here and watch Angelina. I'll be back." Sage didn't know why he wanted them to stand vigil over her. Part of him feared the rabble would eat her body like they had the goat's.

Sage ran to the big cottonwood. Farmer Holland had joined his family in the yard and stood helplessly watching the horde gut their home.

"Come with me. Angelina's been hurt." Sage couldn't bring himself to tell them she was dead.

When they came around the corner and saw her body, splayed unnaturally over the pallets, they somehow knew she had been taken from them. Her father searched for a pulse frantically, sobs coming from deep within him. Her mother wept disconsolately beside him, her hands covering her mouth. Terrence stood stock still, his eyes glazed over.

Sage turned to Terrence. "We need to take the house back. The mob's thinning. We can retake the house if we move now."

Whatever Sage said, Terrence must have heard a call for revenge, because it pulled him out of his grief. He nodded, and Sage motioned for the farmhands to come with them. They rounded the corner of the woodshed and animal pens, seeing that many of the pack retreated with armloads of looted food, scampering back toward the highway to feed. The pace of the larceny had slowed, and the gang's number had fallen to a fraction of its former size as the pillage passed its apogee. The easy food had been taken, and only the mangled bodies of the farm animals remained.

Sage picked Justin out, directing the remaining marauders as they set upon the meat, shifting into a more methodical attempt to render the dead animals into food.

Sage pointed to Justin. "Terrence, that man—the one in the plaid shirt and the beard—he's their leader. Once he's gone, we can take back the house."

In this new world, this world of thin margins and fragile life, a feckless, selfish soul like Justin would take and never give. He would consume people to make his way, as he already had. But Sage's rifle hung at his side, inert.

His eyes ablaze with anger, Terrence asked no questions. He settled against the woodshed corner with his rifle and fired.

Justin spun as though an invisible giant had kicked him in the shoulder, and he slipped sideways to the ground. Terrence looked up from his scope, unbalanced by his vengeance. Justin writhed on the ground for a moment, then climbed to his feet and stumbled away, back toward the highway.

Terrence lined up to shoot again, but Sage rested his hand on the rifle, pushing it away.

"He's gone," Sage said. "He won't survive that wound without medical care. Save the bullet." Sage waved to the laborers and the group fanned out, driving the remainder of the throng before them.

A couple resisted and earned savage beatings at the hands of the farm laborers. After ten minutes, they had driven the looters off and regained control of the farmhouse. The scavengers wandered away toward the highway in small, hobbling knots.

Farmer Holland carried Angelina's body onto the porch, still crying unhindered, repeating "My beautiful girl, my beautiful girl, my beautiful girl..." Thelma walked upstairs in a trance.

The kitchen and pantry were destroyed. Not a single bottle, bag, or can remained. Food was strewn across the floor, ruined. Even the stored animal feed in bins outside had been spilled and cast about. The laborers went to work recovering everything they could. Luckily, the silos of feed corn were still intact, though some had been dumped on the ground.

Sage cleared his rifle chamber, slid the Winchester into his pack and walked back into the barn. Terrence followed.

"We need to save all this meat," Terrence said, "even the horse meat. We're going to starve this winter if we don't."

"I think I saw two chickens out in the field. They must've gotten away from the looters," Sage told him.

"Two's a start," Terrence answered, turning to anything that might distract him from his pain. "I hope a rooster made it."

The two young men stopped at the corpse of the goat, the bloody flesh seeming to clot and gurgle before their eyes. Sage had butchered several large animals with his father: two deer, and once a dairy cow. An animal's body, expertly divided into edible portions, was remarkable in its implicit organization—as if God designed it to be split up and enjoyed by humanity.

An animal's hide pulled neatly away from the meat, a layer of fat smoothing the process. Muscle groups tucked together in sacks of fascia, a plastic membrane that collected and protected them from the oxidizing effects of atmosphere so they could be safely seasoned without hardening prematurely. The organs of a beast and, Sage presumed, a human, were contained in tidy sacks that kept the heart and lungs away from the putrescence of gut and spleen. With a modicum of care and skill, an animal came apart in neat packets for human consumption, clean and efficient; a gift from God to his elegant creations.

What Sage and Terrence regarded before them had once been a goat, but had lately become a wasted mess—an indiscriminate blob of blood and gore. The steely knives of the marauders might have extracted some scant portion of edible meat, but the majority had been left to intermingle with gut and bile, the gravel and dung of the farmyard—a life discarded in exchange for a few mouthfuls of raw flesh, the gift of God defiled.

"Terrence," Sage said, shaking his head, "you know they're going to come back, right? You can't stay here."

"We have to stay here. Our water's here. Our fields are here. This is our land."

"You're too close to the highway. Even if you were willing to kill every one of those people on the road, more will come. They'll walk here from as far away as Yakima. You can't stay here."

"We have to. We'll die anywhere else," Terrence argued.

"You can't afford to feed me, then," Sage reasoned with him. "I'll help you get the meat jerked, but then I should go."

Terrence looked off in the distance. "We could use your gun, but you're probably right. I don't know if we can even feed our own family. It's going to be bad without the animals and our storage."

Even as Terrence agreed with him, Sage knew he was doing them no favors by leaving. Sage didn't need their food for the winter; he had his own. But, if he stayed at the farmhouse, he would doom himself along with the Holland family. It would require an arsenal and an army to fight off the constant gangs of marauders, and they would keep coming until there was nothing left but a burned-out scar where the farmhouse once stood.

Sage would keep his word to his father instead of sacrificing his life for the Hollands. Some tragedies could not be avoided, but they needn't be witnessed.

"Can I stay on the farm? Maybe out by the pond?" he asked.

"Sure. Of course." Terrence's mind seemed to drift toward his grief.

Sage pulled him back to the dismembered goat and the world of the survivor.

"Show me how to jerk this."

MAXWELL CANYON, Hildale, Utah

CAMERON FIGURED the rifle he had stolen was a Mosin Nagant —a World War Two Russian rifle that could be purchased in any of a thousand U.S. gun stores for eighty bucks. He had seen it on *Tales of the Gun* on the History Channel. That probably explained why most of the polygamists carried the same rifle. It was a rifle they could buy by the crate. The box of shells said "7.62 x 54mmR," which meant nothing to him. They looked like big bullets, about the size of his grandpa's 30-06. So long as the little scope turned out to be sighted in properly, it would be perfect for what Cameron had in mind: dealing death from a distance.

You take a man's wife and children, what else can you expect?

Even adrift in rage, Cameron knew he needed supplies. His plan was as simple as it was elemental: kill polygamists until he got his wife and kids back. What the plan lacked in elegance, it made up for in passion. He had never felt hatred like this before. He had done a two-step dance with anger, to be sure, but this plunge into a bottomless rage tasted sweet like whiskey. It burned good; it gave him power. Even his brutal thirst couldn't mute his lust to kill the men who had subjugated his wife and were brainwashing his boys.

To fuel the killing spree he planned, he needed water and camping equipment. Last night had been unbearably cold, as he had only his clothes to keep him warm. The sleepless night had pushed his brain into a brutal turn and any remaining specter of his own death vanished. At last he knew the grip of God's hand on his rage, an instrument of retribution.

He was literally dying of thirst, and the two men he watched sauntering up the canyon on horseback could possibly be the first chords in a symphony of vengeance, in addition to a source of drinking water. Cameron quietly picked his way down the sage and juniper-studded side of the canyon, settling in behind a big rock. The distance to kill the men would be less than seventy-five yards.

More quickly than he had imagined, they appeared

around the bend in the dry stream bed, looking up the sides of the canyon, presumably searching for Cameron, the escaped slave.

BOOM! Cameron's rifle bucked as one man slumped sideways out of his saddle. The gun had gone off before he anticipated, but the shot flew true.

BOOM! The rifle barked again, putting a massive bullet through the second man's chest. The man gurgled and fell into the other horse, sliding between them and face-first into the sandy wash, leaving a broad smear of blood on the side of the horse's buckskin coat. The men had dropped within a few feet of one another. Neither had laid a hand on their rifles, still in the scabbards.

The horses whinnied, reversed course and trotted back toward town as Cameron approached, his rifle covering the dying men. The chest-shot man rasped, frothy blood pulsing out of his mouth.

"Die, motherfucker," Cameron seethed righteously as he got down on his knees and looked the man in the eye from six inches away. "You take what's mine, you go to hell. I'll see you there shortly." Even Cameron was surprised at the forcefulness of the words. The man, wide-eyed and helpless, stared straight ahead until the frothing stopped.

Cameron shuffled through both men's pockets and yanked the backpacks from their shoulders. Ignoring the massive bloody holes in the backs of their shirts, he stripped both men down to their underwear and crammed their clothing, even their socks, into one of the packs. Finished with his predation, Cameron clambered up the side of the canyon, carrying the packs one per side, moving closer to the town of Hildale.

HIGHWAY 274, Confederate, Kentucky

MAT WATCHED as William and Caroline scampered around in the open field of grass, playing a game of tag that didn't make sense. The little window of sunshine, after two days of solid rain, had sent them romping into the field like puppies, gathering vitamin D from the sun and unleashing laughter that had been jammed up behind the wall of their fear and grief. Caroline grinned from ear to ear, finally getting a moment to be a big sister again.

Like most men, Mat didn't understand women. They seemed to have a superpower over him—able to get him to do nearly anything they wanted, except maybe commit himself. He resented their superpower at times. He resented how they didn't always play fair, focusing their inexplicable leverage toward their own ends.

But watching Caroline cavort with her brother, Mat admitted to himself that a woman's superpower came, in large part, from scenes like this one—a woman and her cub, with the sunlight dappling the wet grass. On some primal level, watching them play, Mat could feel in his gut that women brought almost everything *good* to the world. Some part of him longed to be the beast of burden that served them, longed to spend himself in the relentless and insatiable needs of a woman and her brood.

Having dedicated his life thus far to war fighting and tomcatting, the emotional conviction struck Mat a sledgehammer blow. In a flash of sunshine, dew, and sentimentality, nothing mattered in this corroded world beyond what his eyes beheld right there: a woman and her child, playing in safety under a blue window in the cloud-rimmed sky. If all Mat did with the remainder of his life was cast a ring of safety around this scene—guarding space for a good woman to love a sweet boy—his life would not have been wasted. All the death and destruction he had witnessed and dealt clicked into place in his mind. It all meant nothing if not for an outcome where families could be families, without fear of the night.

They had ridden the motorcycles a hundred miles in the rain that day. With the interlude of sunshine, Mat pulled off the highway onto a long strip of open grass underneath electrical transmission towers, their thick copper wires no longer crackling in the humidity.

Mat and his little tribe had just ridden through a junction with a sign bragging a one-horse town called *Confederate, Kentucky*. Mat wondered how long that name would stick, given modern society's compulsion to remove all history commemorating the practice of slavery. Then it struck him: the name of the one-horse town wasn't going anywhere. Modern society and its jangling trinkets of philosophy had just fucked off for the next decade or two, maybe three.

Mat worried as Caroline slowed down in her play, limping a bit on the bad leg, still laughing with an open face and sparkling eyes. She grabbed her little brother and hugged him to her chest. Mat had never seen anything so sexy in all his life. It compelled him to get back to the business of locating safety.

He dug into the stuff sack that contained the maps Mr. Ross had prepared for his daughter. It was high time Mat figured out where they were going. As he organized them, he found a letter Ross had tucked into the bag.

"*My Angel,*

If you're reading this, then things have taken a dark turn. I hoped it wouldn't happen, but I provided all the insurance I could in the form of planning, gear, and training. I pray I guessed well because, if you're using these maps, it means you're traveling in peril. I write in hopes that you will anticipate the danger and prepare yourself for the men of violence who are already prowling for victims..."

Mat read on, unfazed by the dangers predicted by Ross. Mat had already seen those dangers and worse, both in Mosul, Iraq and Louisville, Kentucky.

"*Without fail, you must cross the Mississippi River before disorder becomes widespread. I'm afraid there are too many people east of the Mississippi for there to be any safety that will last in any town or parcel of wilderness. Please run, using every means at your disposal, until you get across the big river. Hopefully, you will make it all the way to Utah but, if you must stop for a time before that, find a farm family and offer them the gold bullion I've sewn into the lining of your backpack. Each coin was worth over $1,000 dollars during good times. During bad times, those six coins should be worth ten times as much. Find a good family who can protect you until things calm down. Then, come home to Utah. As soon as you cross the Mississippi, call me on the satellite phone. Until then, think of nothing more than getting across that river.*"

Having exhausted his prophetic advice, Ross went on, sharing his love for his daughter and family. Mat stopped reading, uncomfortable lurking in the Ross family circle.

He opened the big map of the Midwest, studying the

three-hundred-mile circle around each major city. There wasn't a square millimeter on the map east of the Mississippi that wasn't covered by at least one circle, meaning that *everywhere* was within a tank of gas of a major metropolis. Much of the map was overlapped by three, four, or five circles. As he searched west, the situation wasn't much better, but the overlap lessened, even offering some clear space.

He began prioritizing cities based on his sense of urban danger. He knew for certain he wanted to stay away from Louisville, St. Louis, and Dallas. Guessing at the risk, he deprioritized Memphis, Springfield and Wichita. Oklahoma City stood dead in the middle of their westward path, and he frankly had no idea how much gang culture and urban rot had taken over the town. If only he could Google it.

As much as the gangs seemed like the enemy *now*, Mat reminded himself not to fight the last war. He should prepare to fight the *next* war. Suburbanites would certainly become more dangerous as they starved. At some point in the near future, the "good people" of every city would surpass gangbangers as the greater threat.

He found himself charting a course toward Salt Lake City, accepting the invitation of a family he didn't know. For long-term subsistence, Utah, Idaho, Wyoming, and Montana all seemed like winners in this shitty game of nationwide who-will-die-first.

Mat realized that he had taken reuniting with his own family in California off the board. His family wandered somewhere in the California desert, without a way to communicate with him.

He had tried calling his brother and dad. While he occasionally had cell coverage, the call went to telephone purgatory every time he tried to call California. He knew that going after his family would be like looking for a needle in a haystack, all while the haystack was on fire. Mat would have to trust his brothers to take care of their Mom and Dad.

Salt Lake City would have to wait for Mat to reunite with his Ford Raptor. Not only was the truck his sweetheart, but the Army Ranger in him forbid crossing the vast American heartland on motorcycles. The weakness of Ross' idea of using long-range motorcycles was becoming all too clear. Aside from the fact that one of his party had already laid a bike down, every stop on their trail demanded significant effort to set up and tear down camp just to get any cover from the elements. The cover of the tarp had proven less than ideal in constant rain. In his Raptor, they could've stopped wherever, and slept in the rain, perfectly dry, without lifting a finger.

While the metal and glass cage around the Raptor didn't provide much ballistic cover, it did provide visual cover and made for a less-inviting target. Riding around on motorcycles felt like running through no-man's-land buck naked, begging the enemy to take potshots.

Even though Caroline seemed to be doing okay with her road rash, Mat hated that they were exposing themselves to the degradations of weather for long periods each day; wet, cold, and windy conditions levied a price on the body's ability to maintain itself. Mat stressed over every moment with Caroline in the wet and cold. Even more concerning, without true shelter, he couldn't get her wound clean or dry. Each time he had checked her wound that day, it had been moist, probably from her wet pants and the relentless rubbing and humidity on the road. Mat would have given his left nut for the backseat of his Raptor. At least there, her wound would harden and form a proper scab.

Mat preferred making a quick trip back to Louisville alone on a motorcycle than try to steal another dude's truck. Stealing a truck out here in Sticksville sounded like a good way to get ventilated. Even if he pulled it off, what kind of douchebag steals another man's truck in the middle of the end of the world?

Alone, Mat could get back to Louisville going a solid seventy miles per hour instead of the mind-numbing twenty they had been going. If he wanted to make good on his promise to his Raptor, he would have to modify the plan to reach Utah, maybe waiting until after winter before attempting to cross the passes of Wyoming or Colorado. Without snow plows working the high passes, Utah would be as far away as the dark side of the moon come December, even in the Raptor. As long as he could find a relatively safe hole to hide in, they could winter someplace where only one or two of those three-hundred-mile circles overlapped.

Caroline and William, exhausted by play and driven from the grass field by the returning rain, flopped down beside Mat under the Paratarp. Both smelled like sweaty children.

The maps spread around the sleeping bags made Caroline curious. "What're you thinking, Mr. Army Ranger?"

"I'm thinking we want to end up in Utah. But I'm also thinking that the winter's going to prevent us from crossing the passes until springtime."

"Listen to you!" she exclaimed. "You sound like a mountain man, worried about the winter passes. Are those still a thing?"

"Yeah, babe. We're back in the eighteen hundreds. I wish I'd paid better attention in American History class. I'd love to know how those mountain folks survived without plastics and civil engineering. For now, I think we need to find the safest place possible and hang out for a few months."

"What kind of place?" Caroline asked.

"Old Man Ross had an idea." He handed Caroline the letter from the stuff sack. "He told his daughter to find a farm family as soon as she crossed the Mississippi River and pay them some gold to keep her safe until winter. Sounds like an okay plan to me."

"Gold?" Caroline looked confused.

"Yeah. Read the letter. Apparently there's some gold sewn into one of these backpacks."

"No shit." She marveled at the news. Just like in "mountain man times," gold bullion might be the new American Express.

12

"When there are people crying in the streets.
When they're starving for a meal to eat.
When they simply need a place to make their beds.
Right here underneath my wing, you can rest your
head."

— *CITIZEN/SOLDIER*, 3 DOORS DOWN,
3 DOORS DOWN, 2008

ABOVE JESSOP AVENUE AND JUNIPER STREET, HILDALE, UTAH

CAMERON WONDERED how the man he was about to kill
mattered.

What kind of guy would they put on early morning guard
duty in the middle of a street? He looked to be in his twenties,
like the other three men he had killed so far. Cameron got the

distinct impression this guy was dispensable. Kind of like Cameron.

In the FLDS community, he knew from television, young men were loved by their mothers, but barely tolerated by the old men. When the average sixty-year-old married half-a-dozen wives, that meant five out of six young men needed to be sent away or, in this case, they needed to risk taking a bullet. Cameron had to admit, though, his background information on the religious sect consisted of a barely-remembered show that had probably been more fascinating than factual. But math didn't lie. When old men have more, young men have less.

Which brought Cameron back to the man he was about to kill. He felt zero compunction about taking the life. These guys had put two bullets in Cameron. They had taken his wife and boys. In the calculus of his anger, anyone connected to this shit show was heading for a dirt nap, plain and simple.

What chapped Cameron's knickers, however, was the sneaking suspicion that he was doing the old men—the shot callers in this piece of shit town—a *favor* by offing the kid bobbing around in his scope. Killing him would free up one more piece of fourteen-year-old female ass for the old, perverted trailer trash leaders of this town.

BOOM!

Down went the kid.

Damn! This piece of shit rifle does the fucking job!

As Cameron stumbled back into the mountains, putting distance between himself and the site of the murder, he wondered what the town would do next. The twin towns of Hildale, Utah and Colorado City, Arizona were entirely populated with FLDS polygamists. As far as he knew, they didn't have a habit of sending their young men to serve in the

United States military. As far as he knew, they hated the United States government. What would a bunch of inbred religious extremists do with a sniper-assassin roaming about the fringes of their town, offing anyone who walked the street?

Apparently, Plan A had been to send men out to track him down on horseback. Scratch two pilgrims right there.

Plan B had been to put guards on every street corner. That made it easier for Cameron, giving him stationary targets in predictable locations. Scratch one more pilgrim.

Cameron halted his climb and made his way around to a hide he had scouted above Utah Street and Richard Avenue. He only had to stop twice for the pain of his wounds to abate.

The guard there had run off toward the shooting, so this street corner was vacant. But another guard came charging down the street, probably coming to the rescue. Cameron had never attempted a running shot, so he guessed a bit and led the running man by a body width, fired and missed, causing the guy to run faster. Cameron climbed up the red rock mountain, rolling around behind the towering bluff and climbing away from the killing field. Eventually they would send more kids into the rocks to find him. The time had come to make himself scarce for a while.

He had a lot of pilgrims to shoot before they took him down, and Cameron still harbored hopes of recovering his family. So far, his little "recon by fire" mission hadn't yielded any solid ideas about how to get his family back. He could pick men off from the outskirts of town and probably get away with it for a time, but he still didn't know where they had taken Julie and the boys. Shooting his way into the middle of town to rescue his wife and kids, assuming she even wanted to go, wasn't shaping up as a likely scenario. The town had dozens, if not hundreds, of disposable young men they could throw at Cameron.

His mind flipped back to the itch that wouldn't go away. A few days back in the hospital, Julie had come off really strange to Cameron, like a woman he didn't know. She had talked to him about "the prophet" and "the priesthood" as though they were real things.

If some old fuck in this town had promised Julie safety for her and the boys, Cameron had to wonder if she would turn down the offer. Given the hell they had been through, he could imagine her at least *wanting* to believe their crazy religion, if it meant safety and three squares a day for her and the boys.

Was she really buying into their doomsday routine? Given that the cult had some current events to back up their paranoia and, given that Cameron had put Julie through nothing but trauma since the bomb, he worried.

Could she wear the ugly dresses and the eighties hair? Would she bail on him, taking the boys, even if it meant she had to bang an old dude? He could see that happening. Hell, he could even imagine it. It made him sick.

It didn't have anything to do with Julie. She was a good woman, maybe better than he deserved. It was him. He hadn't been man enough to protect them. Even in the middle of Anaheim in good times, he had plenty of doubts about himself. Now, with America in the middle of *Planet of the Apes*, would she bail on him?

Even if he knew for sure she didn't want to be rescued by him, Cameron still felt just fine about killing pilgrims. They could take his wife and his boys, but he would charge hefty interest. Drilling them, one at a time, felt pretty good right now. Popping holes in the old geezers who ran this place... that would feel even better.

Looking down at the town from high above on the hill, Cameron realized that this town never planned on being besieged by some super-pissed dude with nothing to lose. Part of him was curious to see what the town would try next. He supposed he would keep killing pilgrims until they ran out of plans. He didn't hold out much hope for getting his wife and boys back, but he was flying high on confidence that he could kill a pile of them in the process of working it out.

Play stupid games, win stupid prizes.

Old State Highway 22, Wrinkley Branch Creek, Tennessee

With the return of the driving rain, everything had gone to shit. The most direct route west had taken them to a two-lane bridge crossing the Cumberland River in the Land Between the Lakes National Recreation Area. As Mat had feared, weekend crusaders—probably refugees from Nashville who owned cabins surrounding the lake—had closed the bridge with a formidable barricade. He had worried about this happening. Every middle-class family with a cabin had retreated to their "bug-out location," previously their vacation home, and walled off all ingress from the outside world. It was what Mat would have done if he had been a middle-class family man and not just a coochi cowboy on a mission to bed as many ladies as possible.

Unfortunately, the roadblock across the Cumberland forced Mat and his team to detour farther south around the recreation area to find a bridge that nobody cared to barricade. They finally found a lonesome bridge without a roadblock, and they motored across the Tennessee River unmolested. Mat had been concerned about finding such a bridge across the mighty Mississippi. There would be fewer larger, bridges, and odds of crossing without conflict would be zero.

His more immediate concern was Caroline. They had only covered about sixty miles that day, her fatigue becoming a game stopper for the group. Because of the detour, Mat figured they had only made about twenty miles of westward progress. When he had stopped for a break, her eyes had been glassy, and she had struggled to get the kickstand in place, wobbling a little when she climbed off the bike.

Mat called it a day right then, and had her follow him in search of a hideout. Some nameless asshole had shot at his group outside the town of Bruceton Township. The attack had been ineffective, but still unnerving. Mat had no idea why anyone would want to shoot at them. He took it as a dark omen and decided to keep his group close from then on.

Finally finding a dark chunk of forest outside McKenzie, Tennessee, Mat led the group down a dirt road between a field and another dirt water creek. At least the cursed motorcycles made it easy to ride off-road, well away from pavement.

He simply did not have enough medical experience to know how concerned he should be about Caroline's wound. He examined the wound carefully once camp had been set, staring intently at the jellied scab that refused to dry. He had already burned through their bottled water and alcohol towelettes, and Mat didn't know if the white marbling of the wound was normal or a sign of infection. He had never seen a wound moist for so many days. Nothing smelled amiss, but several smells, including their four days without a bath, made it hard to tell. He couldn't get a lock on the question that terrified him most: was the wound infected?

Caroline's forehead felt clammy, but so did William's. They had been riding in the rain for three days, and the temperature had been dropping the whole time. Everyone shivered, and all their clothes were wet. They had cycled through everything dry in their backpacks. In the night, they strung their clothes inside the steeple of the tarp, but nothing actually dried. Every morning they put on the same, damp clothes from the day before.

Mat wondered if he should remove the gelatinous scab just to get another shot at cleaning the wound. He knew that scabs were good medicine and that the body knew how to heal itself. Mat didn't know anything about wet scabs. Would they do the trick?

Mat split the difference and scrubbed the surface of the scab with filtered creek water and a T-shirt he had set aside for wound care. At this point, he didn't think there was a square inch of cloth in either backpack that was clean or dry by any reasonable standard. Again, Mat lamented the loss of his Raptor and the clean, dry space it would have provided.

He sighed and thought about knocking on the doors of the homes along the country road. It was a crapshoot. Every door would be a chance of death by shotgun. Roll an eleven, they send you away empty-handed. Roll a six, maybe they give you a clean T-shirt and a place to spend the night. Roll a seven, they give you a belly full of buckshot.

He decided to give it another night. Hopefully Caroline would feel okay after a chance to warm up and get a good night's sleep.

Mat dug out the little shortwave radio from his backpack

and flipped it on, scanning through channels for anything to distract the group from their sodden misery. Somewhere in the shortwave bands, a voice crackled with farcical banter, a tone Mat hadn't heard on the radio in two weeks.

"...Kelley Barracks in Stuttgart, Germany is still holding out. They killed a bunch of ISIS fighters trying to rush the base gate. But they're running out of food now, so keep them in your prayers if you're into that.

Here's a weird story: Jennifer Watts, a Drinkin' Bro-ette, off of Galveston, Texas radioed in from a flotilla of boats all tied together in the Gulf of Mexico. They can't make landfall because of the gangs out of Houston, so they're just drifting around, eating whatever fish they can catch. A cargo ship carrying produce out of Brazil called in yesterday and I think I've got it on a rendezvous course with the flotilla. I'm like the Tinder of hungry people now, using ham radio to hook up grub to girls and girls to grub.

Strange days. This is not what I thought I'd be doing when I grew up..."

"Hey," Mat laughed, "I think I know this guy. It sounds like JT Taylor, this one dude I met overseas. We became pretty good friends."

Caroline eked out a wan smile, enjoying Mat's moment of happiness. "Tell me all about JT Taylor," she asked as she snuggled up to Mat, closing her eyes.

Worried, but without anything he could do at the moment, Mat started telling funny stories about JT, the radio quietly mumbling in the background. As her breath deepened, Mat turned off the shortwave and brushed back her dark hair and prayed silently to a God he barely knew.

IN THE MIDDLE of the night, something awoke Mat. He knew instantly it was a threat, and his Glock was in his hand before he fully gained consciousness. He listened intently, hearing nothing.

As he sat up and disturbed the sleeping bag, he realized with a sickening drop in his stomach what had awakened him. He slid the Glock back into its holster.

The smell floating out from under the sleeping bag was undeniable. His beautiful girl's wound had rejected his first aid and he knew he faced an adversary more malignant, more relentless than any Al Qaeda fanatic.

Infection.

13

_____

"No more petty crimes, nickel sacks
Rap shows or raves, sunshine or bullshit
    holidays
Just radiation and tidal waves
Death to the modern-day slaves
Running down the streets without arms raised,
atheists now give praise."

— *EARTHCRUSHER*, MR. LIF, I
PHANTOM, 2002

OLD STATE HIGHWAY 22, WRINKLEY BRANCH CREEK,
Tennessee

MAT STARED into Caroline's wound in the morning light, and
a wave of despondency washed over him. He had never seen

anything like it. The flesh in and around Caroline's wound had puffed up and turned white around the edges, and small dark bubbles had begun to form under her skin. When he touched the skin around the wound, it crackled. He looked carefully for a red line leading from the wound to her heart, but he saw nothing like that. He might have held out hope that it wasn't an infection except for the smell: a sulfurous stench, like the worst foot odor he had ever encountered. He could barely stand to be under the Paratarp.

There was no doubt; she was running a fever and her heart rate seemed high. He struggled to believe that something as simple as road rash could take down a healthy adult in just three days. Even factoring in fatigue, cold and wet, it seemed impossible in this day and age.

He reminded himself that they now lived in another "day and age" and he vaguely recalled stories about Civil War and First World War men dying within days due to minor infections.

"William," he turned to the boy. "I'm not sure what to do here. If we start knocking on doors, we might get shot. We didn't see anyone outside yesterday."

"Because of the rain, right?" William asked.

Caroline turned over and looked at them both. "I'm really sorry about the smell," she smiled. "This isn't the way a lady likes to greet her gentleman callers."

"Well, the human body is good at dealing with injury on its own, and I'm hoping this wound is something your body can handle. How are you feeling?"

"I'm okay," she said. "I'm a little tired and I think I have a fever."

"That's your body fighting the infection. I'm pretty sure

think we need to get you inside a real shelter, sooner rather than later."

"Couldn't that be dangerous?" she asked.

"It's nothing I can't handle." Mat gathered his things.

IN MAT'S MIND, he had accounted for being turned down, and he had even accounted for being shot. He hadn't accounted for *nothing*.

It was almost noon, the rain was coming down in sheets, and Mat hadn't spoken to a living soul. He figured he had walked three miles and knocked on twenty doors, all of them farmhouses. Not a single door opened, no matter how hard he hammered.

He would approach a door, step to the side of the frame where he might have some cover from incoming fire, and knock, gritting his teeth and preparing for the worst. Then... nothing. Twenty times he had knocked on doors and not a single sound had come from a single farmhouse. The rain pounded on the porches, so he couldn't hear small sounds, but no one had answered any door. That was for certain.

Mat considered going back to camp, but he didn't think it would help. He could once again clean Caroline's wound, but after three days he knew his ministrations weren't making it better. If anything, cleaning the wound made it worse.

In one of his loops down the local farm roads, he had come close enough to the town of McKenzie to see the fringes of the city. He hadn't completed any actual recon, but heading into town might be his next best choice. Knocking on farmhouse doors wasn't getting him anywhere.

The town looked small— maybe a few thousand

people—from his vantage point off the highway in the pouring rain. Mat hoped that a town this small might have kept its humanity intact. Without actually deciding, Mat turned toward McKenzie, looking for the best approach.

If he hoped for trust from the townspeople, he figured the direct approach might work best—walking straight into town and making his intentions immediately known. Mat carried his Glock and it was tucked inside his waistband in a concealed holster. He had left his rifle and his military kit back at camp, thinking the weapons would make people less willing to talk to him, if that was even possible.

As Highway 22 reached the edge of town, a five- or six-story grain elevator appeared out of the rainy haze with a roadblock near the base, a harbinger of the town's inevitable fortification. Mat had expected as much. He put his hands in the air and continued walking toward the concrete barriers. Behind the roadblock, twin police cruisers came into view, parked nose to nose.

"Stop right there and state your business," a disembodied voice shouted through the rain.

"My traveling companion crashed her motorcycle and has an infection. She needs medical attention."

"Are you armed?" the voice demanded.

Mat recalled his intention to play this "open kimono," but telling these guys—probably cops—that he had a handgun wasn't going to help Caroline get into a hospital.

"No," Mat replied.

"You have to take her to the medical center in the big town, Paris. They can help her there."

Mat noticed the cop hadn't claimed this town had no hospital, which meant it probably did. Otherwise, the cop would have ended the conversation by telling Mat they didn't have a hospital.

Mat pressed. "She can't travel. I'm worried that she might have gangrene."

"Son, like I said, you're going to have to take her to the medical center. We can't help you here."

"I have money. I have gold," Mat tempted them.

"You could be the goose that lays the golden eggs and it wouldn't make no difference, son. We can't help you."

MAT TURNED and walked back the way he had come, flipping through his options. He couldn't afford to spend the rest of the afternoon walking half a mile between farmhouses, hoping someone would answer the door, and he wasn't desperate enough to kick in a door and risk a gunfight with a family.

Going into the town of McKenzie might make the most sense. The cops had barricaded the big roads, but they hadn't built a moat around the town. There were still a thousand ways in.

Mat cut northeast through a field of sodden grass and headed toward a grove of trees, then turned east, certain he would intersect the town proper in a few hundred yards. As he had guessed, the trees opened up and he walked onto a shaggy grass backyard and a street dotted with small, single-story brick homes. Not a soul was in sight.

He knocked on the first door and nobody answered. After knocking on ten doors without a sound in any of the houses, Mat stopped to think. They could all be dead, but that made no sense short of some kind of biological attack, and even then he would be able to smell it. The people could have left the region, but then why would the cops barricade the roads? The pounding rain limited Mat's five senses, giving him less information than he would normally have in a situation like this.

Frustrated and feeling like he had to do something for Caroline soon, Mat walked down the middle of the street, making his way toward what felt like the center of town. As he worked his way west, the roads grew larger and more defined, and the homes became older and statelier—as though he were moving back in time from the 1970s to the 1900s. Nothing about the town resembled the destruction of Louisville. Everything seemed in place.

Turning a corner onto Georgia Avenue, Mat saw his first human being, a middle-aged woman walking purposefully down the sidewalk. She noticed Mat from a distance and they exchanged waves, which struck Mat as odd until he considered that he was in a Midwestern town of less than five thousand people. Everyone probably waved, even if they didn't know one another. The middle-aged woman looked like a "normal" American out for a walk in her rural town. An observer would never think Armageddon had come.

Mat fell in behind the woman, keeping his distance in case she realized that she didn't recognize him. Also, he was concerned with his state of hygiene after four days riding in the rain. His hair was matted, his clothes were dank, and he had no idea if his face was dirty or clean. He had wiped up that morning, but didn't have a mirror to check himself.

After a couple turns, the woman walked up the front steps of McKenzie Middle School and ducked inside. Mat followed her, acting like he belonged. As soon as he opened the glass doors of the school, the mystery of the empty homes and empty town instantly resolved itself. Somewhere inside the school, a P.A. system blared.

"Folks, quiet down. I'll take your questions one at a time. Now, I believe Mr. Burton stood first. What's your question, Willy?"

Another voice echoed through the halls of the school, presumably "Willy."

"Mayor Tennyson, you mentioned that we will be gettin' water from the well, but how do you plan to run the pump? I mean, we ain't got electricity no more."

Mat followed the woman into an auditorium bursting with people. Approximately two thousand townsfolk sat crammed into the school auditorium, and at least another thousand stood around the edges and into the hallway. Mat could barely see inside, craning to look over the top of the thirty or so people standing in the hallway with him. He became conscious of his body odor, noticing that the townsfolk didn't seem to have missed any showers.

"Good question, Willy," the mayor said over the P.A.. "The energy committee gave its report last night to the City Council, and they have collected eighty-five solar panels from McKenzie and the surrounding farms. We think it's enough to run a small back-up pump. We can recharge the water tower once every two days, give or take. That means we'll have to ration water. Showers twice a week, folks." The townsfolk broke into side conversations. "Next question. Quiet down, please. Let's keep going. MaryAnne, I believe you were next..."

Mat listened as the town went through its critical systems: water, food, sanitation, trash collection, winter heat, electricity, law enforcement, protection, firearms, medical care, snow removal, governance, care for the elderly, care for drug addicts, care for criminals... the list went on and on. Mat could imagine this meeting continuing for days. It had required centuries of planning and implementation of hundreds of systems to allow people to live in towns without getting each other sick; sharing responsibilities, and striking conventions that kept violence and disease at bay. Within a week, all those systems had been thrown up in the air. In small towns all over the world, people were having this same conversation, Mat surmised, rushing to preserve as much of modern civilization as they could.

"What about raiding parties from the big cities?" a disembodied voice thundered over the P.A. system. "Dollars to donuts those city people from Nashville and Memphis are working their way here to McKenzie as we speak. How're we going to hold them off? We're mostly a bunch of retired people."

"I'm going to ask Sheriff Morgan to step up and address that question. Sheriff..."

After a brief pause, a tall, rotund man stepped up to the podium. "Since we don't know how big the possible threat from the cities might be, it's hard to say. As you know, we have twelve uniformed officers and another six in our auxiliary. That's eighteen trained officers, more or less. We've blocked the main roads, but we're going to need a few more men to cover the smaller streets. I hope that'll button up the town pretty tight."

Mat heard himself shouting before he realized he was going to do it. "NOT SO, SHERIFF!"

Three-thousand eyes turned toward Mat as he pushed into the auditorium. Mat swallowed hard, thinking of Caroline. "YOU'RE MAKING A MISTAKE," Mat shouted again, working his way toward one of the microphones.

"And who are you, young man?" the sheriff asked into his mic.

"My name's Mat Best, and I'm an Army Ranger who walked into your town this morning unchallenged." Mat started talking the moment he reached the microphone, knowing that his window to convince them would be very short.

"Officers!" the sheriff bellowed, and Mat noticed several men moving toward him from the edges of the crowd. He resisted the urge to reach for his Glock, reminding himself that he couldn't shoot his way out of this situation.

"Hear me out, sir, please..." The sheriff made a motion with his hand and his officers slowed, pausing to give Mat another sentence or two. "I came into town seeking medical attention for my wife. We come from Louisville and I can tell you with total certainty what kind of opposition you will be facing in the next two weeks. I can promise you that eighteen officers and a couple roadblocks aren't going to be enough. You will lose your town."

The audience rumbled, and Mat wondered if he had gone too far. He looked to the sheriff, knowing that his fate rested in the big man's hands.

"Keep talking, son," Sheriff Morgan motioned, leaning toward Mat.

In that moment, Mat knew he spoke with an officer who cared more about his people than looking good. Mat had known both kinds of officers in the military. It was a fifty-fifty bet that this guy would let Mat challenge the assumptions they were making. He had pulled the ace card.

"Sir," Mat proceeded, "the gangs have already consolidated the suburbs around Louisville and they're pushing out to the surrounding farms. I have direct observation of the enemy and we're facing a more organized force than you would like to believe. The gangs will continue to consolidate men and materiel, and they will begin to probe your town in the next two weeks, give or take."

"You said you were a Green Beret?" Sheriff Morgan tested Mat. "What battalion and regiment, please."

"No, sir. I said I was an Army Ranger. 75th Regiment, 2nd Battalion."

"Officers, take this man into custody. Folk, folks..." the sheriff calmed the crowd. "I'll collect some intel and report back tomorrow morning. Until then, stay calm. We'll be okay."

The sheriff's men closed on Mat, guns drawn, and placed him in handcuffs.

———

"LET'S HEAR IT, SON," the big sheriff sat heavily on the Middle School teacher's desk. Mat was handcuffed to the teacher's chair. It had been a biology classroom; diagrams of dissected animals paneled the walls.

"Four days ago, we fought our way out of Louisville after checking on my wife's parents in Beechwood Village. Gangbangers had already killed her parents, but we rescued her little brother. Some neighborhoods were barricading themselves and killing looters. Let's just say the good people of Louisville were sticking gangbanger heads on pikes. Literally."

"Wait," the sheriff said. "You're telling me that white folks were chopping off heads and putting them on pikes?"

"Well," Mat couldn't help but add a bit of political correctness. "I don't know what race was chopping off heads, but every head I saw was an African-American male." Mat didn't know why it should surprise anyone that "white folks" would decapitate their enemies and display their heads. In the history of warfare, no one on this planet had ever been more vicious than white people.

"How do you know if it was gangs who were doing the looting and killing?"

"For one thing," Mat answered, "we got into a firefight with twenty or thirty gangbangers. I killed or wounded fifteen or twenty."

"How many casualties on your side?" the sheriff asked. Mat got the feeling he was being sized up.

"No casualties on our team," Mat answered.

"You said your wife needed medical attention..." Sheriff Morgan continued his interrogation.

Cops will be cops, Mat smiled.

"She wasn't wounded in the gunfight. She laid her motorcycle down and the road rash got infected. It hasn't helped that we've been riding in the rain and cold for four days. I think her immune system is compromised, worn down."

"Humph," the sheriff looked away, thinking. "Okay. I'm going to send one of my men with you to get your family. If any part of your story doesn't check out—like you telling my men at the roadblock that you weren't armed..." the sheriff pulled Mat's Glock from the back of his waistband, dangling it from the trigger guard, "If there are any more issues with your story, then we'll part ways right then. You read me, son?"

"Then maybe I better tell you now that she's my girl-friend, not my wife."

Sheriff Morgan thought about it for a moment. "Okay. Anything else? Last chance..." After a silent moment and a hard stare, he handed Mat his Glock.

MAT HAD ONLY BEEN GONE eight hours and the wound looked much worse. A blackness crept into the edges of the scab, and it stood up at least a half inch, inflamed and angry. Most concerning were the blisters. They were reddish grey and they had grown larger than they were that morning. Mat had no idea what he was looking at with this wound, but he knew it wasn't good.

"Officer Laherty, can you help me carry her to your cruiser?" Mat asked, hurrying to collect their things and get them packed and stowed in the trunk of the police car. He would be happy to leave the motorcycles behind. If he had the time, he would love to light them on fire.

William helped with the gear, packing up the Paratarp and the sleeping bags, everything sopping wet, and he watched helplessly as Mat and the policeman carried his sister toward the backseat. William opened the door and slid in beneath her, cradling her head in his lap.

"That thing looks like hell," the officer remarked as the door closed. "Smells like death."

Mat sighed. "I hope you have a decent doctor in town."

SHERIFF MORGAN FOUND Mat in the waiting room while the surgeon worked on Caroline. The room was like waiting rooms the world over. Mat, William, and Sheriff Morgan sat in uncomfortable chairs, surrounded by old magazines. The smell of tangy cleaning products and fresh bandages saturated the area.

"I hope you don't mind if I keep you company," Sheriff Morgan said.

"No. You're good. What can I do for you?" Mat wanted to get his mind on something he could control, unlike Caroline's terrifying wound. To him, it was like a merciless alien had taken over his girl's body. He still couldn't wrap his mind around how fast things were happening.

"How many times did you deploy?" the sheriff started with the typical size-up-an-operator questions.

"Five deployments to Iraq and then a bunch of work in Afghanistan as a contractor for the U.S. State Department." Mat watched to see if the sheriff knew enough to know what that meant. To someone with military experience, it meant Mat had done enough gunfighting for fifty lifetimes.

"So, the Agency?" the sheriff interpreted. Mat didn't reply or react.

"Okay, son," the sheriff continued. "I could use your help. How would you go about defending this town from outsiders?"

Mat thought before answering. He could see no reason why this town wouldn't be the same as a Forward Operating Base (FOB) in Afghanistan. If FOB defenses had worked in "Indian Country," they should work here.

He began with a list of questions. "Where's our food source? Where is our well? How many residents live outside the boundary? Will they come inside? What kind of weapons do we possess? Is there a military base we can tap for support or heavy weapons? How many military age men live here? What about other towns? Can we coordinate a defense with them? What other resources are nearby such as explosives, lumber, an auto wrecking yard, a heavy-equipment dealership?"

"Hold on, hold on, hold on. Let's take it one question at a time. Let's start with food... We have a large pig farm about a mile and a half outside of town, plus a couple of dozen smaller farms."

"Mr. Best..." The surgeon came through the double swinging doors from surgery and into the waiting room. Everyone went silent, all eyes on the doctor.

"Gentlemen, Caroline is suffering from gas gangrene. It's not uncommon when soil and debris are involved in a serious infection, especially when there is continued exposure to wet conditions. The bubbles made the diagnosis certain. I had to sedate Caroline to remove the necrotic tissue around the wound. Unfortunately, its reach was extensive, and I've spent the last two hours trying to re-route her vascular system to provide decent blood flow to the affected area. She's on a heavy regimen of antibiotics, but gas gangrene is sometimes known to be resistant to antibiotics. If we had a hyperbaric chamber, we could put her on oxygen therapy, but the nearest chamber is in Louisville. For now, all we can do is wait to see how the wound responds to the removal of the tissue and the regimen of antibiotics."

Mat sighed heavily, not knowing what to say. He considered asking if the gangrene was a threat to her life but, given the level of medical intervention she was getting, he considered it so unlikely that he didn't ask. He had known guys who survived much worse, and he didn't know anyone who had died once they reached a surgical unit. Plus, Mat didn't want to think about the possibility of losing her. "Can I see her?"

"She's still sedated and I want her to stay that way. If you wish to go in, please don't wake her."

Mat stood, and William followed. The surgeon walked them through the double doors and pointed to a mask dispenser on the wall. They put on surgical masks and entered the recovery room.

Mat's eyes went straight to the gaping wound on Caroline's leg, uncovered and draining. The surgeon had removed maybe half a pound of her flesh. He struggled with his emotions, choking up as he turned to William, who stared into the massive cavity in his sister's calf muscle. Mat's throat tightened with a groan and his hand moved to his face.

Gathering himself, Mat put his other hand on William's shoulder and steered him back out the door.

HIGHWAY **89,** Outside Fredonia, Arizona

CAMERON HAD plenty of time to think. He had been watching the roadblock since before dawn—the roadblock where he had been shot.

The sun had set on another day, and he used the mounting darkness to creep up on the spot where the pilgrims liked to take a piss. As far as Cameron could tell, these fanatical assholes had an overblown sense of modesty. Even the men would walk fifty yards away from one another before they got their dicks out to pee. They had fallen into a pattern. Every man on roadblock duty pissed in a sage ditch fifty yards into the brush, the erstwhile bathroom.

Everyone, including the old guy who appeared to be in charge, used the pissing ditch. As Cameron thought about it, he figured they had probably been ordered to piss there. This community wasn't like other communities; they seemed to make a lot of rules and then obey them with extraordinary precision. Like Charles Darwin might have observed, they appeared to select their men across generations for one trait in particular: strict obedience.

Watching them talk, eat, and shoot approaching cars, Cameron marveled at how much he had grown to know them. Even observing from several hundred yards away, his sense of their town culture grew. He began to understand their strange hierarchy and maybe something about their motivation.

From where he sat, tucked under a juniper tree, the math of polygamy looked like the unseen hand guiding everything. The community needed a certain number of productive men to pay the bills and fill the bellies of the town. The women worked hard, but the men ran the businesses and farms— and a baseline number of men were required to keep the hierarchy and town afloat. That number of capable, obedient men had to be kept in a certain numerical range or there wouldn't be enough wives for everyone. He remembered that it took three wives to get into the celestial heaven described by the FLDS, at least according to the television show.

The deliverables that would keep the younger men in the running for their own wives were a combination of productivity and obedience, two character traits that didn't commonly occur in a matching set. Most Type A guys in the real world kept their own counsel and would inevitably run afoul of the priesthood peckerwoods. At the same time, most obedient guys could follow orders, but they weren't go-getters. Any young man who could prove he had the magical combination—competency and obedience—could survive the FLDS selection process and get his hands on some wives. Anything outside that range would get the young man the boot.

So two out of every three of the young bucks had to be eliminated for the racket to pan out. That meant pretty much every man under the age of thirty-five was working to prove his worthiness on one level or another, and that was precisely what it looked like from three hundred yards away beneath a juniper tree. It looked like the young guys were working their asses off to prove they were good enough to have their share of the wivestock.

As a relatively young man of thirty-five years old himself, Cameron compared the shitty deal of the FLDS men with his own shitty deal: working from the bottom up in corporate America, slaving at school to get a degree he suspected would buy him nothing, raising a family he felt like he didn't deserve. Then losing it all when some nameless asshole nuked Los Angeles. He could definitely relate to the young shit-kickers down at the roadblock, kowtowing to the old man.

Over the hours, with a passion fueled by boredom, Cameron chewed through one hair-brained plot after another to screw the old men of the FLDS out of their harems. He would die happy if he could take down this evil empire. If he couldn't have his wife and kids back, he would settle for destroying a bunch of cocksure old autocrats. Killing the FLDS cabal felt analog to killing the thankless world that had already crippled Cameron's soul.

He had been wracking his brain all night, sitting up against that craggy, malodorous tree, about how to jack the FLDS system. He didn't want to kill any more young guys if he could help it. He would rather poison the system and take it all down at once. He spent half the day imagining scenarios where he would abduct the second- or third-in-command

and frame him for the murder of the prophet, tipping the whole shebang into chaos.

Even in his muddled state, Cameron knew the odds were long that he could pull off a coup. But he could certainly try. What else did he have to do with his time?

The old bastard running the roadblock wasn't the head honcho. Cameron knew as much from the television show. The prophet, Rulon Whatever, drove around in a big, blue Cadillac Escalade. Cameron vaguely remembered the guy being in his seventies, with over sixty wives. The old priesthood dude at the roadblock was an underling to the prophet, but maybe an important underling. Maybe he was the Number Two or Number Three guy. The young men at the roadblock treated him like some kind of general, obeying his every command with alacrity.

It had been at least an hour since the old man had taken a piss, and that was a long time for an old geezer. Maybe in his early sixties, General Turd, as Cameron had taken to calling him, was due for a leak.

Cameron skulked down to the piss ditch and wedged himself between a couple of big sage bushes. There he waited.

General Turd wore a big, white cowboy hat, probably to keep the sun off his lily-white skin, and Cameron held vigil, looking for that hat to come bobbing over the sagebrush in the night, backlit by the campfires behind the roadblock. Eventually, the general would want to head home to his harem for some bumping uglies with one of his wives. Cameron wanted to grab the old guy and maybe beat some information out of him. If he got lucky, the old guy might turn out to be the key to derailing the priesthood poontang racket.

Two young pilgrims came to the piss latrine over the next hour and neither of them used a flashlight, probably saving precious batteries. Neither noticed Cameron hiding. Finally, the white cowboy hat bobbed over the edge of the sagebrush and General Turd appeared, hitching up his suspendered pants as he climbed down into the ditch. When he got his pecker out, Cameron stepped from between the sagebrush and pointed his rifle at the General.

"Make a sound and I'll shoot you in the face," Cameron spoke his first audible words in three days. It came out sounding like a croak.

With the camp fires behind him, the general's face was a dark tableau, but Cameron could see from body language that he had scared the living shit out of the old man.

"By the POWER OF THE PRIESTHOOD," the old man shouted, "I CAST YE BACK INTO OUTER DARKNESS! GET YE HENCE, MINION OF SATAN!"

"Shhhh! Shut the fuck up!" Cameron whispered loudly, drowned out by the old man's admonitions.

"BE GONE, DEMON!" The old man shouted again.

Cameron's hand fired the gun of its own accord.

BOOOM!

The rifle bucked and General Turd crumpled to the ground, landing face-first into sand and two weeks of pilgrim piss.

"Fuck me!" Cameron swore as he turned and ran away, stumbling in and around ten thousand sage bushes, fleeing back into the night. His wounds screamed, but he pushed on, plowing through one sagebrush after another, his natural night vision hampered by the giant stain in the middle of his retina left by the muzzle flash. Eventually, he figured out how to run with his head turned three-quarters to one side, giving him a little window of peripheral vision. Encumbered with his backpack and rifle, Cameron went down hard on the ground, over and over, lighting up the still-healing holes in his chest with bright pain before his panic subsided.

After he had run nearly a mile, Cameron slowed to a walk, listening for pursuers. He struggled for breath, his heaving lung jostling the scar tissue inside his chest. He heard increased commotion at the roadblock, probably the ambush crew rendering aid to their fallen leader, but it didn't sound like anyone was on his trail.

"That could've gone better," Cameron whispered to himself, realizing how dumb it had been to imagine he could abduct someone without raising an alarm. He thought about it, and decided there were a hundred ways for that particular plan to go inverted and only a couple of ways for it to go right. Pulling espionage tactics from the History Channel probably wasn't the best idea, now that he'd tried it. The enemy always had a vote and maybe shit *usually* went weird when kidnap or murder was involved. He would have to keep that in mind in the future.

At least he had popped an old dude this time instead of a young buck. Tomorrow, maybe he would get to see the town's Plan C. Cameron smiled and then broke into laughter, the tension of the last couple days bubbling into the night air. As his laughter subsided, and he heard it echoing off the unseen cliffs around him, he scratched his sweaty scalp, considering an uncomfortable possibility.

Was some squirrely corner of his mind trying to get him killed, attempting suicide by revenge?

If so, Cameron didn't find the thought particularly alarming.

14

"Trudging slowly over wet sand
Back to the bench where your clothes were
    stolen
This is the coastal town
That they forgot to close down
Armageddon, come Armageddon!"

— *EVERY DAY IS LIKE SUNDAY*,
MORRISSEY, VIVA HATE, 1988

McKENZIE REGIONAL HOSPITAL, McKENZIE, TENNESSEE

THE NIGHTTIME NURSE woke Mat and William at dawn. They
had slept on the hard floor of the waiting room, the best sleep
they'd had in days, with the dog having been taken in by the

sheriff's family for the evening. Sleeping on hard carpet beat sleeping on wet ground any day of the week.

"Doctor Patel will be here in fifteen minutes, and I thought you'd want to clean up before he comes through to check on Caroline."

Mat thanked her and walked William into the bathroom.

"Mat... how should I brush my teeth?" the boy asked. The magnitude of the disquiet undoubtedly faced by the boy suddenly struck Mat: dead parents, school gone forever, friends likely dead, sister suffering a horrible wound. Mat was the boy's only protection—a tattooed, strange man he had only just met. He put his arm around William's shoulder and pulled him to the sink next to him.

"In the Army, we call this the *field expedient toothbrush*," Mat held up his index finger and smiled. He opened his mouth and began rubbing his teeth and gums vigorously, pantomiming a real toothbrush.

"What about toothpaste?" William smiled as he watched Mat goof around.

"Toothpaste is for POGs, little bro," Mat said with his finger still in his mouth.

"What's a POG?"

"People Other than Grunts. Not you and me. We're grunts. You can't go through the shit we've been through and not come out the other side a warrior. You're a field-hardened killing machine now, my little man."

William's eyes brightened with the idea. "Are you training me to be a soldier?"

"Absolutely. You're on track to become one of the best of the best: an Army Ranger."

Mat grinned. Over the last few days, he had grown to like the little dude. William took orders well and looked for work around camp—the first qualification of a special ops warrior.

If you were the kind of guy who waited to be told what to do, you would never survive the military selection process. If you were the kind of guy who looked for work and got it done, you might just survive to become a top-tier operator. Young William was the second type of guy, and Mat could definitely work with those raw materials.

Doctor Patel stuck his head in the bathroom. "Let's go check on your sister."

The trio walked into her room, the nurse in tow. As they filed in, Caroline looked their way with a beleaguered smile.

"Good morning, boys. You coming to see the Bride of Frankenstein?"

The doctor gently pulled back the lower third of her sheet to examine the leg, and his chest visibly deflated. He held back the sheet for Mat to see, defeat painted across his brow.

To Mat, the wound looked much better than before but, as he focused on the margins of the wound, he could see the reason behind the doctor's despair. The blackish color and dark blisters had renewed their assault on her tissue, nibbling at the edges of the ruthless debridement from the day prior.

Doctor Patel let the sheet fall back in place. "We still have work to do, young lady," was all he could say, unable to hide his disappointment and concern.

After some touches and kisses, the men retreated into the hallway while the nurse helped Caroline with her morning ablutions.

"What the fuck, Doc?"

The doctor looked at the floor and rambled. "I can't remove any more tissue. I probably took too much as it was, and her vascular system isn't strong enough in that region to deliver the antibiotics. The *Clostridium* has probably become systemic. We didn't have a way to run the skin culture, so I couldn't be sure. We need to get her to the medical center or a hyperbaric chamber..."

"Doc. Stop. What are you saying? In simple language?" Mat interrupted.

"I'm saying that she needs an amputation to save her life. I've never done one and we lost contact with the medical center in Paris six days ago. The Clostridium infection is more aggressive than I'd hoped. We're fighting to save her life at this point."

Mat ran his hand through his hair and exhaled hard. He looked at William. "I'm guessing the sooner you amputate, the better, right?"

"Yes, but I'm not prepared to conduct an amputation." The doctor's voice trailed off.

"Sack up, Doc. Pull yourself together. Do you or don't you know how to perform the surgery?" Mat couldn't say the word "amputation" again and not start to crack.

"I know how. I practiced on cadavers. It's a high-risk procedure, with even higher risk given the limits of our medical equipment at this facility."

"Can you do it?" Mat looked him directly in the eyes.

"Yes. I believe I can," the doctor shot a glance at the boy. "I would prefer that you tell her, though."

MAT STARED INTO THE SMOOTH, olive skin of her elegant face. He considered her perfect nose, delicate eyebrows, and almond-shaped eyes. He could spend a lifetime looking at that face, even in the morning, even in the hospital, even terrifyingly sick.

"Here's the problem," Mat began, holding her hand and peering into her eyes. "I've found the girl of my dreams, but I'm not quite done with my bucket list. I'm *so* close. Unfortunately, there's just one last little thing to clear up before I abandon my freedom and tie myself down to a single woman..."

Caroline smiled big, showing her teeth, rolling into Mat's joke. "And what's that one, last, little thing, if a lady might ask?"

Mat gave William a half glance then leaned in toward Caroline to whisper. "I gotta do a one-legged girl."

Caroline's eyes brimmed over with tears. Her beautiful smile held, her suspicions confirmed. "Is that right? And how do you propose to go about that, given the circumstances?"

"Well, Doctor Patel and I have worked out what you might call a win-win." A giant tear rolled from the corner of Mat's eye and hit her hospital blouse with an audible pat.

"Ah, I think I see. She reached up and put her hand on the back of Mat's neck. "Then let's do what needs doing."

"Caroline, it's a risky surgery. I'm with you no matter what, but you should know that this one's a doozy. Even in the best of times—my buddies who lost limbs—it's a game-changer."

"I can do it. I've got some good stuff to live for." She pegged Mat's eyes with hers, then reached for her brother with her other hand. "Good stuff."

"So, yeah." Mat sniffed and blinked away his tears. He knew the passing nature of this world—a world where life was no longer assured. He felt a last internal wall crumble in the urgency of this moment. "I should probably tell you. I'm pretty sure I love you."

"Pretty sure, huh?" Caroline pulled his head down until they touched foreheads. "We'll work on that." The couple embraced, Mat leaning in more and more until he was almost in her bed.

"I should get started," Doctor Patel interrupted. "The anesthesiologist is ready."

Mat stepped back and William took his place beside her, crying into his sister's neck.

"It's all good, Will. It's going to be fine," she said as she caressed his fine, brown hair.

1300 West and Field Avenue, Colorado City, Arizona

Cameron lay on a gentle rise between two big washes, shaded by a clump of prickly tamarisk. By setting the old rifle in the crook of one of the bushes, he could surveil the west side of town. That morning, he had finally spotted the blue Cadillac Escalade, and it had vanished toward this area. The location of the prophet's home could be reduced to just a couple of options, and Cameron thought he had it pegged to one, high-fenced compound.

He didn't know for sure if he had killed the general from the night before, but he chalked it up as another mark on his totem anyway. He carved a notch in the stock of his Mosin-Nagant for every pilgrim he smoked. By his count, it was five.

Still surviving on the water, food, and equipment he had taken off the dead horsemen four days prior, Cameron knew he would need to steal more supplies to keep up his rampage. He was about out of water.

Observing the twin towns of Hildale and Colorado City proved challenging because of its fences and walls. Many homes had seven-foot walls or fences protecting those inside from prying eyes. Most of them were white vinyl fencing, common in suburban America. No doubt, the fencing had been a defense strategy against government authorities who had periodically raided and incarcerated polygamists in the towns since the 1950s.

Looking through the scope of the rifle exhausted him. With only one eye working, and holding the weight of the rifle, he could only glass for a couple of minutes at a time before being forced to rest his eyes. He had discarded a cheap pair of binoculars he pulled from the backpack of one of the horsemen. Now he regretted it. Using two eyes to surveil— and not having to manipulate the heavy rifle—would have made this process ten times more comfortable.

While he rested his eyes, Cameron saw motion at the gates of one of the fenced compounds. He jumped on the rifle scope and watched as the blue Cadillac Escalade pulled out, the gates closing behind it. Dollars to donuts, that would be the Prophet's personal enclave, housing "His Holiness" and his multitude of wives.

"Bingo," Cameron whispered. Now he had a target. Next he needed a plan.

McKENZIE REGIONAL HOSPITAL, McKenzie, Tennessee

. . .

MAT AND WILLIAM talked quietly in the waiting room, as though whispering might help the doctor concentrate in the operating room far down the hall. It had been two hours since they had begun Caroline's amputation, but Mat didn't know how long an operation like that was supposed to take. This whole excursion—from Baltimore to now—made him wish he had known more about medicine and trauma. Maybe if he had known more about how to clean wounds or how to spot infection, he could have acted more quickly and could have saved Caroline's leg.

Mat knew a lot about combat, and he even had training in combat first aid, but it hadn't been his specialty, especially not in situations where a trauma hospital was more than a Blackhawk ride away from the area of operation. He had trained as a breacher, the guy who blew open doors and exploded whatever needed exploding.

While Mat chatted with Will, he mentally scrolled through the decisions he had made over the last five days and second-guessed every one of them. He hadn't even heard of "gas gangrene" before Doctor Patel said those awful words. Mat guessed people would be hearing lots of medical terms almost lost to civilization. Words like cholera, blood poisoning, amputation, maybe even polio and mumps.

The more Mat chatted up young William, the more he liked the kid. Mat hadn't seriously thought about having children. He figured himself for too big of a shit-show to father kids. Plus, why give up his prolific "dating life" for a life of white picket fences and mowing the lawn on weekends. Who the hell would do that? He thought it was Stalin who once said it: *"Quantity* has a *quality* all its own."* Mat had applied the motto to women and it had almost satisfied him. *Close, but no cigar.* Never had Mat been happier to have failed.

The time with the dog, William, and Caroline had opened his eyes. It had taken the Apocalypse for him to understand the metronome charms of depending on others and having them depend on you. It reminded him of being on a squad in the military, only having a wife and child felt sweeter, almost spiritual in nature. Mat found himself suspecting that he might have been born for this—the good knight protecting his family. He smiled to himself, still chatting with William, as he contemplated the radical turn his heart had taken.

Doctor Patel came through the double doors, looking uneasy and doing a hand-washing motion, probably from having just used the alcohol hand cleanser. Mat tried and failed to interpret the Doctor's body language.

"Mat, Will. I'm so sorry, but your sister—and, er, girl-friend—she didn't respond well to the surgery." Mat's eyes went wide and he stood. Will hovered in his chair. "Caroline, er, didn't survive the procedure," the doctor muttered.

"What the fuck do you mean?" Mat barked, louder than he had intended.

"I'm sorry, sir, but we did everything we could, but given the stressed state of her immune system and the compro-mised nature of the arteries feeding the site of infection... we kept losing the attachment points of the vascular system, receding into the tissue around the joint and given the posi-tion of the wound, being that it came so proximate to the joint..."

"Doc!" Mat yelled, looking back and forth between William and the doctor. "We don't understand what you're trying to tell us. Speak English, please." Mat regretted the insult right away, but his desperation overwhelmed any such concern.

"She's gone. I don't know what else to say. She's gone... I'm so sorry. My condolences to you both," Doctor Patel muttered as he retreated through the double doors.

"What did he just say?" Mat begged William. The boy's face had gone white.

"Mat, I think Caroline died." William burst into tears, curling into a ball in the chair, the last of his strength abandoned.

Mat choked, then sobbed, then wrapped himself around William, overflowing the hospital chair, crying into the boy's hair.

The two sat like that, curled around one another in the hospital waiting room, until the nurse came and led them outside the clinic, then down the street, and into a small home that had been offered to them by the town.

Mat didn't really know where he was, and he allowed it, allowed himself to be lost in the arms of a town he didn't know. William was his only anchor, the only point in the universe that presently mattered to him.

Mat and William stayed lost, marooned on a strange couch, in a strange town, fed by strange people, for a long time.

15

"When I looked out the window
On the hardship that had struck
I saw the seven vials open
The plague claimed man and son
Four men at a grave in silence
With hats bowed down in grace
A simple wooden cross
It had not epitaph engraved
It had no epitaph engraved
Come on down and meet your maker
Come on down and make the stand."

— *THE STAND*, THE ALARM,
DECLARATION, 1984

ELM STREET AND FIELD AVENUE, HILDALE, UTAH

. . .

BEFORE DAWN, Cameron stole a set of pilgrim pants and a shirt off a clothesline. Someone had left them out overnight. Except for the missing black hat, he looked the part of a priesthood contender.

Despite the botched kidnapping at the roadblock the night before, Cameron concocted another complex scheme to disrupt the FLDS town. This time, he was going straight to the top, intent on putting a bullet in the head of the FLDS prophet. He convinced himself that odds were better this time around but, truth was, he didn't really care. With his wife and kids a lost cause, Cameron felt content to "wing it" and let the chips fall where they may.

He couldn't shake the conviction that winging it had worked so far because he had been snipping at the margins of the community. Today, he would walk straight into the hornet's nest.

His plan relied on the pilgrims' strange fixation with big gardens. Owing, perhaps, to their doomsday cult, the FLDS surrounded their homes and their residential neighborhoods with miniature farms. Every compound either contained or bordered on an orchard or a garden. While the huge homes had little in the way of architectural style, they had lots of small outbuildings holding grain, fertilizer, and the sundry tools of farm life. Cameron saw dozens of places to hide inside the otherwise Spartan town.

After lunch, Cameron sashayed into town in his pilgrim clothes, covering two blocks on foot before drifting into a maintenance shed on a potato field facing the prophet's main gate. The rifle drew no attention, since every male carried one just like it. Cameron could hang out in the dim shed and make sure the prophet was in-residence before making his move.

The tall wooden gates of the prophet's home opened six times that day, with only a white sedan and an Econoline van passing through, both filled with pilgrim women on their way to work or school. The Escalade remained parked inside all day.

The new community defense plan, it seemed, was to station small teams of young men *inside* the gated compounds, protecting the old men and their harems. Anthropologically speaking, it sounded like the young guys were doing all the work and getting none of the reward. Why would they let themselves be used like that? Cameron didn't understand. Stranger things had happened when it came to religion, he supposed.

Phase Two of Cameron's mission relied upon an odd piece of ammunition he had stolen from the horseback riders.

Other than the occasional shooting trip to the desert to fling lead with his brother, Cameron didn't know much about guns. Wracking his brain, Cameron swore that green-tipped ammunition meant the bullets were steel-core, armor-piercing. Orange-tipped bullets were tracer rounds; they would light up the night with a blur of burning metal. Regular bullets without any markings were copper-jacketed lead-core ammunition—the most common "dumb" bullet.

Cameron found two Mosin-Nagant stripper clips in the backpacks, and every other bullet was painted orange. If memory served, that meant the stripper clips were set for night shooting, permitting the shooter to see where the rounds were striking in the dark. Cameron assumed it meant that one of the horseback riders had worked the barricade on Highway 89, where his 4Runner had been shot to bits. It made him feel a little better about killing those particular men.

Again relying on Hollywood for inspiration, Cameron's plan for sneaking into the prophet's compound depended on a diversion. The community utilized a system of propane tanks mounted outside each home for heating gas, as in many rural towns. A truck normally refilled the tank every month or two. In the Apocalypse, the truck would never come again, but the big tanks would last months, maybe even years, with rationing.

On the *Mythbusters* television show, Cameron had seen a propane tank explode. The "myth" they were attempting to bust was whether or not a bullet going through a propane tank would spark and cause an explosion. A regular, lead-core bullet failed to cause an explosion because it passed straight through without spark, but an incendiary bullet did the trick nicely. On TV, a twenty-pound barbecue tank made an impressive fireball. One of these huge, thousand-gallon propane tanks in the polygamists' yard should go up in a massive mushroom cloud, an ideal diversion to cover Cameron's move.

The only piece that wasn't clear to Cameron had been whether the orange-painted tracer rounds were the same as incendiary rounds. The tracers definitely burned orange, so they must be magnesium-tipped or something similar.

He needed the explosion to cover him walking into the prophet's home. Even then, he couldn't just walk through the gates. At least six young men stood guard inside the prophet's compound. Cameron had seen them peacocking with their rifles, looking tough for the women when the gates opened to let the van out. He couldn't count on all the guards leaving their posts to respond to a fireball. Cameron would have to go in a different way if he didn't want to face any young guards still in the compound.

With all day to examine the situation, Cameron deduced that the fencing around the compound had been built for privacy instead of security. The fence wasn't designed to prevent law enforcement from breaking into the prophet's home, like federal troops had done at the Branch Davidian compound in Waco, Texas. These polygamists weren't spoiling for a stand-off with law enforcement. The fence had prevented prying eyes from seeing the prophet cavorting with his child brides and multiple wives, denying authorities the ability to build a criminal case. The prophet's fence wasn't ballistic concrete or even cinder block. It was stained cedar slats, probably screwed to cross-supports, vulnerable to being kicked to splinters. Cameron knew about privacy fences from his experience as a teen hoodlum in southern California. Residential fences were zero-percent effective against a good boot.

Once he got into the prophet's compound, Cameron would have to improvise. He couldn't see the exterior doors because of the privacy fence, and he wouldn't know where the prophet resided inside the house. Hopefully, aside from the young guards, it would be a house full of women, children, plus one wrinkly, old prophet. Once he had broken in and blasted the prophet with a couple of rounds of 7.62 to the face, Cameron would improvise his escape. Admittedly, that part of his plan was a little fuzzy.

He sat back from his surveillance in the equipment shed, surrounded by shovels, pesticides, and spray backpacks. He considered using one of the spray backpacks as a flame thrower, filling the tank with gas instead of pesticide, then gunning his way around the prophet's compound, lighting everything and everyone on fire.

As he had learned the night before, things didn't always go the way he planned. Without a chance to test his flamethrower idea, he could picture the gasoline eating up the plastic parts in the nozzle, causing it to gum up and fail. Or, maybe the flame would whip back inside the plastic tank, exploding gasoline all over his back and head.

Since leaving southern California, he had gained a master's degree in the fragility of order and the strength of chaos. *What can go wrong, will go wrong.* Things in life seemed to *want* to break and go crazy. If he were being totally honest, the same could probably be said of his mind.

Open disclosure to himself: this was a suicide mission.

He had probably been on a suicide mission since he beaned that pilgrim in the head with a rock.

Quixotically, when a suicide mission goes south, the protagonist survives. When he thought about it that way, Cameron had been mind-fucking the universe for a week or so. If the universe wanted chaos, then Cameron had been its huckleberry. He had delivered a heaping pile of chaos to this town of doomsday polygamists.

Neat trick. He patted himself on the back, realizing his mental stability might not be what it once was. Loneliness wasn't a great condition for a guy like Cameron. Loneliness, anger, and serial murder in combination... that probably wasn't going to end well for anyone.

Some part of his mind tried to talk him out of his plan to kill the FLDS prophet. Part of his mind argued for him to turn west and walk away from this whole, sordid affair. He remembered the technical term for that part of a person's mind that reminded the person not to do stupid shit: *the prefrontal cortex.*

He smiled, pleased with his community college education being applied to a practical life situation. It was his prefrontal cortex telling him that it would be stupid-beyond-stupid to assault the prophet's compound.

The thing that kept him pinned to the ground in the maintenance shed, gearing up to attack against ridiculous odds, was a vestigial piece of the family man he once was. His woman could lose her mind and join a cult if she wanted.

Fuck women and their unreliable affections anyway.

But Cameron wouldn't leave his boys behind. He would rather die killing pilgrims than wake up next week alone and safe. At least killing polygamists, he wouldn't die feeling like a shitbag, the kind of asshole father who bailed on his sons. He could live with many failures, and he had done exactly that. Failing his boys was not a fuck-up he could survive. His father hadn't raised that kind of man. In this one thing, his dad would be proud.

He could see the dusk shadow of the Utah Mountains lengthening over the town, and he knew his time to die grew near. He planned to attack in the failing light, increasing the chaos bearing down on the town. After all, chaos had become his compadre. His amigo. His dark companion and confidant.

Cameron belly-crawled out from the maintenance shed and back into the dry wash, using the shed as a visual screen between himself and the prophet's compound. Once under cover of the desert swale, he scampered south on foot, cutting around a ramshackle compound that must have belonged to a lesser polygamist. Other than the prophet and a half-dozen others, most of the priesthood men lived like trailer trash in oversized

312 JEFF KIRKHAM (SPECIAL FORCES, RET.) & & JASON ...

double-wides. Their homes resembled the beat-down trailer hovels Cameron passed in the middle of the Mojave Desert in his flight from southern California. One of the trailer homes near the prophet's house hadn't completed its privacy fence, and Cameron planned to use its propane tank as his diversion.

Taking up a new position in the dry wash, Cameron perched his Mosin-Nagant between the limbs of a dead sage bush and sighted in on the propane tank—just a hundred yards away. He shucked the backpack, dug out his water bottle and drank the last of it. He checked the rifle's chamber for the third time and confirmed the orange-painted bullet in the breach.

Go time.

AS THE LIGHT FADED, Cameron pressed the trigger.

BOOM!

The Mosin-Nagant bucked in his hands and then... nothing.

No doubt he had hit the propane tank, but there was no explosion. He switched his view to the movement of the family's mongrel dogs mucking about in the yard. A couple raised their heads, curious about the shot. He shifted his view to the shimmering dusk wind in the tops of the cottonwood trees. Cameron searched for clues, still confused at the lack of an explosion, noticing the family barbecue merrily smoking near the back door of the trailer.

With a massive *ka-wump*, the propane tank finally exploded in a giant fireball that churned over and over as it rolled into the orange sky above the town. A wave of heat hit Cameron, even a hundred yards distant. Screams shattered the evening as people ran toward the source of the fireball. Cameron racked the bolt of his rifle, flicked the safety on and stood up, jogging toward the explosion like everyone else.

As he ran in the direction of the burning double-wide trailer, now caught up in the flames, Cameron deviated slightly left, angling toward his true destination, the prophet's compound. He scanned the fire as he loped past. The windows of the trailer were blown in and the curtains inside were burning. Tongues of fire rose out of holes where the windows had once been and they lapped greedily at the roof. The cheap trailer door burst open and a woman in a prairie dress rushed into the dirt yard carrying a little girl, the girl's dress on fire. The mother dropped to the ground and rolled the girl in the dirt, extinguishing the flame. Other women and children poured out of the trailer like a clown car full of burning pioneers, some dancing with flame and others helping swat them out.

"God dammit!" Cameron swore. He had no intention of setting children on fire, but his bedfellow, Chaos, had other ideas. Cameron faced forward, resisting the urge to run to their aid. Townspeople came from every direction, buckets and fire extinguishers in hand.

Cameron's irritation boiled; he hated himself for causing this torment. He hated his wife for betraying him. He hated the prophet for setting this whole cocked-up situation in motion in the first place. Cameron would kill that bastard, and hopefully kill himself in the process. Two assholes for the price of one.

The townspeople didn't notice the stranger among them and, frankly, Cameron didn't care. He reached the back of the prophet's compound and kicked viciously at the cedar planks, blowing them inward and making a hole big enough to slip through. He found himself inside the privacy barrier, hidden behind a storage shed. He slid around the corner and watched as the last of the armed guards headed out the gate toward the fire, eager to accomplish some act of priesthood heroism.

Scanning for a back way into the prophet's home, Cameron spied a young girl peering out a door opposite the storage shed, curious as to the commotion. He jogged across the little strip of lawn and up to the girl, lowering himself to her level. She considered him without a shred of distrust.

"Hello, sweetheart." Cameron smiled. "Where's the prophet?" The girl pointed inside and up. Cameron quietly side-stepped the girl, moving into the house, and confronted a staircase heading upward. He calmed his pounding heart as he ascended, trying to convince his adrenal system that he belonged in the house, just another young guard looking after the prophet. The odds of running into one of the sixty wives was probably a foregone conclusion.

Strangely, the upper floor seemed empty, with all the sounds of commotion concentrated on ground level. Cameron began opening doors and peeking into rooms. One after another, he found small rooms dominated by queen-sized beds, fluffy comforters and an astounding array of home crafts nailed to the walls, proclaiming pithy and whole-some messages like "Choose the Right" and "Love Begins at Home." Cameron imagined this strange bed warren as an old man's sex palace and it made perverse sense—the confluence of innocence and sexuality, a modern variant of Old Testament depravity.

After five empty rooms, Cameron opened a door to find an elderly man gazing outside through a set of French doors, regarding the fire on the next block. The old man turned toward the creak of the door and appraised Cameron with fatherly eyes.

"Yes, my son?"

"Um. Are you the prophet?" was all Cameron could think to ask.

"I am," the old man said with gravity. "Who are you?"

Cameron stepped inside, locking the door behind him. He physically shook off the creepy charisma exuded by the man.

"I'm the guy who's come to kill you," Cameron explained as he locked eyes, now prepared for the man's solemn gaze.

"Ah. You are whom the Lord hath sent." The man stated it as a fact and clasped his hands behind his back. "Please sit."

An invisible tractor beam pulled Cameron into a white upholstered chair. The FLDS prophet lowered himself into the chair's mate. Cameron swung the gun barrel toward the old man and he suppressed the urge to shake his head like a dog, hungry to clear the spell being cast over him.

"Yes. I'm going to shoot you," Cameron proclaimed, as much as a reminder to himself as a threat to the old man.

"I see. Well, I've been waiting a long time for you to come," the prophet announced in his freaky monotone. Cameron began to understand the scam now—this old man played the role of a prophet of old—unflappable, trusting in God, everything a part of his grand plan.

"Drop the act, old timer. You nut jobs shot at my family. You took my wife and boys. Now I'm going to shoot you and you're going to shit yourself on this white carpet as you die. No more porking your sixty wives. No more driving around in your Escalade. No more glossy-eyed maniacs worshipping at your feet. It'll just be you, your brains, and your shit splattered on this ugly-ass carpet."

The profligate swearing seemed to shock the old man, interrupting his schtick. Still, he tried again.

"I see. I see. Perhaps you'd like to confess your sins before we both perish because when you fire that rifle, the servants of the Lord will rush in here to take your life, too."

"Jesus," Cameron smiled an impish grin, "it just never ends with you, does it? You're going to keep up the 'prophet' routine right until the bitter end. Okay. Suit yourself." Cameron raised the rifle to the man's face and flicked off the safety.

"Wait," the prophet begged, his voice jumping two octaves. "Just wait. Wait. I don't want to die yet. I need to say something first. Just wait." The monotone was gone.

Surprised by the shift in demeanor, Cameron lowered the rifle a few inches. "Talk, you horny old fool. I'll give you ten seconds."

The man blinked away the last of his affectation and sighed hard, closing his eyes and breathing deeply, spending his ten seconds in thought. Cameron waited, curious what the old man would say.

"I lost my priesthood thirty-one years ago. I behaved immorally with my sister and then my daughter." The old man opened his eyes and looked at Cameron with a ghostly expression. "I am not the prophet. I never was the prophet, and I have been deceived by the powers of evil. Brother Thomas R. Jessop has been the true prophet since my Father's passing..."

Holy shit, thought, Cameron. *This old fucker's really confessing.* "Go on." He waved the rifle barrel, pressing the man to continue.

"...I have been the most wicked man in this dispensation and in the eyes of God. And I took charge of my father's wives when the Lord God told me not to because I could not hear him, could not hear his voice, because I did not hold the priesthood. As far as I possibly can be, I am sorry from the bottom of my heart. Please tell them all." The old "prophet" deflated in his white, upholstered chair, now a fraction of the pompous being he had been just five minutes earlier.

Cameron hadn't understood half of what the old codger said, but he knew he had heard some shit that would blow this place apart, bringing Cameron back to his earlier scheme to break up the cult. Maybe Cameron was *"he whom the Lord hath sent"* after all. The idea made Cameron chuckle.

"I'm not telling your people shit. You tell them." Cameron gestured at the French doors and the balcony beyond. "Confess your sorry ass to them. And, while you're at it, order them to bring me my wife and boys. If you try and go back on anything you just said, the last thing you'll see will be your brains flying onto your driveway, you perverted old fuck. Get up. Go on. Tell them what you told me." Cameron waved the rifle barrel at the doors.

The prophet rose out of his chair, now just a tired old man. He opened the French doors and stepped out on the balcony. Cameron scooted his chair up so he could cover the old man with his rifle. Nobody below could see Cameron inside the room.

"Brothers and sisters," the old man spoke, returning to his "prophet" act. "Brothers and sisters, please gather 'round." He gestured generously at his driveway and motor pool below. "I have words to share." He waited a few minutes for a crowd to gather for his declaration. Cameron bobbled in his chair, antsy as hell, but more curious than anxious.

A woman knocked at the door and called out, *"Uncle Rulon?"*

Cameron bet that nobody in this community had the stones to kick in the prophet's door, so he remained still.

"Uncle Rulon?" the woman pleaded again through the door. After a minute, Cameron heard her walk away down the hall.

"Brothers and sisters," the old man revved up again, his audience presumably sufficient. "I have words to share. Not words of the Lord, but words of a man who hath sinned in the eyes of God. A man guilty of sins, weighty enough for blood atonement..."

Cameron didn't know what the hell that meant, but it sounded like the old dude was moving ahead with his confession. Cameron laid the rifle across his knee and settled in for the show.

"Many years hence, I committed sins against my sister. Sins against my daughter. My priesthood has been lost these many years..."

The crowd gasped, murmuring. The old man went on, rattling off pronouncements, confessions. He dropped the same truth bomb on the crowd of pilgrims that he had dropped on Cameron.

"Don't forget about my family, old timer," Cameron hissed.

Unwilling to interrupt his flowery confessional, the prophet wrapped up his thought and moved into Cameron's item of business.

"And, though I am no longer your prophet, I ask that ye bring forward the family I once placed with my son Isaiah, the wife and two sons of the man taken at our roadblock. Bring them hence... I declare this marital placement void, committed in the shadow of my sin... bring them hence..."

The prophet then continued with his soliloquy from before.

Cameron grew bored with the prophetic rambling and wanted to get on with it, living or dying. "Hurry it up, old man. Have 'em send Julie and the boys up here."

The orange flicker of the firelight had abated across the street, the light dwindled. By the rumble of the crowd, half the town had assembled to listen to the prophet confess his sins.

The prophet continued with his confession, bowing his head and praying over the community. He even took a moment in prayer to pass his priesthood authority to the Jessop guy, which made no sense to Cameron, since the old man had said he wasn't the prophet in the first place because he had diddled his sister, or some such thing.

"This is a just test of our faith, right?" a man below interjected when the prophet paused in dramatic humility. "This is our chance to prove our loyalty to you, right, Uncle Rulon?"

"No, my son. Alas. I am no longer your prophet. The Lord God hath sent an avenging angel and I say farewell to you forever, you who are worthy for Zion, for I will not be there," the old man held out his hands in celestial surrender.

Just then someone tapped at the door. The ex-prophet moved on into another round of holy-sounding prophet talk, apparently unable to turn it off. Cameron unlocked the door and cracked it open, seeing the anxious face of Julie in the light of the hallway. He opened the door wide and ushered her into the room along with their two boys. He closed and locked the door behind them, shutting out a middle-aged woman in a prairie dress waiting in the hall.

Julie looked at Cameron with wide eyes, confused. The ex-prophet droned on outside on the balcony. Julie looked from the prophet to Cameron and back again.

"Nice get-up." Cameron raised his eyebrows at her full-length dress, buttoned to the nape of her neck. His boys stepped around her skirts and clamped onto Cameron's legs, hugging him. Cameron knelt and hugged them fiercely, filling his senses with their wonderful, sweaty-boy smell. Both boys appeared well—scared, but good. Looking into their eyes felt like finding a waterhole in the desert. Cameron drank deeply, inhaled, and smiled.

"Cameron, what's going on?" Julie asked, bringing him back to the room. "What's happening here?"

Cameron let go of his boys and stood up. "Julie. I don't really know what the deal is here, but I need you to listen to me. This place is going bonkers and you need to take the boys and run. Run west along the road. I'll be behind you. Do you understand?" Cameron grabbed her shoulders, physically trying to pull her forward to a reality he barely understood himself. She nodded once, then nodded again with conviction.

She repeated his instructions. "Run west down the road... Okay, but which way is west?"

"That way is west," Cameron pointed. "Run. Hopefully, I'll be behind you." He opened the door and herded them out of the room. He had to stay focused on current events, not his boys, if they were to have any chance of getting out of this alive. The boys craned their necks around their mom, trying to catch a last glimpse of their father as he shut the door behind them.

A bit of hope garnished Cameron's thoughts. The Chaos about him shuddered, and Cameron forced himself to sit back down in the white upholstered chair.

The ex-prophet continued in his monotone, apparently used to speaking like this for hours. Cameron tried to pick up on the thread of his sermon while the crowd below grew restless, struggling to grasp the eternal import of the prophet's pronouncement—struggling to understand the machinations of God's strange Church on Earth. Cameron didn't blame them for being confused. He had set this whole thing in motion, and he didn't understand what the fuck was happening, either.

Cameron remembered that he was supposed to kill the blathering old man on the balcony, now speaking in the dark, lit blue by the light of a xenon flood lamp. But, in truth, all the murder had gone out of him. To Cameron, it felt like when those softball games turned into fights, spending their savage magic, and then receding back into brotherhood and sport once again. It felt like *Miller Time.*

Maybe it had been the prophet's pathetic confession. Maybe it had been breathing in his boys. Maybe it had been the sudden revelation that Julie hadn't been entirely brainwashed into dumping him. All his insecurities struck their moorings and floated into the night sky and left him wondering why he had, moments before, felt so compelled to murder this old man and destroy this bizarre town.

Suddenly, the door burst inward, kicked hard. Eight men, all of them with six-shooters in their hands or on their belts muscled into the room. Cameron was caught sitting in his chair, eyes wide, his rifle drooping toward the floor.

Fortunately, he had never seen any of the men before, which meant none of them had ever seen him, either. Cameron assumed they were the secondary leaders of the town because their ages ran from late fifties to early sixties. A couple of the men glared at Cameron, but one tipped his hat like a Western movie lawman. The men clearly didn't recognize Cameron as the *assassin about town.* They moved through the white-carpeted room like they were on a mission

322 JEFF KIRKHAM (SPECIAL FORCES, RET.) & & JASON ...

from God, stomping past onto the balcony and confronting the prophet. They shouted something about Rulon being the "fallen prophet" and about the need for "blood atonement."

With a jolt, Cameron returned to himself. This would be his best chance to leave. *Exit stage left.* With a burst of energy that shattered his ennui, Cameron bolted from the room and into the hallway, now choked with confused pilgrim women.

"Excuse me," he said politely as he made his way through the hallway full of the harem of the prophet. "Pardon me." Cameron snaked his way down the hall, then took off at a gallop as he hit the stairs.

He raced around to the front of the house, now packed with pilgrims, and slowed down to work his way through the crowd toward the open gates of the ex-prophet's driveway. Confusion reigned and no one spared Cameron any notice. The men on the balcony made some booming pronounce-ment and then their six-guns sounded in unison. Cameron looked back to see Prophet Rulon fall sideways beneath the railing of the balcony, his body peppered with splotches.

"Was the Prophet Rulon translated into heaven?" he over-heard one pilgrim woman ask another.

Cameron shook his head in disbelief as he cleared the gates and broke into a run, loping west out of town.

As he cleared the last of the trailers, it felt like he might make it, family and all. He could see the figures of a tall, blonde woman and two struggling boys ambling west, away from the town, on the road before him.

The feeling of threading the gap—between *bad man* and *good man*—struck him as both strange and heaven-sent. He didn't understand the whys and wherefores of the last week of mayhem, but Cameron knew this: he had been faithful to his boys. And when their eyes called him to return to the land of the merciful, he had returned.

Maybe that was all this new world would ask: to fight like a savage when the battle raged, but then return to hearth when the flags lowered and the blood vanished into the ground.

Cameron knew he was a slow learner. He couldn't expect this one, absurd victory to paint his life in tones of wisdom and calm. Running west as the last light fled the sky, gaining ground on his family, he filed it all away as proof of a new reality. Maybe it would be a reality more suited to a man like him.

EPILOGUE

SAGE HAD KILLED and butchered hundreds of rabbits; it had been his token responsibility on his dad's hobby farm. He had worked mightily to avoid any other kind of labor or responsibility, always making himself scarce when he knew his dad might need him. But try as he might, he could never get out of butchering the rabbits.

In the last two weeks, Sage had become someone he barely knew. At his feet lay a dead rabbit, and Sage glowed with pride. He had finally caught a cottontail in one of his snares, and the meat was still warm. The rabbit had probably run through the snare earlier that morning.

He found himself looking forward to gutting, skinning, and cooking the rabbit over a fire. These skills—skills he had earned honestly—would fill his belly tonight.

Back in his old life, no matter how loudly he had barked about his independence and argued with his parents about making his own decisions, Sage had always known himself to be a fraud. He had always known he was a boy in a man's body. He hadn't earned the right to stand for himself, though that never stopped him from trying. All his old bluff and bluster, false confidence and bravado sounded in his ears like the clanking of tin. It had all been bullshit and he smiled, knowing now that his dad had listened and tolerated it with patience.

Becoming a man, he discovered, was far more than growing some chest hair and banging a girl for the first time. As he hefted the dead rabbit in his hands, he felt the magnitude of this moment. With competence and skill, he would feed himself. Maybe this was becoming a man.

He would never have asked for the fall of society. His heart would probably always be heavy with the deaths of Angelina and Penny, and heaven only knew if his parents and siblings were still alive. But he wondered if he would have found the path of manhood without the collapse.

He had grown so good at manipulating his friends, his mother, and his father's wealth that he might never have reached this moment, when he and the earth wrestled for survival and he emerged alive.

Sage knew he would never be victorious, since Mother Earth would always come around to take another poke at him. But perhaps being alive for one more day was the ultimate endgame, the final stamp of competency of a man, moving across the skin of life.

Sage reset the snare and headed back toward his hide, the comforting weight of the rabbit hanging from his belt.

The words of the old man back on the highway turned out to be prophetic. OPSEC—operational security—had truly become a life-and-death factor for Sage. As the masses

stranded on the highway became increasingly vicious, being
discovered equaled death. If a mob didn't kill Sage straight-
away, they would certainly kill him by taking his supplies.
With just ten rounds of ammunition left for the Winchester
.30-30, staying hidden from the roaming masses meant
staying alive.

Sage got a small fire going and went to work on the rabbit.
He peeled away the skin, the thin fur coming off the flesh
with ease. Then he carefully slit the belly with the head
hanging down so that he could surgically remove the bladder
without getting a single drop of urine on the meat. With the
bladder out, he flipped the carcass and dumped the guts onto
a chunk of sagebrush wood, thinking he might use them later
as bait for his deadfall traps.

He carved the rabbit into six parts: two rear quarters, two
front quarters, the breast and the midsection. Cut up in parts,
the rabbit laid flatter in the frying pan. His grandpa had
forgotten to send him with cooking oil, but that was something Sage figured he would get used to sooner or later. The
lack of oil and butter would be an adjustment, especially
since game meat had so little natural fat. He plunked the
rabbit pieces down in the pan and set it on the sagebrush
coals. He added four small onions for flavor.

After salting and flipping, he dug into the rabbit and
onions. It required discipline to choke down the bland meat
—he had nearly reached his max on cooked onions after the
first week of eating them—but Sage forced himself to eat
every bite. He wasn't sure if cooked rabbit would be good the
next morning, and he wasn't willing to risk getting sick from
eating bad meat. He still didn't know how cold it should be to
preserve meat.

He spent the rest of the afternoon on overwatch of the

pond and the road. He could barely see the Holland farm-house, just a pinnacle of green in the distance punctuated by their huge cottonwoods. Sadly, those cottonwoods would beckon the hungry and desperate like an oasis in the desert. Sage hated to even look at the farmhouse, knowing that the marauders would come again and again. He decided to stay away. His heart couldn't take another bout of tragedy.

The clouds built on the eastern horizon and, if they kept on their way toward him, the afternoon would bring more snow. While Sage loved his hand-built shelter, he knew it wasn't a tent and that it would leak. He had a tent bundled in with his supplies, but he was afraid that its geometric lines would be too easy for wandering eyes to spot. He thought he would be stranded here for the winter, so he decided to hole up in his stone-and-tarp shelter for as long as the mobs kept coming. Staying hidden took priority over staying comfort-able or even dry.

Something at the bend in the road caught his eye. He dug around for his binoculars and took a careful look. Three figures made their way closer, walking half a mile out. He could tell they were all men, throwing up feathers of dust as they marched toward him.

Ten minutes later, the men were almost to the pond, and Sage couldn't believe what he saw. Without a doubt, one of the men, the one leading the trio, was Justin. Somehow, he had managed to survive the wound to his shoulder, and had found medical treatment, with clean bandages and a sling for his arm.

From this distance, Sage couldn't hear their conversation, but he could see Justin motioning toward the onion field, describing to his companions the advantages of the pond. A gnawing feeling grew in Sage's gut. Justin would keep coming. He would keep pressing and keep showing up, until one day Justin would find Sage asleep or unaware.

How Justin had remained alive for this long flummoxed Sage. Justin had no skill of his own. His only ability was to manipulate others, bending their minds to his will and enticing them to jeopardize their survival for his own. Watching him now, directing the men toward Sage's onion fields and trap lines, he realized Justin would never go away.

When the three men turned toward the onion field, Sage slid out of his observation hide and slipped over the rocks, putting the ridge between himself and the men. He had imagined that harvesting rabbits and mice would be enough, that Mother Nature would be satisfied with the blood of small animals. He had assured himself that she would require no more than to follow the life of a hunter, to shed blood only so that he could eat, as his father had taught him.

Sage had withheld the part of him that could become a killer of men, and had hidden that part deep within, where maybe she wouldn't notice the hoarded piece of his childhood, tucked between his loving heart and his innocent soul. At last, with a plunging grief, he held it out to Mother Nature, complete in his surrender.

Sage checked the breech of his 30-30 and took off at a slow trot, jogging around to their back trail. He would approach them from where they had come, where they would least expect an attack.

There had been many occasions where Sage could have killed Justin, but he had sidestepped them all. He had no desire to kill anyone, much less someone he knew. He had possibly killed men and women from the farmhouse window, but he didn't know that for a fact.

Killing Justin would be different. He would face the deci-

330 JEFF KIRKHAM (SPECIAL FORCES, RET.) & & JASON...

sion squarely. He could see no alternative. If he didn't kill Justin and the other two men, they would end up killing him.

Sage cut their back trail and slowed to a walk. He could see the men several hundred yards distant, with their backs turned toward him. Using the sagebrush for cover, he moved forward quietly, cutting the distance. The scoped .30-30 rifle was most accurate under a hundred and fifty yards. To make a sure kill, he would have to close to within a hundred yards.

He wanted to turn back. Sage knew the ghost of Justin would haunt him and he knew that killing these men would forever change him. He could justify it, but he sensed that the justification would wear thin over time. Like the coming snow would overwhelm the land, truth of murder would overwhelm Sage's self-deception. Yet Justin was a true threat to Sage's own survival, and no amount of wishful thinking would change that reality.

Maybe it was like the rabbit. Perhaps Mother Earth demanded this final sacrifice on the altar of survival. Maybe she required the forfeiture of his fresh, teenage heart—his innocence, his childhood. Perhaps Mother Earth demanded that those relics of the old world be left here on the stony plain of Idaho for Sage to live. Perhaps this dark act of murder was a toll Mother Earth had forever demanded of men, and she had grown tired of forbearing the rite of passage. Maybe, with the collapse of society, she had come to collect for the last hundred years of modern civilization, this time with interest.

Sage moved up to a large sagebrush and nestled into the heart of the branches, a hundred twigs jabbing his skin. He ignored them and arranged the execution of Justin and his companions with no chance of failure. The rifle was rock-steady, anchored against the trunk of the bush.

Sage clicked off the safety, committing himself to the honesty of killing, the siren song of Mother Nature. He settled the crosshairs on the center of Justin's back.

Then he squeezed.

BLAIRE STREET, McKenzie, Tennessee

MAT AND WILLIAM stood atop the crappiest HESCO barrier Mat had ever seen, the terrier alongside. Mat drank a mug of coffee, graciously supplied by the town to their newest favored sons. Two tides had flowed together in the currents of human bonding between Mat Best and the town of McKenzie: grief and gratitude. Mat was both a figure worthy of sympathy and a figure worthy of grace, as Mat held the military knowledge that might save them all. A dead girlfriend and a lethal threat turned Mat and William from intruders into honored guests.

The coffee mug and the morning mist lulled Mat into thoughts of combat in Iraq. The low-lying mists of the late Kentucky fall enshrouded the rolling grasses, shooting skyward where distant refugee camps burned their morning fires, the tendrils of smoke punctuating the otherwise benign fog, slightly off-color and dangerous.

He remembered Master Sergeant Menendez, the hardened warfighter who had taken Mat under his wing during Mat's first deployment to Iraq. The sergeant had died in Mat's arms on his second deployment, coughing blood onto Mat's fatigues after a bullet slid underneath Menendez's body armor and perforated both lungs.

Over more deployments than Mat knew, Menendez fought Al Qaeda like a savage. At the same time, Menendez brewed beautiful coffee. The cup in Mat's hand couldn't compare with the slightly-fruity, Ethiopian blend Menendez would share with Mat and no one else. While delicious, the Ethiopian coffee hadn't changed Mat's life. It was Menendez's stumpy warfighter's hands on the plunger of the French press that Mat would never forget—the picture of those hands worked its way into Mat's soul like yeast in bread.

Each morning, with the mist still covering Mosul and their morning physical training behind them, Mat and Menendez would fade away from the team and drift back to a nook in the forward operating base where they kept their beans, grinder, and press. While Menendez hand-ground the beans, Mat—the bushido apprentice—fired up the stove and boiled water in a weather-worn aluminum camping pot that had long ago lost its percolator cap. With the water just north of boiling and the beans ground to shavings the precise width and breadth of a grain of sand on the beaches of the Euphrates River, Menendez poured hot water down the side of the press with sufficient velocity to churn the grounds without need of a spoon. After four minutes, the grinds would sufficiently engorge with water, allowing the screen of the press to pass through the darkening brew.

Menendez's hands cupped one another and cupped the plunger in turn, like a father blessing the head of an infant child. Patiently, he coaxed the screen downward through the press, taking more time than the operation probably required, enjoying the final moment before the coffee poured.

Mat could see those hands, scarred, scraped, and veined from ten thousand hours wrapped around barbells, working explosives, and manipulating the unforgiving edges of weapons of war.

When those two hands cupped one another and the plunger—the grace of power restrained—Mat understood the purpose of war in a way that would open like a flower over the years that he would spend killing men. Mat would awaken, petal by petal, to an understanding that killing without grace brought only death. Killing with bushido protected life.

As he prepared to kill again, standing on a HESCO barrier in western Tennessee, Mat sipped his coffee and remembered Menendez.

He and Will hadn't had time to grieve Caroline. In war, one rarely does. The town needed Mat's leadership, as the first groups of desperate refugees and vicious gangbangers had already begun to run up against the feeble defenses of McKenzie. If the town were to survive, he would have to set his grief aside and teach the people how to defend themselves.

The town had cobbled together several miles of deer fence—wire mesh with four inch gaps. When wired together, they wouldn't hold sand like a military HESCO bastion, but they would hold lumber. McKenzie had a lumber yard just outside of town, along with a fleet of front-end loaders and backhoes. At Mat's direction, they filled the hasty HESCO cages—six feet thick and six feet tall—with trees, cut lumber and anything else they could throw in the HESCOs to give them weight and stopping-power. Mat doubted anything other than a tank could punch through. Climbing over would prove difficult, slowing any attack.

Mat had already improved the town's roadblocks with Z-shaped concrete passages, using every concrete barrier in and around town. Mat placed overwatch shooters to back up the roadblocks. Then he started on the HESCOs, walling in the fields and forests around the town to give security to their flanks. Little by little, the defenses took the shape of an FOB, *Forward Operating Base,* like a walled city of the Dark Ages.

They had been forced to divide their defenses, building another HESCO wall around the pig farm outside of town. McKenzie would keep a small garrison at the pig farm and swap men out every couple of days. Additionally, Mat spent a few hours each day training a Quick Reaction Force with their best weapons to respond to an attack anywhere along the wall or at the pig farm.

The town pooled its firearms, and Mat figured he could field almost five hundred men and women with some sort of firearm in a pinch, more than half of them retirement-age men. The town had extremely limited ammunition, since nobody had stockpiled and because the town was too small for a gun shop. He would have to train them without live ammunition.

Mat sipped his coffee, the morning chill and the dark aroma combining in existential perfection.

Maybe tomorrow he would look for a French press in town. The boy should see Mat's hands on the plunger. Like Caroline, Mat's own life was anything but a foregone conclusion, especially with many weeks of killing still ahead. He might die and, if he did, he would like to leave William with something to remember him.

Mat would kill Americans this time. He would kill criminals, but he would also kill desperate citizens, the kind of people who had paid taxes and registered to vote; the very people he had fought to protect by killing Al Qaeda. Mat would kill outside the HESCO walls of McKenzie, and maybe inside the HESCO walls as well. He would kill those Americans to protect the people of his town, but he would mostly kill them to protect the boy standing beside him.

"Gallantly will I show the world that I am a specially selected and well-trained soldier."

After Mat had found a French press, and after many repetitions of the slow grinding and steeping ritual, he hoped to prove with his hands that it had mattered that Caroline had lived. Mat would wordlessly share that Will was Mat's ultimate act of bushido, a warrior's firm and gentle touch on another human soul, a stranger's monument to a sister's love.

Gallantry. Maybe for the first time, Mat knew the word as more than a flourish.

Mat put his free hand on Will's shoulder, shucking the rifle around to his back, out of the way.

"So what are we, you and me?" Mat asked with a smile in his voice. "Brothers? Father and son?"

Will looked up at Mat with sadness dragging at the corners of his eyes, but with a smile spreading out from his mouth, reaching toward his eyes but not quite arriving. "I don't know, sir. Maybe we could both be Army Rangers?"

Mat grinned and sipped, slowing himself and enjoying both the coffee and the company of the boy.

"Don't get ahead of yourself, tiger. You gotta make it through Ranger School first."

MEANWHILE...

Filadelphia Hotel,
Antigua, Guatemala

WHOEVER SAID "CRIME DOESN'T PAY" MUST NOT HAVE KNOWN MANY smart criminals.

Gustavo "Tavo" Castillo drifted in and out of thought as the coming dawn filtered through the coffee plantation and quieted his restless soul. The rich light touched off the emerald greens of the leaves and the brilliant white of the blossoms one degree at a time, like an awakening after too much sleep.

Each of the hundred million blossoms granted a minuscule breath of fragrance, mingling in the slight breeze and washing the hillside in alternating waves of vanilla and jasmine.

Nothing in the world touched Tavo more deeply than this place, during this time of year: the flowering of the coffee in Antigua, Guatemala. Tavo had set the annual business meeting with his daughter for this place and time—the Hotel Filadelfia in late September.

"Buenas dias, Papi." His daughter kissed him on the head, careful not to jostle his coffee, and took the seat across from him at the wrought iron patio table.

Well, Tavo corrected himself, there was one thing in the world that touched him more deeply than the coffee bloom. He looked at her and felt mesmerized by his daughter, as Latin American fathers had for eons.

Somehow, even without makeup and at the cusp of dawn, she lit up the patio like a Roman goddess. Her airy white blouse floated around her shoulders and set off her rosy, latte-colored skin and her blush lips, delicately closing on the edge of her coffee cup. She smiled at Tavo silently, as if to acknowledge the perfect morning.

Loving his daughter was one of the few ways Tavo felt human. Mostly, he didn't. He felt like an alien wearing the skin of a man; an infiltrator, passing through the world, harvesting the weakness of humans. Tavo preyed upon them —except for this gut-punch-beautiful woman.

He pulled his eyes away from the coffee bloom to watch her pour half-and-half into her coffee. Were it not for her, he would be no different than any other predator; living only to kill and eat. Because of Sofia, his predations meant something: that the spoils of his life would pass to this light-dappled creature. As far as life purpose went, Tavo knew that many men had far less.

She waited on his pleasure. She sipped her coffee without a sound, honoring his enjoyment of the dawn and the mist-dusted coffee flowers. It was something he might do, himself, to soften a target of manipulation—feigning grace and open-heartedness. Pretending to respect the other man's pleasure and taking time to indulge the petty contentments of his target. Tavo was ninety-nine percent certain that his daughter did it because she sincerely cared for him. Either way, he respected her self-mastery. It was a rare trait among twenty-nine year old women.

He set his coffee cup quietly on the patio table and straightened in his chair, signaling his willingness to get to work.

"Will you tell me what you think about the troubles in America?" she began.

Good, Tavo thought. *Always start with a question. Draw the other person in. Make them feel heard before maneuvering toward your objective.*

"We've seen big swings in the stock market six times in the last year," Tavo recalled. "This could just be one more of those."

"Yes, but the dirty bomb attack on the Saudi oil pumping station might make this stick. We haven't seen the New York Stock Exchange circuit breakers close trading until now. The market troubles in the past have been herd panic. This one's founded on an actual loss of capital infrastructure."

He couldn't help but take pride in her nuanced understanding of the global financial situation, but it also unsettled him. She'd done her undergrad at Vanderbilt and then whipped through her MBA at Wharton. Since then, she'd been building her way up to running all his legitimate enterprises, and she'd had unbelievable success. Of course, his legitimate businesses could never compete with drug trafficking for profitability. But until she'd taken the helm of his corporations, they almost all lost money. They were money

340 JEFF KIRKHAM (SPECIAL FORCES, RET.) & & JASO...

laundering schemes more than anything else, so losses hadn't been an issue. But she'd turned that around. Now they were making money on their money laundering.

He wondered how much her analysis of the stock market had been lifted from a class she'd taken at Wharton. The alternative—that her genius approached his own in magnitude—brought with it another set of problems. He'd made it a personal mantra: never work with anyone as intelligent as him. A smart enough person would see through his well-manicured humanity and peg him for the sociopath he was. Had his daughter already turned that corner?

"American financial trouble has always been good for us," Tavo threw out the statement, more interested in keeping her talking than anything.

She chuckled. "It's been good for *you*. My businesses take damage when markets fall. They're only worth what people will pay for them and that depends on private equity funds and the cash they have on hand, which relies heavily on their investors' stock gains."

Tavo received it for what it was: an intellectual parry. She was fully aware of the drug trade that had funded all the family's legitimate enterprises. At the same time, she had worked tirelessly to firewall the two sides of the family fortune. In theory, her policy fit perfectly into his empire strategy. In practice, her relentless fence-building between his "dirty work" and her "clean work" tasted like last night's garlic.

And yet, he reminded himself, it had always been just the two of them. Father and daughter, forever driving toward the same outcome; her long-term wealth, and hopefully, the well-being of his grandchildren at some point. The thought of grandchildren made him think of a male counterpart for Sofía. *Just another person I would have to eventually kill,* he worried. He knew everything about every man she'd ever been with, and thankfully, she had never taken any of them seriously. There hadn't been one equal to the challenge of becoming a Castillo.

Tavo realized that his long silence had revealed his discomfiture and he regretted his lapse in control. "I'll make sure you have the capital to weather any storm, Sofi. If American investors take losses, that's our time to buy. Did they teach you at business school about how the industrialists expanded their empires on the back of the Great Depression? We should be so lucky."

She enjoyed her coffee and her eyes lingered over the plantation.

She's suppressing her first response, Tavo noticed. *Her first response had probably been to take a jab. But she didn't go with that. She refrained.*

"We may not need the expansion. I'm getting close to our exit threshold," she reported, returning to the agenda. "Our net worth is running just above thirty-five million on my side. We can cut over to purely legitimate businesses and we'll be good."

Tavo leaned back in his chair and chuffed. *Thirty-five million.* The glacial pace of profit accumulation in the corporate world always amazed him. He could generate thirty-five million in three days with narcotics. It'd taken her four years.

Sofía always came back to "the exit threshold." *Our* exit threshold, Tavo noted. She presumed his consent to her strategy—that someday they would abandon his drug operation in favor of legitimate enterprise. When they hit their "exit threshold" of clean cash, they would move off together, Tavo and Sofía, respectable business partners, welcome to walk among the elites without any taint of criminality.

Every time she said it, his disdain for "the elites" arose. Tavo ground his teeth, eager to pulverize the useless upper class between the twin stones of his formidable intellect and his hatred for aristocrats. He had sent his daughter into their world to study at their schools and master their markets, but he had never ceded one inch to the oligarchs. In the end, he longed to see them burn.

She must've noticed the foul wind pass across his face because she tacked an anxious footnote to her statement. "Papi. Nobody survives forever as a *narcotraficante*. You need to get out while you can."

He held up a finger, hearing something in the breeze. A dog barked at the edge of the plantation. After a moment's pause, he replied, "Nobody *yet* has survived. Everyone who has tried, so far, has been a fucking idiot. I apologize, *mi amor*, but you need to leave right now. Don't pack. Go to your helicopter now. I'll see you in Los Mochis soon. Go." He stood and lifted her from her chair, her face beset with momentary confusion. He kissed her on the forehead. "Go."

Sofía left her coffee cooling and walked back into the hotel without another word.

As soon as she disappeared around the plaster-spackled columns, Tavo slid the Glock G26 from the low-viz holster on his waistband and reflexively press-checked the chamber. Brass glinted back at him.

He moved to another patio table, this one surrounded by stone and adobe columns, the same columns that once ringed the hacienda of the Filadelfia before it had become an ultra-lux hotel. He left his coffee alongside his daughter's and dragged a wrought iron patio chair from behind a table and over to a column. To the staff, Tavo would look like he was being discrete. To another shooter, Tavo would look like he was taking cover and concealment.

There were no other guests. When he visited the Filly— one of his few, secretly-owned Latin American holdings—he ordered all other guest reservations cancelled, if for no other reason than to protect his quiet time in the morning. It was one of the few financial indulgences he allowed himself south of the American border.

This visit to the Filly had been a close call. Tavo's personal "Egghead," as he jokingly called his pet millennial Octavio, had flagged an up-tick in Guatemalan electronic chatter around one of Tavo's nicknames, *"El Mentor."* *"Mentor"* was a common enough word in Spanish, but *El Mentor* was a term worthy of note. The fact that the phrase had been bouncing around the Guatemalan Ministry of Defense had elevated the possible threat sufficiently that Octavio had raised the red flag. That, together with the barking dog, had set off Tavo's finely-tuned situational awareness.

Something was wrong.

Later, he might feel bad about possibly losing the Filly to the Guatemalan government. For the moment, his heart rate picked up and his endocrine system flooded with one of the few highs he actually enjoyed: *combat.*

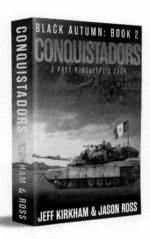

*[Excerpt from **Black Autumn Conquistadors**, the sequel to Black Autumn Travelers. Continue reading **Black Autumn Conquistadors** on Kindle, paperback or free on Kindle Unlimited.]*

A WORD FROM JEFF AND JASON

Thank you for reading **Black Autumn Travelers** and we hope you had as much fun reading it as we had writing it.

If you know Mat Best (from Black Rifle Coffee), then you can guess how much fun we had telling his (*mostly* fictional) story. We're betting Mat won't read this—we're not sure he knows how to read—but we wrote a post-apocalyptic version of Mat's personal journey, going from Army Ranger playboy to a husband and a man of inspiring honor. The Mat we know today is the Mat who stands with young Will, sipping coffee, at the end of the novel. Mat's own non-fiction book, *Thank You For My Service*, is available on Amazon and it's a hilarious ride through the scandalous moments of Mister Best. It tells Mat's gritty true story with all the action and hijinks you might imagine. *Not* suitable for children or pastors, mind you. You'll notice that we stole liberally from his book to inspire the post-apocalypse version.

Sage Ross is well on his way to finding a path of honor in this modern world. He currently, serves in the United States

Air Force (and his father could not be more proud!) *Following winds, my son.*

Meanwhile, in Black Autumn Conquistadors, a genius cartel overlord pours into the gap left by the collapse, amassing invincible weapons in a push to rule Southwest America. But no matter how powerful his tanks and machine guns, no weapon can force trust with the people closest to him. Nor can military force alone exterminate the relentless spirit of America, which is anything but dead.

And where is the President of the United States as the economy takes a blistering nose dive? The Last Air Force One reveals the desperate struggle of Dutch McAdams, President of the United States, as he fights the forces of destruction massed against the U.S.A. in its moment of weakness. During the death struggle of the largest empire ever seen on Earth, Dutch must confront his responsibilities as a father as well, pitting the needs of the millions against the life-or-death of his beloved wife and children.

The first five books of the **Black Autumn series** rampage through the seventeen days of the Black Autumn collapse, chronicled coast-to-coast through the eyes of thirty-one desperate survivors.

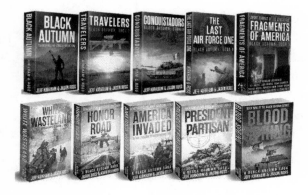

Series in order:
1. *Black Autumn*
2. *Black Autumn Travelers*
3. *Black Autumn Conquistadors*
4. *The Last Air Force One*
5. *White Wasteland* (same characters as Black Autumn)
6. *Honor Road* (same characters as Travelers)
7. *America Invaded* (same characters as Conquistadors)
8. *President Partisan* (same characters as The Last Air Force One.)
9. *Blood Spring* (all characters from all books.)
10. *Fragments of America* (short stories)

While the unique book order can be a bit confusing, it helps to think of the five "black cover" books as a single, epic novel covering the same seventeen days of collapse, then the four "white cover" novels telling the story of the following, impossible winter. Then, Blood Spring culminates all storylines and characters. Like *Game of Thrones*, or *The Stand*, the Black Autumn series breaks down an epic tale with dozens of characters, fighting for their survival.

Our apologies for any head-scratching that may ensue. We couldn't think of a better way to tell the massive, 2,000 page tale bouncing around in our brain buckets. As usual, I blame it all on Jeff.

— Jason

ABOUT THE AUTHORS

Jeff Kirkham (right) served almost 29 years as a Green Beret doing multiple classified operations for the US government. He is the proverbial brains behind ReadyMan's survival tools and products and is also the inventor of the Rapid Application Tourniquet (RATS). Jeff has graduated from numerous training schools and accumulated over 8 years "boots on the ground" in combat zones, making him an expert in surviving in war torn environments. He spent the majority of the last decade as a member of a counter terrorist unit, working in combat zones doing a wide variety of operations in support of the global war on terror. Jeff spends his time, tinkering, inventing, writing and helping his immigrant Afghan friends, who fought side by side with Jeff. His true passion is his family and spending quality time with his wife and three children.

Jason Ross (left) has been a hunter, fisherman, shooter and preparedness aficionado since childhood and has spent tens of thousands of hours roughing it in the great American outdoors. He's an accomplished big game hunter, fly fisherman, an Ironman triathlete, SCUBA instructor, and frequent business mentor to U.S. military veterans. He retired from a career in entrepreneurialism at forty-one years of age after founding and selling several successful business ventures.

After being raised by his dad as a metal fabricator, machinist and mechanic, Jason dedicated twenty years to mastering preparedness tech such as gardening, composting, shooting, small squad tactics, solar power and animal husbandry. Today, Jason splits his time between writing, international humanitarian work and his wife and seven children.

Check out the Readyman lifestyle...search Facebook for ReadyMan group and join Jeff, Jason and thousands of other readers in their pursuit of preparedness and survival.

Black Autumn

Travelers

A Post-Apocalyptic Saga
The Black Autumn series, Book Two
by Jeff Kirkham, Former Army Green Beret
& Jason Ross
© 2018

� Created with Vellum

72147891R00208